ANNE BARBOUR is the recipient of the *Romantic Times* Award for Best Regency of the Year for her novel *Lord Glenraven's Return*. Her most recent Regency is *Step in Time*.

CARLA KELLY is a popular Regency author who won the 1995 RITA Award for Best Regency for *Mrs. Drew Plays Her Hand*. Her most recent Regency is *Reforming Lord Ragsdale*.

EDITH LAYTON, historical romance and Regency author, is the winner of numerous awards, including the first *Romantic Times* Award granted for Best Short Story in 1992.

PATRICIA OLIVER is the recipient of the Romantic Times Award for Best First Regency in 1994 for her novel *Lord Harry's Angel*. Her most recent Regency is *An Immodest Proposal*.

PATRICIA RICE is an award-winning author of historicals and Regency romances. Her most recent historical is *Paper Moon* from Topaz.

A WEDDING BOUQUET

ANNE BARBOUR
CARLA KELLY
EDITH LAYTON
PATRICIA OLIVER
PATRICIA RICE

A SIGNET BOOK

SIGNET
Published by the Penguin Group
Penguin Books USA Inc., 375 Hudson Street,
New York, New York 10014, U.S.A.
Penguin Books Ltd, 27 Wrights Lane,
London W8 5TZ, England
Penguin Books Australia Ltd, Ringwood,
Victoria, Australia
Penguin Books Canada Ltd, 10 Alcorn Avenue,
Toronto, Ontario, Canada M4V 3B2
Penguin Books (N.Z.) Ltd, 182–190 Wairau Road,
Auckland 10, New Zealand

Penguin Books Ltd, Registered Offices:
Harmondsworth, Middlesex, England

First published by Signet, an imprint of Dutton Signet,
a division of Penguin Books USA Inc.

First Printing, May, 1996
10 9 8 7 6 5 4 3 2 1

Ⓡ REGISTERED TRADEMARK—MARCA REGISTRADA

Printed in the United States of America

CONTENTS

SOMETHING OLD

~

Patricia Oliver

PROLOGUE:
The Unclaimed Dance

London, April 1806

Jane glanced about her self-consciously, and her heart shrank.

It was going to be yet another of those humiliating experiences, she realized, sensing the familiar constriction building in her throat. Once again, Lady Jane Sutherland would play the role of wallflower, while other young ladies of her acquaintance flirted, and giggled, and fluttered their eyelashes daringly at the elegant bucks who ogled them from across the room. Tonight's gathering of the *ton* would be no different from a score of such events she had attended last year with equally painful results. At nineteen she was no wiser, no less gauche and tongue-tied, than she had been at eighteen. And not a whit more beautiful, Jane thought with uncharacteristic cynicism.

Tugging self-consciously at the amber tasseled shawl

clutched across her bosom, Lady Jane grimaced at the thought of this offending piece of anatomy. Only her bosom had changed since the year before, burgeoning forth in an abundance that had become a source of constant embarrassment to her. Her mama had been delighted at this evidence of her daughter's increasingly prominent female assets—as she had modestly referred to Jane's changing shape—and had insisted on displaying them—despite Jane's blushes and heated protests—in the low décolletage of a new jonquil silk gown, ordered especially for this occasion.

Jane sighed. She should never have allowed herself to be bullied—gently, and with the very best intentions, of course, but bullied nonetheless—by her family into attending the opening ball of the Season. Had she not already endured one London Season, her first and—she had sincerely hoped—her last. But her father, the Earl of Weston, had disregarded her entreaties to be allowed to stay in the country with her beloved dogs and horses. No, the earl had said in that dry tone of voice he used when he had already made up his mind, his dear Jane must make a push to establish herself creditably.

When Jane heard that note of finality in her father's voice, she had ceased to argue and bowed to the inevitable. Her elder sister, Lady Margaret, was to blame for their father's intransigence, as Jane knew only too well. Maggie had caused the rafters at Sutherland Park to rattle in their four hundred-year-old sockets when she had insisted upon accepting—among a host of suitors that included two earls and the heir to a dukedom—the stunningly handsome James Driscoll, Viscount Scovell.

Not that Lady Jane blamed her sister for a moment. She had developed an embarrassing *tendre* for Lord Scovell herself, although she was sure this handsome gentleman had not even noticed her existence when he came courting her lovely sister. That had been the story of her life, she mused, wondering what it might be like to be the object of such a dashing gentleman's devotion. Jane sighed again, well aware that such an eventuality belonged to the realm of daydreams.

The sound of the musicians tuning their instruments in the minstrel gallery above the Countess of Mansfield's glittering ballroom brought expectant smiles to the faces of the young ladies clustered in giggling groups around their hostess like so many fluttering butterflies.

Excitement was in the air. Lady Jane could feel it, but she knew from past experience that the faintly dizzy sensation of expectancy she was feeling would slowly fizzle away as the evening progressed and her dreams of meeting that special gentleman who would change her life forever dwindled and died with the last note of the last dance, a dance that would—if the past were to repeat itself—remain unclaimed.

"Oh, do come along, Jane," her sister, Lady Amelia, said in an excited whisper. "Lady Mansfield is going to find dashing partners for us. How absolutely thrilling! Do you not agree, Jane?"

Lady Jane looked down at the radiant face of her younger sister. At seventeen, Amelia was showing signs of becoming the beauty their Mama had been in her prime. She seemed never to be at a loss for words—a feat that Jane envied most deeply—and her vivacious, outgoing manner would guarantee her a partner for every dance of the evening. Jane felt an unexpected twist of envy that she quickly suppressed.

Reluctantly, she moved forward with her sister to join the cluster of five or six ladies who followed the countess down the room. Lady Mansfield was everything Jane wished to be and knew she had no hope of becoming. Cool, poised, and utterly charming, the countess paused before one eligible gentleman after another to introduce her charges and secure for each of them—with an enchanting smile that seduced the youthful gallants into blushing compliance—the coveted partner for the first cotillion.

As Lady Jane watched her hostess deftly cajole a nervous young man into leading a suddenly shy Amelia to join the nearest set, she wondered how Lady Mansfield—whom everyone knew had been a country vicar's daughter before her unexpected marriage to Phineas Ravenville—one of the *haut monde's* most eligible and unobtainable bachelors—had learned to go on so comfortably in this highly critical milieu that never failed to reduce Jane to tongue-tied confusion.

Idly she wondered if perhaps even her ladyship's undeniable charm and amiability might not falter when faced with the task of procuring a willing partner for the unremarkable Lady Jane Sutherland. But her ladyship did not appear at all concerned at the prospect. She linked her arm through Jane's and smiled up at her with genuine friendliness.

"I realize how much you must be looking forward to your second Season, my dear," she said cheerfully, quite as though Jane's first appearance in London had been a raging success. "First Seasons are usually so painful, are they not? One never knows what to say to a gentleman; at least I never could think of anything remotely witty. So I am sure you will wish to be more particular in your dancing partners than these fledgling misses." The countess waved a gloved hand in delicate dismissal of the giggling group of young ladies she had dispatched so effortlessly.

Jane blushed and murmured something quite incoherent. Privately she suspected that the diminutive countess was indulging in a Banbury tale, for no tongue-tied miss could possibly have won the heart of the darkly handsome, stern-faced Lord Mansfield, whom she had heard referred to as *Raven* by his intimates. The sobriquet was very apt, Jane thought, for the earl possessed a predatory air about him that frightened her.

Lady Mansfield's smile became more intimate, and her pleasant voice dropped to a conspiratorial level. "Now that you have had time to look around, my dear, perhaps there is a particular gentleman who has caught your fancy?" One eyebrow rose inquiringly, and Jane's blush deepened.

"I . . . I do n-not . . . that is . . . " Her voice failed her. How could she tell this charming creature, who evidently knew how to entrance the most fastidious of men, that Lady Jane Sutherland would be happy to have any partner at all for the first dance? That she would not dare to presume to set her sights on a certain gentleman, as many young ladies did, much less throw out lures to him.

"Come now," the countess cajoled. "You cannot persuade me that there is no gentleman in this room who deserves a second glance from those splendid eyes of yours, my dear. Such an unusual shade of amber. Quite captivating, if you do not mind my saying so, dear."

"T-thank you, my lady," Jane stammered, taken aback by this unexpected frankness. "But my hair is quite dreadful."

The countess let out a delighted tinkle of laughter. "Nonsense, child," she said gaily. "If truth be told, I envy you your coloring. Such a dramatic shade; not a mousy auburn like mine. One must carry it with pride, dear. There is nothing equivocal about red hair," she added with a wry smile. "We must find a partner worthy of you," she continued, and the intimate moment was gone. "Tell me which one it shall be."

Jane wished it might be that simple, but in truth none of the elegantly dressed young men she had met so far that evening appealed to her in the slightest. She knew their kind from the year before. They had come to the ball to ogle the latest crop of young ladies let loose upon the *beau monde*, and would spend the entire evening trying to cut one another out with the two or three acknowledged beauties of the Season. They would waste no time on wallflowers.

"I really have no preference, my lady," she began, her eyes scanning the crowded room with a perfunctory glance. "I would be quite content with anyone you care to . . . "

And then she saw him, and her voice faltered into silence.

Quite distinctly, Jane heard herself draw a deep, shuddering breath, as though she had been deprived of air for too long. When her lungs protested, she let her breath out with a whoosh, feeling suddenly light-headed. Unable to tear her gaze away from the tall man who stood on the threshold of the ballroom, Jane heard, as if from a great distance, Lady Mansfield's murmured protest.

"Ah, yes," the countess said softly. "Magnificent is he not? But too old for you, dear. And far too set in his rakish ways to be caught in parson's mousetrap."

Jane shut her mind to this unwelcome advice. "Who is he?" she whispered breathlessly, her heart in her throat.

"Viscount Hammond," Lady Mansfield replied after a short pause. "Heir to the Earl of Ridgeway. But let me warn you, Jane . . ."

But Lady Jane heard none of the countess's warning, her eyes reaching across the room to drink in every detail of the viscount's manly form. He was indeed superb, she thought, almost reverently. Not even Lord Scovell, the handsomest man Jane had ever expected to see, could hold a candle to the classical perfection of the godlike creature lounging in the doorway, accompanied by two friends, whose appearance Jane could not have described had her life depended upon it.

"That is the one I want," she whispered, as if her heart had spoken of its own accord.

For a brief instant, Jane could not believe that she had actually given voice to that sudden, secret longing. She felt herself blush furiously, but could not drag her eyes away from the mesmerizing vision of the man who had triggered this extraordinary outburst.

"Are you quite sure of this, Jane?"

Of course she was sure, Jane told herself firmly, believing every word of her own argument. How could a female feel this strongly about a man and not be sure?

The viscount's languid gaze drifted over the crowd of guests, and Jane imagined she felt the heat of his glance brush her face briefly. But then he turned to say something to the rotund gentleman beside him, and she knew that he had not noticed her. No doubt Lady Cartwright's ostrich plumes had blocked his vision, she thought crossly, resisting the urge to tear the offending ornaments from the old Tabby's purple headdress and grind them under the heel of her dancing slippers.

Luckily for Lady Cartwright, Jane felt the countess's light touch on her arm. "If you are set upon it, then," Lady Mansfield said with a rueful smile, "I shall certainly make you known to the viscount. But do not expect miracles, my dear. Gentlemen of his stamp rarely pay court to very young ladies."

"I am not a very young lady," Jane murmured half to herself, but her thoughts were centered on the viscount as they made their way toward him through the throng of guests already on the dance floor. All she could think of was the longed-for moment when she would stand before him and look up into his eyes. What color would they be? she wondered, wishing the countess would make haste to present her before the set began. They had appeared light blue, almost gray in the brief glimpse she had caught of them. Whatever color they were, Jane knew they would be warm on her skin. She could almost feel the heat of his admiring gaze on her face, her neck, her bosom. In a rush of unprecedented recklessness, Jane wished she had not stuffed the lace handkerchief into the revealing cleft between her breasts.

Would her naive prudery amuse him? Jane wondered, as she followed the countess across the last steps toward her goal. Or would the viscount find her missish and immature? The immodest thought crossed her mind that she could always allow her shawl to slip off her shoulders and reveal what her mama had once called the glory of her feminine form. Without appearing to expose her charms too blatantly, of course, she amended quickly.

The fear of appearing too forward caused her cheeks to flare with color again. Now of all times, she thought desperately, when she most wished to appear to advantage, her emotions would betray her.

And then her doubts and fears were miraculously forgotten, for the Viscount Hammond was smiling. Not at her, of course, but the warmth of his smile included her in its radiance. He smiled down at Lady Mansfield, bowing gracefully over her hand and placing his lips for an interminable moment on the tips of her gloved fingers.

Lady Jane writhed in an agony of envy.

And then the countess was murmuring the name of the rotund gentleman to the viscount's right and Jane was forced to drag her gaze from the dark cluster of curls that she longed to touch. She caught the name Hampton, and found herself being observed by a pair of twinkling brown eyes. She smiled faintly and extended her hand. The rotund gentleman executed an elegant bow, carrying her fingers to his lips with an exaggerated gallantry designed to charm the most pampered Beauty.

Jane was singularly unimpressed. She was listening avidly to the sound of the viscount's mellow voice exchanging pleasantries with Lady Mansfield, whom he obviously knew well. She was poised for the moment when those eyes, that voice, those lips would be turned on her, a moment that seemed to be drawing out unbearably.

When it came, the moment was nothing like the enchanting encounter Jane had envisioned. The viscount repeated her name in a stiff, bored voice, and his lips did not so much as brush the yellow kid gloves she wore. Worse yet, he hardly glanced at her, and Jane was unable to decide whether his eyes were the iciest of blues or the bleakest of grays.

The third gentleman, tall and blond and offensively haughty, who appeared to be cut from the same marble stamp, showed her even less enthusiasm and quickly made his excuses, sauntering off in the direction of the card room.

Lady Jane stood silently beside her hostess, mesmerized by the sensuous smile on the viscount's well-shaped mouth, but already sensing in the pit of her stomach the familiar bitterness of defeat.

The countess rallied instantly, suggesting—with an astonishing frankness that brought the color rushing to Jane's cheeks and caused her to lower her eyes to the viscount's impeccably arranged cravat—that her dear Hammond might oblige her by leading Lady Jane out in the first set.

There was an infinitesimal pause, during which Jane sensed the brief, dismissive brush of those cool blue-gray eyes against her skin. Where, oh where was the warmth she had longed for? she wondered dispiritedly, knowing the answer must have been obvious from the moment she had dared to imagine such a man would notice her.

Lady Jane deliberately closed her ears to his litany of excuses. She had heard them all before. Instinctively, she pulled the shawl closer about her, all desire to display her attractions to this odiously complacent, conceited oaf dissipating like dreams upon wakening.

"Perhaps later?" she heard Lady Mansfield's voice insisting gently. "I am sure dear Jane can save you a dance after supper, Hammond. Is that not so, my dear?"

Jane wished she had the courage to deny this possibility. To deny it in such a way that the wretch would know she had seen through his feeble excuses and despised him for his lack of common civility. But she had no experience in deception and deliberate rudeness, so could only nod her head and force her lips into a tight little smile.

"I shall look forward to it, my lady."

Jane could not tell if these clipped words were addressed to her or to the countess, but she hoped the others did not hear the hint of impatience in the viscount's voice as clearly as she did.

Lady Mansfield twitched Jane's dance card from her flaccid grasp, and Jane watched miserably as the viscount scribbled his name with a careless flourish and handed it back without a word, without even a glance to soften the sting of rejection.

Jane's heart curled up into a tight knot of pain. Through a mist of despair, she heard the viscount's deep, cool voice deftly smooth over the awkward moment with the meaningless pleasantries *de rigueur* in such situations. But even the knowledge that the gentleman had definitely not wished to stand up with her, and had only signed her card under pressure from his hostess, could not prevent Jane's eyes from following his tall figure stride off across the room in search of his sister. At least that was the excuse he gave them. Jane knew differently, of course.

Well, she thought to herself with a sigh of resignation, her second Season had certainly started on a low note, and would predictably get no better if last year's fiasco was any indication. Jane found herself smiling at her own stupidity in imagining—even for a minute—that things might have been otherwise. What a goose she had been to allow her romantic yearnings to overcome her common sense. How the delectable viscount—so fully aware of his own magnificence as he undoubtedly was—must have squirmed at the notion of being paired off with a tongue-tied long-Meg like her.

Not for the first time, Jane thanked her lucky stars for her irrepressible sense of humor. This ability to see the ridiculous in awkward, embarrassing, often painful situations was truly a blessing, she mused, and had carried her through life with at least a semblance of serenity. Nineteen years of being the ugly duckling—for so she always considered her-self—in a family noted for its beautiful women had given her a fortitude that served her well now.

She would survive very well without the odious conde-scension of the Viscount Hammond, she told herself firmly. She would have to, for Jane knew, as surely as she knew her own limitations, that this gentleman would never claim the dance that had been forced upon him.

And she was right.

"Hammond?" Lady Margaret had exclaimed, with a hint of waspishness that Jane instantly recognized as envy. "Never say you have promised that rakehell a waltz, Jane? How very indiscreet of you. Mama will have something to say about that, you may be sure."

Jane did not greatly care what Lady Sutherland might have to say, and she merely smiled enigmatically. She had gone into supper with Lord and Lady Scovell, and had made the mistake of showing her sister the scrawled name on her dance card.

Jane instantly regretted succumbing to this vanity.

As the guests began to drift back to the ballroom, Jane glanced longingly down at her card. That careless scrawl—as brash and arresting as the man himself—had seemed to promise so much, but when the viscount's party strolled past her table without so much as a glance in her direction, Jane knew that she had lost again.

I
Reckless Driver

Lark Manor, Sussex, 1816

"Oh, do pray slow down, Jane dear," Miss Margery Milford exclaimed as the extravagant vehicle tooling down the country lane came perilously close to hitting the ample posterior of old Mrs. Munster, who had chosen that unwise moment to bend down to pat her dog, Bones.

Miss Milford removed a large pocket handkerchief from the voluminous reticule she clutched in her gloved fingers and mopped her brow. "You almost murdered poor dear Mrs. Munster, child," she said in accusing tones, focusing her pale blue stare on the young female sitting beside her on the precarious seat.

"Rubbish!" Lady Jane replied, casting a smiling glance at her trembling passenger. "Mrs. Munster did not come close to being dispatched, Aunt, although I must say I was sorely tempted. Only consider how invitingly she protruded herself into the public road."

Miss Milford sniffed loudly. "I do declare, Jane, you grow more like that reckless father of yours every day. I shall always maintain that he did you a disservice when he taught you to outride and outdrive your brother. 'Taint ladylike I say."

Lady Jane laughed at her aunt's long-standing quarrel against the Earl of Weston. "Papa always was an out-and-outer, a regular paragon of a horseman," she countered with obvious enthusiasm. "John is too cautious around his cattle, and besides, he has no flair at all with the ribbons. So Papa turned to me when he wished to discuss horses. It was only natural that he took an interest in fostering my love of the sport."

"Your love of danger, I would call it," Miss Milford interjected crossly. "You will never convince me that a high-perch phaeton is an appropriate conveyance for a well-bred female, particularly since she defies all rules of proper deportment by driving it herself."

"Would you deny me my only indulgence, Aunt?" Lady Jane replied without rancor, her eyes scanning the narrow lane ahead for approaching vehicles.

"A deucedly expensive indulgence, if you ask me," her aunt replied shortly, and Jane sensed the familiar pattern of her aunt's thoughts. She sighed softly and dropped her hands a fraction, reveling in the surge of power she felt as her horses responded instantly, increasing their already alarming pace to a speed calculated to paralyze all but the most hardened whips.

"Jane! You will land us both in the ditch, child." Miss Milford's admonition was not unexpected, and Jane smiled broadly as she risked another glance at her aunt.

"Have I ever put you in the ditch, Aunt?" she cried, her voice high with excitement. "Besides, dusk is falling, dear, and you know how Mrs. Porter hates it when we are late for dinner."

Scarcely had the words left her lips when she heard the sound of rushing hooves and wheels behind her. Jane glanced quickly over her shoulder, curious to see the daring driver who had come up behind her so unexpectedly, but a bend in the lane hid him from view. It was rare to encounter any equipage on this narrow lane other than Mrs.

Robinson's ancient landau or Squire Morris's smart gig.
But Jane knew that her cantankerous neighbor's overfed
slugs could never have passed her own team even in their
heyday, and Squire Morris's cob—as rotund as his master—never moved faster than a sedate trot.

Torn between her first instinct to spring her horses and
show the impertinent whipster a clean pair of heels, and her
natural curiosity to learn the identity of the reckless driver
who thought nothing of endangering life and limb on wind-
ing country lanes, Jane glanced back again as she heard the
racing carriage closing the distance between them. What
she saw caused her to pull her team up hastily, edge the
phaeton onto the grassy verge, and call sharply to her two
wolfhounds who stood, ears alert and tails motionless, in
the middle of the lane.

"Dido!" she called again, fear edging her voice with
panic. The great dog gave a languid glance in her direction,
then turned to observe the approaching noise. Aeneas
moved obediently toward the phaeton, but Dido stood
rooted to the road. Only at the last possible moment, when
the hound must have sensed that the racing curricle was not
about to stop, did she leap for safety, but not before Jane
heard her anguished yelp as one of the wheels jostled the
dog's flank.

"The devil fly away with the oaf!" Jane exclaimed angrily, her attention and skill fully occupied in wrestling her
team back into a semblance of calm. The grays were not accustomed to being outdistanced on the road and had taken
instant umbrage at the four superb chestnuts that had
dashed past in grand style. As Jane eased them back onto
the lane, they showed every sign of wishing to bolt.

Jane glanced at her aunt and saw that Miss Milford had
suffered a severe shock. Never comfortable around horses
of any kind, her aunt was particularly wary of the four
bang-up bits of blood her niece insisted upon tooling
around the countryside. At the moment she sat, back rigid

and eyes screwed shut, clutching her reticule to her bosom as though it offered some slight comfort in her hour of need.

"Aunt Margery," Jane said, a hint of anxiety in her voice, "you may open your eyes now. The reckless rogue has gone, but I think he hit Dido. Tobias"—she called over her shoulder at the groom who rode behind them—"hold the ribbons while I get down to have a look, will you?"

But Tobias had already swung down and was looking around the carriage for the dog, which appeared to have disappeared.

"There she is, poor dear," Miss Milford cried out, pointing to the deep ditch beside the lane where the top of Dido's massive head could be seen above the long grass.

"Come, Dido," Jane called. "Come here, old girl. What has that nasty man done to my baby?"

The dog rose to her feet but made no move to approach her mistress until the groom took her by the collar and pulled her out of the ditch. Jane let out an angry exclamation when the dog whimpered as she limped toward the carriage.

"Got a nasty scrape on her right flank, milady," Tobias said, leaning over the big dog and running his hand gently down her side. "Going to feel mighty sore for a few days, I would say. But no bones broken, as far as I can tell."

"Can you lift her into the carriage?" Jane inquired, looking dubiously from the old groom to the great shaggy dog. "We cannot allow her to walk home in that condition."

With some assistance from a passing farmer, the groom was able to hoist the dog into the phaeton, where she settled down at her mistress's feet, her huge head on Miss Milford's lap.

By now twilight had set in and the thought of Mrs. Porter waiting impatiently to set dinner on the table caused Jane to urge her horses forward. They had covered less than half the distance to the gate leading to Lark Manor when the evening air was pierced by the ominous splintering sound of two vehicles colliding, followed immediately by the shrill scream of frightened horses.

As Jane gave her horses their heads, the thought uppermost in her mind was that the mad whipster who had passed them a few moments ago had paid the price for his recklessness. At the speed he had been driving, he might well have broken his neck, she thought, and no doubt destroyed one or more of that splendid team of chestnuts.

As she swept past the entrance to Lark Manor and raced toward the curve in the lane leading down to the old wooden bridge that crossed the stream a mile away, the thought did occur to her that the stranger had received his just desserts for hitting poor Dido, and had no one to blame but himself if he had maimed himself for life.

The sight that met their eyes when the phaeton dashed around the bend and came in full view of the bridge made Jane gasp with horror. The wreckage of the curricle lay all over the road, completely destroyed by its violent encounter with the back of old Mr. Logan's heavy dray cart. Three of the chestnuts were rearing and snorting, while the fourth lay tangled in the broken traces, screaming in panic.

Of the reckless driver there was no sign.

Without hesitation, Jane thrust the ribbons into her aunt's nervous hands and jumped down, calling to Tobias to help Mr. Logan, who was trying to calm the chestnuts and disentangle them from the jumbled traces. Jane cast an anxious glance around the scene searching for the madman who had caused this havoc. It was difficult to see anything in the deepening twilight, but finally she tripped over a booted foot protruding from the grassy ditch.

She went down on her knees and gingerly removed the gentleman's head from a shallow puddle of water and brushed the dark soggy hair away from his face. She could not make out his features clearly, but felt the warm blood oozing from a deep cut in his forehead.

"Tobias!" she called, fearing that the stranger might be seriously hurt. "Here is the driver. Help me get him out of the ditch, will you?"

The gentleman made no sound at all while he was lifted out of the tall grass and deposited on the road, but Jane saw at once that one shoulder was twisted unnaturally and appeared dislocated.

"We must get him up to Lark Manor immediately," she exclaimed, noting that the unconscious gentleman wore an incongruously large posy of daisies in the button hole of his coat. A Town Tulip no less, she thought disgustedly. She had seen several such dandies during her uneventful Season in London many years ago, and had always thought them a care-for-nobody lot whose only concern was amusement at any cost.

What perverse fate had brought this one to her doorstep? she wondered. And what on earth was such a man doing in this quiet corner of Sussex?

II
Uninvited Guest

The cavalcade that wound up the elm-bordered driveway of Lark Manor twenty minutes later would have caused considerable comment had the summer dusk not shrouded it from prying eyes.

Lady Jane Sutherland led the slow procession in her phaeton, and only when the flickering flambeaux beside the door became visible did she hasten her pace and pull up beneath the narrow porte cochere, throwing the reins to a young groom. She ran up the shallow steps to instruct the old butler to have one of the guest rooms prepared, but was not surprised when the carved door was thrown open and a plump-faced lady, dressed with more style and elegance than usually seen in the country, bustled out to greet her.

"Oh, Jane, my love. There you are," the lady exclaimed—rather superfluously Jane thought. "What delayed you so long at the vicarage? Mrs. Porter is in *such* a taking, dear. We quite thought you had come by some terrible mishap."

Jane smiled encouragingly. "What could possibly happen to us in such an out-of-the-way place as Ditchling, Aunt Prudence?" she inquired teasingly.

Miss Prudence Milford did not reply, her attention suddenly caught by the approaching horses, led by Tobias. "Do not tell me you have acquired yet another team of horses, Jane?" she demanded testily. "Wherever shall we put them all, dear?"

"They are not mine, Aunt," Jane assured her quickly. "Although I must admit that I would not mind it if they were. But we have other things to worry about besides horses, dear. Would you mind asking Mrs. Collins to prepare one of the guest rooms immediately? We have an unexpected guest."

"A guest?" Jane's aunt repeated in astonishment. "At this time of night? Who is this inconsiderate person, dear?"

"A gentleman," Jane corrected her. "At least I assume from his attire he must be a gentleman, although his reckless driving labels him a whipster of the worst kind. He ran over Dido," she added bluntly.

At the sound of her name, the wolfhound raised her head and gave a long, low whine.

Aunt Prudence let out a little squeal of horror and bustled down the steps to make a huge fuss over the wounded dog, who seemed to relish the added attention, while Jane regarded the scene fondly. A moment later, however, the approach of Mr. Logan's heavy wagon brought her mind back to the present dilemma.

Who was this stranger who had fallen into their midst so unceremoniously? she wondered, moving forward to stand beside the low wagon which Mr. Logan had been persuaded to put at the stranger's disposal. Not surprisingly, her Aunt Margery—who had a well-earned reputation as the neighborhood healer—had insisted upon riding with the unconscious man.

Looking down at the pale face of the gentleman, Jane realized for the first time the upheaval this stranger had abruptly brought into her life. His low moan reminded her that she must send to the village for Dr. Middleberry immediately, deal with an irate Mrs. Porter in the kitchen, and instruct the housekeeper to ready a bed for the invalid.

During the next hour Jane took charge with her usual efficiency and by the time the family finally sat down to dinner, Lark Manor had returned to a semblance of order. The unconscious stranger rested comfortably in a guest room in the West Wing, his dislocated shoulder set by Dr. Middleberry. It had been determined that the stranger's horses had suffered no serious damage, and Dido was installed before the drawing-room hearth—quite one of her favorite places—with one of Aunt Margery's secret concoctions plastered all over her hindquarters.

"The wretched man should be thankful he is still in the land of the living," Miss Milford remarked as she cut resolutely into the overcooked portion of roasted lamb on her plate. "Had Mr. Logan been going about his business when the accident occurred—instead of standing in the middle of the lane chatting up that hussy Rosie Tucker until all hours of the night—that wretch might have lain in the ditch until morning with no one the wiser."

"And it would have served the scoundrel right if he had drowned in a ditch among the tadpoles like some penniless waif," Aunt Prudence added with considerable gusto. "I can only wonder what would bring a gentleman—if indeed he does not turn out to be an impostor—to this lonely part of England so late in the evening. I cannot imagine where he proposed to rack up for the night, can you?"

"In all likelihood the villain is absconding with the family jewels, or running from the bailiffs, or something equally disreputable," Jane put in with a smile.

In point of fact, the stranger had appeared more than a little suspicious when they had finally got him cleaned up and into his nightclothes, she thought. His face, once free of the green slime from its immersion in the ditch, had revealed none of the elegant lines or softness she had expected to see. The patient had been older than she had anticipated—in his late thirties, perhaps early forties, Jane estimated—and his features showed evidence of dissipation and hard living. He was definitely not the type of gentleman who frequented her restricted circles. The stranger was as out of place in the quiet village of Ditchling as she had been in London all those years ago.

"I consider it more than likely that he was rushing to an illicit rendezvous with some brazen ladybird he is probably laying siege to," Aunt Prudence added with her usual flair for the bizarre and outrageous.

"Prudence!" her sister exclaimed sharply. "No self-respecting lady should know about such goings-on, and I must ask you not to contaminate our dear Jane's tender ears with your unseemly talk."

"Pooh!" Jane scoffed. "I have known any time these past twelve years what a ladybird is." She chuckled. "They are also referred to as bits of muslin, birds of Paradise, and *amourettes*, I believe. So it is unlikely that my ears will be harmed in any way by the mention of such poor unfortunate creatures."

"Jane, dear," her eldest aunt chided, "I cannot but blame your father for the quite scandalous vocabulary you seemed to have acquired. You most certainly did not hear those low-bred expressions in this house."

"Of course not, Aunt," Jane agreed gently, disregarding the obvious truth that the younger Miss Milford was often given to expressing herself without inhibitions on any number of subjects. She winked across the table at the culprit who had the grace to blush.

The ladies did not linger over dessert, but repaired immediately to the drawing room upstairs, instructing Harvey to bring up their tea tray earlier than usual since they had a long night ahead of them, sitting with the patient.

"I shall take the first shift," Aunt Margery announced, no sooner had she finished her first cup of tea. "Prudence can relieve me at midnight, and perhaps Mrs. Collins might be persuaded to take over at four in the morning."

"And when shall I take my turn?" Jane wanted to know, well aware that, if allowed to do so, Margery would take most of the patient's care upon her own shoulders. "Why not let me take the midnight shift? You know how Aunt Prudence likes to sleep late in the mornings."

Miss Milford gave her a quelling glance. "Certainly not, child," she said firmly. "Your dear mama would never forgive me if she heard I had allowed you to spend the night in a gentleman's bedchamber. Alone."

Jane bristled. "I am hardly a child, Aunt. And what harm do you suppose I can come to if the gentleman is unconscious? Besides," she added prosaically, "our guest does not strike me as the kind of gentleman who would look twice at a plain-faced spinster of uncertain age."

"You never know with these town beaux, dear," Prudence put in sententiously. "I have heard that they will indulge their beastly passions with any willing female. And often enough with those who are not so willing."

"You may rest assured that I am not one of those willing females, Aunt," Jane cut in quickly, before Margery could rebuke her sister for this piece of plain speaking. "And I promise you that if this rogue should take me for one, I will cosh him over the head with the chamber pot, dear."

And so it was that Jane found herself sitting by the stranger's bedside at four o'clock that summer morning, waiting for the birds to start their daily choir, and listening to the breathing of the man in the bed.

She had drawn the high-backed fauteuil close enough to allow her to observe the patient comfortably. He was still unconscious, but his breathing appeared easier, and Jane was relieved that he no longer tossed and turned about as he had when the footmen first laid him on the bed. Stout fellows though they were, Thomas and James were sweating profusely by the time they had carried the stranger up the two flights and along the corridor to the West Wing guest chamber Mrs. Collins had prepared for him.

Jane let her eyes wander over the large frame outlined under the light coverings. Yes, she mused, he was certainly tall, and when divested of his damp coat and soiled shirt, the uninvited guest had displayed an impressive expanse of shoulders and chest. Jane found herself wondering if the gentleman was one of those fashionable bucks who made a cult of their athletic prowess by working out regularly in Jackson's Saloon with the master. Her own father had often boasted of going into the ring with Gentleman Jackson in his heyday, but her brother John had flatly refused to have anything to do with such a vicious sport, intended—or so he would have it—for bloodthirsty commoners and sadistic, bored nobles.

A movement from the bed aroused Jane from her musings, and she rose to tuck the covers more securely under the patient's chin. He moaned, as if in protest, and Jane noticed that his forehead was damp with sweat. Dr. Middleberry had warned of a fever setting in, so Jane dipped a cloth into the bowl of lavender water by the bedside and gently wiped the patient's brow. This action elicited another moan from the gentleman, who moved his head away.

Not to be outdone, Jane grasped his chin firmly and finished her task, discovering in the process that the patient's nightshirt was damp. Alarmed, she turned down the covers, and applied the cool cloth to the heavily muscled neck and what she could reach of the shoulders.

Without warning a strong hand shot out and grasped her wrist, and a harsh voice cut into the silence of the room.

"Not now, Lydia, my sweet," the stranger growled, bringing Jane's hand to his lips for a brief caress. "I am not in prime twig at the moment, I fear. But I shall make it up to you, love. I promise."

Jane felt her face turn scarlet as the import of the stranger's words became clear. He spoke as though he were addressing a lover, she realized with a shock, one of those ladybirds Aunt Prudence had spoken of earlier. Someone called Lydia, who evidently had expected him to come to her last night. Jane shied away from examining too closely the purpose of such a clandestine assignation, but she was certain it could not have been anything but clandestine, and that the man who lay clutching her hand in his viselike grip had been up to no good when he drove so rashly through Ditchling yesterday evening.

Unless, of course, the mysterious Lydia was the gentleman's wife.

The thought struck her without warning, and Jane felt rather foolish for having instantly judged the stranger so harshly. She was becoming as impressionable as Aunt Prudence, she thought. Always ready to leap to some fantastic conclusion without the slightest thread of evidence. Perhaps the poor man had been rushing home to his beloved wife, who might—for all she knew—be in childbed, or laid low by some mysterious malady. Perhaps—and here Jane experienced an odd chill—the stranger had a houseful of little ones looking forward to his arrival.

Jane glanced at her fingers, still pressed against the warmth of the gentleman's mouth and shivered. No, she thought, this did not look like a man tied to any female's apron strings. Besides, she had to admit, the explanation involving the lascivious lightskirt awaiting her lover was far more intriguing. And credible, too, she thought, feeling the stranger's lips pressing another kiss on the tender curve of her palm.

Gingerly, Jane tried to free herself from the stranger's grasp, but instantly his grip tightened.

"Why so skittish, love?" he said in a low voice that made Jane's spine prickle not unpleasantly. "Be a good girl and lie down beside me, Lydia. I want to feel your lovely curves. After all, I paid enough for the privilege, would you not agree, my sweet?"

With a gasp of shock, Jane tried to jerk free of the relentless grip, but the iron fingers only seemed to dig more deeply into her tender wrist. She knew herself to be blushing furiously and was thankful that the outspoken guest appeared to be talking in his sleep. At least she hoped that he was not fully conscious.

She glanced quickly up at his face and froze. Two gray eyes held her in their heated stare, and it took Jane several uncomfortable moments before she realized that the gentleman did not actually see her at all. He saw only what he had evidently expected to see, a female called Lydia.

"Get me some water, Lydia," he said hoarsely. "I am dying of thirst, love."

"Not unless you release me, sir," Jane murmured, hoping that her voice would not give her away. She felt his hand grow slack and was able to pull away, rubbing her wrist, which showed the red marks of his fingers. Her first instinct was to flee the room, but she brushed that cowardly thought aside and reached for the water jug instead.

His eyes were closed when she leaned over to press the glass against his lips, but he drank greedily, then subsided against the pillows with a sigh.

Jane echoed the sigh, but hers was one of relief. She went to work with the cool lavender water, bathing his face gently, avoiding the ugly gash that had sliced into his right forehead and still bled sluggishly. She should sprinkle bascilicum powder on it again, she thought, making a mental note of it.

"Hmm," she heard the stranger murmur, as she ran the cooling cloth down his neck. "Here, love," he mumbled sleepily, tugging at the neck of his nightshirt until it opened to reveal a large expanse of chest, thickly matted and damp with sweat. "Cool me here, too, sweetheart. I am burning up." Abruptly he threw the covers off, revealing the cotton nightshirt stuck damply to his belly and thighs.

Jane quickly averted her eyes from the masculine form outlined beneath the clinging damp cotton, and drawing a deep breath to steady herself, resolutely pulled the sheet up again.

Glad that her Aunt Margery had not been present to witness the stranger's immodest display of gentlemanly unmentionables, Jane turned to search for the bascilicum powder, wondering if perhaps she should administer a few drops of laudanum left by Dr. Middleberry to help the patient rest.

When she turned back to the bed, the uninvited guest was breathing deeply and regularly. He had fallen fast asleep again.

III
Initial Skirmish

The unusual sound of a cock crowing awakened him, and Martin Douglas, sixth Earl of Ridgeway, imagined himself a boy again, waking up in his room at Ridgeway Park in Dorset. It was clearly summer, and for one brief, invigorating moment he was once more filled with youthful eagerness and wonder at the world that awaited him outside on his father's sprawling estate. The euphoria dimmed, and the earl felt the eagerness ebb, taking with it the energy and adventure of youth.

He felt the familiar weight of boredom settled on his chest. The world had not lived up to his youthful expectations, he thought morosely. Or perhaps he had not lived up to the world's expectations. Either way, it mattered little at this stage in his life, for the best part of it seemed to have escaped him anyway.

He resolutely put these morbid notions aside. Self-pity was abhorrent to him, but increasingly of late he seemed to find himself wallowing in it. Impatient at the direction of his thoughts, Martin threw off the covers, which seemed to be suffocating him. The sudden movement brought a groan to his lips. What in Hades was the matter with him? he wondered, gingerly attempting to sit up in bed. He discovered that such a feat was impossible unless he wished to

endure excruciating pain in various parts of his body. He
groaned aloud and sank back into the feather pillows, suddenly aware that he was covered with sweat and had a
crushing headache.

And where the devil was Lydia?

The earl closed his eyes and tried to order his thoughts.
Even that was painful and the room appeared to be swaying
alarmingly. He opened them again quickly, and the room
settled down around him. It was then he noticed that this
was not Lydia's room—a room that had always inhibited
him with its nauseating pinkness. Ruffles, flounced curtains, bows and curlicues, embroidered cushions on every
available space—all in various shades of pink, very like
Lydia herself, he thought cynically.

Nor was it the guest room she kept especially for him
in her Brighton residence. And he was in Brighton, was
he not? The seaside resort had certainly been his destination, but he had no clear recollection of his arrival there.
But he did recall Lydia fussing over him, bathing him
with lavender water of all things, and touching him rather
intimately, as Lydia was prone to do at the slightest
provocation.

Ever insistent on getting her pound of flesh was Lydia,
Martin remembered grimly. Insistent, avaricious, and
grasping. He wondered suddenly what had inspired him to
accept her coyly worded invitation to spend a week or two
with her in Brighton. Undoubtedly boredom with London,
so pitifully thin of company in summer. And had he not already begun to tire of the luscious Lady Pamela, his latest
light-of-love? Lydia's note had arrived at a propitious time,
and he had taken off without pausing to reflect on the futility of it all.

Martin closed his eyes again, but the room resumed its
dipping and rolling, quite as though he were aboard his
yacht, the *Seabird*, making a particularly rough crossing to

Calais. He opened them in time to see a tall, rather regal female of definitely unmarriageable age sweep into the room.

At least she was not Lydia, a point in her favor, Martin thought with grim humor.

"Where the devil am I?" he inquired without preamble.

The female ignored him and set the small tray she was carrying down on the oval table beneath one of the open windows. When she turned and approached the bed with a bowl in her hands, Martin saw that he had fallen into the clutches of one of those managing females he had tried to avoid all his life.

"I asked you a question," he said in a tone intended to sound firm and authoritarian. To his horror he sounded merely pettish to his own ears.

"Good morning to you, sir," the female said in a mellow, faintly ironic tone, quite as though he had not spoken at all. "I have brought some cool water to relieve that fever." She set the bowl down on the small table beside the bed and calmly proceeded to wring out a linen cloth. The pungent smell of lemon filled the room.

"Lemon?" he remarked crossly. "What happened to the lavender?"

She glanced at him then, a faint smile touching her lips. "You prefer lavender, sir?" she asked as though addressing a child. "I shall try to remember next time."

"I care not a fig for either," Martin growled, wincing at the pain that shot through his head. "And furthermore, I am dying of thirst." In actuality he felt increasingly unwell, and his body seemed to be burning up.

The tall female appeared not to have heard him, for she methodically wiped his face and throat with the cool cloth. In truth her touch was gentle and the coolness soothed his aching head, but Martin was unaccustomed to having his commands disregarded.

"Water," he repeated in a voice that sounded more like a croak.

"All in good time, sir," the managing female replied, passing the cool cloth over his face again, then down his neck and across his left shoulder beneath his damp nightshirt. The gently probing fingers made him groan aloud as an unexpected flash of pain engulfed him.

"Ah! I see your shoulder still pains you," she remarked calmly, as though impervious to his suffering. "Doctor Middleberry will be along shortly to examine you again." She poured a glass of water and, raising his head with one hand, held it to his lips.

Martin gulped the water eagerly, and it was not until he had emptied the glass that he thought to glance up at the lady who was leaning over the bed. What he saw gave him considerable pause. The wench was comely, for all she must be at her last prayers by London standards. She smelled of lavender and her skin was a flawless cream marred only by faint laugh lines around her eyes. And her eyes! Good God, Martin thought, staring into the startling amber depths and seeing something there he had not seen in a woman's gaze before.

"Would you like some more?"

Her voice, low and entirely lacking in the cloying simper he was used to hearing in female chatter, brought him back to his senses, and he found himself thinking—quite irrationally and with a strange longing he could not identify— that yes, indeed, he would like a good deal more than water from this clear-eyed nymph who seemed so utterly unaffected by his notorious charm and good looks.

"What is your name, my dear?" he said, ignoring her question.

She regarded him quizzically for a moment, as though she would rather not identify herself. "Lady Jane Sutherland," she said finally, turning away to replace the glass.

"And this place is?"

"Lark Manor, in Sussex, some fifteen miles north of Brighton."

To Martin's surprise she showed no interest in his identity, and before he could reveal it, the door opened, and a gray-haired gentleman with long, carefully groomed whiskers entered the room briskly.

As the good doctor introduced himself, Lady Jane Sutherland slipped quietly out of the room, without so much as a backward glance.

Jane paused for a moment after closing the door to the patient's chamber. Something about the stranger had disconcerted her. Why, for instance, had she felt that odd reluctance to tell him her name? she wondered. Why had she not demanded to know his? Absentmindedly she rubbed the faint marks his fingers had left on her wrist five days ago. He had called her Lydia, but the identity of this female with whom their guest appeared to be on intimate terms was still a mystery.

After sending one of the footmen up to help the good doctor change the patient's damp nightshirt and bedsheets, Jane made her way to the sunny breakfast parlor at the back of the house.

"Well, dear," Aunt Margery inquired, "how is our gentleman feeling this morning?"

"He was finally conscious when I went upstairs, Aunt, so I left him alone with Dr. Middleberry. He is still feverish and seems to be in severe pain."

"Did he tell you his name, dear?" Aunt Prudence demanded, pouring her niece a steaming cup of tea.

"I did not think to ask," Jane admitted, wondering again at her lack of curiosity in this regard. But no, she thought, it was not that she did not wish to know who the stranger was. It was a growing sensation, which had intensified as the days went by, and she had assumed an increasing share of the sickroom duties, that she had encountered the strange gentleman before. And this morning when, for the first time in five days, the stranger had regained consciousness, she had felt it again.

She spread a thick layer of currant jelly on her toast, her mind still occupied with the enigma of the strange gentleman upstairs. The likelihood of her ever having met a man of that stamp was too remote to be considered, yet there had been something about his eyes—particularly their elusive color, somewhere between gray and blue—that had stirred unpleasant memories.

Jane shook off this notion as too fanciful by half, and smiled cheerfully at the doctor, who was at that moment ushered into the breakfast parlor by the stooped and silent Harvey.

"Well, Dr. Middleberry," she inquired, "how do you find our invalid this morning? Does he show any signs of improvement?"

"Ah, yes, indeed, my dear Lady Jane," the doctor replied in the clipped, pompous tone he affected with the ladies at Lark Manor. "Your Mr. Martin is well on the way to complete recovery, although he is still somewhat feverish, and his shoulder, which as you know sustained a nasty wrench, will pain him for some time to come, I imagine."

"And his poor ankle, doctor?" Miss Prudence Milford inquired solicitously. "Will he be able to walk now that he is conscious again?"

"Once the fever subsides, my dear lady," the doctor replied, accepting the cup of tea offered by his hostess. "But until that happens, I do not want to see him out of his bed, and so I have told him."

So, Jane thought with an odd feeling of disappointment, the stranger was a stranger no more. He was—in the doctor's words—*their* Mr. Martin. And since she was certain she knew no one of that name, should she not feel relieved? she reasoned, wondering why she did not. She could not repress a smile at the doctor's assumption that his word would be law to the autocratic Mr. Martin.

"Mr. Martin tells me he was on his way to Brighton to join his family for the summer. I imagine he will wish to send a message to them to allay their fears for his safety."

The ladies heartily agreed with the doctor's suggestion, and Jane was delegated to arrange for a letter to be taken down to Brighton by one of the grooms. With this charitable errand in mind, Jane entered Mr. Martin's bedchamber ten minutes later bearing her writing case and a freshly sharpened pen.

She paused by the bed, vaguely alarmed at the patient's appearance. His eyes were closed, and his face, drawn and feverish, glistened with a sheen of perspiration. On the point of retiring to leave the gentleman to his rest, Jane suddenly became aware that Mr. Martin was observing her from beneath his drooping lids.

"I have come to help you write a message to your family, Mr. Martin," she said briskly, taking a seat in the nearest chair, with the writing case on her lap.

"I have no wish to write to anyone."

Jane ignored the surly tone and settled herself more comfortably in the chair, her lips set in a bland smile. "Oh, I am sure you do, sir," she remarked encouragingly. "You would not wish your family to worry about you now, would you?"

This was greeted by what Jane took to be a grunt of amusement.

"Now if you will just give me your family's address in Brighton, I can do the rest for you," she continued.

After a slight pause, Mr. Martin said in a dull voice, "I have no family in Brighton, my dear."

Jane looked up from the sheet of paper she had taken from the case. He was observing her with a cynical smile on his lips, as if contemplating an unpleasant private jest. "But . . . " she began, startled at a sudden flash of memory in which a similar cynical smile had played a significant part. "I understood Dr. Middleberry to say you had."

For a long moment Jane felt Mr. Martin's smoky eyes—

blue or gray, she could not decide which—bore into hers, and once again experienced a faint quiver of recognition. It annoyed her to think that perhaps her advancing years were beginning to impair her mind.

"The doctor is mistaken," Mr. Martin said bluntly. "I have no family in Brighton."

"But Brighton was your destination, I take it," Jane insisted patiently.

The patient sighed and closed his eyes. "Perhaps," he murmured. "Perhaps not. Who is to say what our ultimate destination will be."

Surprised at the hint of despair she detected in these odd words, Jane laid the writing case aside and stood up. Reaching for the damp cloth, she rinsed it out and applied it to the patient's hot face.

"Have you no one you would wish to inform of your accident, sir?" she inquired softly after a while, thinking of the Lydia he had spoken to with such intimacy during his delirium earlier that morning.

She felt him tense immediately.

"I shall be on my way soon enough," he muttered. "A letter would only alarm m-my mother."

At least he did have a mother, Jane thought, strangely comforted by this admission. But Mr. Martin was deluding himself if he imagined he would be able to travel in less than a sennight.

"I would not count on leaving us for another week, sir, perhaps two, depending on how soon the fever subsides," she said firmly, watching a frown crease the wide expanse of his brow. "And your ankle will not yet bear your—"

"Two weeks!" The harshness of his exclamation made Jane jump. "That blathering sawbones assured me I was on the mend," Mr. Martin added, his eyes wide open and their expression forbidding. "I have no intention of being molly-coddled for another week, much less two. If you will order my team poled up, I shall take my leave tomorrow morning."

The effort of this prolonged speech seemed to take all the fire out of him, for Mr. Martin slumped back against the pillows, his eyes closed.

"Regardless of how much you wish to be rid of us, sir," Jane said curtly, annoyed at the gentleman's deliberate rudeness, "it should be obvious to anyone with an ounce of wit that you are in no condition to travel. Furthermore, I should also advise you that, as a result of your execrable driving, you no longer have a curricle in which to travel."

The patient's eyes flew open again, and Jane felt a perverse sense of satisfaction at the alarm she saw in them. That would teach the odious man to be more mannerly, she thought, fascinated by the changing color of his eyes, which now appeared almost slate-gray. And furiously angry, she saw with an involuntary shiver.

"What happened to my curricle?" he barked coldly.

Jane laughed in his face, delighting in the impotent fury clouding the gentleman's grim countenance. "What is left of it, I presume you mean, sir? The pieces are piled in the stable yard, and I was tempted to use them for firewood, but thought it might be a salutary lesson to you to see how nearly you escaped death."

"And my horses?" he snapped, his face cold.

"I wondered when you would ask," Jane responded accusingly. "Such a splendid team does not deserve a cowhanded whipster, sir, that I can say. They are superb goers, and I would not mind owning them myself."

Mr. Martin glared at her, dawning horror in his eyes. "Am I to understand that you have been driving my team, madam?" he inquired in a harsh voice.

"There was no reason not to, sir," Jane replied acidly. She was more than a little proud of her skill with horses and did not take kindly to criticism. "I do not trust the grooms with blooded horses."

"And I do not trust a female to drive my team, madam," came the curt response. "You will not do so again."

Jane bristled. "How do you intend to stop me, sir?"

She returned the patient's furious glare without flinching. Finally her sense of humor got the better of her, and she laughed. "You should not make threats you cannot enforce, sir," she said teasingly, half enjoying the battle of wits with a gentleman as formidable as Mr. Martin.

The gentleman's eyes lost some of their fury, and Jane tensed when she saw the cynical amusement reappear in their gray depths.

"I presume you are at your last prayers, my lady," Mr. Martin drawled with studied insolence. "There can be no other explanation for this desperate waspishness, derived, no doubt, from spinsterish frustration at not having snared yourself a husband."

Jane felt herself blanch at this unexpected attack. The unkind words came too close to the truth for comfort, and it took all her inner fortitude to refrain from flinging the damp cloth, which she still clutched in one hand, in the odious creature's smug face.

Something in the gentleman's expression of disgust jogged her memory again, but Jane could not imagine any acquaintance, however casual, subjecting her to the insult the insupportable Mr. Martin had just thrown at her.

"Yes," she said with deliberate calm. "I am most definitely at my last prayers, sir—as you so kindly express it. And every morning when I awake, I thank my Maker from the bottom of my heart for saving me from the unhappy fate of being tied to a loathsome creature like you."

She had expected him to return a scathing retort, and was startled when he laughed.

"Well spoken, my dear. I like females with spirit. But are you not forgetting the nights, love? When you go to your cold bed at night, do you not secretly wish for a loathsome creature like me to warm your blood for you? Can you honestly say that you have never . . ."

But Jane did not stay to hear the end of this scandalous suggestion. With a haughty tilt to her chin, she turned and walked out of the chamber, closing the door forcefully behind her.

IV
The Wedding Gown

No sooner had the door closed behind Lady Jane than the smug smile faded from the earl's face. In the heat of argument he had ignored his throbbing head and aching shoulder, but now he felt drained of energy, and the verbal scuffle with the lady had left him with a bad taste in his mouth. There had been no call to insult a gently-bred female. Had he sunk so low that he could do so without flinching in disgust at his own perversity? he wondered, wishing the harsh words unsaid.

More than anything, Martin wished for a chance to retract his offensive comments, but that was out of the question. Some instinct told him that Lady Jane would not come near him again, and he did not blame her. And in his present weakened state, there was no chance that he could seek her out and press his abject apology on her. In all likelihood the lady would fling it back in his teeth, and he smiled to himself at the prospect of witnessing once again the fiery glitter in those magnificent eyes.

He glanced longingly at the bowl of cool water she had used to bathe his face, and cursed himself for the flare of temper that had driven her away when he needed to feel that gentle, cooling touch on his burning skin. He closed his eyes, trying to imagine what it might be like to feel those cool hands on his whole body, bringing relief from the fever that consumed him.

This thought led to others, considerably less innocent, and by the time he dropped off into an uneasy sleep, Martin promised himself that before he left the shelter of Lark Manor, he would try his hand at seducing an amber-eyed termagant at her last prayers.

A cool sensation on his forehead brought him out of his fitful slumber and Martin examined the female who was bathing his face from between lowered lids. Her touch alone told him that she was not his Lady Jane, and when she turned to rinse out the cloth, he saw that she was considerably older and less lithesome. He sighed, and the lady turned a pair of shrewd blue eyes upon him.

"Awake, are you, sir?" she remarked sternly. "I shall ask Mrs. Porter to send up your chicken broth, although heaven knows, you do not deserve it."

Martin opened his eyes and regarded the lady's censorial expression curiously. "I do not care for such tasteless slop," he growled, wondering what he had done to incur this dragon's wrath. "Where is Lady Jane?"

The lady's expression became suddenly several degrees cooler. "My niece is out driving, sir," she said stiffly. "And if you know what is good for you, you will drink your broth and like it," she added belligerently. "I want you out of this house within a sennight, so put your mind to it."

Her dislike was so patent that Martin was taken aback.

"You cannot wish it more than I, madam," he retorted, stung by her unexpected rejection. "And I trust your niece is not driving my horses, for I have expressly forbidden her to do so."

To his surprise, the dragon let out a hearty laugh that set her angular frame aquiver. "Which only goes to show how little you know my niece, Mr. Martin," she remarked, evidently enjoying a secret jest. She chuckled, regarding him all the while with her critical blue gaze.

"Forbid her to drive your nags, did you, sir? That's like waving a red flag at Squire Morris's Jersey bull, if you know what I mean. No wonder the sweet lass ran straight down to the stables as though all the devils in hell were after her." She paused to gaze at him pityingly. "Had those chestnuts of yours poled up quicker than you could say Jack Robinson, did our Jane. No doubt she is kicking up a rare dust at this very moment. Not one to take orders tamely, is our Jane. No, sir. Has a mind of her own that girl and no mistake."

The notion seemed to give the dragon considerable pleasure, for her face was wreathed in smiles when she left him a short time later in the care of Thomas, the footman.

So, Martin mused—looking with distaste at the bowl of thin gruel Thomas was spooning into his mouth—the fiery Lady Jane was one of those impudent females who considered themselves equal to men was she? And she was out there driving his best team in direct defiance of his orders. Well, he thought savagely, she was about to learn that no female trifled with Martin Douglas, not even one with eyes the color of polished amber.

The challenge of devising a plan to bring a disobedient female to her senses became so engrossing that when Thomas stood up to leave, Martin found that he had finished every last drop of the insipid gruel without a protest.

By the time Jane returned from tooling Mr. Martin's chestnuts around the countryside at speeds that had the locals shaking their heads in dismay, her spirits were considerably restored. She had derived particular delight in imagining Mr. Martin's fury when he discovered her deliberate disregard for his orders. As a result she was smiling when she joined her aunts for the ample nuncheon spread for them in the small dining room.

"How was your drive, dear?" her Aunt Margery demanded as soon as Jane had accepted her plate from Harvey.

Jane met her aunt's shrewd glance and smiled. "Wonderfully invigorating, Aunt," she replied lightly. "Those chestnuts are superb goers. I am sorely tempted to make our rakish guest an offer for them."

"I would not do so, if I were you, dear," Margery remarked blandly. "I fancy our Mr. Martin would take pleasure in denying you."

"You are so right, Aunt," Jane acknowledged ruefully. "And since I have promised myself not to set eyes on the odious man again, I cannot very well make him an offer for his horses, can I?"

"No, indeed," Margery agreed noncommittally.

"What has the dear man done to send you into the boughs, Jane?" Prudence exclaimed, pausing in the act of serving herself another wedge of pigeon pie, her forget-me-not eyes clouded with concern.

"He was unpardonably rude to her this morning," Margery responded before Jane could find a suitable answer. Jane had not given her aunt a full account of their guest's scandalous remarks, of course, but she had a suspicion that Aunt Margery—who was wide awake on all counts—had come to her own conclusions regarding the autocratic Mr. Martin's dubious character.

Her decision to play least-in-sight where their guest was concerned was put to the test that very evening, when Thomas came rushing downstairs, his face and livery dripping with Mrs. Porter's gruel.

"Threw it in me face, 'e did, milady," the much aggrieved footman exclaimed after the ladies had been summoned to the kitchen to witness the debacle.

"A wicked, willful rogue 'e is, too," Mrs. Porter expostulated, her round cheeks flushed with righteous indignation. "And 'e will starve to death, 'e will, before I lift a finger to cook another morsel for the uncouth wretch."

"Hush, Mrs. Porter," Prudence said, shocked at the belligerence in the cook's voice. "Mr. Martin is an invalid, and I am sure there must be some other explanation for his odd behavior."

"Odd indeed?" Margery exclaimed sharply. "I would call it plainly malicious and irresponsible. I shall go up and have a serious talk with the gentleman on the instant."

Ten minutes later Miss Milford was back, and Jane could see from her smug expression that her assertive aunt had emerged victorious from her skirmish with the hardened rogue upstairs.

"Asking for you, he is, the impertinent scoundrel," Margery exclaimed in scathing tones, as she joined the ladies in the drawing room before dinner. "Actually had the effrontery to demand that you go up to him, Jane, like some servant wench he can order about as he chooses. I informed him that no one in this house will take orders from some mannerless jackstraw who comes out of nowhere to throw our household into a tizzy."

Jane could well imagine Mr. Martin's chagrin at being called a jackstraw, and only wished she had been there to see it.

"You did exactly right, Aunt," she observed, handing her aunt a glass of sherry. "We are too set in our ways here at Lark Manor to put up with any gentleman's foibles," she added. "And the sooner Mr. Martin recognizes that he is not master here, the sooner he will get tired of playing lord of the manor and go back from whence he came."

Miss Prudence Milford delicately wiped her lips on her white embroidered serviette and focused her dreamy blue eyes on her niece. "We should not be too hard on the poor gentleman, Jane, my love," she began. "It cannot be very comfortable for a strapping young man like Mr. Martin to be confined to his bed for so long. I am only surprised he has endured the uninspiring company of three spinsters so tamely. I cannot but imagine he is accustomed to livelier company."

"Pooh!" Jane exclaimed. "That man is no gentleman, Aunt, take my word for it," she added darkly, the memory of Mr. Martin's scandalous suggestion still fresh in her mind. "And he is hardly in the first flush of youth. I confess I agree with Mrs. Porter, the rogue can starve to death before I will come running at his every beck and call. Who does he think he is?"

So the contentious Mr. Martin went without his supper that night, and as Jane blew out her candle and climbed into bed, she wondered how long this absurd stubbornness on the part of their troublesome guest would last. It was nothing to her, of course, that the arrogant oaf was probably lying there suffering pangs of hunger, but for some obscure reason, Jane could not get Mr. Martin out of her mind. His last words to her still titillated her memory and drew her thoughts along paths she had long ago abandoned as fruitless. Did she indeed regret not having made more of a push to attract a husband during that disastrous Season in London ten years ago? Did she—as that lecherous rogue obviously assumed—secretly wish for a loathsome creature like Mr. Martin to warm her bed at night? she wondered, feeling herself blush in the darkness at this immodest notion.

Alarmed at the direction of her thoughts, Jane turned over and settled her cheek more comfortably into the soft pillow. She could manage very well without a husband, thank you, she told herself. And while Mr. Martin was right to consider her on the shelf, it was not as though she lacked suitors. The Reverend Frederick Coulton had become rather pointed in his preference for her company of late, and Aunt Prudence—the eternal romantic—had taken to twitting her about the lanky, soft-spoken vicar, and speculating upon the likelihood of bringing him up to scratch.

Jane shuddered and pulled the sheet more closely about her. It was not that she disliked Frederick Coulton. Actually she enjoyed their philosophical discussions. But if she were to wed—which naturally she had no intention of doing, she told herself firmly—and if she could indulge her most secret fantasies, Jane had to admit that Reverend Coulton came nowhere close to making her heart sing.

Only one gentleman had ever come close to fulfilling these foolish fantasies, and Jane had cast him out of her mind ten years ago, she remembered. It had been a long, long time since the handsome, arrogant image of Viscount Hammond had invaded her memory. She had endured heartbreak and humiliation on his account, and the agony of that first impossible love had lingered for months after her abrupt return to Sutherland Park after Lady Mansfield's fateful ball. And it had probably been for the best anyway, she told herself once again, as she had so often in the past. She had always been an awkward dancer, tense and self-conscious of her height and budding womanhood. And she would have been tongue-tied to boot.

The bitterness of the viscount's careless cruelty had faded away with the years, but Jane had preserved the damning evidence of his perfidy. Her dance card, faded and worn around the edges, still lay at the bottom of her jewel box, together with the pressed rose she had worn in her hair.

Jane sighed at these old memories, which no longer had the power to hurt her. Many years had passed since she had stolen a glance at that arrogantly sprawling signature, traced it longingly with her finger as only a young girl in the throes of her first love would do. Since she had conjured up the memory of that imperious gaze, from eyes that were neither quite blue nor entirely gray, but a curious mixture of the two. And cold, as only a bored gentleman's eyes could be.

*   *   *

The memory of blue-gray eyes was still with her when Jane rose the following morning, but she was not thinking of the lost viscount but of the gentleman in the West Wing. Would he eat his breakfast this morning? she wondered. And would he demand her presence as he had last night? The notion of a gentleman summoning her to his bedchamber brought a faint flush to her cheeks as she sat before the beveled mirror watching Lucy arrange her hair.

"You are in looks this morning, milady," the abigail observed, tucking one recalcitrant auburn curl into place. "Miss Prudence asked me to remind you that Mrs. Munster will be here at ten to fit your masquerade gown."

Jane frowned. Her thoughts had been so occupied with pointless speculation about their autocratic guest, that she had forgotten all about the masquerade ball.

"Tell my aunt that I will be along directly, Lucy," she said. "I am still not convinced that we should cut up her old wedding gown just to make me resemble a medieval queen. It seems such a sacrilege."

"I can see as how it might be took for a sacrilege, milady, but look at it this way," Lucy said in her practical way. "Miss Prudence is fifty-two if she be a day, and the likelihood of her ever needing a wedding gown is pretty slim, if you ask me. Besides, milady, with your coloring you will look a proper treat in all that creamy lace and satin. Trust me."

Jane was not convinced, and when she entered her aunt's sunny sitting room later that morning and saw the heap of lace thrown casually over the back of a chair, she could not help expressing her reluctance to destroy such a beautiful gown.

"But you will be doing no such thing, dearest Jane," her aunt answered promptly, lifting the lacy gown and measuring it against her niece's slender figure. "Of course, it will have to be lengthened, but Mrs. Munster should be able to do so easily. And do not look so downcast, dear. The gown has only sad memories for me, since my poor dear Raymond never lived to see me wear it." Prudence paused, and her dreamy blue eyes gazed out of the open window as though searching for a face that was no longer there.

Jane knew better than to commiserate with her aunt's tragic loss of her betrothed, Major Raymond St. Cloud, so many years ago. Prudence belied her romantic nature when it came to mourning the past, refusing to indulge in what she called senseless whining over what was not meant to be. Much as Jane admired her aunt's fortitude, she had been shocked when Prudence had first suggested turning her treasured wedding gown into a frivolous make-believe disguise for a masquerade ball.

Gingerly she touched the satin with her fingertips. Except for the outdated style, the gown was as fresh as though it had been made up last week, and Jane was struck—as she always was when the subject of her aunt's blighted hopes came up—by the multitude of unfulfilled dreams this mass of lace and satin must signify for her aunt. Surely after all these years it must still hurt to remember what might have been, she thought. Compared to what her aunt had suffered, Jane felt her own disappointment in love was very insignificant indeed.

And, unlike her aunt, she had Frederick Coulton standing in the wings if she ever changed her mind. Jane wished she might have remembered to mention her unprepossessing suitor when that obnoxious gentleman in the West Wing had called her an ape-leader. That would have wiped the smug grin from his face, she thought, seeing in her mind's eye the taunting laughter fade from those smoky eyes.

Blue-gray eyes. Was it a trick of the Fates or merely coincidence that Mr. Martin's eyes awoke a long-dormant and highly improper yearning in her heart? Jane wondered.

V
The Kiss

By the time Mrs. Munster had measured, pinned, tucked, and basted to her satisfaction, the hour was so advanced that the ladies were late in joining Miss Milford in the dining room for nuncheon.

"Well?" Margery demanded as soon as Lady Jane had taken her seat at the table. "How does our dear Jane look in a wedding gown?"

"Beautiful!" Prudence exclaimed, her eyes dewy. "I only wish that she might wear that old gown to her own wedding instead of to a silly masquerade."

"Nonsense, Aunt," Jane cut in before the sentimental Prudence could expand on this fruitless line of conversation. "That is balderdash, and you know it. The gown is the most beautiful thing I have ever seen, of course, and I shall love wearing it at my birthday ball, but it is no longer a wedding gown, dear. It is a masquerade gown, designed to make me look like a medieval queen or something equally improbable."

Prudence only smiled her misty, secretive smile, and helped herself to the cold duck Harvey was holding for her inspection. "It will always be a wedding gown in my eyes, Jane dear, and I hope that our Mr. Coulton will see it that

way too, and take you to the altar in it. How very romantic
that would be, do you not agree, Margery?"

Miss Milford sniffed audibly. "I rather think our vicar
lacks your sense of the romantic, Pru," she remarked dryly.
"I cannot see him doing anything that takes the least bit of
imagination, my dear. Call me unfeeling if you will, but
Fred Coulton strikes me as being far too much under his
sister's thumb to make a push to take on a wife unless Mary
were to suggest it to him."

"But Jane and Mary Coulton are good friends, are you
not, dear?"

"Friends perhaps," Jane replied with a laugh. "But hardly
bosom-bows, Aunt, and I doubt Mary would want me running the vicarage."

Prudence pooh-poohed this objection, saying that if
Mary could not see the advantages of becoming related to
an earl's daughter, she must have windmills in her head.

The conversation turned to other things after that, mostly
concerning the arrangements for the masquerade ball, and it
was not until later that afternoon, that Jane heard rumors
from the housemaid that Mr. Martin had refused both his
breakfast and his midmorning bowl of gruel.

"Let the cantankerous creature starve, I says," Mrs.
Porter declared crossly when Jane went down to the kitchen
to investigate these disturbing rumors. "Dr. Middleberry
told me I was to give him nothing but thin gruel for the rest
of the week," the cook announced in her strident voice.
"And thin gruel is all he will get from me, let me tell you,
milady. Feverish as the rogue is, it would be foolhardy to
give him the beefsteak and ale he is calling for."

Jane had to agree with the irate cook, but she thought it
prudent to send for the doctor. She had no desire to have a
gentleman—even the odious Mr. Martin—expire on the
premises through any negligence on her part.

Dr. Middleberry assured her that the patient was in no
danger of giving up the ghost in the immediate future, but

he did advise Lady Jane—in that prosy voice of his that Jane despised—to humor the gentleman's request that she attend him rather than Miss Milford.

At first Jane was incensed at what she saw as outright blackmail on the part of a gentleman determined—like most others she had known—to impose his will at all costs. By the middle of the afternoon, however, after the patient had again refused to eat his nuncheon, she relented and climbed the stairs to the West Wing.

The sight that met her eyes when she opened Mr. Martin's bedchamber door made her wish she had not come. The man sitting on the bed, clad only in his buff-colored breeches, attempting fruitlessly to pull the freshly starched shirt over his head, evidently had not heard her knock. His struggles with the garment, which he appeared too weak to position correctly, caused him to utter a litany of curses that made Jane's ears tingle.

Her first impulse, upon casting her astonished gaze on this broad expanse of masculine anatomy, was to withdraw with all maidenly haste. A instant of reflection made her change her mind, and her lips thinned dangerously as she strode into the room and seized the mangled shirt with both hands. Her temper thoroughly aroused, Jane yanked the offending garment out of Mr. Martin's flaccid grasp and threw it onto a chair behind her.

"Just what do you think you are doing, sir?"

She glared at him for an interminable moment, noting that the initial flash of anger in his eyes—definitely gray and dangerous—began to subside, replaced by a glint of amusement that gave them a bluish tinge. Jane felt her bravado waver when the gentleman's lips, which she had not given much thought to before, curled into a slow smile that made her insides flutter alarmingly. This was ridiculous, she thought angrily, the rogue was attempting to cut her up sweet, was he? Well, Mr. *Odious* Martin would soon discover that he had picked the wrong female to bamboo-zle. Her frown deepened as his smile broadened.

"I thought that must be pretty obvious, love," he drawled caressingly. "I was trying to get into my shirt. But I do understand how you might prefer me undressed, sweetheart," he continued with deliberate provocation. "And naturally, I am happy to oblige a lady."

Jane gasped at the implications of this ribald pronouncement. Instinctively she stiffened, unwilling to let this unprincipled rake see how he had shocked her sensibilities. "And why, may I ask, sir, are you deliberately disobeying the doctor's orders?"

He laughed then, but in spite of the brave front he put on, Jane detected signs of strain around his mouth and in the depths of his smoky-blue eyes. Mr. Martin was still a very sick man, and should not be exerting himself in this way. Her concern overcame her outrage, and she picked up his crumpled nightshirt from the floor and advanced toward him purposefully.

"Get back into bed this instant, sir," she said sternly. "You will catch a chill sitting about like that." She gestured at his disturbing state of undress.

His only response was a weak grin. "And you intend to put me there, do you, love?" he murmured gently.

"Indeed I do," Jane responded bravely, shaking out the nightshirt and throwing it over his head. Avoiding any contact with the grinning rogue, Jane held it while he thrust his arms into the sleeves. "There," she said with some relief that he had not protested her orders. "Now get into bed, sir, and I will bathe your face for you."

His grin broadened. "What about my breeches, love? Have you a mind to take them off for me?"

Jane felt herself blush hotly, but she met Mr. Martin's challenging gaze squarely. "No, of course not," she scoffed. "Take them off yourself."

"Very well, my lady. Anything you say, sweetling."

Before Jane realized what he was about, Mr. Martin had risen shakily to his feet and stood, swaying slightly on the balls of his bare feet, a challenging grin on his face as he raised the nightshirt to fumble at the fastenings to his unmentionables.

Shocked to the very core of her being, Jane whirled to run out the room, but a groan from the man by the bed stopped her. Mr. Martin had taken an unsteady step toward her, but his ankle had buckled under him, forcing him to grasp the bedpost with both hands.

Jane did not stop to consider the consequences. She clasped both his hands, pulling them gently away from the bedpost. When she turned him toward the bed, he seemed disoriented, wavering about alarmingly.

"The devil fly away with it," he muttered under his breath, "I feel as weak as a kitten. Here," he added throwing an arm about her shoulders and pulling her against his side, "give a dying man a helping hand, love."

"You are not dying, sir," Jane said calmly, although the sudden close contact with a man in his nightshirt was doing strange things to her breathing. "Do get back into bed, Mr. Martin," she continued, slipping an arm around his waist and pushing him in that direction. "You are still a very sick man."

So closely pressed against him was she, that Jane both heard and felt the rumble of his laughter. Was he indeed as weak as he looked, or was he only pretending? The thought flitted through her mind, but she shook it off instantly. This man was really feverish, and it was up to her to protect him from further harm.

"Come, sir," she said coaxingly, putting her other arm around him and urging him backward. "Please do as I say."

He did not budge, but his lips, more drawn and white than before, twitched into a smile. "Your wish is my command, love," he murmured in a low, weak voice that scared Jane by its very lifelessness. The arm he had placed around her shoulders abruptly slid down to her waist, and his other hand came up to press the flat of her back. Without warning, Jane found herself flattened, from hip to breast, against Mr. Martin's muscular body, which suddenly appeared, to her heightened senses, to be very much alive indeed.

Before she could collect her wits enough to pull free, the gentleman's head fell forward onto her shoulder, and Jane felt his warm lips and breath against her neck. The resulting sensation was so unexpectedly pleasant that Jane stood for an interminable moment, drinking in the smell, the touch, the feel of his hard length against her own unresisting body.

Abruptly she realized the depraved spectacle she must present to anyone entering the room, and stiffened, pushing on the gentleman's scantily clad chest. This was a mistake, she discovered, for the warmth of him seeped through the thin nightshirt, and beneath her frantic fingers, Jane clearly felt the excited hammering of his heart.

Tentatively she squirmed, but the pressure of his arms only increased, until Jane was convinced that he intended to break all her ribs.

"Release me at once, sir," she demanded, but the forcefulness seemed to have gone from her voice. She tried again. "Please let me go, Mr. Martin. This sort of behavior is highly irregular"—she argued patiently—"and I am convinced you would not wish to have to explain it to my Aunt Margaret should she suddenly appear. Would you, now?"

"What a scold you are, love," he murmured against her neck, the warmth of his breath creating a delicious sensation of wantonness in her breast. "And you know what they say about shrewish females, do you not? They never get husbands, love. So be a good girl, and give me a kiss."

Before Jane could react to this quite shocking proposal, Mr. Martin's lips had settled possessively on hers, and when she tried to protest this arbitrary invasion of her person, his mouth opened and his tongue slipped between her parted lips.

To her everlasting mortification, Jane felt her arms—quite of their own accord and without so much as a by-your-leave—find their way up Mr. Martin's broad chest and twine themselves around his neck as though they had been there many times before.

VI
The Gift

That evening, adamantly ignoring her Aunt Prudence's gentle suggestion that their dear Mr. Martin was anxiously awaiting her appearance with his dinner tray, Jane retired to her room with the beginnings of a megrim. This alone should have warned her that something was amiss. Jane Sutherland never suffered from megrims. It took her several hours of tossing and turning in her rumpled bed before she finally faced the scandalous truth about herself. She lacked the courage to confront the one man who had awakened the dormant wanton streak in her soul; the man who had discovered—and worse yet forced her to admit to herself—that Jane Sutherland was nowhere near as self-sufficient as she had imagined.

What a complacent fool she had been! This revelation shattered what remained of her self-control, and—for the first time since that heart-rending humiliation she had suffered ten years ago—Jane let her tears flow freely.

The worst part about this whole highly improper affair, she thought wryly, blowing her nose with unnecessary force, was that she did not even like the man. Mr. Martin did not fit any of her notions of romance. He was much too old, for one thing. Over forty at the very least, although he still wore his dark hair in the fashion of a much younger man, curling around his ears and over the collar of his nightshirt in careless disarray. The memory of just how soft those curls had felt between her wanton fingers this afternoon brought a flood of warmth to her cheeks.

She had behaved with unpardonable license, of course, that was what galled her. She had lost control of herself with a man she hardly knew. Almost a complete stranger. Yet hardly a stranger to her fingers, her lips, her eager body pressing itself against him with the abandon of a paid hussy. Jane shuddered at the unflattering picture she painted of herself. And no stranger to his heart, she remembered suddenly, feeling again the pounding of that organ beneath her fingers, against her breast as he held her firmly, nay crushingly in his arms.

And all this emotional upheaval over a man she did not like, she reminded herself perversely. A man who was odious on all points; arrogant, dictatorial, full of self-consequence, and highly immoral. How could she have enjoyed being kissed by such a man? Jane refused to pretend any longer that she had not enjoyed Mr. Martin's embrace. And his kisses. Dear Lord, how could she have so forgotten herself as to cling to him in that shameless manner? she wondered. He had kissed her like some serving wench with no morals to speak of. And Lady Jane Sutherland had enjoyed being kissed like a serving wench. The though appalled her, and Jane resolutely focused her musings on the gentleman's all too apparent deficiencies.

He was a lecherous brute, of course, and undoubtedly dissipated beyond anything an elderly female such as herself could possibly imagine. No sooner had she come to this unflattering conclusion, however, than Jane found herself trying to imagine the depths of Mr. Martin's depravity. When she came to the scene of seduction in which she herself was the object of the gentleman's amorous assaults, Jane wrenched her thoughts back to sanity.

Only after bathing her heated face with cool lavender water from the bowl on her dresser was Jane able to fall into a fitful slumber that left her, the following morning, heavy-eyed and restless.

It did not help Lady Jane's disposition to find, sitting beside her plate in the breakfast parlor the following morning, a short, apologetic note from Mr. Martin begging the favor of her presence.

Again disregarding her Aunt Prudence's intercession on the rogue's behalf, Jane ordered her grays brought around and offered to accompany Margery on two or three errands in the village. The pleasure of driving her own team and of watching a much improved Dido romping with her fellow playmate Aeneas beside the phaeton went a considerable way toward restoring her spirits.

By mid-afternoon, having written long overdue letters to her mother and sisters, picked a basketful of roses from the garden, arranged them tastefully about the house, and consulted with Mrs. Porter about the evening meal, Jane had convinced herself that she was being unreasonably missish about an incident that might not have held any significance whatsoever for the gentleman in question. What gentleman worthy of the name, she told herself, and bored by a long convalescence, would not consider a little dalliance with any female within reach entirely natural? So when Thomas took up Mr. Martin's tea tray at four that afternoon, Jane entered the invalid's bedchamber in compliance with his summons, her two wolfhounds at her heels.

As she had hoped, the dogs provided the distraction she needed to feel comfortable again, although Mr. Martin's first remark as soon as Thomas had left them was obviously designed to remind her of their previous intimacy.

"How wise of you to bring two such formidable defenders, my dear," he drawled, reaching out to scratch Aeneas's huge head that the dog had rested hopefully on the bed.

"Did you imagine you would need protection from me, love?"

He looked better today, Jane saw immediately, as he examined her quite frankly from his reclining position against the pillows, a relaxed, teasing light in his eyes. Ignoring this leading remark, Jane smiled politely. "I see you are much recovered, sir," she said dryly. "I understand you wished to see me?"

His smile broadened, and Jane felt her heart flutter irrationally. "What are their names?" he inquired, ignoring her question.

"That shameless rascal is Aeneas," she said, gesturing toward the bed. "Always ready to sell his soul for food or attention. While this"—she placed a gentle hand on Dido's head, as the dog sat close to her mistress, long tongue dangling, and black eyes fixed on the stranger in the bed—"is Dido. Faithful and loyal."

"How appropriate." He laughed, and Jane tried not to look at his mouth or the laugh lines at the corners of his eyes. "I see she does not like me. Perhaps because I ran her down with my carriage."

"Undoubtedly," Jane said shortly. There must be dozens of people who do not like you, Jane felt like adding. Most of them females, she imagined.

"I swear I never saw her. Surely you cannot believe I would knowingly harm an animal?"

Jane smiled faintly. "I hardly know you well enough to answer that, sir. But hurt her you certainly did. She will not easily forgive you." Something in Jane's voice caused Dido to move closer and lay her shaggy head on her mistress's lap.

After a slight pause, Mr. Martin said in a different voice. "And will *you* forgive me, Jane?"

Jane raised her eyes from the dog and stared at him coldly. "I do not believe I gave you permission to use my name."

"After what happened between us yesterday, my dear, do you imagine I need your permission?"

Jane felt herself blush. This was exactly the kind of remark she had feared, and she should have known he would not resist reminding her of her shameless behavior. Angry at her own foolishness, Jane rose to her feet. "If that is all you have to say to me, I shall leave you," she said stiffly. "I have better things to do."

He raised a hand in protest. "Please do not leave me so soon, my dear. I have a request to make that your Aunt Prudence assures me you will not deny."

"Aunt Prudence is too tenderhearted for her own good," Jane retorted, resuming her seat. "What is this request, sir?"

He smiled quite charmingly, and Jane felt the insidious pull of attraction. "I would like to come downstairs for tea tomorrow. Dr. Middleberry assured me this morning that it might hasten my recovery to start moving about a bit. Your Aunt Margery seems to be anxious to be rid of me."

Was the wily patient putting words into the good doctor's mouth? Jane wondered. She did know that Aunt Margery had expressed a desire to send Mr. Martin packing as soon as possible, however, so she said nothing. "I see no reason why you could not spend an hour or two on the terrace in the afternoons," she said cautiously. "I imagine you must be anxious to join your family, too," she added facetiously.

His only response to this leading remark was a rueful quirk of his lips. When Jane once more rose to leave, he spoke again. "I understand from your Aunt Prudence, bless her charitable soul, that you will be celebrating your birthday soon," he said. "She also tells me that the event will be marked by a masquerade ball here at Lark Manor."

"That is true," Jane said shortly, wondering how much else her romantic aunt had revealed to this stranger.

"It is a monstrous shame that I will not be here to claim the first dance with you, my dear," Mr. Martin said, quite as though he really meant it.

"I am sure we shall do very nicely without you, sir," Jane could not resist retorting with deceptive sweetness. "By then you will no doubt be disporting yourself in Brighton . . . with your family, naturally. Now, if you will excuse me—"

"One more thing," he said quickly. "Since I shall, as you say, not be here to wish you well on your special day, I beg you will allow me to give you this small token of my esteem. Something to remember me by, my dear," he coaxed when Jane could find no immediate excuse for refusing this unexpected request.

Jane rose to her feet and stared suspiciously at the unmistakable jeweler's box Mr. Martin held out to her. How could the rogue possibly have obtained a gift for her if he had not left his bed in over a week? she wondered, intrigued in spite of herself.

"I hardly think it appropriate sir—" she began.

"Nonsense, my dear girl," he cut in before she could frame an acceptable excuse. "The merest trifle, I assure you. Do not deny me the pleasure of seeing you smile, Jane."

There was a strange wistfulness in his voice that reached out to Jane's heart. He sounded unhappy, although she could not imagine why. In spite of his rough, overbearing manner, Mr. Martin appeared to be a gentleman of some standing in the world. His clothes were of the best, and his pockets must be deep indeed to afford those chestnuts, she reasoned. Why then did she hear an echo of sadness in his voice that did not sit well with his carefree appearance?

Gingerly she took the slim black case and stood for a moment gazing into his smoky eyes, which held—she could have sworn to it—a glimmer of apprehension. Jane was amused at the notion that the brash Mr. Martin might be apprehensive about anything, but when she opened the case, she understood the reason immediately. There, in a bed of black velvet, lay the most expensive ruby necklace she had ever seen. The perfect, blood-red gems, set in a bed of diamonds too numerous to count, glinted back at her with an opulent arrogance that took her breath away.

When Jane had recovered from her astonishment, the first thought that burned itself into her mind was that this magnificent, ostentatious bauble had not been purchased for her, as the wretch had implied. The recognition of that truth pained her more than she cared to admit; it also aroused the full fury of her temper. She should have known it, she thought, not daring to look at the vile perpetrator of this insult. What else could one expect from a roué of Mr. Martin's stamp? However he might deny it, Jane knew in her heart that this extravagant gift had been purchased for a different kind of female, one who would expect such a tribute from men like Mr. Martin. No doubt in tacit payment of services Jane refused to put a name to.

She felt suddenly quite ill with disappointment. She wanted more than anything to throw the offensive gift back in his teeth. How dare he treat her like . . . like . . . Jane refused to finish the thought. She closed the case with a snap and handed it back to him without a word.

His surprise was almost comical, and Jane might have laughed had she not been so hurt. How like a man to imagine that any female could be dazzled by gaudy gifts.

"You do not like it?"

With enormous effort, Jane dredged up a faint smile. "It is very pretty, sir," she said mildly.

"Then why will you not accept it, my dear?"

Jane sighed. Did he really think her a flat to be taken in by his rakish tricks? she thought. "It was not purchased for me, Mr. Martin," she said in a cool voice. "And please do not argue the point. I appreciate the gesture, of course, but I cannot accept a gift that was obviously intended for quite another female." She turned toward the door, where she paused, the two huge dogs brushing past her into the hall.

"Jewels are like women, Mr. Martin; they are not interchangeable. I am surprised you did not know it."

VII
The Good-bye

Had one of his tonnish London cronies suggested a month ago that Martin Douglas, the sixth Earl of Ridgeway, might find contentment in a rural setting, he would have found the notion ludicrous. But the balmy June weather at Lark Manor seemed to be perfect, and as the days drifted by, Martin discovered that country life offered unexpected pleasures to his jaded spirit.

It took him several afternoons spent on the south terrace in the company of Lady Jane and her two aunts to recognize that the sunny weather was not by any means the main cause of his well-being. In that family setting, even Miss Margery Milford, whom Martin had secretly nicknamed the dragon, revealed a side to her nature that was every bit as congenial as that of her gentler sister. All three ladies were well-read, and Martin was occasionally hard put to keep up with their lively conversation. Not since his own long-forgotten days at Oxford had he discussed the Greek dramatists, but one afternoon he found himself stoutly defending the irreverent tone of Euripedes against Miss Margery's decided preference for the more formal Aeschylus.

"I prefer Sophocles myself," Lady Jane interjected, raising her auburn head from the embroidery that Martin suspected she employed as an excuse to remain on the periphery of the conversation. "Euripedes could never have penned anything as moving as *Antigone*. Why, even his portrayal of that unhappy queen Phaedra does not touch us as deeply as that of Antigone's unselfish loyalty to her brother."

It was through such revealing remarks that Martin came to know the female who had piqued his interest enough to keep him idling away his time in the country. No, he thought, it was more than that, much more. Exactly what he could not say, but when he was near Lady Jane, Martin felt a vital energy and love of life flowing from her that he had not encountered in a female before. Lady Pamela had not possessed it, he thought, smiling at the notion of that languorous lady romping with the two wolfhounds on the manor lawns like some schoolgirl. Neither had the promiscuous Lydia, for whom he had purchased the rather indecently expensive ruby necklace.

Not for the first time, Martin wished he had not offered that bauble to Jane. She had instantly recognized it for what it was—a tawdry payment for intimacies permitted with just such a reward in mind. Jane had made Martin Douglas feel ashamed of himself for the first time in many years. Her amber eyes had held such open contempt that Martin had vowed to redeem himself with a gift more suitable for a lady of quality.

But to do so, of course, he would have to leave Lark Manor, and with each passing day Martin became increasingly reluctant to give up the unexpected contentment he had found there. The ladies had made him feel at home, he thought, watching with delight from his privileged position on the terrace between the two Misses Milfords, the uninhibited gambols of their niece with her dogs. Fastidious as he had always been about his women, Martin could not fathom the pleasure he took in Lady Jane's tumbled auburn curls, and her simple, outmoded afternoon gown, her delighted laughter as first one wolfhound then the other knocked her to the ground with their rough play. All this was a mystery to him, one that he was reluctant to examine too closely for fear it would fade away into boredom again.

"Hoydenish but charmingly, would you not agree, Mr. Martin?" Miss Prudence remarked softly. "'Tis a pity . . ." Her voice dwindled into silence.

"Yes?" Martin prompted gently, intrigued by the speaking glance Miss Margery threw at her sister.

"Oh, nothing, really," Prudence murmured. "Only that 'tis a pity the Fates dealt such a bitter blow to our Jane. Tragedy runs in the family you must know. First it was my own dear Raymond's death in India before we could start our life together. Then it was Jane's disappointment in love—"

"Prudence!" Miss Milford's voice held a note of warning Martin could not mistake. "I do believe Mr. Martin is ready for another cup of tea, dear."

So his Jane had been crossed in love, Martin mused later that evening, as Thomas helped him into his dark blue coat and handed him the ebony cane Miss Prudence had brought down from the attic for him, and which Martin still used as an excuse to prolong his stay at Lark Manor. Perhaps the romantic Miss Prudence might be induced to reveal Jane's secret, he thought, as she had so many others. Quite irrationally Martin felt the desire to smash his fist into the face of this unnamed cad who had caused her pain.

The violence of his reaction surprised him, and as he made his way downstairs to the drawing room before dinner, it flashed across Martin's mind that the time had come to leave. If he stayed much longer, he told himself ruefully, he would not want to leave at all, and he could hardly stay here forever, could he?

Could he? The notion of spending the rest of his life in the country was so *outré* as to be positively laughable. Even before he came into his title, he had visited Ridgeway Park as seldom as possible, preferring his lavish residence on Grosvenor Square. His stay at Lark Manor had altered his perception of country life, Martin had to admit, but not enough for him to embrace it as a regular thing, surely?

These misgivings made him uneasy. What maggot had got into his head to trigger such maudlin notions? he wondered. He was beginning to sound like a damned country squire, as senile as that old codger Morris who extolled the virtues of country life every time they met. No, he must leave before he became so hopeless enmeshed with the ladies of Lark Manor that he could not escape at all.

The following morning found Jane down at the stables an hour earlier than usual. Mr. Martin's sudden announcement of his departure the evening before had upset her equilibrium, and she had been unable to rest. He had accepted the loan of her own curricle, and had ordered the chestnuts brought around to the front door at ten o'clock.

"Give them extra oats this morning, Tobias," she instructed the old groom. "They are to carry their master home today."

"If it is Brighton 'e intends to visit, milady, these fancy prads will get 'im there in less than an 'our I warrant ye. There be no need to pamper 'em with extra oats. Only make 'em sluggish it will."

Somehow the thought of Mr. Martin driving down to Brighton to resume his interrupted assignation with the mysterious Lydia distressed Jane so much that she decided not to join her aunts and that perverse gentleman for breakfast, but to take her mare out for a solitary gallop to restore a little good sense to her world. She had grown altogether too fond of the rogue, she thought, and Jane knew too well the hurt that could result from such reckless infatuation. Had ten years taught her nothing? she fumed, angry at her own foolish flirting with disaster. Mr. Martin was not a gentleman any sensible female would—or should—look at twice. Unless of course she wished to ruin her reputation forever, Jane mused, not a little alarmed that she was even contemplating such an event.

Jane sighed and began to ply the currycomb on Star's gleaming haunches with dogged determination. She must nip these dangerous notions in the bud, before her foolish heart had time to weave fantastic dreams around a charming rogue who would not hesitate to break every one. Under no circumstances would she repeat the fiasco of ten years ago when her romantic dreams—admittedly built on shifting sands—were withered by a contemptuous glance from the viscount's mesmerizing smoky-blue eyes.

Mr. Martin's eyes were even more mesmerizing, she thought, and equally unreliable. The uneasy thought struck her that their handsome guest was but an older version of the viscount: the same charming smile, the same gray eyes, even the same coloring, except that Mr. Martin's dark hair was touched with silver at the temples, and he was probably unmatched for debauchery, she thought wryly. Could it be that she was destined to be fatally attracted to ineligible or unattainable gentlemen?

"So here you are, my dear," a familiar voice, soft and unnervingly intimate spoke from the stall doorway. "Avoiding me again, I see."

Jane jumped, causing the mare to sidle nervously. Suddenly she felt shy and gauche as a young girl, and after one quick glance at the intruder, kept her eyes firmly on her task. Mr. Martin looked particularly elegant this morning, she noticed, his broad shoulders filling out the blue superfine riding coat as if molded there. In the dim interior of the stall, she could smell the familiar fragrance of his shaving cream, an intimate detail that she had unwittingly come to treasure. One she would dearly miss.

"You flatter yourself, sir," she retorted, setting down the brush and reaching for Star's bridle. "I thought to take my ride early today since it is supposed to rain later."

"Do you not have grooms to do this for you, my dear?"

he remarked in that lazy drawl of his that seemed to suggest forbidden intimacies. He took the bridle from her limp fingers and slipped it on the mare, who nuzzled him playfully. Inexplicably stung by this small betrayal from her favorite, Jane turned to reach for the saddle. She had barely grasped the smooth leather before she felt him behind her, his arms brushing the sleeves of her primrose riding habit as he lifted the saddle down from its rack and placed it on Star's sleek back.

The mare nickered softly, and turned her small head to nudge him playfully. How had this man weaseled his way into everyone's good graces so effortlessly? she wondered. Aeneas fawned on him quite shamelessly, and even Dido, who was not given to toadying to strangers, had taken to lying at his feet every evening after dinner. Aunt Prudence had remarked upon it only last night, and Mr. Martin had only grinned engagingly at her and winked, reminding her—as he often did—that they shared a scandalous secret, one that still made Jane blush when she thought of it.

Would he kiss her again? she wondered, feeling her pulse increase alarmingly. She must certainly slap the rogue's handsome face for him if he dared to do so, Jane told herself firmly. But what if he did not? Could she bear it if he ignored her? If he showed no desire to tease her into responding to his improper advances? Into opening her lips for him? Into throwing her arms around his neck and pressing herself into him as though her very life depended on the comforting feel of his body against hers?

Abruptly Jane knew she had to get out of the stall before she disgraced herself beyond redemption. The sweet scent of the fresh hay, the soft munching of the mare, the enveloping dimness of the stall, all these were familiar things to Jane's senses, but the added intoxication of the stranger's presence made her dizzy, and she did not trust herself to deny the yearning she felt churning in her heart.

She reached for the mare's reins, but before she could escape out into the early sunshine, Jane felt her fingers enclosed in Mr. Martin's warm grasp. "Jane," he murmured, his voice oddly uneven. "My dear Jane, I am only an uncouth, odious fellow. You have told me so yourself often enough, love," he hurried on as she opened her mouth to protest. "But I want you to know that you are the sweetest shrew I have ever met, and I fear I will miss you quite dreadfully, my dear."

Jane did not quite know what to make of this odd declaration. The pressure of his fingers said one thing, as did the deep intensity of his voice; but he had quite distinctly called her a shrew, which she could hardly take as a compliment. She was hovering between indignation and pleasure when he bent his head and placed a lingering kiss on the palm of one hand, then on the other. Her indignation melted away, replaced by a surge of delight. He was going to kiss her after all, she thought, knowing she should withdraw her hands but finding she had not the will to break the magic of his touch.

He raised his head and Jane trembled as he pulled her closer, cradling her hands on his chest. She dared not raise her eyes from the pristine folds of his cravat, and she feared he must surely hear the wild hammering of her heart. The moment seemed to go on forever, suspended in time, and Jane found herself listening to his uneven breathing and wishing—against all reason and modesty—for the feel of his arms about her.

Just when Jane thought she could bear the suspense no longer, she heard him sigh and felt his chest quiver. "Tell me, Jane," he murmured so softly she wondered if he had meant to speak aloud. "Tell me, love, will you miss me, too?"

Miss him? she thought, mesmerized by the tenderness in his voice. How could she not miss this rogue who seemed to know exactly how to breach every one of her defenses until she felt herself entirely at his mercy. Jane searched in vain for the strength to resist the erotic lethargy that crept through her body, but all she felt was her growing need for this man who promised her delight beyond her wildest dreams.

"Look at me, Jane," he whispered, his breath moving the wayward tendrils of her hair.

Jane raised her eyes and from his arrested expression knew that Mr. Martin had read the truth in them; they had betrayed her sinful thoughts. With an anguished groan he gathered her into his arms and held her close for an endless moment of joy. Then he kissed her, and Jane forgot about everything except the taste of him, and the rush of pleasure she experienced from his lean body crushed against hers. Nothing else existed except this man, this kiss, this moment of sensual pleasure that Jane opened herself to with complete abandon.

Abruptly he released her and Jane murmured in protest and opened dazed eyes. His hands clamped on her shoulders, and he glared at her with eyes blazing with passion.

"Come away with me, Jane," he muttered hoarsely. "Please come away with me. I have a small estate on the coast in Dorset, where one can hear the sea from the bedchambers and see the waves in the moonlight, sweetheart." His eyes devoured her face, willing her to surrender to his outrageous proposal. "I will give you everything your heart desires, my love. Everything. Anything you wish for will be yours, Jane. I will cherish you forever. Only say you will come to me there."

For a dizzy, intoxicating moment Jane allowed herself to believe him. She had always loved the sea, and the picture he painted was so exquisitely tempting, she had to fight hard to throw off the seductive vision that had blossomed in her mind at his words. He made it sound so utterly romantic and perfect. The two of them hand-in-hand walking on the sand in the moonlight, roaming the cliffs in the summer

sun, listening to the waves in bed at night . . . Ah, she
thought, pulling her mind out of the delicious, sensual
quagmire that threatened to engulf it. That was the rub. She
was looking at ruin, and for a dreadful moment, had actually contemplated embracing it. The realization of her own
weakness shocked her, as the implications of Mr. Martin's
offer began to sink in. So this is what it felt like to be offered *carte blanche*, she thought. Humiliated, and stripped
of all sense of decency. And who could she blame but herself? she reasoned. Had she not led him to believe she was
willing? As indeed she was, a small voice in her heart
pointed out unerringly.

Jane stepped back resolutely, and Mr. Martin's hands fell
from her shoulders. "I have everything my heart desires
right here in Sussex," she said in a voice that sounded like a
little girl's. And in a roundabout way this was true, she told
herself. As long as he was here with her, she could ask for
nothing more. "And besides," she added in a stronger
voice, "such arrangements as you propose do not last *forever*, sir. I suspect you are offering me a fool's paradise."

Before Mr. Martin could reply, or the stricken expression
on his face induce her relent, Jane led the mare out to the
mounting block, literally threw herself into the saddle, and
turned Star's head to the farthest corner of the estate, her
eyes blinded by tears.

VIII
The Masquerade

The morning before Lady Jane's thirtieth birthday dawned brilliantly clear. A perfect English summer day, she thought, leaning out of the open window of her bedchamber with blithe disregard for appearances. A prelude to a perfect evening for her aunts' masquerade ball. She drew in a deep breath and let it out slowly, savoring the sweetness of the air. All around her the manor stirred with activity as the upstairs maids put the finishing touches to the guest chambers, and the footmen carried in the potted palms from the hothouse, and Mrs. Porter set the scullery maids to preparing the potatoes, and carrots, and vegetables she intended to serve at the formal dinner that evening.

All was well with the world, Jane thought wryly, or so she had made herself believe. The invitations had been sent out, the menu had been selected days ago, the orchestra would arrive later that morning from Brighton, the lobsters had been delivered yesterday and were even now being transformed into Mrs. Porter's celebrated patties. And her masquerade gown hung in her clothes press waiting for the magic hour when Jane was to metamorphose into the Lady Guinevere and become the Queen of the Masquerade.

But there would be no Sir Lancelot. The illicit lover who had tempted the queen to sin and broken her heart.

Jane brushed the insidious thought away impatiently. Queen Guinevere had been her Aunt Prudence's choice, but Jane had also been intrigued by the woman caught between the passions of two great men. That had been before the advent of Mr. Martin, of course. Now she rather wished she had chosen a more innocuous female, one who did not remind her so forcefully of her own Sir Lancelot, the sweet seducer who had almost caused her own downfall.

Jane sighed and moved away from the window. Did every female carry the seeds of her own destruction deep within her heart? she wondered. Seeds that would spring forth into deliciously sinful blossoms if the right Lancelot came along?

Sin had blossomed quite shamelessly in her own heart ten days ago in the stables, she recalled. Jane still did not comprehend how she had found the strength to deny the wild, unfamiliar longing that had surged through her when Mr. Martin had spoken of his love nest by the sea. By now she might have been in Dorset with him, she mused, her heart heavy with regret. With *him*. Her very own Sir Lancelot. Except for her inconvenient attack of prudishness, she might be indulging in a forbidden love with a forbidden gentleman, whose magnificent smoky eyes had awakened long forgotten dreams in her spinster's heart.

Jane shook herself impatiently at this maudlin train of thought, and went over to select a gown from the clothes press. Lucy would be coming up soon with her hot chocolate, and there were any number of tasks that must be seen to before their first guests began to arrive by mid-afternoon.

The thought of these guests banished the blue devils that had threatened to overcome her. Jane particularly looked forward to seeing her parents, although she would dearly love to know how her mama had persuaded Lord Weston to attend a masquerade ball—even one held in his daughter's honor—dressed as Captain Kidd. Her brother John was coming. Would not miss it for the world, he had written only last week. And her eldest sister Lady Margaret with her four little darlings and her dashing husband, Viscount Scovell.

No, she told herself firmly, there was no time to mope. Had she not moped quite enough already over a handsome rogue who had quite likely forgotten her very existence by now. By midnight tonight, Lady Jane Sutherland would be thirty years old, and must learn to put all romantic notions out of her head and settle down to a life of tranquil contentment that would carry her into old age. This had been her goal for the past ten years, had it not?

Why, then, did it suddenly make her want to weep? Jane thought.

The curricle drawn by four flashy chestnuts was making good time, although the gentleman handling the ribbons had not indulged in the neck-or-nothing style of driving for which he was famous in London circles. His leisurely progress along the coast from Dorset into Sussex had been—in the words of Matt Turner, the gentleman's groom—boringly sedate, quite as if his lordship were entering his dotage. Either that or headed straight for Bedlam, Matt added as an afterthought.

His lordship had not taken offense at this plain-speaking from his groom, who had been in his family's service for as long as he could remember.

"Mayhap you are right, Matt," he said somberly, wondering if perhaps his old groom had not spoken truer than he intended. For the decision he had reached after much soul-searching during the past ten days—spent in virtual isolation at his small estate near Osmington on the Dorset coast—scared him half to death.

Never in his whole career as one of London's most elusive and intemperate bachelors had he contemplated such a drastic step. The finality of it made his blood run cold. And caused it to run hot, too, he had to admit with an ironic smile. And gave rise to tender yearnings so unlike his usual cynical self that he was moved to think Matt might be right. He must indeed be raving mad.

Mad and certainly moonstruck. Yet there was still time to turn aside from his course and keep his original assignation in Brighton. If he knew anything about females—about *most* females, that is—he would be forgiven and things could go on as before with nary a ripple to show for the aberration that had taken hold of his mind during the past weeks. And of his heart, too, he thought, still not entirely ready to admit that such farradiddle might actually be true.

He would soon find out, he thought, pulling into the yard of *The Swan*, the only inn that the tiny village of Clayton seemed to offer. He could easily have made his destination in time for the formal dinner he knew had been planned for this evening, but, for reasons of his own, he did not wish to arrive much before midnight. The witching hour, he thought irrationally, wondering if his recent accident had not addled his brain beyond repair.

What if he merely managed to make an utter fool of himself? he thought. Why did he not turn his horses toward the delights of Brighton and forget this fever that had taken possession of his soul?

Even as the notion flitted through his mind, the gentleman dismissed it. He had to discover if what he suspected about himself was true. He had to look into the lady's magnificent eyes again and convince himself that he had not misread what he had seen there.

But above all, he had a pressing engagement to keep, long overdue.

The evening had turned out to be everything the morning's perfection had presaged, Jane thought, looking down the long table at her dear papa, engrossed in a political discussion—she was sure of it—with bluff Sir Henry Rothingham, seated beside Lady Biddleton on his left. She caught his eye and smiled. In spite of his loud protests at the indignity of being draped in a truly abominable coat of bright blue, and swathed in studded belt and pasteboard scimitar around his waist, Papa looked rather dashing in his pirate's costume. He had drawn the line at having a stuffed parrot pinned to his shoulder, and Jane had supported him in this, although Lady Weston had argued heatedly that no self-respecting pirate would be caught dead without his parrot.

As the guest of honor, Jane was scheduled to open the ball with her father, who had scrawled his name on her dance card as they stood together at the top of the stairs to welcome those guests who had arrived later for the ball. The Reverend Coulton had also claimed the dance she had promised him several days ago, as did other gentlemen acquaintances, and before Jane knew it, her dance card was full.

How different from that disastrous ball in London, she recalled wryly, when her card had been so painfully devoid of partners. Except for the arrogant viscount, who had signed her card but neglected to claim his dance.

Jane brushed that ugly memory aside and turned to take her father's arm as the strains of the opening cotillion filtered out onto the landing.

"I shall feel mighty peculiar dancing with Queen Guinevere dressed as a buccaneer, m'dear," Lord Weston muttered under his breath as they took their place at the head of the set. "Must have had maggots in my head to let your mother talk me into this absurd rig."

"You look perfectly splendid, Papa," Jane replied with a smile. "But you were right to stand firm on the stuffed parrot. Not at all the thing. Regardless of what Mama says."

Her father glanced at her fondly. "Always knew you had a good head on your shoulders, Jane, m'dear." He had a slight frown on his face when next they came together, and Jane knew instinctively what he would say. "Are you sure you would not like me to look around for a suitable match for you, dear? You are still a mighty fine looking lass, Jane, and there must be any number of fellows who would jump at the chance—"

"No, Papa," she replied firmly, as she had so many times before. "I am quite content here at Lark Manor with my aunts. And tonight, at the stroke of midnight, I will be thirty years old. Quite on the shelf, would you not agree? in spite of Aunt Prudence's attempts to marry me off to poor Reverend Coulton."

"The vicar? Never say so, Jane. I see I shall have to have a serious talk with Prudence. No mere reverend is good enough for *my* daughter, and so I shall tell her." He paused to observe her keenly. "You have not set your heart on him, Jane?"

Jane laughed outright. "No, indeed, Papa," she replied dryly. "The vicar is rather too sober for my taste." Having cavalierly dismissed Mr. Coulton as a possible suitor, Jane's thoughts flew to that other gentleman who was so opposite the vicar in every way. But that would not do either, of course, for no serious offer might be expected from that quarter, as she had found out to her sorrow.

By the time Jane went in to supper on the arm of Sir James Rathbone, to the intense chagrin of the young Misses Biddleton, who were both visibly smitten with the startlingly handsome blond baronet, she had dismissed all thoughts of the philandering Mr. Martin from her head.

Jane had hardly glanced at her dance card all evening, enjoying the heady sensation of knowing herself to be—in spite of her advanced years—truly the belle of this ball, with not a single dance unspoken for. She sighed, feeling a rush of affection for the two ladies who had made this unusual triumph possible.

Aunt Prudence had been right, she mused. Her aunt's wedding gown—lovingly designed so many years ago for that most joyful occasion in a woman's life—had turned plain Jane Sutherland into a vision of beauty. That promise of magic that had been denied her aunt with Major St. Cloud's death had come to blossom in her niece. If only for one enchanted evening, Jane knew the heady power of her own beauty. No longer inhibited by her regal height, no longer self-conscious of her shapely bosom, no longer exasperated by the color of her burnished red hair, Jane felt herself emerging—under the admiring glances and unabashed flattery of every man in the room—from a lifelong cocoon of shyness and self-effacement.

She smiled at this fanciful notion, but the idea of shedding her old, retiring self amused her. Yes, Aunt Prudence's refurbished wedding gown had provided the magic for this moment of happiness Jane would treasure forever. And if she could not be a bride, she thought philosophically, at least she could be—for a few glorious hours of make-believe—the beautiful queen who had captured the heart of King Arthur's bravest knight.

And if Sir Lancelot was not here to see her in all her glory, Jane thought, with a brilliant smile at the stunningly beautiful young Sir James who was handing her another glass of punch, then she had only to remember that gentlemen—even such a legendary true and gentle knight like Sir Lancelot—were all too often disloyal and traitorous, and not to be depended upon to bring joy and happiness to a lady's heart.

The tall knight standing half-concealed behind the potted palms across the room grimaced at the blinding smile the queen bestowed on the obviously besotted Robin Hood in brown hose, green doublet, and jaunty feathered hat, who presented her a glass of punch with an elegant flourish. The notorious outlaw's face was hidden behind his black mask, but his slender, elegant form proclaimed him a youth in his early twenties. Half his own age, the tall gentleman realized, grimacing again behind his own mask of black silk.

Had he come on a fool's errand after all? he wondered, fighting the irrational urge to wring the impudent stripling's neck for him.

His unorthodox entrance through the kitchen had been achieved with no trouble at all, thanks—he was sure—to the good offices of Miss Prudence Milford, his friend and willing cohort. That lady's tenderhearted complicity in this mad scheme, and her fertile, romantic imagination in suggesting he come dressed as Guinevere's lover had seduced him into believing that it might be a great lark to arrive unexpected and incognito to right a wrong committed so many years ago.

For by the time Martin left Lark Manor he had known who Lady Jane really was. Miss Prudence had—in a moment of effusive sentimentality, and without knowing that she spoke to the villain in the affair—confided her niece's sad tale of unrequited love. Otherwise he might never have recognized the shapely, sharptongued virago for the gauche chit at Lady Mansfield's ball. A chit as unremarkable as a score of other hopefuls he had met and eluded and promptly forgotten that Season.

The revelation sobered him as nothing else in his dissipated life had ever done. For a fleeting, nostalgic moment his mind speculated on what might have happened had he seen the lady as he did today, in all her womanly glory. A fruitless exercise, of course, to be dismissed as maudlin beyond bearing. But from that nostalgic moment had sprung the germ of the mad scheme he was embarked on tonight.

Except that suddenly there was so much more at stake

than retribution for past sins, Martin realized with an unfamiliar twinge of uneasiness. Abruptly he was glad of the black mask that concealed his face.

The musicians began to tune up for the after-supper waltz, and Martin knew he could delay no longer.

He stepped out from behind the potted palms and strode forward with a swagger he was far from feeling.

IX
The Unmasking

"I believe this is my dance, my lady."

Jane smiled dismissively at the young man in Sherwood Forest green who still hovered about her, and turned her glittering smile on the gentleman who had appeared unheralded at her side.

What she saw caused her smile to falter. The gentleman who claimed the dance was tall and extraordinarily broad-shouldered, and the costume he had chosen made her catch her breath in sudden alarm.

He as all in black. A rich velvet tunic fell below his knees over tight black hose and soft half-boots, girded with a thick silver-linked belt clasped loosely about his waist, and studded with bright scarlet stones that winked blood-red in the candlelight. About his shoulders swung a short ermine-collared cloak that emphasized their width, fastened carelessly at the throat with a huge broach of beaten silver. But it was his chest, emblazoned with a vermilion coat of arms, that drew Jane's fascinated gaze.

She gasped. The boldly displayed vermilion against the black of the tunic was the heraldic signature of Sir Lancelot du Lac.

Slowly she rose to her feet, bracing herself against the table. "I do not seem to recall . . ." she began hesitantly, fumbling for her dance card. Surely she would have remembered granting this gloriously costumed medieval knight a dance earlier in the evening, she thought. Her eyes skimmed the list of scrawled names and came to rest on the heavily inked signature immediately following the supper hour. She stared at it a full minute before her dazed mind admitted what she saw.

Hammond? How had that despicable name got on her card?

The name seemed to dance before Jane's confused gaze. This simply could not be true, she thought, feeling herself go cold with shock. The Viscount Hammond *here?* Either Aunt Prudence's champagne punch was a great deal stronger than usual tonight, or she had imbibed more than was good for her.

She raised her eyes and stared up at him. "May I know your name, sir?" she heard herself ask breathlessly.

She saw his mouth quirk beneath the mask into that slow, sensuous smile she had thought to have erased from her memory years ago. Evidently she had not done so, for it still had the power to make her knees weak.

"Hammond," he said softly. "I am Viscount Hammond."

The sound of his name, spoken with none of the arrogance she well remembered, touched a raw spot in her heart. But something about the caressing tone of his voice disturbed her, and Jane glanced up at the tall knight beside her. This man was not the Hammond she had known. Jane was sure of it. But she had the odd impression that she knew him very well indeed. By the gleam in his eyes, barely visible behind the slits in the black mask, she knew he was laughing at her.

"You are not Hammond," she said stubbornly. "That much I do know. He was a very different kind of man."

His amusement faded. "Yes, you are right, my dear. He was an arrogant fool, was he not?"

Something about the intonation of the stranger's voice when he spoke the endearment made Jane's heart jolt uncomfortably. The familiarity of that caressing, teasing, half-seductive tone brought a rush of color to her cheeks. Had she wished so desperately to see Mr. Martin's face again that she was seeing him now in this other stranger? she wondered, her mind spinning dizzily. Was she so besotted that any man's voice became *his* voice? Any man's eyes *his* eyes?

Jane grasped awkwardly at the back of a chair, thankful that her half-mask hid some of her confusion. Drawing a shaking breath, she forced herself to look up into his eyes. No, she thought, repressing the increasing dizziness that threatened to overcome her, this could not be *her* Mr. Martin. Had she not sent him away after he had made that quite indecent proposal? Why would he come back? she wondered frantically, when there was nothing at Lark Manor to hold the attention of such a gentleman. No, she told herself again, this was not the man who had come so close to seducing a lonely spinster ten days ago.

And then, as she placed her hand in the warm palm he held out to her, and felt his lips tease the tips of her fingers with a lingering kiss, she knew—against all reason, beyond all sanity, Jane knew—that the knight with the vermilion arms blazoned on his chest was indeed her own true knight. Her very own Sir Lancelot.

The shock of it was too great to be borne, and Jane did something she had never done before. She gave a little gasp of surprise and swooned.

When Jane opened her eyes, her first thought was that she had been transported to Bedlam. She found herself reclining on the leather sofa in the library, surrounded by a crowd of her aunts' guests, all talking at once. She heard her Aunt Prudence trying, with less than her usual patience, to clear the room, while Lady Scovell repeated to everyone who would listen that there must be some mistake, because her sister Jane never, *never* fainted. Jane suspected that

Margaret was rather put out that, for once in her life, she was not the center of attention.

Someone was rubbing her hands vigorously—no doubt her practical Aunt Margery—while Lady Weston dabbed rather ineffectually at her daughter's face with a damp cloth, exclaiming all the while that her darling Jane's behavior was most odd indeed, and that the poor girl must be coming down with something.

"What fustian you do talk!" Margery interrupted curtly. "The child has merely swooned, no doubt from the heat, which is rather oppressive for June. If you want to be useful, Penelope, you may tell that husband of yours to clear this room at once. Our darling Jane needs fresh air."

Above the chatter around her, Jane heard her father's voice raised authoritatively, and within minutes the noise subsided as the guests drifted back to the ballroom.

"You, too, my dear," she heard him say in his no-nonsense tone, presumably to Lady Weston. "And take your sisters with you. I wish to be private with Ridgeway here before Jane wakes up."

Ridgeway? The name sounded vaguely familiar. Where had she heard it before? Jane wondered.

There was a sudden, uncomfortable silence. Jane longed to open her eyes, but the lids seemed unnaturally heavy.

"Now, my lord," Lord Weston said in an odd tone she had never heard him use before, "perhaps you will explain to me exactly why my daughter fainted. As you have no doubt heard, Jane is no wilting violet with missish starts and die-away airs."

Jane heard the man her father had called Ridgeway laugh deep in his throat. "No, indeed, my lord. A refreshing change from too many of today's females, if I may say so. A treasure I have unfortunately been distressingly slow to appreciate."

Jane made little sense of the words that washed over her during this speech. All she heard was the voice. *Mr. Mar-*

tin's voice. She must indeed be ready for Bedlam, she thought incoherently, to hear that libertine's voice in every man she met. Advancing age had addled her brains, as the village crones were wont to say.

"Forgive me, my lord," her father said with sudden stiffness, "if I presume to ask you to clarify the nature of your interest in my daughter."

This blunt demand was followed by another silence. Jane froze. Surely Mr. Martin would not—no, he *could* not confess the scandalous offer he had so recently made to Lord Weston's daughter. She held her breath for an interminable moment before uttering a soft moan of protest.

Instantly the cloth was removed from her eyes—no wonder she could not open them, she thought—and a fresh, cool one used to wipe her face with infinite gentleness.

Jane opened her eyes, and there they were, the teasing, smoky eyes she had thought never to see again. He had removed his black mask and the cloak, but the embroidered vermilion coat of arms was alarmingly close to her. Mr. Martin must be kneeling on the floor, Jane thought, quite irrationally gratified at the idea. His eyes regarded her intently, and her heart fluttered irrepressibly at the warmth she read in their gray depths.

Her father's dry voice abruptly interrupted this silent communication. "I must ask you to leave us now, Ridgeway," Lord Weston said. "There are certain things I wish to discuss with my daughter." He paused, then added in a warmer tone, "I trust we may speak again before the evening is over."

It was not a request but an order, Jane knew, having experienced just such a tone in her father's voice before. She was not surprised when Mr. Martin rose and bowed, a faint smile on his lips.

"As you wish, my lord," he said, and glanced down at Jane. His smile broadened and he winked. "You look like a scared rabbit, love," he murmured, quite as though they were alone. "Never fear, my pet. I shall take care of everything."

Before pausing to consider the impropriety of her action, Jane flung out a hand to him. "Do not leave m-me," she murmured weakly. "I c-cannot bear it if you go away again."

There was another pause, during which Jane distinctly saw his gray eyes acquire a hot, hungry look. Strangely this predatory stare did not frighten her in the slightest. She had seen it there before.

He took her outstretched hand in both his, raising it to his lips and placing a feather-light kiss on her fingers. Then he glanced up at her father. "If you have no objections, my lord, perhaps it might be better if I had a few moments alone with your daughter. With your permission, naturally."

Jane held her breath at the temerity of the man. Few gentlemen of her acquaintance would dare to stand up to the Earl of Weston so coolly as her Mr. Martin.

Quite unexpectedly her father relented. "Very well," he said gruffly, casting an anxious glance at Jane, whose hand was still clasped quite firmly in Mr. Martin's. "This is rather irregular, of course, but I trust you will not forget that you are a gentleman, Ridgeway." He paused, one hand on the doorknob. "Ten minutes then, that is all I shall give you."

No sooner had the door closed behind the earl than Mr. Martin let out a crack of laughter. "Your father is a total innocent, my love," he explained in answer to Jane's questioning look. "He has no idea how much I can do to you in ten minutes."

The expression in his smoky eyes, which raked her quite ruthlessly, was so intense that Jane never doubted that Mr. Martin was quite capable of carrying out this vaguely titillating threat.

"What are you doing here?" she demanded in a quavering voice, suddenly self-conscious at being alone with him. "And exactly who are you, anyway? How dare you presume—"

"Hush, my dear," he soothed, getting down on his knees again and proceeding to kiss each of her fingers quite thoroughly. "Which question would you like me to answer first? What am I doing here? I should think that must be rather obvious, love. Even for a silly, adorable widgeon like you. I am kissing you, sweetheart." He proceeded to place a very warm kiss in the middle of her palm, much to her secret delight.

"As for who I am," he continued more soberly, "now that is rather more complicated, my dear. I trust I will not disappoint you too much if I confess that I really am Viscount Hammond. At least I was until five years ago. I am now the Earl of Ridgeway, as your father knows."

Jane gazed up at him and saw that he was uneasy. "In other words, you lied to me, sir," she said bluntly. "You are not Mr. Martin at all." She had almost said *my* Mr. Martin, but caught herself in time. "I liked you better as Mr. Martin," she added irrelevantly, staring at the ceiling.

She saw him wince at her accusation and would have gladly withdrawn it. What did a name matter, after all? she thought, when he had called her an adorable widgeon.

"Then I shall be Mr. Martin, my love," he murmured, his voice suddenly low and throaty. "I will be anything you want me to be, Jane. Anyone at all. Even Sir Lancelot. If only you will come and live in Dorset with me. My son can be an earl if he wants to, but I hereby renounce all my titles if they displease you, love."

His words lulled her with their sweetness until she realized what he had said. "You have a son?" she asked carefully, determined not to show how the very notion froze the blood in her veins.

"No," he answered promptly. "But I shall just as soon as

I can convince you to come to Maple House with me. That is where I have spent the past ten days, love," he continued when Jane gazed at him in disbelief. "Thinking about you. And about me. And about all the things we could be doing together." His voice had grown softer and softer as he spoke, and now it ceased altogether, leaving a silence so pregnant with erotic images that Jane blushed.

Jane discovered she had a lump in her throat. "I thought you were in Brighton," she confessed, feeling the ghost of Lydia materialize between them.

"You should not harbor naughty thoughts about your own true knight, my dear." He lowered his head to brush her lips gently with his. Jane knew she should protest this indecorous familiarity. but all she felt was disappointment when he raised his head and grinned at her.

"But that reminds me, love. I have something for you."

"For me?" Jane wanted only his heart from this man, but the notion that he had thought to bring her a birthday gift made her quite giddy.

"Yes," he said, pulling a small velvet pouch from his pocket and placing it in her eager hands. "And I swear that this one is not interchangeable."

Jane blushed hotly, remembering the lavish ruby necklace he had tried to give her. This time it would be different, she thought. She had no idea how she knew, but she was absolutely certain that Mr. Martin would not make the same mistake twice.

She was right. The sapphire necklace that slipped out of the pouch when she loosened the silk cord was as delicate and lacy as a cobweb. A single, pear-shaped sapphire—rather modest when compared to the rubies, Jane was glad to see—hung in a web of gold threads studded with a starburst of tiny diamonds that twinkled bewitchingly in the candlelight.

Jane let out a long, contented sigh of pleasure.

"Do you like it, love?" His voice had a note of anxiety in it that charmed her.

She gazed up at him, her heart so full she could not speak.

"If you would prefer something more impressive, you have only to say so, Jane. I promised you anything your heart desires, remember?"

Jane felt her smile freeze. Was he really toying with her after all? Was this masquerade only an elaborate sham to amuse a gentleman so bored with the world that he would sink this low? Perhaps Viscount Hammond had not changed his spots after all. She refused to look into the chasm of misery that seemed to open suddenly at her feet.

"Yes, I remember it well, Mr. Martin," she said dryly. "Anything my heart desires if I would run away to live by the sea with you." Jane lowered her eyes to the exquisite necklace, a mist of tears obscuring her vision. She should have known better than to fling her heart away on an arrogant, care-for-nobody. Was it to be trodden underfoot twice in one lifetime? And by the same gentleman? This was entirely too much for an aging spinster to bear.

Resolutely Jane swung her legs to the floor and stood up. That was a mistake, she soon discovered. Mr. Martin slipped an arm about her waist and pulled her against his chest. It was difficult to think of resisting the wretch when her heart, her lips, her entire body yearned for his touch.

She drew in a long, steadying breath. "I suggest you get back on your charger, sir knight, and ride off to Brighton," she said in a level voice. "Even *you* can scarcely have the audacity to propose such a scheme to my father."

For answer he laughed deep in his throat, his smoky eyes burning with a fire Jane had despaired of seeing in them again. Then he kissed her. There was nothing even remotely gentle about that kiss. Jane was bewildered at the desperation with which his mouth opened over hers, imprisoning her, invading her, tantalizing her with the force of his passion, tempting her to succumb to the heady surging of her own desire. To her shame, she found herself quite incapable of even a token resistance. Her arms instinctively fastened themselves around his neck, and her body behaved with shocking license, curling into him as though it could not get close enough.

When it was over, and Jane was able to breathe again, he did not release her. He smiled lazily at her as though he had read her immodest thoughts, and Jane's heart fluttered wildly.

"There is nothing for me in Brighton, love," he said against her ear in that caressing tone that Jane dreaded most, for it demolished all her defenses. "Everything I want is here." He paused for a moment, drawing back to regard her with unusual seriousness. "I want *you*, Jane."

How was a female supposed to maintain a modicum of decorum, a semblance of respectability, a trace of decency when a gentleman presented his case so thrillingly? Jane wondered, feeling the seeds of her own downfall moving with quiet determination within her foolish heart.

"My poor papa will disown me," she murmured, not particularly concerned with this indisputable fact.

"Really?" Mr. Martin's eyebrows rose in amusement. "I was under the impression that Lord Weston would rather welcome my offer. Arrogant of me no doubt, my love, but there you are."

Jane felt herself stiffen in his arms. She simply could not—*would* not—allow herself to assume what she so desperately wanted to assume he meant by those suggestive words.

"You are a wicked tease, Mr. Martin—"

"Martin," he interrupted gently. "My real name is Martin Douglas."

She threw him a withering look. "Martin, then. It is a relief to know that you do have a real name like everyone else."

"And I am not teasing, love. Never more serious in my life. Actually I am scared out of my wits," he added, tracing her cheek gently with his knuckles. "I intend to ask your father if he will give you to me, Jane."

Jane took a moment to digest this astonishing news. She was reluctant to believe she had heard aright. "*Give* me to you?" she repeated breathlessly. "As in . . . " Her voice trailed off. She could not bring herself to imagine the bliss of being married to Mr. Martin.

"As in marriage," he completed the half-formed thought. "Yes, my love. Marriage. A truly awesome step, is it not? One I never anticipated taking to tell the truth. Unless you will have me, Jane." He paused for the merest fraction of a moment, during which Jane held her breath in terror least he think better of it.

"*Will* you have me, Jane?"

She stared at him for quite a full minute before she let out her breath slowly, a knowing, totally feminine smile transforming her fears into a sweet glow of contentment. She dropped her eyes in a provocative gesture as old as Eve's. "How can I possibly take you seriously, my lord?" she murmured, savoring her moment of triumph.

He appeared nonplussed. "The deuce take it, woman," he protested. "I have just offered to put my head in the noose for you. What can be more serious than that?"

Jane smiled and kissed him on the chin, watching in delight as his glance dropped to her lips. Gently she untangled herself from his arms. "If you are serious, my lord," she said teasingly, "you will surely wish to do the thing properly."

She seated herself primly on the leather sofa and pointed to the floor. "Down on your knees, sir knight, and learn how to ask a lady for a boon."

His gaze raked her from head to foot, pausing with a lazy grin on the low neckline of her gown. "You will pay dearly for this tonight, my lady," he drawled. "I shall look forward to teaching you how to treat a loyal, self-sacrificing, devoted knight."

Jane felt herself grow uncomfortably warm. "Tonight?" she whispered, unwilling to believe the impudent suggestion.

He grinned then, and his smile was suddenly tender. "Did you not know, my sweet innocent, that Queen Guinevere took Sir Lancelot into her bed without all this rigmarole? Let us follow her example, love. You already have a wedding gown, and with a special license, which I shall obtain later today, you may have me in your bed by tonight."

Jane blushed deeply, partly at the audacity of Mr. Martin's words, partly at the audacity of her own desire.

"Not unless I hear an offer that takes my fancy, sir," she heard herself respond with a daring she did not recognize.

She watched in wonder as he got down on his knees yet again and took both her hands in his. This humble posture, Jane did not fail to notice, was belied by the gleam of triumph in his smoky eyes.

He was going to ask her to marry him, she thought, her joy almost too much to bear. To run away with him to his love nest by the sea, to walk with him in the moonlight, to lie with him in bed, listening to the waves kissing the shore. She had been waiting all her life for such an offer from him.

Jane could not wait to give him his answer.

SOMETHING NEW

Carla Kelly

"There is no new thing under the heaven."
ECCLESIASTES

There is no pleasure quite like the pleasure of sitting naked in hot water, secure in the knowledge that I will not be summoned to fire a round at anyone or anything, thought Major John Redpath of the Royal Horse Artillery. He carefully sank lower in the tub and contemplated his bare knees. I will lie here up to my neck in hot water, and if anyone knocks, I will say fearful things such as . . .

Knock.

"Come in," the major said with a sigh, quite unable to break six years of habit. "This had better be very good," he added, before the door opened. "Oh, it is you. Parkhill, go to hell."

The lieutenant grinned and leaned against the doorjamb. "Yes, sir! But only after my wedding, sir, and that is what I have come to see you about."

"Not interested," the major said, looking for something to throw. "Not even if your fiancée were to come in here and scrub my back."

"She would never!" said Lieutenant Sir Edmund Parkhill, shocked. "Not Emmeline! I'll be dashed lucky if she scrubs mine!"

What is it about me that no one thinks I mean what I

say? the major asked himself, as he regarded his most junior lieutenant. When we are serving the guns, no one questions me. But put me in a tub, or a bed, or a bordello, or a church, or even a necessary, and I am fair game to all my officers. I am entirely too accessible, he decided as he stood up to soap himself, then sat down quickly when Lt. Parkhill was followed into the room by one of the laundresses. The water sloshed from the tub and he sighed again.

"Sir, I have a matter to discuss with you that can't wait," she said, glaring at the lieutenant, who knew when he was outranked and took up a defensive position in the window. "It is about Marie Deux."

"Mrs. Hurley, could you not wait until I at least cover my privates?" he grumbled, reaching for a washcloth.

"And about your privates," she began.

Ed Parkhill started to laugh as the major looked down into the water then up at the laundress, who probably outweighed him, particularly in her current condition.

"Major Redpath, the ones outside! The ones who are getting drunker and more disorderly by the minute."

"I didn't think you meant the ones in the water, Mrs. Hurley," the major said, smiling in spite of himself. "Leave them alone—the ones outside—and let them celebrate Boney's abdication, please. Marie Deux? What is that little puss up to?"

The laundress looked less sure of herself as she came farther into the room. She rubbed her belly, big with another of Sergeant Hurley's botherations. "Sir, I just can't take her along to Belgium. I didn't win in the lottery so I have to travel overland, and it's too much, Major Redpath."

"I expect it is," he agreed. "I'll see what I can do, Mrs. Hurley," he said, absently scratching himself.

"I knew you would, sir," she said as she left the room.

The major looked at the lieutenant balancing in the window. "There she goes, certain that I will solve her problem," he complained. "Why do people do that around me?"

"Because they know that once you are acquainted with their problem, you will solve it for them," the lieutenant said promptly. "There is something about you that inspires complete confidence. It is a knack you have. Now, sir, about my wedding . . ."

"Aye, the answer is aye," Major Redpath sighed, fishing for the washcloth. "Since I am so obliging, I will oblige." He stood again to soap himself, after a wary glance at the door. "Now tell me what I have agreed to."

"A simple matter."

"It always is," the major said wearily.

"You and I are going on leave to England at the same time, sir. I wish you to accompany me to Kent and be my best man," Parkhill said. "That's all."

The major soaped himself thoughtfully and motioned for his lieutenant to hand him the bucket. He poured the cold water over himself. "If that's all there is to it, Ed, I'll do it."

I wish everything were that easy, he thought, as he shaved, dressed, and kept an eye on the clock. Beau Wellington was particular about his officers arriving on time for functions. Redpath leaned his cheek on his hand, stared at the heaping mound of unfinished paperwork in front of him, and said a monumentally dirty word in French. He got up and went to the window.

The church bells in Toulouse had not ceased to ring since announcement of Napoleon's abdication had reached the town from Bordeaux. He could not begin to describe the gratitude that welled in his heart. He was alive, he was healthy, with furlough home in Scotland coming up, following a wedding in Bath. He looked out the window again. "Marie Deux, what am I to do with you now, lass?" he asked.

As it happened, she was seated in the courtyard below with the other laundresses' children. Hands folded, feet together, back straight, she watched the Hurley's toddler fall and rise, and try to join the others in their chase after a ball.

Patiently she retrieved the squalling child, wiped his face like the little mother she was, and resumed her watch.

He smiled as he observed her. "Marie Deux," he murmured, "were you ever young?"

He knew she couldn't be much more than four, herself. Ed Parkhill had told him how they had found her among the French guns after the third siege of Badajoz, too starved to cry as they approached to look at the French battery, English artillerymen on a coachman's holiday. "She was all eyes on a scrawny neck," Ed had told him several months later, when he joined the Second Battery. "She just sat there and watched us." Then Ed shook his head, amazed all over again at the perspicacity of little girls. "And then she held out her arms to us. Damn how it is: I suppose daughters of the guns know sons of guns, eh, sir?"

Poor Marie Deux, he thought, watching her, you were flotsam in the sea of war. Parkhill admitted to him later that his first inclination was to pass her by. "She would have been dead in a day, Major," he remembered in the telling. "But we couldn't. Call it artillerymen's courtesy."

Major Redpath understood. It was the same humanity that always compelled him to tour the remains of all Froggy batteries following a battle. He had dispatched more than one horse struggling against death, or French *bombardier* ghastly with wounds, begging and pleading for a quick end. Artillery was unforgiving, and cruel to victim and server, he knew. He found a perverse fascination in sitting on a French limber and looking across the field, wondering about that point of view.

"We artillerists are always concerned about point of view, Marie Deux, for it is our business," he said, looking out of the window. "What would be best for you, now that your country is ours, and Boney is gone?"

It was a question he carried with him to the town hall, where Wellington had ordered dinner for his officers and allies. He had to watch his steps in the streets of Toulouse.

Everywhere enterprising Gallic merchants were busy dis-
carding any signs of Bonaparte from shop windows and fa-
cades, and throwing the remnants into the street. He stood a
moment to watch masons chipping the carved N and B
from the front of the town hall. Everywhere bells tolled.

He joined the dinner guests, quickly locating Sir Thomas
Picton, his division commander, all hearty and foul of
mouth, and wearing his top hat even indoors. I wonder
what gentry at home would think if they knew we would
and did follow that smelly lump of leadership all over
Spain, and gladly, too? he thought.

"Sir, I need your advice," he asked, before the dinner
began in lengthy earnest.

"Well, damn me, John, speak up. Don't know why you
artillerists are so soft-spoken."

Standing with his commander in an alcove off the dining
hall, he told him about Mrs. Hurley and Marie Deux.
"She's been mothering Marie since her husband found her
on the field at Badajoz, sir. Now she wishes to be released
from the obligation, and I, for one, think she deserves to be
heard."

To Redpath's relief, Picton listened with interest. The
general himself had proved vulnerable to Marie's considerable charms, as he lay recuperating from wounds of Badajoz, so Parkhill had told him. Mrs. Hurley had been pressed
into service as a nurse, and she made the rounds of the
makeshift ward within the breeched walls of Badajoz, tow-
ing little Marie after her, nursing her, too, with an open-
bloused generosity that saw no enemy in a hungry child.

"Is she still a pretty minx, John?" the general asked.

"Aye," Redpath said, thinking of the times he had been
very nearly skewered by her dark eyes and way of watching
him so carefully, as though she knew he commanded and
must be cajoled, and perhaps obeyed. "Aye," he said again.
"She has her French ways of getting to us all."

The general leaned against the wall. "Have you thought of a Spanish orphanage?"

Redpath had, and the idea found no favor with him. Marie was French from her name to her accent, and he feared her treatment in an orphanage in Spain. "It doesn't seem wise, sir," he said. He shrugged. "Neither does a French orphanage. She has been with the Second Battery for so long now, that I do not know how happy the Frogs will be about her, either. It's a dilemma."

Both men were silent, letting the continuing toasts to Wellington and euphoria of victory swirl around them. "I don't know why it's your problem," Picton said at last.

"It's my battery, sir," Redpath responded quietly. "I may not have been there to approve or disapprove the whole thing in the first place, but when I assumed command from poor Williams, I took on all the Second, not just the guns."

General Picton nodded. "So you did; so we all do. Well, sir, are you married? Maybe your wife would like a remembrance of Spain besides your sorry self."

Redpath laughed and shook his head. "No to both charges, sir! Even if I were leg shackled, I can't fathom springing a four-year-old on an unsuspecting wife."

"Nor I, John." He leaned against the wall, his hand raised as if painting a picture. "There is your loving wife, hands on her corset strings, dying to see you after . . ." He looked at Redpath.

"Six years . . ."

" . . . six years, and you walk in with a child and say 'Surprise!' "

"I can't imagine it," John said. He was silent, waiting for Picton to continue.

"Very well, damn your eyes, Redpath, I'll see what I can do," the general said at last, and then managed a rueful laugh. "Now it's my problem?"

John Redpath grinned, and stepped aside for a waiter staggering under a tray of bottles. "That's what Horse

Guard pays you so much for, General. Cheers, now." He snagged a bottle from the tray as the waiter struggled past. Ah, me, champagne in dusty bottles, he thought, as he nodded to his general and went to take his seat. It's about time we took France.

After the dinner—all toasts and well-deserved applause for Beau Wellington—John Redpath strolled back to his quarters. The bells were silent now, but men who had found dusty bottles of their own leaned against each other, or slumped in corners. All the stars were out, and probably even more than usual, considering the victory celebration, and he walked slowly, savoring the idea of peace and a return home, if only for a brief furlough.

Not for the first time, he wished there were a wife waiting for him, hands on corset strings, as Picton so baldly put it. He had been at war almost twenty of his thirty-six years, serving the guns all over India, and then Portugal and Spain. He couldn't complain, really. The time had passed quickly, and beyond a little deafness in one ear—an occupational hazard—he was healthy and the possessor of all his parts, no mean achievement for a gunner. Of course, there had been scant opportunity to seek out a wife. In the rush and fervor of war, he had not minded, really. His urges for women he could satisfy anywhere in Portugal or Spain, as long as the ladies continued to favor the men who served the guns. He sighed, thinking of his orders to Belgium following furlough. Likely the *femmes* of Brussels would be as compliant as their French and Spanish sisters.

He sat down on the steps of the cathedral to enjoy the champagne buzz that filled his head, even as he scrutinized his solitary life, and found it wanting. I am tired of one-night women, he thought, and different cots in different bivouacs, and food served in a mess hall, or on a stick over a campfire, and washing myself in a gun bucket, and drinking out of empty shell casings. Chin in hand, he sat on the steps and wondered what it would be like to read the morning paper seated across the breakfast table from someone who smelled good, or wake up to children running into his room and jumping on the bed, as he used to do as a small boy.

He wasn't too drunk to realize that he didn't have the slightest idea how to go about the getting of a wife. It was knowledge ungleaned in all those years of war. He considered asking Ed Parkhill, who seemed to have navigated those shoals successfully, then discarded the idea. No, no, he thinks I know everything, the major reflected sourly. "I do know a lot, but somehow I do not think elevations, azimuths, and apogees will get me a wife," he told the drunk soldier snoring nearby. "I wonder what will?" he asked, as he got up and headed in a more or less straight line toward his bed.

General Picton was as good as his word. Two weeks later, he skirted around the battery as the men of the Second discharged their final rounds, preparatory to swabbing out the guns thoroughly and readying them for transport to Belgium. Redpath, his interest trained on his lovely six-pounders, was startled out of his black-powder reverie by Picton's hand on his shoulder.

"Yes, sir," he said, removing the cork plugs from his ears and leaning close to his commander.

"I've found the place for your Marie Deux." Picton shouted over the guns. "My family donates a cartload of money each year to St. Pancras Orphanage at Austell. I've already sent a letter and they will be expecting our French minx."

Redpath nodded, his attention on his guns again as one of the gunners spilled a casing of powder. "Sergeant Mathey," he shouted, leaping to his feet from his perch on a caisson. "On report! It's a wonder Soult didn't mash you in the last engagement!" He returned half of his attention to

General Picton. "Excuse me, sir? St. Austell's out of St. Pancras?"

"No! The other way around! Austell!" The general grabbed Redpath by the neck and towed him away from the guns. "St. Pancras out of Austell. You know, near Land's End. For God's sake, Redpath, pay attention!" He shrugged, his irritation momentary. "At any rate, my ADC is drawing up a letter of introduction for you."

"Have him give it to Lt. Parkhill, sir," Redpath said, replacing his cork plugs. "Better yet, Parkhill is already packed and his case is in the courtyard. Have him put it inside, if you please, sir."

Picton nodded, grinned, and gave Redpath a shove back toward the battery. "Letter to Parkhill, it will be. And I am interested in a report on this." He held out his hand and Redpath removed one plug. "Let us clap hands, Major. I've never thanked you for six years of the best."

Redpath shook his commander's hand, felt himself amply repaid, wondered why his eyes were brimming over—particularly since he was used to all that smoke—and returned to his guns. It was late that night before he reluctantly left the loading area, feeling out of sorts and melancholy as he always did, when he was going one way, and his guns another. Toulouse was quieter now, settling into the routine of peace. He passed the ambulance trains taking wounded back to the convalescent hospital at Fontarabia. He, Parkhill, and Marie Deux would ride with them tomorrow, leaving for home from the port in Spain. He looked up from his contemplation of the cobblestones to see Mrs. Hurley waiting for him outside his quarters, bundle in one hand, and Marie Deux in the other.

"Here she is, Major," the woman said, bending down to straighten the cotton fichu on Marie's tidy bodice, and give her skirt a twitch. "Now, do as you're told, miss, and I'm sure you'll find a good family in England."

You might as well tell her she's going to the moon, Redpath thought, as he watched Marie's eyes well up with tears. His heart did a little flop as he saw her sniff them back, shudder, and then grab Mrs. Hurley in a tight embrace. Awkward in her pregnancy, the sergeant's wife knelt on the cobblestones, her own grip strong. "I wish it could be different, dearie," she murmured into Marie's ear as the child clung to her. She looked up at the major, her eyes appealing for help. "Gor, Major, it's hard to leave, but I don't know what else to do."

She wrenched herself away finally, handed the bundle to the major, and put Marie's hand in his. What small fingers, he thought, as he nodded to Mrs. Hurley, wished her the best of luck, and stood with the child until the woman had turned the corner. He winced inside, waiting for Marie to cry, but she only took a tighter grip on his hand and leaned against his leg.

"Where is this England?" she asked suddenly. "Can I ride there on the caissons with the other children?"

He knelt beside her in the courtyard, amazed at the impact of her words on his heart, as he saw in his mind's eye the children, dusty but uncomplaining, riding the caissons or balancing on the limbers as the Second Battery, Picton's Third Division wound its way the length of the Peninsula. That and walking was all she knew of transportation.

"Lass, you will be two weeks traveling by ship, and then you will be in England," he explained, knowing that his words meant nothing to someone who had never seen more water than the often-stingy rivers of Spain. He ignored the familiar catcalls and comments of his fellow officers returning to their quarters, surprised that it should matter so much to him that Marie Deux understand what was happening to her. He could tell she did not; she sighed heavily.

Two weeks and six years has been this journey, he amended to himself as he lay in his cot later that night. He had made a pallet for Marie Deux out of his discarded clothes, patting it smooth for her and giving her his pillow. She was asleep now, breathing quietly and evenly in the little room, and he smiled that her evening's work to organize him had worn her into solid slumber.

"I am now going to pack six years of Spain," he had announced to her as she perched on his hat case, eating the mush and milk he had cajoled from the mess hall. "Of course, I should have done this much sooner—you may only consider Lt. Parkhill's much better example—but dash it all, Marie, I am a busy man. *Muy ocupado*."

He had held up one of his powder-burned shirts, and was vastly amused when Marie set down her bowl, shook her head, and declared, "*Mais non, monsieur*," in the firm tone of one who knows, counseling one who doesn't.

"Oh, you are my fashion arbiter?" he murmured as he discarded the shirt. "How French of you!"

She did not understand sarcasm any better than any other four-year-old, but she was obviously waiting for him to hold up another shirt. He did, and she rejected it, too, and the next one, and the next.

"Marie, I will go to England naked!" he protested.

"You can have more shirts made, monsieur," was her imperturbable reply as she returned to her mush and milk, all the while keeping him under close observation, lest he should sneak in a shirt she did not approve.

She shook her head over his trousers, too, restoring his good humor by her Gallic contempt of his wardrobe. "Monsieur does not for one moment think he should take holes to this England?" was how she phrased it, with an expressive cut of her hand that made him turn away and cough, so she would not think he was laughing at her.

"I wouldn't dare," he replied promptly, and his beloved campaigning trousers, powder burns, holes and all, ended up on the growing discard pile. "I know, I know: I can have more made in this England!"

To his huge amusement, she nodded seriously, as though relieved he was finally showing a lick of sense. "You should know these things, Monsieur," she commented as he coughed some more. "Mrs. Hurley claims that you lead the Second," she added, great doubt in her voice.

He couldn't help himself then, laughing out loud and wondering why on earth he had never considered the splendor of his raiment before as he and the Second had blasted their way through Spain. He sat on his packing case, contemplating Marie, and trying to imagine himself through her eyes.

"I was pretty shabby, wasn't I?" he asked her finally.

She nodded. "I will overlook it," she said generously. "Maybe you were *trés ocupado.*"

Maybe I was *"trés ocupado,"* he thought later as he listened to her sleep. She had been properly impressed with his dress uniform that he carefully put last into the packing case. She had even hopped off the hat case to finger the epaulets and rows of gold braid, her eyes wide. Then she looked at him, mystified, as though she wanted to ask why on earth he didn't wear this, instead of his usual campaigning rags. She must have thought better of it, because she confined her remarks to a whispered *"C'est bon,"* that got him back into her sartorial good graces.

He watched as she smoothed down the deep blue fabric, her fingers light on the gold trim. To his amusement, she rearranged the two tassels on the front in a more pleasing design. "There," she said, like God resting on the seventh day. "It will do."

Ah, there is a lucky family in England that doesn't even have any idea of the good fortune shortly to come its way, he thought as his eyes began to close. St. Pancras or St. Austell's or whatever that place was called will have no difficulty placing this charmer. She will go to an unsuspecting family, place herself in charge, and organize them beyond their wildest dreams.

* * *

It was a short crossing from Irún to Portsmouth, rendered palatable by Marie Deux. Impervious, apparently, to seasickness, she had calmly wetted a cloth and wiped his face after his bouts at the bucket, and he was reminded of the care she took of the Hurley's children younger than she. It gave him some perverse satisfaction that she ignored Ed Parkhill, moaning and groaning in the other berth. I have a devoted and efficient handler, Redpath realized, as Spain receded from his vision and his heart, and he allowed himself to think of Scotland, and home.

When he could function, he rewarded Marie by taking her on deck frequently, where she stood like a little admiral, admiring the view from the poop deck, and capturing the loyalty of most of the watch. "Your daughter?" the captain had asked him, and it almost gave him a pang to say no, and explain Marie Deux's origins. "We keep cats," was the captain's only comment, and he realized how extraordinary had been the Second Battery's salvage of a dying child from a French battery. His appreciation for his mush-hearted gun crew welled up all over again, and he longed to see them, and his guns, in Belgium. He frowned. It will not be the same without Marie Deux there, he thought.

Portsmouth was no more than a welcome spot to feel the ground again, engage a post chaise, allow Lt. Parkhill time to dash off a brief missive to his fiancée in Bath, and start for St. Pancras, near Land's End. "At least, I am almost certain the village was St. Pancras," he said, as he and Lt. Parkhill sat in the post chaise and waited for the postboys to stow the luggage.

"My God, Major Redpath!" Parkhill burst out. "You're not sure? I mean, sir"—he gulped—"I mean, I just wrote my fiancée that we would be in Bath in three days, sir!"

Redpath frowned. "I think it was St. Pancras. Yes, I am certain. Well"—he paused, looking at Marie Deux, who leaned against his sleeve, asleep—"it's a simple matter,

Ed! I told General Picton to have his ADC put the letter of introduction in your packing case. Just get it out and look at it."

Parkhill nodded. "A simple matter." He stuck his head out of the window. "Boy, there, boy? Bring down that packing case, there's a good lad." He started from the vehicle, then gasped and sat down suddenly on the top step as though someone had yanked his legs from under him.

"An old wound, Ed?" Redpath sympathized, his eyes full of concern. "It won't do to go bum butt a week before your wedding."

His lieutenant was silent for a long moment. "The packing case in the courtyard," he said, striving to keep his tone conversational, to the major's ears, but unable to keep the rising panic from his voice. "My packing case."

"Well, yes. You were already packed," Redpath explained.

Parkhill turned around slowly to look at him, his face as pale as though he still pitched and tossed in the transport. "Major, I gave my packing case to Jack Beresford in exchange for his, which was larger. You see, I had presents for Emmeline and her sister and needed more space, and Major Beresford had lost most of his personal effects in that fire. We traded. Oh, God."

The two men stared at each other. "I am almost certain it was St. Pancras," Major Redpath said slowly. "Of course, I had those cork plugs in my ear, and the guns were going off . . ."

" . . . and they've always claimed your full attention, sir," the lieutenant concluded, shaking his head mournfully. "Oh, Major Redpath."

"St. Pancras," Redpath said decisively. "I'm sure of it." He ran a finger around the inside of his collar, surprised suddenly how warm it was for May in England. "Well, maybe I'm not so sure."

* * *

There, now, thought Audrey Winkle as she folded the last of Emmeline's trousseau petticoats and stuck her needle back in the pincushion. I have hemmed everything in this house except the butler's trousers. Every frock and walking dress and ball gown has been oohed and ahhed over, tried on and ironed. Mama has given Emmeline "The Lecture" and scared her to death. The mints and marzipan are cooling in the milk house. Cook and housekeeper are still speaking to each other. It only remains for Ed Parkhill to get here and marry my wretched sister before she turns into an ogre fit only to frighten bad children into good behavior.

Audrey laughed out loud at the image of Emmeline, all blond, pink, and sweet-smelling being used as a disciplinary object lesson. She went to the window, pulled back the drapes—newly cleaned and restored—to look out on the gathering darkness of late spring. I wonder if I was so terrible before Captain Winkle so kindly married me? she thought, wondering why, after all these years, she still thought of him as captain, and seldom as Matthew.

She leaned against the drapes, sniffing the sunshine still held in them, even as the moon rose like a benediction over the newly planted fields. If I had known him better, perhaps I would think of him today as Matthew, she considered. As it is, I do not remember what color his eyes were, but then, eight years is a long time to recall so brief a husband and lover.

She knew from time-honored experience that she could still close her eyes and see him as though screened through her wedding veil, handsome, confident in his naval uniform, hand resting self-consciously on his sword. But his eyes? Were they gray or blue? Not that it mattered. The next time she saw him, they were closed in death. He wore the same uniform, the peaked hat tucked at his side, all cozy and big shouldered in a coffin that seemed too narrow to contain the life that had been his. Admiral Lord Kitchen of the Blue Fleet had presented her with his sword, which now hung over the fireplace in her room, looking supremely silly with its background of pale green walls, white-trimmed mantel, and china doodads. She wanted to put it away in the closet, but Mama would have been aghast. As it was, she would go days and days now without even a glance at the miniature of him that rested on her bedside table.

She never told Mama, of course, any more than she would have admitted to her or even Emmeline how it set her teeth on edge when they looked at her with profound sympathy still, even after eight years. They didn't need to know how she resented the lingering, loving way they spoke his name occasionally, as though Captain Winkle of His Majesty's Royal Navy was someone soft and effete to be remembered in hushed tones. She closed the drapes. They never understood how robust he was, how fun, how lovely, how blasphemous, how naughty.

"Ah, well," she said out loud. "I wonder that anyone knows how to mourn." She had grieved and suffered and buried her husband of two months, replacing the highest joys with the deepest pain, enduring it and willing it to take her, too. And when she could finally stare down death and not shudder at the remembrance of its cold pall on the one she loved, she knew that she was through mourning. When she could remember the joy without the sorrow, and feel something close kin to peace, it was over. She knew she had been ready for some years now to find another husband. She had thought at first to never marry another military man, but Audrey Winkle was open to suggestion.

And now the world was at peace again, and Napoleon on Elba. The gentry of her circle would return to the concerns of business and land, and if an older widow of twenty-eight years held some attraction over the young sprites who dressed in light muslin and practiced dance steps and how to pour tea, her prospects were at least sanguine.

She knew she had a pretty face; that sort of thing ran in the Caldwell family. True, not everyone could be blond like Emmeline, but there was room in the world for brunettes with brown eyes and graceful carriage. It gave her a little perverse pleasure to note that her own figure was neater than Emmeline's, even at her advanced age. Several respectable widowers had come to call and gaze down at her fine bosom when they thought she wasn't aware, but Audrey Winkle smiled, flirted gently, and knew that somewhere in the world, there had to be younger men still. They weren't all dead on battlefields, or drowned in the sea, or victims of sudden illness like Matthew.

Of course, the reality that one of these paragons with ginger in his step and a twinkle in his eye would ever appear on her doorstep was unlikely in the extreme. This will be the difficult part, she considered, as she gathered the last of the petticoats and folded them. I must eventually convince Mama that I am quite able to set up my own establishment, and in a livelier locale than a house on the outskirts of Bath, where gouty old men come to drink the waters, belch, and complain about the government.

She had the income from her dear dead Papa, and all of Captain Winkle's prize money, too, so the issue was not financial. She needed her own place, and soon, what with Emmeline already chattering on about how wonderful it would be to have Aunt Audrey close by to help with new babies. A pox on Aunt Audrey, she thought, as she took a deep breath and prepared to venture into the rest of the house with its visiting relatives and wedding plans. Aunt Audrey would rather have babies of her own, and they didn't grow in succession houses under strawberry leaves. A husband was essential for that, she thought, and fun in the bargain.

Petticoats draped over her arm, she stepped in the hall

and discovered too late that tactical error as her mother bore down upon her. Too bad that one cannot press a hand against a door to detect heat and looming mothers of brides, she thought with resignation as she smiled at her mother.

"Where have you been hiding?" her mother demanded, taking her by the arm and hurrying her toward the dining room.

"Mama, I was not hiding," she protested gently, knowing the truth of that question and owning to a touch of guilt. "I was finishing the last of Emmeline's petticoats. Mama, where are you taking me?"

Tight of lip and pale of face, Mrs. Caldwell's fragile appearance was belied by the strength of her grip on her elder daughter. Amused, Audrey hurried to keep up, wondering what Dr. Welch would say if he could see his most constant patient practically trot down the corridor without even breathing heavily.

Mrs. Caldwell stopped in front of the dining room doors and flung them open with the strength of ten. "There!" she exclaimed, her voice filled with ill usage. "Can you imagine?"

Audrey couldn't, particularly since she could see nothing out of place in the impeccable room, set with several smaller tables for the bridal dinner. "Mama, perhaps it's a little early to set the tables for . . ." she hedged.

"Audrey, you are so dense at times that I could scream!" Mama said. "I had the servants set it up to see the effect." She paused dramatically. "How can we face all our relatives and friends?"

"Mama, there is nothing wrong!" Audrey said.

Mrs. Caldwell burst into noisy tears, turning to sob on her elder daughter's shoulder while Audrey looked closer.

"My dear, you can't be concerned because the tablecloths are just slightly yellow?" she asked at last.

Mama sobbed louder. "And the goblets!" She raised her hand helplessly and let it fall.

"Oh, Mama, the patterns are so close no one will notice," Audrey assured her. She tried to make a joke of it. "I will be amazed if Ed notices anything but Emmeline."

It was a foolish effort, and she should have known better. Mrs. Caldwell gasped and heaved herself off her daughter's shoulder as though it burned. "Sir Edmund! Sir Edmund! Not Ed! Audrey, where are your manners?"

Audrey looked behind her. "I thought I brought them into the room with me. Mama! Don't be silly! It's been Ed for years." Years, indeed, she thought, trying not to smile at her mother. They had all watched Ed Parkhill grow from a skinny lad with a stutter, into a firm of jaw, clear of eye young man whose title had always sat lightly on him. Orphaned young and living on the nearby estate of a now-dead uncle, Ed Parkhill had spent more time at their place, keeping company with the Caldwell brothers and worshipping the ground Emmeline glided over. "Mama, Ed doesn't give a rap about tablecloths or goblets," she soothed. "I doubt he's even seen anything so refined in the last few years. It doesn't matter!"

Mrs. Caldwell dried her eyes and glared at her daughter. "It matters a great deal, Audrey! We have a certain standing to maintain in Bath, I will remind you." She stared at the offending tablecloths and goblets as though willing them to shrivel away, then turned her displeasure on her daughter. "I am determined to have a wedding that no one ever forgets. You will find new tablecloths in the morning in Bath and check every china shop in town for that pattern." She jabbed her finger at the goblet closest to her. "A rose etched on the side."

Audrey gritted her teeth and kissed her mother's cheek. "Certainly, dearest! I will not rest until everything matches. Oh, dear! Whatever will we do about Uncle Eustace and his eye patch?"

Mama was still in no mood for frivolity. "Don't try me!" she exclaimed. "You and Matthew may have settled for something a bit more jolly—oh, those Winkles were a trial at times—but I intend for my only daughter marrying into the ranks of the nobility to have a memorable wedding, one unequaled in the annals of Bath. That is all."

Audrey knew this was no time to mention to Mama that a baronet was hardly coin of the realm. Oh, when did Ed go from being just old Ed to Sir Edmund? she wondered. And why is this wedding starting to turn into a monster? And where is Ed?

The whereabouts of her fiancée was certainly on Emmeline's mind in the morning. The two of them teetered and balanced on stools in Mama's sewing rooms while the seamstresses crawled the floor and measured hems. (The only hems I have not finished, Audrey thought with amusement.)

"You don't think he has cried off?" Emmeline asked, as the seamstresses released them from tyranny and they removed their wedding finery.

"No!" Audrey declared. "We know Ed better than that, Emmy, at least, I do."

"I still wonder where he is," she said while Audrey buttoned up her work dress. She frowned. "He scribbled something about 'a little business to take care of,' and then he would be here. That should have been yesterday."

"Wasn't he traveling with his commanding officer?" Audrey asked, turning around for Emmeline to button her now. "Major Redpath must be an older man; perhaps he took sick."

"Perhaps," Emmeline said slowly. "Still, I think it is rude and inconsiderate of him and so I shall tell him."

Audrey shook her head. "Don't waste your time on things that don't matter, Emmy. Trust me on this one."

Emmeline rested her cheek on her sister's shoulder. "But it does matter to me! What will people think if the groom is late?"

What, indeed, Audrey thought later as she sat in the kitchen mulling over the week's menu. Sometimes I wonder if Emmeline really loves Ed, or if she just likes the idea of a wedding. She owned to a twinge of guilt. I suppose if Captain Winkle and I hadn't hurried to Portsmouth for a quick wedding before he prepared to embark for the West Indies, Mama and Emmeline would not feel the need so much for an elaborate affair that no one will ever forget. She smiled to herself and looked at the menus again. As it is, Emmeline will probably not remember anything of the day anyway, and Mama will have spent a lot of guineas solely for the entertainment of relatives and friends who will only talk and gossip about us. She grinned. As we gossip and talk about them. Oh, Lord spare me from this small society!

They were still waiting and wondering after dinner, and long after the lamps had been lit. Emmeline stalked back and forth in front of the window while Mama languished on the sofa and Audrey pretended to read. Emmeline's mood changed with the minute, from "He is dead in a ditch and I have wasted the best years of my life writing to him!" to "Mama, why must men be such a trial? Do you suppose he became lost and didn't want to ask directions? Men are like that, you know." Audrey kept her eyes on the book and tried not to laugh out loud, considering that her stock was low enough anyway with Mama.

"Audrey, you will go into town tomorrow and match the goblets and find new tablecloths," came Mama's firm voice from the depths of the sofa. "And if you see Dr. Welch, tell him my heart is palpitating all over my chest."

"Yes, Mama."

They were beginning to think of bed, when Emmeline halted her forced march in front of the window, threw up the glass—which brought faint cries of anguish from Mama—and leaned out. "I know I see a vehicle," she said. "Oh, Audrey, come look."

Audrey looked and felt a measure of relief. No question there was something coming. Carriage lights glittered through the newly leafed trees, and soon they could hear the horses.

"If it is horrid Uncle Eustace and Aunt Agatha come early, I will scream," Emmeline declared. She grabbed her sister's hand. "Audrey, do you think he will have changed? It's been two years."

Audrey took her sister by the shoulders and gave her a gentle shake. "I know he will have changed, my dear." She put her forehead against her sister's. "That's one thing else we need to talk about. It's been a long war, and war does things to men."

And women, she thought as she watched the vehicle turn into a post chaise much muddied from travel. War has robbed me of a husband, and babies, and old age with someone I loved. I do hope Napoleon is vastly uncomfortable on Elba.

The post chaise stopped in the driveway. Audrey waited for Emmeline to fling the door open and run outside and into her fiancé's arms, but she did not. Oh, I would, thought Audrey, feeling anguish wash over her, as though Captain Winkle were but newly dead. I would throw myself into his arms and have to be pried out for meals and baths. "Go to him, Emmy," she whispered, when she could get her lips to move.

Emmeline shook her head. "No. I am angry at him for being late."

And so it was the butler who welcomed Lieutenant Sir Edmund Parkhill into his love's home. Audrey steeled herself for the pain she knew would come when Ed gathered her sister into his arms and forgot the war. If I dig down deep enough, I can stand this, too, she thought as she moved slowly toward the sitting-room door to greet her future brother-in-law.

What happened next wiped out any pain she anticipated. With an expression more unreadable than usual, the butler opened the door, and in walked Ed Parkhill, carrying a sleeping child in his arms. He was followed by another man as shabbily dressed as himself, but with more gilt on his uniform. Audrey knew she would remember forever the light in Ed's eyes which changed to open-mouthed astonishment as Emmeline gasped and staggered toward him, jabbing her finger in his direction.

"Edmund! A child! How could you!" she shrieked, in dying tones that would have done Mama proud, except that Mama had already lapsed into a quiet faint. Before Audrey could move, her sister pressed her hands to her temples, uttered an unladylike noise, and sank gracefully toward the floor.

That Emmeline did not land on the parquet and do herself an injury, she owed entirely to the other officer, who stepped quickly forward and snagged her on the way down. To Audrey's further astonishment, he grinned at Ed. "I told you to let me carry Marie Deux, you simple simon."

"But . . . but . . ." the dumbfounded lieutenant began, then stared at his love lolling in his commanding officer's arms.

"Where should I put this darling lass?" the man asked. He settled Emmeline more comfortably in his arms and looked toward the sofa, then at Audrey. "It appears your mother has jumped to conclusions, too. Goodness, what a fainting family. Ed, close your mouth. You'll catch flies, you know you will."

It was all so artless, and spoken in the most wonderful brogue that Audrey had ever heard. It had heather, and sheep, and bracken and burn, and short days and long nights in it, brisk, bracing, and cheery and totally in command, no matter how softly spoken the words.

"Over here, sir," she said, collecting her wits one by one, which seemed to have rolled out of her ears and onto the carpet. "Goodness, indeed! I don't think we quite expected to see Ed with child so soon."

The officer grinned at her choice of words. "I warned

him, but 'pon my word, he's a naive soul, isn't he? Even after two years in Spain. Ah, me. Ed, put Marie down somewhere and come here and prepare a mighty explanation for your . . . sister-in-law, is it?"

Audrey nodded, suddenly and surprisingly shy. She held out her hand. "Mrs. Winkle."

He set down Emmeline and took her hand in his. "Charmed, indeed."

She couldn't think of anything to do with her hand at the moment, so she kept it in his. He was a man of some height, and up close, even shabbier. What distinguished him in the quiet room was the uniformity of his coloring, which was the light mahogany of a warmer climate. It matched almost perfectly the red of his hair, and blended with a fair sprinkling of freckles. I am looking at a Celt cast ashore from some tropic location where surely nature never intended him, she thought with amusement, her hand still in his.

His eyes were a brilliant green, a delightful contrast to his hair and complexion. She thought him handsome beyond words. "Major Redpath?" she asked, even though she knew it could be no one else. No Englishman ever looked so much like the soil he sprang from; nature designed Scots to be permanently marked with their homeland, she decided, as she observed him and forgot her swooning relatives.

"John Redpath," he replied, his voice cheerful, and so soft she had to lean closer. He still didn't seem inclined to release her hand, and she couldn't understand why that didn't bother her. "Sorry, Mrs. Winkle. We gunners tend to speak softly. I think it's a consequence of all that shouting to be heard over loud noises."

His reply was so ingenuous and his accent so charming that she wanted to hear it all over again, from the top. And did she step closer to him, or was it the other way around? She couldn't be sure. Well, she excused herself, as she released his hand, if he wouldn't speak so softly, I would not need to tromp on his boots to hear him. He smelled of wool and travel, and John Redpath.

Ed deposited the sleeping child on the carpet and Audrey came closer to look at her. What a pretty child, she thought, as she hurried to Ed and grasped him in her arms. She stood on tiptoe to give him a loud smack on the cheek.

"Oh, Audrey. Should we revive them or should I offer a brief explanation to you first, so you won't think me a complete rake?"

"Explain, you rascal." Audrey separated herself from Ed's returning embrace and looked at the butler, who stood like Lot's wife in the doorway. "Ames, bring some wet cloths, and some whiskey, please." She twinkled her eyes at Ed. "This is not a sherry occasion. Tell all now."

"I should, for it's my doing, considering that I command," the major said, stepping over Marie to stand beside her. "Members of the Second found Marie Deux after Badajoz and raised her in the battery. I command a soft-hearted gun crew, Mrs. Winkle. Now that the war's over, I'm on furlough, and General Sir Thomas Picton told me of an orphanage." He looked at Ed and shook his head. "I'm the guilty one; I misplaced the directions to the orphanage."

"And we've been traveling all over Land's End looking for a St. Pancras, or St. Austell, or St. Anybody, until we are sainted out," Ed continued picking up the story.

"No luck?" Audrey said.

Ed shook his head. "I knew Emmeline would be wondering where we were, so we came here. Major Redpath said he'd take up the hunt after the wedding." Ed took Audrey's hand again and kissed her fingers. "And that's the truth of it, my dear."

Audrey grinned. "I never doubted for a moment. Here now, have some refreshment while I revive my family. Major, take off your cloak and make yourself comfortable, please!"

* * *

She had to hand it to the artillery, which moved in promptly with explanations, blandishments, and apologies enough to remove the suspicion from Emmeline's eyes, when they opened again. Mama was a more difficult subject, to Audrey's embarrassment.

"This won't do, Major," she told Redpath as she leaned against Audrey, sniffing at her vinaigrette. "I can't imagine what our friends and relatives will think when they hear of this. You must find that orphanage at once, sir, or keep that . . . that . . ."

"Wee lassie?" the major suggested.

"French camp follower trash is more what I think," Mama said roundly. "At any rate, I'll not have such leavings strewn about to wreck a most perfect wedding, Major!"

"Of course not, Mrs. Caldwell," the major said, as Audrey burned with humiliation. "I don't know what got into my lads, to save a two-year-old from a bombed-out French battery, but there you are. Marie Deux and I will keep ourselves scarce."

Mama nodded. She looked at Audrey. "I don't know where we'll put her. All the relatives will be arriving tomorrow." She began to pick at the handkerchief in her lap, as the tears welled in her eyes. "This is so upsetting!"

"Oh, Mama, we'll manage." Audrey swallowed her shame and looked at the major. "She can sleep with me tonight."

"Audrey! Suppose she has fleas or some disease."

"Mama, this is a little girl and she must go somewhere," Audrey said, her voice firm. "Major, tomorrow I can get a cot for her in my dressing room, but I am certain we will be fine tonight."

"Mr. Winkle won't mind?" the major asked as he carried the sleeping child upstairs.

"Captain Winkle is dead these eight years, sir," Audrey replied, holding her candle so he could see the steps over his burden.

"I'm sorry," he replied. "Was he Army?"

"Navy, sir. Here's my room."

The child woke when he set her on the bed. How pretty you are, Audrey thought, as the captain removed her little traveling cloak, obviously cut down from an army coat. She reached out to finger the child's curls. "Hello, Marie Deux," she said, her voice soft so as not to startle her. "I always wanted curls."

The major sat beside her on the bed. "You don't need them," he said, and turned slightly to look at her. "Everything works as it is."

It was an ingenuous statement, but somehow it did not startle her. Sir, our acquaintance is too brief for such a compliment, she thought. But say on, anytime you choose, and let me soak in your marvelous accent. "Well, I thought I wanted curls," she amended.

"You'll sleep here tonight, Marie," the major said as he helped the little girl from her dress. The child only nodded, accepting her, the room, and the arrangement with a matter-of-factness that touched Audrey. Here is a little one who is used to anything life throws at her, she thought, as she took the dress from the major and draped it over a chair. My family should study this instead of reject it.

The major got up then. "Well, I'll leave the rest to you ladies," he said. He bent down to touch Marie's cheek. "All right, Petty Chew, don't snore."

The child smiled at him. "You snore, Major, not me."

The major laughed. "So I do, lass!" He looked at Audrey. "We've been making a pallet for her on the floor in too many inns, Mrs. Winkle."

She nodded. "One does what one must." She glanced at Marie, whose eyes were closing already. "'Petty Chew?'"

It was the major's turn to blush. "I started calling her *'mon petit chou'* and that was more than the gunners could handle," he murmured, and she could almost feel his embarrassment at such a homely, intimate nickname. "'Petty

Chew' she is." He patted Marie again, then to Audrey's surprise, picked up the miniature of Captain Winkle on the bedside table. "A handsome man."

"I thought so, too."

His eyes went to the sword over the mantelpiece. "It doesn't really fit in here, do you think?" His voice was soft, but full of that same confidence of command that she remembered vaguely from Captain Winkle.

"No, it doesn't," she agreed, surprising herself in an evening of surprises. "I've been meaning to take it down for a year or more now, but I'm not tall enough to reach that last bracket."

"I am," he said as he put the miniature facedown, went to the fireplace, reached up and removed the sword. He leaned it in the corner. "Good night, lassies. You say I'm two doors down?"

She nodded, wondering at all the feelings playing tag in her head. She thought she should be offended, but couldn't imagine why. *He comes in my bedroom, turns down Matthew's miniature, takes his sword from the wall, changes everything, and I let him. I have known him less than an hour, and I am in the middle of something. I wonder what it is?*

Puzzled with herself, she gently shook Marie awake and helped her from her petticoat, smoothing down her wrinkled chemise. "I'm sure I can find you a nightgown that fits in the morning," she said. "Mama never threw out anything." She readied herself for bed, tying on her cap, her eyes on the miniature still lying facedown. She righted it, then picked it up, took a long look, and put it in her drawer under her handkerchiefs and stockings.

As Audrey blew out the lamp and lay down, Marie moved close to her with a sigh. It was an easy matter to put her arms around the child, and enjoy her warmth. She looked at the bare spot on the wall over the fireplace, thinking that one of her watercolors would look fine there. I hope Major Redpath is comfortable in that bed, she thought, as she rested her head against Marie's curls and listened to her even breathing. She closed her eyes, wondered outrageously if he had freckles everywhere, and was glad the room was dark.

He woke early, as he always did, startled awake by the silence of the room, and wondering briefly where Marie Deux was. He relaxed against the pillow, remembering that she was two doors down, where he wanted to be. Lucky Petty Chew, he thought, as he got up, washed, and shaved himself, gazing into the mirror with some dissatisfaction that he was not as handsome as Captain Winkle. As he dressed, he toyed briefly with the idea of tiptoeing back into Mrs. Winkle's bedroom and repositioning the sword on her wall. He could throw himself on her mercy and apologize for his presumptuous behavior in removing it last night. He had the good sense to reject such a stupid idea. I am sure she would love to see a strange man walking about in her room, benevolently and contritely rehanging her husband's sword, he thought sourly.

As he sat on his bed to pull on his boots, he was struck by an odd idea. He had been nineteen years at war, and deep into the routine of it all, knowing that nothing new would ever happen to him. War had robbed him of everything except more war, and it was all he knew. But something new had happened, and his logical, mathematical, practical artilleryman's mind could not begin to explain it. I will not try, he thought.

Emmeline and Ed sat in the breakfast room, and despite his own relative inexperience with women, he recognized tension without requiring a manual. He nodded and smiled to them both and hurried to the sideboard, wondering if the silly widgeon was going to continue to punish her love for bringing home a French waif from the wars.

Apparently she was. "Edmund, I wonder that you and Major Redpath didn't just leave that child."

"Marie Deux," Redpath said quickly, not meaning to interrupt what was certainly not his quarrel, but unable to stop himself, "she has a name." *And nicknames, and some of us are fond of her.*

". . . that child at any orphanage in Land's End!" she concluded. "Surely it would not matter to General Picton, even if he did take some interest."

He sat down at the table, struck by the good sense of what she said, and chilled by it at the same time. "Well, no," he agreed, looking to Ed for help. "I don't suppose we even thought of that."

Then you are an idiot, her expression told him, even if she said nothing.

The lieutenant gazed at his fiancée. "Maybe we weren't really taken with any of those institutions we saw, Emmeline, my love."

"I cannot feel that is important, Edmund," Emmeline replied. "Why am I thinking that Mama and I will have to explain that child—"

"Mary Deux," Redpath interrupted.

". . . over and over to everyone who shows up? It is too much to ask, and will be hard for some to believe. You know how people like to think the worst and jump to conclusions."

You certainly did, he thought dryly.

She dabbed at her lips with her napkin. "I have to ask myself if you are determined to scotch—excuse me, Major—my plans."

The major watched her expressive face and was curious what trick of light had made her seem so attractive last night as she swooned in his arms. *I must have been overly tired,* he thought, as he held up his cup for tea from the footman.

Emmeline stopped her tongue until the footman closed the door quietly. "I think that the sooner you find a place for . . . for . . ."

"Marie Deux," the major filled in, his voice sounding dangerously patient to his own ears, and obviously to Lieutenant Parkhill, too. His subaltern shifted uneasily in his chair.

". . . that child, the more comfortable Mama and I will be," she finished, with just a trace of a pout in her voice that made him begin to pity Lieutenant Sir Edmund Parkhill.

The return of the footman with muffins and toast stifled the hot words that bubbled up in him, and then Mrs. Winkle and Marie Deux came to breakfast. He rose when they entered the room, happy to admire Mrs. Winkle in morning light. She nodded to him and blew her sister and Ed a kiss, then helped Marie at the sideboard, while he was content to regard her and let his breakfast get cold.

I have been missing English skin, he decided, as he watched the light play on Mrs. Winkle's marvelous rose complexion. She wore an attractive lace cap that covered her glorious dark hair, but brought emphasis to her eyes, warm brown like Marie's. He noticed how she touched Marie's cheek, and then rested her hand lightly on the child's shoulder. I would like to be touched like that, he decided, as he looked at his food again. And return the favor. I would wager she is as soft to the touch as she is gentle on the eye.

"Major Redpath."

He glanced up in surprise at the barely spoken words to see Emmeline watching him, her eyes full of amusement. "To spare you any possible disappointment," she confided, her voice low as she watched her sister across the room, "my dear Audrey said years ago that she would never marry a military man again."

"Emmy!" Lt. Parkhill hissed. "Mind your manners! This is my commanding officer."

"I know, my love, I know," she replied quietly, the soul of complacence. "It is merely that I do not wish to see Major Redpath unhappy."

I doubt you care at all, he thought, but he nodded, and returned his attention to food that held no attraction for him now. Her words were food for thought, however, and he chewed them along with the bacon. Am I that interested, he asked himself, and so obvious? He almost shivered with pleasure as Mrs. Winkle sat beside him. You are too late, Emmeline, he thought, as he smiled at Audrey Winkle. I am already unhappy.

She turned her attention to Marie Deux, seated next to her, and saw her organized with napkin, spoon, and bowl before she looked at her own plate. She ate as a hungry woman ought to, pausing once to inquire if his food was not to his liking.

"Oh, it is fine," he hastened to assure her. "I suppose I am still used to weevily porridge, or fried hare, or whatever we scared up from the bushes in Spain."

I sound like an idiot, he thought desperately. Would anyone here mind if I suddenly let out a roar, grabbed Mrs. Winkle, threw her over my shoulder, and carried her upstairs to have my way with her? The prospect was so appealing that he could feel himself turning redder than his uniform collar. To his relief, Lieutenant Parkhill laughed, and pushed back his chair.

"So am I, sir! Do you know I even had trouble sleeping in my bed last night?"

Oh, Lord forgive me, so did I, he thought. Please keep talking, Ed.

His lieutenant did not fail him. "And when the maid came in with hot water and jerked the draperies open with that zipping sound, I nearly climbed under the carpet!" Parkhill toyed with his fiancée's loose hair around her neck. "Emmy dear, it takes a while to readjust, I am discovering. Things change."

"Do you change, Edmund?" she asked, brushing away his fingers impatiently. "I am sure I never do."

Parkhill said nothing, but he continued to watch her thoughtfully when she returned her attention to her toast.

"Well, my dear sister, I am going to gird my loins now," Mrs. Winkle said as she crossed her knife and fork on her plate. "Mama insists that I turn Bath inside out in my search for tablecloths white enough for the finest wedding ever seen in this shire, and goblets that match each other. Marie, will you accompany me?"

"I'll come, too," Redpath offered.

"Excellent!" she said. "I am sure Mama and Emmeline cannot spare me a footman or a maid to give me countenance. You will do."

Oh, I would, he thought. I would do most splendidly, Mrs. Winkle who-thinks-she-should-not-like-military-men.

"While you are in town, stop at the Foundling Home on the High and the workhouse," Emmeline said, as calmly as though she suggested that Audrey pick up a new scent at the perfumers.

"I will not," Audrey said quickly, then blushed. "Excuse my presumption! Of course, I suppose you are right. This *is* what you want, isn't it, gentlemen?"

The major looked at his lieutenant. "It must be what we want," he said finally. "That was the original plan, at any rate," he temporized.

"And nothing has changed, has it?" Emmeline asked so sweetly that he wanted to leap across the table and throttle her.

Everything has changed, he thought, everything. "No, nothing has changed," he mumbled. He sighed and glanced at Marie, who was watching him with an unreadable expression. "At your service, Mrs. Winkle."

* * *

Major Redpath decided by noon that if a bomb were to suddenly drop on him—an eventuality he had anticipated for years now—he would die a happy man. He had just spent the best morning of his life, going from shop to store to warehouse, looking for tablecloths and goblets. If only Picton could see me now, he thought, as he offered his opinion on the relative whiteness of damask that all looked the same to him.

He took wicked delight in the realization that Mrs. Winkle seemed to care as little about tablecloths as he did. Marie did the final selecting, to the amusement of the clerk. "Your daughter is remarkably perspicacious," the clerk told him as he bundled the tablecloths in brown paper and string.

"She is, isn't she?" he agreed without a qualm. "She takes after her mother," he added, his unholy glee increasing as Mrs. Winkle blushed and looked down at her shoes.

"I do not mind telling you, sir, that you are a rascal," she said as they left the shop, Marie skipping ahead.

"You could have denied it," he said reasonably.

"And create a scene in a shop?" She laughed then. "Well, is she your daughter? I've heard Ed's story."

"Then believe it," he said. "I came to the Second from the Torres Vedras lines after poor Captain Williams lost his neck at Badajoz. It had a terrible effect on his head."

She grimaced, and he had the good grace to blush in his turn. "Excuse an artilleryman's humor, Mrs. Winkle, but we've earned it," he apologized. "Sergeant Hurley found her. The men named her Marie Deux after the Second, and Mrs. Hurley let her suck." He shook his head. "I do remember that she was almost two then, we think, or maybe more, but so thin and scrawny. Mrs. Hurley thought it best."

"I wonder that she did not wish to keep her," Mrs. Winkle said. They were walking slower and slower now, but there seemed no need to hurry.

"It's a hard service, Mrs. Winkle," he explained. "Mrs. Hurley lost the lottery and has to travel overland to Ostend. The guns and her husband were going by sea, and she is not, and there are three bairn and another in the making."

When Marie came skipping back to tug on his sleeve, he realized that they were just standing there on the sidewalk. She stopped in front of him, her hands on her hips. "Major Redpath!"

Goblets were a problem. Mrs. Winkle would hold one after another up to the light for him to see the design, and he would stare at her instead. He couldn't help himself. She was the most beautiful woman he had ever seen, and she stirred him to the depth of his heart in a place he hadn't dreamed existed.

"I know why you are doing this," she said finally, after looking in another shop.

"Oh?" he asked, certain he was guilty with whatever she charged him.

"You want to make sure that I never trouble you with another shopping expedition during your stay," she accused.

And there they stood until Marie reminded him that the clerk was expecting some response. "We'll take the whole lot, pitcher, plate, and all," he said, drawing out his wallet. "It will be my wedding present to the happy couple." He directed the packing crates to the Caldwell's Bath address, and offered his arm to Mrs. Winkle again.

After a jovial lunch where they all laughed too much and earned stares and whispered comments, they knew they could not avoid the next stop. "I'm sure I do not like this, but Emmeline is probably right," Mrs. Winkle said as she clutched his arm tight this time and directed him up the High Street beyond the shops to where the avenue turned into a narrow lane of overhanging houses and sewers smelling of centuries of use. "We can at least check it out," she concluded, doubt evident in her voice.

St. Elizabeth's Foundling Home was even more grim inside, low-ceilinged, cold, and dark, as though denying spring in bloom everywhere outside. While he spoke quietly to the matron, a cadaver of a woman dressed in unrelieved black, he noticed that Marie Deux had backed herself up against Mrs. Winkle until she could get no closer. Audrey's hands were laced strong across the child's chest, and her eyes filled with dread.

"Major, this child of yours . . ."

". . . not mine . . ."

"Whatever you say. This child is too old for our institution." With a flick of her hand, the matron motioned them after her down the cramped hallway, ill-lit and echoing with the cry of small children. "However, if she is capable, we could use her in here." She opened the door on a large room where cheap tallow candles smoked and burned and babies sobbed.

He forced himself after her into the room, grateful in his soul that Mrs. Winkle refused to enter with Marie, but stood anchored in the doorway, the child tight in her grasp again, her face turned into the widow's skirts this time. I can't do this, he thought, as he watched with anguish as girls not much older than Marie tended the babies, their hair unvisited by a comb or brush and their eyes redrimmed from the smoking candles. One or two of them looked at him with hope, but the others didn't even glance up as they hurried to change babies and feed them.

The matron was looking at him expectantly, and he fought to subdue the disgust that rose in him and return some civilized comment. "I . . . uh . . . I wonder that you can remember all their names," he managed finally.

The matron gave a humorless laugh. "We do not name them, Major! They are numbered. If they live to a year old, then we pick Bible names for the wretched little sinners. It is our Christian duty."

He closed his eyes against loss of life and dignity worse than any battlefield, spun on his heel, and left the matron standing there, her mouth open. "See here, sir, we do the best we can!" she hurled after him.

"You'd be kinder to line them up and shoot them down," he shouted, setting off more babies crying. "Come on, Audrey, let's get out of here!"

He almost ran into the street, speechless with horror, striding rapidly along until Mrs. Winkle protested. "I'm sorry," he said then, slowing his pace and letting her tuck her arm through his. She leaned against his arm, and he touched her face, then quickly picked up Marie. The child burrowed her head into his shoulder, her grip so tight on his neck that he winced. "Don't worry, Marie Deux," he said into her ear. "That's not the place we had in mind." She said nothing, but only clung tighter, her legs wrapped around him now.

It was a long, wordless walk home, but neither of them felt like hailing a hackney. Mrs. Winkle clutched his arm, her knuckles white on his sleeve, Marie dug into his neck, and he could think of nothing to do now except hold them both and wish, like a coward, for the simplicity of artillery.

Mrs. Winkle released him as they came up the front steps, looking around in surprise at the post chaises and carriages that lined the drive. She sighed. "The relatives have descended."

They entered the house quietly, Audrey tiptoeing down the hall, listening to the buzz through the sitting-room door, and motioning him down the hall to the servants' stairs. He followed her down to the kitchen, presided over by no one more intimidating than the cook.

"I cannot face any of them, even my brothers," Mrs. Winkle said as she removed her pelisse, took off her bonnet, and fluffed her hair. She sat down and Marie perched on her lap. "My dear, what would you think of some milk and biscuits?"

Marie did not answer for a long time. She leaned against Mrs. Winkle, who gathered her close. From the security of the widow's arms, Marie Deux looked at him. "Please, sir, you would not—"

He did not allow her to finish. "I would never, Marie Deux," he said, his voice so fervent that it shook. His heart cracked as she sighed and relaxed in Mrs. Winkle's strong embrace. "Then yes, I would like milk and biscuits." She smoothed down her worn dress with a womanly gesture that cracked his heart again, and allowed Cook to pour her some milk.

He left her at the table, cosseted by Cook, and followed Mrs. Winkle down the hall to a storage room, where she directed him to take down a dress box. She knelt by the box and opened it, smiling for the first time since luncheon and pulling back the tissue. "Mama kept all my clothes. Do you think this will fit Marie?"

He nodded, touched at her generosity of spirit. "She will be lovely."

Mrs. Winkle nodded, folded the dress, and put it aside. She tugged out several others, as well as petticoats, chemises, and a nightgown, which she held up and looked at for a long time. "Major Redpath, what are we going to do?" she asked out of the blue.

"Well, we know we are not going to throw her to the Christians at St. Elizabeth's! I can't imagine the workhouse would be much better." He sat down beside her on the floor and leaned against the wall. "I could kick myself for mislaying the address and location of that orphanage General Picton recommended!"

Her smile was strange and disquieting. She reached for his hand and he grasped hers gladly, partners in confusion. "You do not for a moment think that General Picton's choice would be any better than what we saw this afternoon, do you?"

He considered her question, and could not look at that strange smile. "You are likely right, Audrey. If we are thinking to confine her to a British orphanage, then

Sergeant Hurley and the others should just have passed her by and let her die in the French battery at Badajoz. It would have been more humane."

"Could you keep her?" she asked, releasing his hand.

He shook his head. "I'm not married, I am due in Belgium in a month, and I cannot see how I can manage it. What about you?"

"Mama would never permit it."

"Ed and Emmeline?"

"I think not," Audrey said quietly, the shame evident in her voice. "I fear my sister is not given much to charity, sir."

"And neither are we, if we don't think of something," he said frankly. She looked so young and small, sitting there on the floor Indian-style, with children's clothing around her. "You could marry, Audrey. In fact, I can't imagine why you are not married. Captain Winkle may have been a good man, but it's been eight years." *My, but that was personal and plain-spoken,* he thought. *I haven't even known this woman twenty-four hours, and already I am prying into intimate corners where no one invited me.*

"My offers have been from older men and widowers," she said simply. "They want companionship, someone to mind their children, or a woman to look pretty at social functions. I have become wary of men with a plan, sir." She hesitated. "I had something more in mind."

"Love again, lass?" he asked, his voice soft. "Some people want the moon and stars, too."

She reddened. "Silly, isn't it?"

He couldn't think of anything else to do but kiss her then, lifting her onto his lap and kissing her so long that he had trouble breathing and finally had to stop before he really wanted to. *I'm not so good at this,* he thought, as he put his arms around her and let her rest her head against his shoulder as Marie Deux had done so recently. *I didn't kiss* women in Spain; I just used them. This woman I want to kiss, and I'm not very good at it.

But I could learn, he thought, as Mrs. Winkle took his head in her hands and kissed him. Her fingers so protective of Marie Deux were strong in his hair and then on his back as she made little sounds in her throat and acquainted herself with his mouth in an extraordinary way. I think I just learned, he decided, as he reciprocated in kind and duration. Of course, we artillerymen are the brightest branch of the service.

He was more than ready to relieve the strain and attempt something that would either get him slapped or satisfied, when he heard steps coming toward the storage room. "Cease firing," he murmured, and set Audrey Winkle off his lap. I wonder if I look as disheveled as you do? he thought, and decided that he did. He combed his hair with his fingers, and hoped that whoever came through the door was blind.

Oh, dear, thought Audrey, trying to smooth her hair back under her cap again and calm the wrinkles in her dress at the same time. She glanced at the major, and decided, with a blush, that perhaps she had better step into the hall and close the door after her. Men are so inept at times like this, she thought. My knees may be weak, but that will never show.

To her relief, it was Uncle Eustace meandering down the hall, he of the eye patch earned forty years earlier in the retreat from Lexington. Oh, the relatives, she groaned inwardly as she came forward with her arms outstretched. Uncle Eustace seemed startled at her embrace, and she needed no more confirmation that his other eye was none too vigorous anymore.

"Audrey!" he exclaimed at last, holding her off for a better look. "My, how you've grown."

"I sincerely hope not," she said with a smile. "We only saw each other at Christmas!"

He had the good sense to laugh at himself, then inquired after the wine cellar again, holding out a battered tankard that he always traveled with, to Aunt Agatha's disgust. "I know it is here somewhere and there's rum in it. Your mother serves nothing but sherry, which gives me wind," he complained. He moved to the storage room, and she leaped in front of him.

"No, Uncle, not that door," she said hastily.

He grinned at her and pinched her cheek. "You act like you have a lover in there, missy!"

She joined in his laughter, hoping that he was overlooking the wild expression she knew was in her eyes. "My dear, uncle, let me show you to the wine cellar," she said, taking him firmly by the arm and steering him past the storage room. She helped him down the short flight of stairs, and saw him seated comfortably in front of a keg of rum before she hurried back to the storage room door.

She was debating whether to open it, when Major Redpath came out, looking more himself, except that his lovely red hair still stuck out in several directions. I should not do this, she thought, but she did it anyway, standing on tiptoe to smooth back the hair behind his ears. "There now, sir! Unless you and Marie Deux wish to meet my incredibly proper . . ."

Uncle Eustace was already singing something decidedly lusty in the wine cellar. The major let out a shout of laughter before he covered his mouth with his hand. She pushed him against the wall and giggled into his sleeve. "Stop it now!" she ordered, when she could talk. "Well, most of them are high sticklers. I recommend you and Marie make yourselves scarce until dinner."

"Very well, my dear," he said.

Oh, please don't kiss me again, she thought, already amply well-acquainted with that look in his eyes. "You realize of course, that we have to forget what just happened in the storage room, Major," she began, striving for a dignified tone.

He continued to regard her with that same disquieting expression she remembered from her few memorable nights with Captain Winkle. "I am not sure there is that much amnesia in the entire universe, Mrs. Winkle," he said. "I still think you should marry."

Marry you? she asked herself. Well, propose, and let us see what I do, for even I am not sure. "I've already told you I have no prospects right now," she found herself saying, when he made no more comment.

"It shouldn't be hard," he said, and she knew from his expression that amnesia hadn't set in yet.

"Well it is," she assured him, sounding more tart than she wished. "Do I just go up to someone I hardly know, introduce myself, and say, 'Marry me?' I think not, Major."

That is precisely what I wish to do, she thought mournfully, after she left him and Marie Deux safely hidden in the kitchen. I am certain men have proposed on less provocation than I offered in the storage room—heavens, did I do all that?—and yet he does not. She went up the stairs, slowly. True, I have only known him twenty-four hours, but my heart tells me that I know him well.

Her attempt to escape upstairs to the solitude of her room was foiled by Mama, who bore down on her, wringing her hands and ripping at the little scrap that used to be a lace handkerchief.

"Drat Major Redpath and that child!" she stormed, stopping Audrey's route of escape.

"Mama, you are unfair!" she protested as she worked her way past her mother and started up the stairs.

Mama followed. "What I am is severely exercised! Half of our plaguey relatives are winking and nudging each other, sure that Edmund is the father, and the other half hold with Major Redpath, and wonder why you, of all people, were hanging on his arm!"

"When did you . . ."

Mama sighed and dabbed at her eyes. "My wretched cousin Loisa peeked through the draperies and saw you in the driveway! Really, Audrey, I don't know what has gotten into you! It will not do. That child must go!" She began to sob. "I would send the major away if I could, but he is the dratted best man!"

She cried in earnest, a storm of tears that brought several heads popping out of open doors to gawk and stare. Mrs. Caldwell glared back and the doors closed. "And now the ladies' maids will spread tales all over Bath!" she whispered, almost stamping her foot in her rage.

Audrey took her mother in her arms, and crooned to her like she would comfort a distressed child. "Mama, trust me. It will still be a fine wedding, one nobody forgets! In fact, if you wish, I will spend all day tomorrow getting the flowers ready in the church, so that is one less worry."

Mrs. Caldwell's sobs turned to sniffles, and then stopped. She blew her nose hard on the handkerchief Audrey gave her. "And that child?"

"She will not go to St. Elizabeth's, Mama," Audrey said firmly. "But yes, something must be done, and we all know it."

Mrs. Caldwell was satisfied. "Soon, Audrey, soon. Surely there is one adult among you who can get a little girl into an orphanage! How difficult can this be?" Her attention was distracted by a relative calling to her from the first floor. "I don't know why all my plans are turning to mud, Audrey," she said mournfully, then turned a smiling face on the woman looking up at her on the landing. "Coming, dear Matilda, coming!"

Dinner was the unrelieved trial Audrey dreaded, and she had just cause to feel shame for her relatives. There was

Mama, tight-lipped and white-faced, glaring at Major Redpath and Marie Deux; and Emmeline and Ed sitting close together like conspirators, far from the major. And there were the relatives, looking, tittering, and talking among themselves about how ill-bred a man could be to fling such a wartime souvenir in the faces of good women everywhere, and little realizing their own vulgarity. She knew what they were thinking, despite mounds of explanation— she was sure—from Mama and Emmeline, and it pained her.

After a day in her delightful presence, she knew Marie Deux was a child of considerable nuance, one who must be fully aware that she was an object of derision. She ate her dinner in silence, eyes on her plate, despite the remarks that Audrey directed at her in kindness. She inched herself closer and closer to the major until she was almost sharing his chair with him.

Audrey could hardly bring herself to look at the major. She knew him well enough to know that he would never say anything untoward to her relatives and reinforce their rudeness with his own. She tried to see him as they were seeing him, someone shabby, silent, and dour ("He has been at war, you idiots! There is no tailor on the front lines!" she wanted to shriek. "And if he seems dour, you have made him so!") They would never know the depth of him, and the huge kindness that refused to allow him to jettison his burden at the nearest foundling home or workhouse. They saw only a Scot to fit the stereotype, and missed the man of passion, honor, and rightness.

She was hardly surprised when Major Redpath and Marie disappeared upstairs after dinner, and she had to suffer alone through a long incarceration at the whist table, exchanging pleasantries with people she wanted to flay, and drinking tea when she wanted to grind her teeth. She tried to catch Ed's eye several times, but he avoided her glances, as though ashamed of the part he was playing.

It was easy, finally, to plead a genuine headache and drag herself upstairs. She went wearily into her room, kicking off her shoes and flinging away her cap. Her heart lifted momentarily at the watercolor of spring flowers she had hung over the fireplace, and then lifted still more when she heard Marie Deux singing in her dressing room.

She went in quietly, and Marie looked up and put her finger to her lips. Major Redpath lay there sound asleep, stretched out on the cot. Marie was curled up on the pillow beside him, her knees drawn up to her chest, taking up the little space he left her. "He was telling me a story to put me to sleep," she whispered to Audrey.

"I would say he was not successful," Audrey whispered back, her eyes lively with good humor again. "Your lullaby seems to be more effective." She held out her hand to Marie, who quietly left the cot, stood a moment over the major, then carefully unbuttoned his uniform jacket.

"Should we leave him there to sleep?" she asked Marie doubtfully as they stood in the dressing-room doorway, watching him.

Marie nodded. "He's grouchy if you wake him," she said.

I wonder if he would be grouchy if I woke him? Audrey thought, then made an unsuccessful attempt to coax her mind into other channels. Captain Winkle never complained when I woke him in the middle of the night.

This is not a profitable topic, she told herself, but she was content to watch him and see how the lines smoothed out in his face when he slept. She noted with quiet amusement that he tucked his thumbs inside his hands like a child, asleep in full confidence. I wonder if you ever dream about battle? she thought, and decided that he did not. A man who could relax that completely was someone who put his cares away when he closed his eyes, and did not recruit them again until morning. Well, sir, let us make you more comfortable, she thought, as she gently reached for the side buttons on his trousers and undid them. I can't have you thinking that all the dreadful Caldwells wish you ill. I know I do not.

She helped Marie into the hand-me-down nightgown, touched to see how well it fit. The sleeping cap enchanted Marie, who looked at herself this way and that in the mirror, while Audrey undressed. You're such a Frenchwoman, Audrey thought, as she sat in her own nightgown. She kept half an eye on the dressing-room door, and watched Marie retie the bow under her ear and prance about some more.

"Oh, you are a vain little flirt," she teased finally, and crawled into bed. She held up the covers for Marie, who jumped in, lively with the pleasure of a new outfit, even if it was just another's nightgown. "You have to help me with flowers tomorrow, so let us sleep."

Marie cuddled close to her and she sniffed deep the fragrance of the little girl, and the spice in which Mama had packed her old clothes. "I cannot help with the flowers," Marie said finally, drowsy and warm in Audrey's embrace. "I promised to help Cook with more biscuits tomorrow."

"Oh, my, you are in good hands then," Audrey murmured. There was no answer. She smiled into the dark, silently blessed Cook, and closed her eyes, trying not to think of the major in her dressing room.

He left it some time before morning, because he was gone when she woke. She thought she knew when he left; those warm fingers on her cheek couldn't have been her imagination, or the hands a dream that tucked the covers closer about her and patted her hip in a gentle gesture she could only call husbandly.

She spent the day in the church, arranging and rearranging the flowers that came, expensive and pampered, from Bath succession houses. It was one thing to put them in tall vases, but quite another to determine if the effect was pleasing to the viewer. She longed for Marie Deux's discriminating eye, and even Major Redpath's comfortable presence. She knew if he were there he would contribute no more to the project than stretch himself out in one of the pews and agree with whatever she wanted. And he would do it with that slight smile on his face that she was familiar with, the one that made her want to kiss him and see what developed.

The brevity of their acquaintance made no difference to her. This was the man she loved. She could know him two days or two years, and it would be the same. "Well, in two years, I would probably know if he picks up clothes or leaves them strewn about, or if he objects to changing baby's nappies," she murmured into the roses. "I know already that he is kind and honorable, fond of children and artillery."

She laughed out loud, then looked around to make sure that the vicar was not about. I have it from unimpeachable sources that his guns are his chief delight, she thought. I wonder if he would give them up for me. And if he will not, I wonder if I could follow the guns like Marie Deux, uncomplaining and flexible, inured to hardship and sudden death.

It may not come to that, she thought, grateful suddenly to Napoleon for having the good sense to abdicate and change his address to Elba. Now John Redpath is merely to be stationed in Belgium, and what can come of that? Living on a major's income will be no hardship, she decided, even if he has no other money of his own. I have my inheritance, and we can rub along on that. Thank goodness I never told anyone but Emmeline that I would never marry into the military again. It astounds me how fast the right man can change one's mind.

"Then, sir, I think you must propose," she said, getting up off her knees and lifting the vase to the stand beside the prie-dieu. "It is your fate. We will be Marie Deux's parents."

John and Audrey Redpath and Marie Deux. How well they go together, she thought, as she tacked satin rosettes to the pews. We'll have children of our own, I am certain, but Marie Deux will be loved as much as they.

There was more to do, but she was hungry for luncheon and the sight of Marie and the major. She walked home, at peace with herself, admiring the blooming hawthorn and wondering if Emmeline would consider it too plebeian to poke here and there among the roses. She sighed over the increase in carriages and strange servants at the house, and decided that lunch in the kitchen would be more comfortable.

It was, except that the major was nowhere about. She sampled Marie's biscuits and smiled over Cook's praise, as proud as any mother. As she ate lunch, she listened in delight to Marie's description of the biscuit-making process, told in her breathless combination of English and French, with the occasional Spanish word to give it flavor, hands gesturing in Gallic emphasis. Audrey's heart ached a little as she thought of the hollow-eyed young girls in the foundling home, scurrying from baby to baby. Not for you, Marie, and thank God for that, she thought, pulling the child close for a kiss on the top of her head. Of course, I am depending on the major to propose.

Marie looked at her in surprise. "I love you, Marie Deux," she whispered, then got to her feet and held out her hand. "Come with me to the church this afternoon. I need your good opinion."

"Sister, I must borrow Marie Deux," said Emmeline from the doorway.

Audrey turned around with a smile. See there, Emmy, she thought in triumph, you are not immune to Marie Deux's charms. "Well, I don't know," she said in a teasing voice.

"Marie has already promised me she will show me where the tablecloths came from," Emmeline explained, joining them at the table and accepting a biscuit from Marie. "Um, good! You and the major were one short yesterday." She made a face. "Silly me! I broke the pitcher when I was taking it from the crate. Marie said she can show me where to get another." She kissed Audrey. "See there! You have to share!"

"If I must," Audrey teased back. "Does Ed go with you?"

"No, the wretch, I get only a footman! I have sent him and the major to hunt gifts for the groomsmen, and then see about some really good blacking for their boots. Oh, Audrey, think how magnificent they will look tomorrow in their regimentals!" she sighed, then put her arm around Audrey and gave her a squeeze. "It is going to be a perfect wedding."

"I don't doubt that for a moment, Emmy," Audrey said as she rose to go. "I will see you all later this evening then, at the rehearsal." She blew a kiss to Marie Deux. "Emmy, send some nieces and nephews to help, if I cannot have Marie."

"You cannot," Emmy replied with a smile. "And yes, I will send them!"

Her heart light, she spent the afternoon with what the vicar, dear old man, called "relative assistance." *I think that when the major finally proposes, we will dispense with flowers and too many relatives,* she thought, as she separated nieces, nephews, and quarrels, and attempted to turn their energy to good use.

Hunting the wild hawthorn proved to be a sensible diversion. She sent them into the trees by the church armed with dull pruning hooks so they would take lots of time, and give her the calm she craved. She was joined by the organist, who added to the serenity of the church, and her own peace of mind, by liberal applications of Bach, Handel, and Purcell. Soon she abandoned the flowers altogether and seated herself in a pew, happy beyond words for Emmeline and Ed. *Only treat Emmy well, Ed, and I* will forgive you for distancing yourself from your major and your little embarrassment, she thought. Why must people think the worst of those whom they should love and admire the most?

She perked back into action when the nieces and nephews tromped in, dirty from climbing the trees, but laden with flowering hawthorn. She thanked them, sent them back to the house to clean up, and barely finished arranging the last sprig among the roses before everyone arrived for the rehearsal. In perfect charity with her relatives, she endured the scolds from her sisters-in-law for the disrepair to their children. She looked about for Marie Deux, and almost asked about her, but thought it best not to remind her relations of gossip fodder.

Emmeline was splendid, even in an ordinary dress. She waited with what Audrey considered remarkable forbearance for her fiancé and the best man to arrive from their expedition to town for boot blacking. "They may have had to go farther afield than they originally intended," was her only comment, as she arranged her bridesmaids to her liking, waved the vinaigrette about for poor Mama, and indulged in a little mild flirtation with the groomsmen.

And then they were there, Ed all smiles, and Major Redpath keeping his own counsel, as usual. He joined Audrey in the pew. "Don't know why we had to go to the ends of the earth for blacking," he grumbled. "Everyone will have their eyes on Emmeline tomorrow." He glanced sideways at her with a look so warm that her throat went suddenly dry. "And you."

Say on, sir, she thought, but he was looking about the sanctuary now. "Where is that little scamp?" he asked.

"I thought perhaps she would come with you," Audrey said, getting up when her sister motioned to her. "Emmeline needed her help to buy another tablecloth."

"Ed and I came right from town," he explained, rising, too.

"Then I must assume that after she and Emmy returned, Cook found her totally indispensable," Audrey said with a smile. "Onward, now."

Emmeline surprised her with her serenity. Audrey minded her steps, took her place near the altar below the best man, and remembered her own nerves eight years ago. Dear sister, you are obviously made of sterner stuff, she decided, as she watched Emmeline, on the arm of her eldest brother, glide up the aisle. I was quaking in my shoes, she remembered with amusement, afraid of the person I loved the most.

She thought of Matthew Winkle and the great care he had taken of her tentative love. "I thank you for that, Matthew," she whispered, her lips barely moving. Your grace in love gives me confidence to try again. Tears welled in her eyes, the last she would ever cry for her late husband, as she contemplated Emmeline and Ed standing together at the altar. With a glad heart, she folded the memories of Captain Winkle deep within herself, and knew without a qualm that all was well.

The feeling persisted as she strolled home with Major Redpath, even though he did not take the opportunity to propose, as she had hoped. In fact, he was strangely subdued. "I still do not know what to do with Marie Deux," he said finally, as they approached the house, and both of them slowed their steps.

Propose to me, you slowtop, she thought, and this will resolve itself promptly. After a moment's hesitation, she put her arm through his, leaning against him a little—but only a very little—as they stood in the driveway. Surprised, he looked down at her, his smile uncertain, which puzzled her.

"Audrey Winkle, I never took you for a tease," he said, gently removing her arm from its comfortable niche within his. "I know I owe you a great apology for what happened in the storage room. You must think me a thoroughgoing rascal, particularly in light of your own inclinations. I hope you'll forgive me."

"I . . ." I what? she thought in sudden irritation. "My own inclinations?" What do you mean? She felt her newfound serenity dribbling away, and decided that she did not know what to think. He was moving again, and she moved forward with him, wanting instead to tug at his arm, dig her heels into the gravel of the driveway, and talk to him. He must think I kiss men like that all the time, she thought in misery.

She was about to grab him by the shoulders and tell him that she loved him, when the door opened and Mama called to her. She looked around in real irritation, uttered a strengthy oath under her breath that she had overheard from Captain Winkle, and hurried up the front steps.

"Mama, what is it?" she said, hoping that her misery did not show, and longing for her own room.

"You know you should not linger so long in the night air," Mama scolded. Her chin quivered and she burst into noisy tears. "Audrey, Emmeline is my baby!"

Audrey sighed and let Mama cry. "There, now, I'm here," she soothed, all the time her own heart was breaking. And I'll be here a long time, it seems, because a certain Scot is less interested than I thought, she considered. "Now, blow your nose, Mama, and remember that Emmeline will be with Ed in Ostend, or Brussels, and you have always wanted to visit the Continent."

"You'll come, too?" Mama asked anxiously.

No, I will not, she thought. I could not bear to see the man I love again, especially since he seems so little inclined to love me. "Oh, Mama, someone will have to watch the house here," she managed, on the edge of tears herself. "Now, what can I do for you before I go to bed?"

Mama blew her nose again, thought a moment, then nodded her head decisively. "Count the silverware in the dining room one last time." She leaned closer to Audrey. "One

can't be too careful with ragamuffin French army leavings
about."

"Mama! Marie Deux would never steal anything!" Audrey exclaimed in exasperation. *Only my heart, and Scots
majors of artillery are equally adept at that,* she thought, as
she directed Mama back to the sitting room and went to the
dining room.

Everything was there, of course; she counted every knife,
fork, and spoon twice. Even in the middle of her misery,
she was able to admire the elegance of the dining room, all
set up for the wedding breakfast after the ceremony. The
crystal goblets that Major Redpath had purchased sparkled
even in the low light, as servants hurried to lay down the
last place setting. She glanced at the extra glassware still
sitting on the serving table, and looked closer, frowning.

There were two pitchers now. *Odd,* she thought. *Emmeline told me she broke one, and that she had to buy a new
one this afternoon, with Marie Deux's help.* She came
closer, picking up both pitchers. They were the same.
"Emmy, why on earth would you tell a fib, then pick up another pitcher?"

I shall ask Marie, she thought, as she closed the door behind her. *And come to think of it, I have not seen her all
day.* She went slowly up the stairs, stopping halfway up
when the front door opened, and resisting the enormous
urge to turn around and see if it was the major. *No, Audrey,
you're not so hard up for a husband that you need to fling
yourself at a man who obviously just wanted to flirt. Try
for a little dignity.*

She hoped that Marie would still be awake and lying in
her bed, but the bed was empty. Quietly, she tiptoed to the
dressing room, and leaned against the doorjamb, smiling
despite her unhappiness. "Worn out, are you?" she whispered, looking into the gloom at the child who slept on the
cot, hair tucked tidily into her sleeping cap. She closed the
door quietly. *I do not know what Major Redpath plans to*

do with you, but you must certainly take my hand-me-downs with you, she thought. And my heart.

I wonder if I can break myself of this stupid habit of rising with the roosters, Major Redpath thought with irritation as he lay on his back and stared at the ceiling. Probably not, he decided. I have been at war too long to change anything after all, I suppose. What I thought was something new yesterday, is just the same old routine today, he decided. I wake up early, and there is no one here beside me to play with. I dress, and there is no one who needs me to button her up the back. I eat, and I see no pretty face across the table, buttering toast for me or asking my opinion about mundane household duties. And when I go to Ostend in a month, I will go by myself. After a long day of gunnery drill, there will be no one to incline me to skip an evening of cribbage, and think up creative excuses for an early bedtime.

There will not even be Marie Deux. I will have to find an orphanage for her, no matter how I despise the idea, he decided as he got up, stood naked at the window, and regarded the beauty of the morning. It struck him as remarkably short-sighted of the Lord to provide so lavishly for this wedding day when he, Major John Redpath of His Majesty's Royal Horse Artillery, was sunk in such misery.

"Damned inconsiderate, I call it," he said as he washed, shaved, and dressed in his regimentals. He usually took some pleasure in putting on the handsome uniform, serene and somewhat arrogant in the knowledge that none of the other services looked half so good as the artillery. This time, once he got past the doeskin breeches so white that he squinted, everything reminded him of Marie Deux. As he buttoned it, he remembered that the frilly shirt was the only dress shirt she had permitted him to pack. He remembered with a pang her fingers gentle on the rows and rows of gold braid that spanned the breast. He knotted the scarlet sash about his waist, shrugged into the jacket, and glowered at himself in the mirror.

As he pulled on his boots, shined with care and a good thing, too, considering how long he and Ed had chased about finding blacking, he wondered if his old housekeeper at home could keep Marie. He sighed. Maudie McCormack must be past seventy now. I simply have to do what I said I would, he told himself, and resign myself to the unalterable fact that I am every bit as softhearted and mush-brained as those wretched, magnificent gunners I command. Of course they should have left Marie Deux to die in the heat and waste of the ruined French artillery. Now we have saved her for an orphanage or a workhouse.

He hesitated a moment outside Audrey Winkle's door. I could fling it open, throw myself at her feet, tell her to please overlook that she does not wish to marry into the military again, and propose. I could assure her that goodness, no, a major of artillery runs no risk of death, but that would be a damned lie, and she is not stupid. She is a wise woman who does not wish to throw herself away twice on dead meat, and I cannot fault her for that. But, Audrey, take a chance on me!

It was stupid, and he knew it. He went to breakfast, glared at the relatives assembled, and played with his food, hardly looking up when his lieutenant, all jitters and blood-shot eyes, came to sit beside him.

"Well, Lieutenant, you look terrible," he said finally, as the assembled relatives tittered.

Ed said nothing, which surprised him into a closer look. Lieutenant Sir Edmund Parkhill had all the appearance of a man about to change his mind. I can see being uneasy at the contemplation of marriage . . . no, no, I can't, he contradicted silently. I can imagine no joy greater than the thought of splicing myself body, soul, and heart to Audrey Redpath. Ed, what is your problem?

He did not ask, of course, deciding that all men face the

eventuality of wedlock differently, and it was Ed's right to suffer, if he chose. He sat there indecisive, of half a mind to go in search of Marie Deux, or run upstairs, rip out his heart, and throw it at the widow's feet, when the door opened.

Redpath looked around hopefully, and met the frantic eyes of the butler. He stared in surprise, knowing that he had never seen a butler look like that before. "Ames, are you well?" he asked, as the other relatives and friends gathered there swiveled around, too.

Ames was not. He opened and closed his mouth several times, uttered strangling noises that could have been speech in an earlier anthropologic age, and stepped aside for the constable.

"Major John Redpath?" said that worthy.

"Yes?" Redpath answered, his voice wary, as the relatives all leaned closer. He contemplated his various sins, and decided they did not fall within the provenance of a constable at law. "What can I possibly have to do with you?"

The constable drew himself up taller, as though he could hardly wait to unburden himself before such an audience. "Mrs. Audrey Winkle wishes me to inform you that she is being detained by the law and hopes you will bail her out."

Redpath blinked. Audrey's brothers gasped out loud. One of the sisters-in-law began to wave about her vinaigrette as the other gathered her children close and tried to clap her hands over their ears. Uncle Eustace let out a whoop and Aunt Agatha seemed to have trouble breathing. The others began to chatter among themselves.

"May I ask what she did?" Redpath questioned, even as Ed cleared his throat. He was on his feet now, towering over the constable, who backed up into the jam cart.

"It's not my doing!" the man protested as he wiped at the seat of his pants. "I think she's one part lunatic to try to get some little waif out of a workhouse! Created a real scene, she did! But we've got her locked up now, and the child's right where nature intended her." He smiled at the astonished assemblage, the picture of legal complacency.

"My God," Redpath said, his voice perfectly toneless, his mind traveling a thousand miles an hour. He felt a chill run down his spine and then back up again, as he thought of Marie Deux and all his promises of a good family. *Someone has put you in a workhouse and I let it happen.* He picked up the constable by the front of his jacket and held him against the wall. "How did the child get into the workhouse?" he asked quietly.

"Sir, I can—"

"Shut up, Lieutenant," he snapped. "I want to hear from this gentleman. Tell me now," he repeated as he lowered the little man to the floor again.

"You don't need to get violent about it!" he declared, brushing off the greasy front of his jacket. "The beadle told me a blond-headed lady brought her by yesterday afternoon, and that's all I know!"

Suddenly it was all clear. *Someone sent Ed and me on a wild-goose chase for bootblacking,* he thought, as he turned around slowly to contemplate his lieutenant. *And didn't Audrey tell me that Emmeline borrowed Marie for some last-minute shopping?*

"Sir, you know we were only postponing the inevitable."

Redpath stared at his lieutenant, who blanched under his gaze, but did not falter.

"You were determined to find fault with every single orphanage we looked at in Land's End," he continued, his face pale but determined. "We had a duty to discharge, and heaven knows enough tongues were already wagging about Marie Deux . . . and us."

"And you," Redpath amended. "You see, Ed, I didn't mind the gossip because I knew it wasn't true."

"Perhaps you should worry about such things, Major,"

the lieutenant replied. "Think how all this reflects on the Caldwells."

"It reflects on no one but hypocrites," he declared roundly, "people who are happy enough to have us keep them safe from Napoleon, but who have no charity for the weakest among us, the children of war, whatever side." He ignored the gasps of indignation around the table.

Ed had nothing to say.

"Do tell me this, Lieutenant Parkhill," he asked formally, "was this your idea? I would have thought better of you."

Parkhill hesitated. "No, it was not," he said at last. "I knew what she was doing, however, and—"

"And dragged me all over creation for bootblacking." The major looked around the table. "If you all will excuse me, I have to bail a lady out of jail."

He left the breakfast room, taking the stairs two at a time back to his room to retrieve his hat and wallet. *I wonder how much it takes to bail out a lady?* he thought, finding himself amused, now that he did not have to look at her relatives.

Uncle Eustace waited for him at the bottom of the stairs. "I'm coming, too," he said. "No, I am!" he insisted when the major shook his head. "She's my niece, and by Gadfrey, sir, you might need some help to spring the little'un from the workhouse."

He stopped in his headlong rush from the house, touched by Eustace. "It doesn't bother you that I am ruining the perfect wedding?" he asked.

Eustace flipped up his eye patch, scratched, and lowered it again. "I'm damned tired of so much perfection among the Caldwells. Lead on, Major!"

From the glances, stares, and titters that followed them from the edge of town to the center of Bath, the major could only assume that people would have plenty to talk about through the coming summer, and likely well into autumn. Everyone seemed to have business at the magistrate's that morning, he thought, shouldering through the crowd that parted like ripples around a boulder, then closed in again after the two of them. Knowing that he looked perfectly intimidating in his best uniform, and much over six feet tall with the hat on, he strode to the magistrate's desk and slapped his hand on it.

"I'm here to bail out Mrs. Audrey Winkle," he said. "She's matron of honor at a wedding in"——he paused and pulled out his pocket watch, the one that had seen duty in battles less important to him now than this one—"in forty-five minutes."

The magistrate blinked and tugged on his wig. He settled himself behind the high desk, but was unable to achieve much intimidation, because the major appeared even more formidable. Elaborately he looked at the notes in front of him, until Redpath itched to grab him by the wattles of his fleshy neck.

"She was disturbing the peace, General," he said finally, and looked over his shoulder. "Bring out the prisoner!"

As the major watched appreciatively, Audrey Winkle was led forward, distracted, flushed, militant, and beautiful all at the same time. Her lovely hair was independent of any braids or pins and he felt himself growing weak in the knees.

"Twenty pounds!" declared the magistrate.

The crowd gasped. Eustace flipped up his eye patch again for another scratch. "'Pon my word, niece, what did you do?" he asked. "Kill two or three of them and burn down the place?"

"I wanted to," she said, her voice firm and not in the least repentant. "And it's a dashed good thing it wasn't the Foundling Home!"

The magistrate looked at the ledger in front of him. "Says here, Mrs. Winkle, that you swore a round oath, threw an inkwell at the beadle, and then beat him with his own mace when he would not produce a waif named Marie Deux."

What a woman, John thought, as he tried not to laugh.

"The beadle is an idiot, and I don't scruple to tell you so," she replied, biting off each word, a tigress fighting for her cub. "I would do it ag—"

"She'll be silent now," the major said, with a warning look. He opened his wallet. "Twenty pounds? You'll release her to me?"

"Depends, General," said the magistrate. "What's her relationship to you?"

He took a deep breath, grateful that the men of the Second who looked to him for guidance, wisdom, and leadership, were not there. "She's my lover from the wars and the mother of our unfortunate child you have so wrongly allowed to be incarcerated in the workhouse!" My, that was a stunner, he thought, as soon as he uttered it. Who'd have thought I had such an imagination?

Apparently the citizenry of Bath who frequented magistrate's halls had no quarrel with his declaration. Admiring glances from some of the more lived-in looking women, and ugly murmurs from the men directed toward the magistrate, assured him that his cause was just among the lower class of Bath. There was scattered applause.

"I have come to claim that which is mine alone to claim!" he declared in ringing tones, liking the sound of it all, and wondering just briefly if he ought to throw over the army for a career in Commons. "I demand justice!"

He would have said more—he was just warming up—except that Audrey took him by one arm, and Uncle Eustace by the other.

"Quite so, lad," Uncle Eustace said. He looked at the magistrate. "When does my plaguey niece have to reappear?"

"Quarter sessions!" the magistrate said, banging down the gavel. "Unless she can wheedle the beadle into dropping charges."

The crowd seemed to like his alliteration and applauded him, too. The magistrate beamed down on them, the soul of benevolence again as he waved the major away.

"That was stunning," Audrey told him as they hurried along, hand in hand. She looked over her shoulder at the crowd following them to the workhouse. "Do you realize every Caldwell within shire boundaries will be snickered at from now until at least the next century? My reputation is gone."

"Yes, isn't it? You may have to move," he said, all complacency as they hurried him along.

The beadle was less trouble than any of them anticipated. One wary eye on the crowd, and the other on Audrey Winkle, he listened to a reiteration of Major Redpath's speech, blanched, and summoned Marie Deux from the bowels of the workhouse. "I had no idea," he murmured over and over.

Neither did I, Redpath thought. This is turning into such an interesting day. He glanced at Audrey, who stared back, then startled him by running her tongue over her lips and giving him such a look that he wished—not for the first time—that it was his wedding in thirty minutes now.

Then Marie Deux was there, hesitating in the doorway, poised to run if the chance developed. She rushed toward them with a shriek and a cry that brought him to his knees. Audrey was beside him, trying to gather as much of Marie into her arms, and catching him, too, until his uniform sleeve was quite wet with someone's tears. They could have been his.

"Terrible mistake," Audrey was saying into Marie's ear, except that it was his ear, and her lips made him tingle all over. "My darling, forgive us. We had no idea this would happen yesterday."

Even the beadle appeared to be affected by the scene before him, dabbing his eyes with the handkerchief Uncle Eustace offered him. While they could only hug Marie in love and relief, Audrey's uncle proved his worth.

"Now, there, sir, you don't really want to bring charges against this lovely lady, who only wanted to reclaim her child?" he asked, ignoring the startled look Marie Deux gave him.

"Well, no," the beadle agreed, his eyes going to the ink-stained wall behind him. "But there are damages . . ."

"Which I am certain this will cover," Eustace murmured. There were guinea-sized sounds and then silence as the coins disappeared in the beadle's uniform jacket. "Come, niece," he said. "There's a wedding in half an hour, I would remind you."

Eustace hurried ahead while the major and Audrey Winkle followed, each clutching tight to Marie Deux's hands. "When did you find out?" Redpath asked.

"I'm such an idiot," Audrey said. "I thought she was sleeping in my dressing room on that cot, but it was one of my nieces! I confronted Emmeline, told her what I thought, then ran to the workhouse." She looked down at Marie and stopped her long enough to kiss the top of her head. "Emmy took her to town yesterday on those errands as an excuse to pitchfork her into the workhouse, and I was none the wiser! I could kick myself."

Redpath sighed. "I fear my lieutenant was in on the whole scheme, even though he did not plan it. I suppose I cannot fault either of them too much. We were supposed to find that orphanage for Marie Deux, and your sister did want the wedding no one forgets. Things change."

I wonder if you can change enough, he thought, as they hurried up the steps of the church. "I know how you feel about military men—" he began, then stopped as Mrs. Caldwell, her face a shade of gray not found in nature, yanked Audrey away from him and Marie and hurried her inside, scolding and trying to brush her hair at the same time.

He sat on the steps of the church with Marie between his long legs. "My dear, I suppose we will have to go to Belgium, after all."

Marie looked dubious. "I do not think Mrs. Hurley will have room for me."

"I will, Marie Deux, I will," he said. "I'm not exactly the family I promised you, but . . ."

It was his turn to be hauled away, this time by Uncle Eustace, who told him that Lieutenant Sir Edmund Parkhill was already standing at the altar, and from the looks of him, in need of support. Eustace slapped a ring in his hand. "Don't lose this," he muttered. He took Marie Deux by the hand. "You can sit with me and Aggie, m'dear, and hang the relatives."

He whisked her away. Major Redpath took a moment to run a comb through his hair, pull his sash back around where it belonged, tuck his hat under his arm, and walk slowly and deliberately to the front of the church to stand beside his lieutenant, who had been weighed in the balance and found decidedly wanting.

"I hope you will forgive me, Major, for being an idiot," Parkhill said out of the corner of his mouth as the triumphal entry began, everyone rose, and the flower girl strewed rose petals down the aisle.

Audrey came next, her hair in order now and under a beautiful headpiece of roses that made his heart beat even faster. The bridesmaids followed, and then the bride, a vision of purity, loveliness, and irritation as she caught his eye and he made a face at her. I feel better now, he thought.

"Sir?"

"Ed, this is not the time for remorse or conversation," he whispered back. "Save it."

"But, sir. I need advice—"

"Ed!"

And then it truly was too late for conversation. Audrey stationed herself a few steps below him. He looked down on her and wondered how much fun it would be to unbutton that dress. I wonder if she knows what I'm thinking? he asked himself with amusement, as he noticed the flush spread around her neck. He directed his eyes forward then, and knew that he would have to take his chances with Mrs. Winkle. He thought about Marie, and came to the startling conclusion that with such a wealth of love and friendship, he could possibly even do without his guns. And there was a good-sized estate near Dumfries that could use his attention, after so many years of neglect dictated by war.

"Sir? I have to—"

"Ed, really!" he whispered back. "Stow it!" He nudged Ed forward to take his place beside Emmeline, who continued to glare at him.

He half-listened to the vicar go on and on, his mind seeking courage to propose to Mrs. Winkle. The majestic phrases of the Church of England wedding ceremony unfolded around him, pausing at the memorable question when the vicar asked if anyone had any objections.

"I do, sir."

It was Ed. He was stepping away from Emmeline awkwardly as she gasped and tried to tighten her grip on her fiancé. The major blinked in surprise, as his lieutenant started toward him. "That's what I was trying to tell you, sir! I don't think Emmeline wears well in a crisis."

He may have been well-trained to plot the course of canister, case shot, and shell through clouds of battlefield smoke, but Major Redpath knew he would be hard-put to remember the precise sequence of what followed next. It was possible that Mrs. Caldwell leaped up from her front row pew with a scream worthy of Boadicea, but that may have been after Emmeline, fire in her eyes, grabbed one of Audrey's lovely vases of rose and hawthorn and slammed Lieutenant Sir Edmund Parkhill over the head with it. That was when Ed dropped like a clubbed mullet onto the steps leading to the altar, and the vicar leaped back and fell over the prie-dieu behind him. The acolyte performed a juggler's act with the book that went flying in the air, lost, and started to laugh, which seemed to be the cue that set off the entire assemblage.

To their further entertainment, Emmeline threw off her veil, snarled at him as though he was to blame for the whole turn of events, and stalked down the center aisle. Her dress must have caught on a nail or something, because he heard a fearful zip. It sounded enough like a Congreve rocket misfiring to make him drop to his knees out of instinct and pull Mrs. Winkle down with him. It would have been a good time to faint or die—which would have suited Emmeline—but he was made of sterner stuff. He started to laugh instead, sitting on the steps and wiping his streaming eyes.

He was still sitting there a half hour later. Uncle Eustace had taken pity on Ed and carted him off to a nearby inn, figuring that his appearance in the house of his former loved one would cause only mayhem. "I tried to tell you, sir," Ed managed to gasp as Uncle Eustace summoned two groomsmen to carry him off. "Emmeline's changed, or . . . or maybe I have."

The soul of equanimity now, Major Redpath nodded and patted his subaltern. "Best go on to Ostend right away, Ed. You might be safer with the Channel between you and the Caldwells."

The major stayed where he was, content to breathe the scent of roses and hawthorn that filled the almost-empty church. He glanced over at Marie Deux, who rested her head against Audrey Winkle's legs as she sat on the steps, too. *If Ed is brave enough to speak his mind, I should take a page from his book and try it.* He opened his mouth to speak, but Audrey was whispering something to Marie, who nodded, added a little earnest commentary of her own, then walked to him and sat down. He touched her hair, and smiled at her.

"Mrs. Winkle thinks you should marry her."

He stared at Marie, and then at Audrey, who was grinning at him as she twirled her nosegay of roses around her finger. He leaned toward Marie, "Well, tell her . . . oh, this is silly. Audrey, I have it on good authority that you have sworn never to marry a military man," he said, lifting his voice to be heard above the organist, who, through some musical perverseness, had continued to play doggedly.

"I never . . ." she began, then her eyes became militant again. "I could strangle Emmeline," she said.

With a sigh that went all the way down to his well-blacked boots, he leaned back against the chancel rail and regarded his dearly beloved. "You didn't mean it?" he asked. "Emmeline told me."

"Emmeline should be taken out and shot," Audrey said, getting to her feet and brushing off her dress. She came to his side of the church and sat down well within range of his arm. "I said that once, a few weeks after Captain Winkle died. I think it was an understandable reaction."

He pulled her close. The organist stopped, assessed the situation, and began a tentative replaying of the wedding processional.

"You don't mean it, then?" he asked, hardly daring to imagine his good fortune.

"Of course not. I love you," she said, so matter-of-fact that tears came to his eyes. "And how else will I ever get Marie Deux as my daughter, if I don't marry her father and my lover from the wars! Really, John, who'd have thought you to tell so many tales in one morning? I own I didn't."

He didn't answer because he was busy kissing her. Pretty soon I can do this anytime I want, he thought, his brain busy. And other stuff, which will probably mean I won't spend much time at trout streams this month. Lucky fish.

"Very well, then, I'll do this but once. Audrey Winkle, I love you . . ."

" . . . even more than your guns?" she teased.

"You know, I think so. Will you . . . will you marry me?"

"Yes," she said immediately, and gathered Marie Deux into the embrace. She laughed into his shoulder. "I think Ed even has an unused marriage license."

"Nope. It's registered in his name," the major informed her. "I'll tell you what. If you can pack quickly—I'm sure Emmeline will help—you and Marie and I can be in Gretna Green sometime tomorrow, and I'll marry you promptly like a good Scot, over the anvil, with a proper Church of Scotland ceremony." He fished Ed's ring out of his uniform front. "As the wife of a frugal Scot, you won't cavil at wearing this ring, will you? I'm sure Ed won't need it anytime soon."

She kissed him this time, seriously troubling his breathing, his mind and his body. "That sounds irregular, vulgar, and calculated to send my mother and all the other Caldwells into spasms," she said, her lips close to his. "You're right, of course. It's certainly the least we can to do make this a wedding day that no one ever forgets."

"Just as Emmeline wanted," he added.

"And you can write to General Picton and tell him that you were a clunch and couldn't remember the name of that orphanage, and tell him that Marie Deux is ours now."

"It was St. Pancras at Austell," he said promptly.

Audrey pulled away from him, looked into his eyes, and burst into laughter. "You rogue! You never forgot it!"

He got to his feet, and pulled his women up with him. "No, I didn't. I just couldn't give her up." He bowed to the little girl elaborately, as she clapped her hands in appreciation. "And now, Mademoiselle Marie Deux, will you do me the honor of becoming our daughter, now that I have a wife promised?"

As pleased as he was with himself, there was something new in the look that Marie Deux gave him that brought tears to his eyes. She observed him solemnly, and he realized with a pang how much of his heart he had already lost to her. *And now I will have a wife and a daughter,* he thought. This *is* something new, indeed, for I did not know there was so much love in the world. I am a lucky son of the guns. He picked up Marie, so he could look into here eyes. "Well?"

She patted his cheek. If she had just said *oui*, or *si*, or yes, he would have managed, but the huge sigh that came up from her toes, and the way she nestled against his chest filled his cup to overflowing. He could only sit down on the steps again and hold her close.

Audrey, bless her, sat beside him, resting her cheek against his arm, her hand light—but possessive—on his thigh. "I think Marie and I will both give you sufficient reason to stay in Scotland," she said, her soft words tickling his ear. He suddenly knew with all his heart that she was right.

After a moment, Marie pulled away enough to look at him. "It is a good thing, Major," she said, her hand gentle on his face. "Someone needs to tell you when to throw out shirts."

Audrey laughed. "I had thought I could help there, Marie," she protested, her eyes bright with amusement.

Marie regarded her. "Perhaps," she allowed cautiously, "but I have been looking in your wardrobe, and I think you could use some advice, too." She made that dismissing gesture with her hand that Redpath was already familiar with, and which Audrey was destined to discover now.

Audrey laughed and kissed them both. "John, I fear we are in the hands of a tyrant!"

"Aye, my bonny love," Redpath agreed, totally at peace with the idea. "I believe the French are well known for that, wouldn't you say?"

SOMETHING BORROWED

~

Patricia Rice

The dusky light from the high church windows created an aura of stillness through the stone nave. Melanie savored the quiet, the dusk, the scent of lighted tapers, and the small bouquet of wild roses she had wrapped gently in her handkerchief before entering the church. She didn't think Jane would remember flowers, but weddings ought to have beauty.

Already seated in her dark pew, she watched as the two elegant gentlemen paced the nave, and she sighed contentedly. She refused to envy her lovely older sister's good fortune in capturing a man like Damien Langland. With her beauty, wit, and vivaciousness, Jane could grasp the world by the hand and dance with it. Surely, after marrying that old man for her first husband, she deserved a handsome young man for her second. It didn't matter a whit that Damien, Earl of Reister, had always been the next best thing to penniless. Jane had fortune enough for both of them. And Damien not only had a title and looks, but he also possessed intelligence, character, and the kindness not to scorn his fiancée's crippled sister.

The wooden bench made Melanie's hip ache uncomfortably. She should have brought a pillow but she had thought the service would be over quickly. She didn't know what was keeping Jane. Surely she knew Melanie's absence would be discovered soon and their parents would go looking for her. She was flattered and more than a little surprised that Jane had even thought to ask her as witness knowing how difficult it was for Melanie to escape their parents' doting care. She understood Jane's secrecy, though. Their parents had prevented this marriage once before. A penniless earl wasn't good enough for their diamond of a daughter.

Melanie shifted uneasily again and noticed the gentlemen glancing impatiently at the closed church doors. They had arrived fashionably late. Jane was even later. Only Melanie had arrived on time. She hadn't relished hurrying up the aisle with her clunking cane. The vicar had assured her she could remain in her pew throughout the service. She didn't literally have to stand up with Jane, just witness the ceremony.

The vicar in his vestments excused himself to see to a parish matter, assuring them he would return as soon as he saw the carriage arrive. Melanie couldn't blame the man for tiring of standing idly between these cold stone walls when the sunshine beckoned brilliantly outside. She cast a worried glance to the anxious groom who had taken to staring at a sunbeam through the stained glass window above the altar.

The earl's best man pulled out his pocket watch and whispered something to Damien. The earl stopped his staring long enough to check his own watch and shake his head. He wouldn't leave yet. Melanie gave a sigh of relief. Damien wasn't the faint-hearted sort. He would trust in Jane. Idly, she let herself drift into daydreams of herself as bride. A husband like Damien could take her to London, show her the sights, introduce her to people who would appreciate her character and not scorn her disabilities. A husband would give her freedom.

As the hour grew later, Melanie became as increasingly nervous as the groom, who now paced back and forth in front of the altar. In his fitted frock coat and tight pantaloons, with the long tails of the coat flapping, Damien made an elegant figure as he strode back and forth. She couldn't imagine why Jane tarried so long. She worried some accident had overcome her between here and London. She worried their parents would discover Melanie's prolonged absence and come after her.

Occasionally, it had occurred to Melanie to wonder if her parents' suffocating concern for her had more to do with their embarrassment at having a lame daughter than any real anxiety for her welfare. Most days, she shut off those ungrateful feelings. Today, her fear for Jane's happiness made her resentful of her father's refusal to allow Melanie to do anything on her own.

She didn't really think her father would prevent Jane's marriage a second time. After all, Jane was thirty years of age now, an independent widow. Surely this time she could marry for love and happiness. Melanie didn't know why Jane had insisted on this secrecy, or involved Melanie in it, knowing the disaster that would happen if their father found she had left the house without his knowledge. It was almost as if Jane wished the worst to happen.

Melanie breathed a sigh of relief at the sound of a carriage arriving. And then she had the panicky thought it might be her father after all. He could still interfere with the marriage. Or he could just drag Melanie away before Jane could get here.

She had never done anything on her own in her life. From the day she had contracted the fever that had left her left leg withered and weak, her parents had hovered over her every movement. They had never returned to London, choosing to send Jane to an aunt for her Season rather than leave Melanie by herself in the country. She had never gone to London, or any farther than the village church. She had no life of her own, no friends other than those from the village thought suitable by her parents. She had wealth enough for a hundred people and nowhere to spend it since her parents saw to her every material need. She ought to be grateful, but she was twenty-five years old and as frustrated and rebellious as any adolescent.

Melanie's hands tightened around her walking stick at the thought that the carriage's arrival might signal an end to this precious moment of stolen freedom. It took only a moment to react to a lifetime of frustration, bringing Melanie to her feet without shyness. Damien had seen her limp before. Though five years older than she, he had visited their neighboring estate often enough that she needn't hide from him. As she limped into the aisle, he cast her no more than a worried look when others often looked away to hide their repulsion or embarrassment. His best man gave her a friendly smile as he hurried to the church doors to escort the bride.

"Damien!" Melanie whispered urgently, catching the earl's nervous attention. "It could be my father. They'll have missed me by now."

He looked momentarily alarmed, no doubt remembering the last occasion he'd had the audacity to ask the wealthy baronet for his daughter's hand. Sir Francis respected only wealth, and the Earl of Reister had none.

"Where can Jane be?" she whispered with concern, accepting his arm to help her up the step to the raised area before the altar.

"No doubt enjoying herself too much somewhere to break away," the earl replied bitterly. "Do not harbor any romantic illusions about this affair, Miss Melanie. Your sister and I have been old companions for too long."

At the sound of loud voices outside the door, Melanie feared the worst. The worried look the other gentleman sent their way after he peered through the leaded glass confirmed her fears.

For this past hour or more she had sat here idly dreaming how it would feel to stand beside a well set-up gentleman like the earl and to share vows sealing them for a lifetime. It really didn't matter to her if the earl's flaxen hair did not curl rakishly like her daydream's, or if his classically bridged nose had a hump in it. Appearances meant little to her. She craved companionship. She craved freedom. She craved a life of her own. The Earl of Reister represented all that—only he belonged to Jane.

Almost. The earl's friend slipped out the door to delay the family longer. No doubt her father raked the poor vicar over the coals for not notifying them at once that their poor, lame daughter had wandered loose, unaccompanied. What in heaven's name did they think could happen to her in a church?

Outside her own anger, Melanie felt sympathy for the man beside her, dressed in his finest blue frock coat with his cravat gleaming white and elegantly starched and folded. She had always thought him handsome, but then, she admired any man who could talk to her without averting his eyes. She felt his arm stiffen beneath her fingers and knew he braced himself for the tongue-lashing to follow. She could curse Jane for her thoughtlessness. Damien deserved better. She wished she could borrow him for just a little while. Jane had so much, and she had so little . . .

The instant she thought that, a notion of such amazing audacity overcame her that Melanie nearly staggered beneath the impact. Her father would deliver a scathing tirade no matter what they did. Why not gain some advantage for both of them out of it?

She had never uttered a bold thought in her life. She thought them all the time, but she never had anyone to speak them to. She knew she could say them to Damien. He was too devastated at the moment to scold her.

She clutched her bouquet of roses against his arm and tugged a little to gain his attention again. She saw him dart a look to the side door and knew his desire to depart, but he wouldn't desert her to the hands of her parents. Damien wasn't that kind of coward.

Gathering her courage, Melanie whispered, "We could walk out there now and pretend the service is already over. I think if you slip the vicar a few coins, he will keep quiet. My father is very clutch-fisted when it comes to charity. The vicar knows I had to contribute my own funds for the church roof."

Damien looked at her, but he didn't seem to comprehend. He wasn't a stupid man. He just didn't see things the same way she did. She'd had lots of experience developing devious means of escaping her father's authority. The elegant Earl of Reister had never done a devious thing in his life. She had no doubt whatsoever that this secretive marriage was all Jane's idea.

"We can pretend we're married, Damien," she explained impatiently. "We can go into London and look for Jane. My father can't stop us if he thinks you're my husband. I'm of age."

"Melanie Elaine Berkeley! Have you lost your wits? If you go into London with me without benefit of vows, you will ruin your reputation. Devil take it, woman! No wonder your father keeps you on such short strings if that's the way your mind works."

She took no offense. Damien had always treated her like a little sister, scolding her deservedly more than once. She shrugged off his protests.

"What is a reputation for but to catch a husband?" she asked carelessly. "They'll never let me marry. So what is the purpose of maintaining something of no value? If society scorns me, how would I know while locked up in the library staring out at the lawns day after day? I just want a little freedom, Damien. You needn't shackle yourself to me for life. I'm not quite as wealthy as Jane, but I have enough to pay your ticks, I daresay. While Jane was spending her allowances, I was saving. I'm willing to share."

She saw a wild look of hope and incredulity flare in his eyes, and she knew she'd finally captured some small measure of his interest. "Just imagine walking out of here with me on your arm. My father's face will fall clear to the ground. He'll turn too purple to speak."

A chuckle escaped the earl's compressed lips at the picture she painted, but he immediately followed it with a frown. "Of all the irresponsible behavior—"

"You need the blunt, don't you?" she pointed out inexorably. "And I want to see London. I don't care how long we get away with it. I just want to see parliament, and the libraries, and a museum or two. And Hatchard's. Maybe Elgin's marbles. Anything, Damien. I'm quite desperate."

He stared at her a moment or two, absorbing the desperation that must have driven her to such a plea. Melanie knew she wasn't spectacularly beautiful like Jane, but she wasn't hard to look upon. Her plain nut-brown hair couldn't compare to Jane's glorious blond tresses, but their features were similar, except Jane's lips always smiled and laughed while her own often pulled tight with pain. She could learn to laugh easily enough, given an opportunity. She felt her lips quivering now while she waited for his answer, but not with laughter.

"If you mean what you say, Melanie Elaine, I'll marry you in truth," the earl answered fervently, covering the hand holding the roses with a strong brown grip. "Let's get out of here before your father rips James into shreds."

Melanie felt she could float down the aisle on winged feet. She heard angels sing and church bells ring as they solemnly proceeded through the empty church as if it were filled with well-wishers weeping happily. She couldn't have felt more married had the special license in his pocket had her name on it instead of Jane's. She was going off to London with the Earl of Reister!

The scene outside dampened some of her joy, but Damien had learned a few things in the years since he'd last encountered the baronet, she realized. He took control of the situation immediately.

With a firm air of authority, he placed Melanie's hand in the care of James. "See my lady to the carriage, please, James, while I speak to Sir Francis."

The vicar gaped. Laughter lit his friend's eyes as he bowed over Melanie's hand. Sir Francis went so purple he couldn't speak, just as Melanie had predicted.

In that brief, shocked silence, Damien turned to the vicar, pressing a small pouch of coins—the last to his name—into the vicar's hands. "I'll take care of her properly," he promised with an urgency he hoped the other man understood. "The lady has told me of her love for this church. We will return often. If you ever have need of anything, you must let us know."

The man was shrewd enough to know a bribe when he saw one, but cautious enough to check on Melanie first. When she threw him a kiss and waved before climbing into the carriage, the vicar pocketed the coins and nodded. "I'm certain you'll do what's proper, my lord. I've never known you to do elsewise."

"Proper!" Sir Francis shouted, finally coming to his senses. "This young pup knows nothing of proper! That's my daughter he has there! My little Melanie. He hasn't a twig to light on and he thinks he can take care of a young female of her delicate constitution—"

"Melanie's constitution is about as delicate as Jane's," Damien interrupted rudely. "It's her leg that's damaged, nothing else. I'll not cosset her, for she doesn't want it, but I'll see her safe and happy. They aren't always the same things, you know."

Without waiting for any further reply, Damien strode off in the direction of the waiting carriage. He'd borrowed it from another friend, the upkeep of carriages much too expensive for his hollow pockets, but it made a good appearance now. He could still hear old Francis screaming as he climbed in and James shut the door behind him. There wasn't a damned thing the old man could do this time.

It felt good to know he'd bested the surly old goat for a change. With a smile of exaltation, Damien sat back against the squabs and turned to share his pleasure with the dainty woman beside him. As the driver took up the reins and the carriage lurched forward, he found himself looking into vivid violet eyes instead of pale blue ones. Staggered at the immensity of what he had just done, Damien wondered what in bloody hell he'd got himself into now.

"I meant what I said about marrying you."

Melanie turned her gaze from the thrilling melee of carriages, horses, carts, and wagons threading through the London streets back to the man who had remained stoically silent most of the journey. She gave him an understanding smile and reached across the aisle to pat his arm. "You'll marry Jane, just as you wanted. I'm certain there's a good reason for her delay. Shall we stop at her house first and see if she's in?"

"It's four of the afternoon, Melanie. If she's in London, she's driving in the park. She has her own rig. I don't think it wise for us to take a closed carriage into the park right now, still wearing all our traveling dirt. You'd never escape the scandal. As it is, there is some chance we can keep this quiet if Jane will take you in."

Melanie wondered if perhaps Damien was ashamed to be seen with her. She had worn her best rose-bedecked bonnet and a cunning sprigged muslin that draped her figure rather nicely, she thought, but she was well aware she looked as wilted as the roses in the seat beside her. She nodded agreement to his decision not to go to the park, but before he could give the driver directions, she disagreed with his second notion.

"Jane never invited me to visit, my lord," she said quietly, hoping a soothing voice would make her refusal go down easier. "I would not wish to intrude where I am not wanted. I have a house of my own. My aunt left it to me. I asked the solicitor not to let it this year. I had hoped to find some way to see it for myself. Now seems an excellent opportunity."

He'd moved to the seat across from her to give her more room as they journeyed. Now she wished he hadn't. The position made it much too easy for her "husband" to glare at her.

"You're near as wicked and deceitful as your sister," he declared. "If I hadn't happened along, who would you have chosen as victim?"

He was beginning to feel uneasy about his role in this charade they played. She could understand that. She just didn't know how to reassure him. The enormity of the city passing by their window right now overwhelmed her. Would she be able to get about by herself?

"I'm not certain," she answered honestly. "If I could have learned to handle the ribbons, I could have taken myself off, I suppose, but father wouldn't hear of my learning any such thing. I thought of bribing one of the stable boys to borrow the carriage and take me here, but I feared my father might have him transported or some such. Besides, they're all terrified of him; they would never agree. But I would have found some way. I am determined to see something of the world before I retire to knitting stockings for Jane's children for the rest of my life."

"That certainly wouldn't keep you busy for long," Damien responded dryly. "Jane isn't particularly fond of children. I can't imagine she'll want many."

Melanie gave him a surprised look. "Jane couldn't help it if George was too old and ill to father more than one child.

I'm sure she'll be happy to give you an heir or more. I'm looking forward to meeting Pamela." She sat eagerly upright in her seat at just the thought of meeting Jane's only child.

Damien shook his head and regarded her strangely. "When was the last time you saw your sister?"

Indignantly, Melanie replied, "She writes every chance she gets. She tells the most amusing stories! I can't wait to see her again. What time do you think she will return from the park?"

Damien leaned forward and tapped her forehead with his finger. "You aren't listening to me, sugar plum. When did you last actually *see* your sister?"

He had already given the driver directions to her own home, so Melanie didn't resent his attitude. Men had to feel as if they had the upper hand once in a while. Still, she squirmed uncomfortably before giving him the answer he wanted.

"Well, she must visit her in-laws at Christmas because of Pamela," she hedged. "And she never did have a fondness for the country. She swore she'd never return once she escaped."

"You haven't seen her since she married, have you?" he answered for her, leaning back against the seat with his hands on her walking stick as if it were his own.

"But she writes," Melanie protested vehemently. "I know all about sweet little Pamela and how she looks just like Jane. It is just as good as visiting. Better, since I don't have to listen to her argue with our father."

Damien nodded and glanced idly out at the street they now traversed. Melanie could see tall stone homes adorned with expensive windows and iron fences to keep out the uninvited. This street had considerably less traffic than the others they'd traversed. They passed a stately barouche with an elderly lady being helped into it by a footman in scarlet livery. Even in her inexperience, Melanie realized they had reached a wealthier part of town.

"We're almost there, I think," Damien murmured, not looking at her. "Will you have servants in residence?"

"The caretaker and his wife. We can hire some tomorrow." She watched him anxiously. "You do know how to hire servants, don't you? I have no notion at all."

He finally sent her that warm smile she remembered so well. "You've left your wits to let, gosling. I'll see if I can borrow someone's chambermaid for the night so you can pretend you have some sort of chaperonage. I'll come back around in the morning and we'll talk of hiring a real companion for you then."

Alarmed, Melanie stared at him. "You're not staying? You'll leave me alone with complete strangers? You can't do that to me, Damien Langland." She hesitated instantly, realizing of course he could do that. They weren't really married. She'd let her daydreams get the better of her. A feeling of mixed resentment and fear welled up within her as she realized Damien had no obligation whatsoever to continue this charade. Fear was a great motivator, however. Shrewdly, she asked, "Have you somewhere to go? You must have thought you would be returning to Jane's."

She caught the earl's bleak expression before he carefully shuttered it behind his gentlemanly demeanor. If her lameness had taught her nothing else, it had taught her to sit quietly and watch how people really felt. Damien was in hot water right now. She sensed it immediately.

"I have friends. You needn't worry, Melanie. I've been on my own for quite some time now. I fend for myself."

Melanie set her lips and ignored this foolishness. "Well, I haven't and I can't. Come in with me now so I don't look a complete ninnyhammer. We'll send someone around to Jane's house to see if she's there and what she wants us to do. If she's not there, there's no reason we can't continue this a little longer. I can't get about London on my own, and it is rather senseless for me to come all this way and not see the sights. Couldn't we pretend just a little longer, Damien?"

As the carriage came to a halt before a stately town house, Damien gave her a long, thoughtful look that made her shiver in her shoes. She'd never particularly noticed how long-lashed and brown his eyes were until they seemed to penetrate her very soul. She feared he wouldn't very much like what he saw there.

"Melanie, you are twenty-five years of age and perfectly cognizant of what will happen shall I stay here with you. Jane left me standing at the church today, so I owe her no obligation. No one knows of our betrothal. We never announced it. I am perfectly free to marry you. Since, as you have obviously surmised, I am in dire need of the ready, I am more than willing to marry you instead of Jane. Actually, had I thought of it sooner, I might have sought you first, but Jane knows the way of things and you're an innocent. I hate to tar you with the same disillusionment that we suffer. After spending some time in London and in my company, you may wish you had never come. I would not tie you or your dreams to someone of my ilk if it can be prevented. If I go into that house with you now, I go in as your husband, with all the accompanying folderol. I will allow you some time to decide if this is what you want, and if you choose otherwise, we'll find some way to get you free of both me and your parents. But I warn you now, I will spend these next weeks trying to persuade you that we should wed in truth. I have sunk just about as low as a man can go, Melanie. I'm quite capable of seducing an innocent at this point."

Melanie felt a momentary frisson of alarm at the warning tone of his voice, but then she looked up and saw Damien's familiar face—neither threatening nor seductive—and she relaxed a little. No man would want her for a wife when

Jane was available. He was just being gentlemanly as usual. She managed a smile and took back her walking stick. "That sounds quite enticing, Damien. Shall we begin?"

A shadow of a smile curled the corner of his lip, and he shook his head at her obstinacy, but he climbed down from the carriage and helped her alight.

When the caretaker finally opened the door, Damien caught Melanie's waist in a strong grasp, stooped to catch her behind the knees, and literally swept her off her feet to carry her across the threshold. So totally startled by his action that she nearly dropped her cane, Melanie managed to grasp it with one hand while clinging to Damien's strong shoulders with the other. She had never thought of Damien's greater height and weight in comparison to her own smaller stature. The manner in which he casually carried her into her own home made the differences terrifyingly clear. It was a good thing she wasn't afraid of Damien.

As it was, he left her so breathless she couldn't speak to the astonished servant stepping back from the door. Damien had to do the honors.

"We realize we have caught you unprepared, but my lady needs to rest and wash after her journey. Some clean linen and hot water, if you would. We will make amends later." He spoke courteously but with firm authority, never doubting that the poor man could produce what he wanted without question or complaint.

Marveling at the ease with which he took command, not only of her house and her servants, but herself, Melanie grew restive in Damien's hold. He declined to put her down but carried her easily up the stairs, following the caretaker to a room adorned in Holland covers. By this time, the caretaker's wife had appeared, taken in the situation, and started stripping back the linens.

"We were not apprised of your arrival, Miss Berkeley," the woman said breathlessly, hurrying to ball up the huge sheets and remove them to the hallway, "or we would have hired staff and had all prepared." She sent them a look of curiosity over her shoulder.

Once Damien set her down, Melanie could speak again, but he spoke for her. "Miss Berkeley is now the Countess of Reister. You need not apologize for lack of preparation. We will see about staff in the morning, or if you know of a few willing to come in this evening, send around for them. We will fend for ourselves for now."

Melanie watched in amazement as he drove the servants out, leaving her alone in a strange bedchamber with this man who had suddenly begun acting suspiciously like a husband. Wide-eyed, she watched as he turned back to her. She watched for an amorous or determined glint in his eyes, remembering his warning all too clearly. It had never occurred to her that Damien might take advantage of the situation to do *that* to her. She didn't think any gentleman had any such inclination toward a cripple like herself. An odd feeling crept through her midsection as he inspected her thoroughly with hooded gaze.

Then he nodded, gave a smile of approval, and indicated a delicate blue velveteen chair. "Sit, gosling. I'll not woo you yet, although I admit, I felt quite possessive carrying you up those stairs like that. Is that how a husband feels, do you think? You roar so loudly sometimes, I thought you much stouter than you are. You're a veritable feather."

She gave this ingenuous monologue a look of suspicion, but took the chair offered so he might sit and capture his own breath. "Don't you begin treating me like some fragile piece of porcelain," she warned him. "I *am* quite stout. It is just that my one leg is weaker and slightly shorter than the other. It tires me to walk any distance hobbling about like that."

He took a large wing chair across the fireplace from her and regarded her through narrowed eyes. "A horse's gait can be corrected with the proper shoes. I see no reason we cannot do the same with people. You'll have to see a modiste first thing in the morning. You have no clothes. We'll find a bootmaker at the same time."

Melanie brushed aside the mention of boots but smiled with delight at the idea of new clothes. "I will have my choice of the latest London fashions! That hadn't occurred to me. Oh, Damien, do you know the very *best* modiste? Or will Jane? I want to feel like the best dressed female in all London. The Countess of Reister ought to be, don't you agree?" Then reining in this pleasant fantasy, she added, "Should you go 'round to Jane's now? We really can't continue this silliness until we know what happened to her."

"I know perfectly well what happened to her," Damien replied dryly, "but I shall go around and verify it for your sake. Have a bit of a rest, and I'll see what your caretakers can do about summoning up some food. Do they have a household account?"

From that, Melanie quickly deduced that bribing the vicar had cost Damien his last coin. For a proud man, that must be an embarrassing circumstance. She nodded toward the reticule she had left on the night table. "The grocers and such send the bills to my solicitor for payment. I don't believe the Harrises have much coin. I certainly have enough for a meat pie or two. I had hoped to find Jane a pretty present in the village, but I got away too late."

Nodding curtly, he rose and emptied the reticule, folding the bills into his pocket. "As a fortune hunter, I soon must get used to this, but for now, I shall just relish the thought that I am spending Jane's wedding gift on something that we will appreciate more than she would."

He walked out, leaving Melanie with little opportunity to find words of reassurance. She ached for the pain he must feel, finding some similarity with her own. In a way, they were both handicapped, but Damien's disability crippled his pride more than hers. She had grown accustomed to pitying looks. He never would. She must find some way to help him stand on his own, as she did.

Damien watched with amusement as his new "wife" exclaimed over the multitudinous bolts of cloth set before her. She behaved as if he had just given her Christmas a hundred times over. Silks and satins, velvets and muslins lay scattered around her chair in a rainbow of colors, and still she squealed with delight each time the modiste brought forth a new one. He hadn't known spending someone else's money could be so pleasant.

He knew himself for a cad and a bounder, an unscrupulous fortune hunter with every intention of trapping this enchanting innocent in his web. He'd thought he'd lowered himself as far as he could go by persuading Jane she would make an excellent countess, that the title would add to her prestige. He and Jane were two of a kind, predators in the society that fed them. He had come to loathe her as much as he loathed himself, but he needed the money and she was the quickest way to it. To substitute Jane's innocent sister for Jane was the most caddish thing he could do, but it was too late to turn back now. Jane had escaped his net. Melanie wouldn't.

He rationalized his actions by telling himself he would do everything in his power to make her happy, but he knew ultimately, he would destroy that happiness. It couldn't happen any other way. The reason he needed Melanie and her money would be the very thing that destroyed her.

Still, he would give her what he could, while he could. She had time to run away. The one thing he wouldn't do was take her to his bed until the vows were said. He could seduce her with a million little lies, but not the final one. He would return her whole to her parents if she chose against him. Unless he behaved like the cad he was, he didn't think she would go against him. Melanie had a loving heart. She would have him.

As they left the modiste's and headed for the bootmakers, she looked up at him anxiously. "Should we check at Jane's again? Perhaps she has had second thoughts and returned home."

He'd told her Jane had left for an extended stay with a friend in Hampshire. In reality, he'd returned to his former rooms and found a message in Jane's furious scribbles calling him every name in the book and some he hadn't heard before. Some bastard had obviously revealed his little secret ahead of schedule. Damien wondered who hated him that much. Or perhaps the fates worked against him, as they always had. He wondered how to keep the apostles of fate away from Melanie. Keeping Jane away from Melanie wasn't any problem. She'd gone to Hampshire just as he'd said, only the friend she went with wasn't female.

"Jane may send 'round a note when she returns," Damien answered doggedly. "I have sent the appropriate announcements to the papers of our marriage. Your father will be expecting them. I daresay you'll hear from Jane then." It took every ounce of his pride to keep from asking her to marry him in truth again. He didn't know what Jane would do when she discovered her little sister had fallen into his clutches.

"It's so unlike Jane." Melanie fretted beside him. "Are you quite certain the note was in her writing? Perhaps someone has abducted her to keep her from marrying you. I know she must still love you. I just cannot understand this at all. Are you sure we shouldn't wait a while on those announcements? She will simply be devastated if she sees them before we have time to explain."

Damien leaned forward and tipped her chin upward so she met his gaze. She had the most amazing heart-shaped face, with wide violet eyes and the sweetest lips when they weren't pursed with concern as they were now. He wondered what she would do if he kissed her. He had no wish to diminish his prospects by rushing his fences. He merely brushed his thumb reassuringly over her bottom lip and watched it tremble. Good. She wasn't immune to desire.

"You have not seen your sister in ten years, sugar plum. I assure you, Jane knows precisely what she is doing. We meant to marry this time around for the same reasons we meant to marry the first time: my title and her money. I don't like to hurt your harmless dreams, Melanie, but love is not a commodity easily traded in society's market. Should you and I marry, the trade is the same one, only perhaps I can earn my way a little better with you since I can also trade experience. Jane never needed that."

She gave him one of those shrewd looks that reminded Damien all too uncomfortably of her papa, and he removed his hand from her chin, sitting back in his seat. He knew she'd led a sheltered life. Her parents had seen to that. He just kept forgetting that innocent face disguised an all too creative mind.

"You are trying very hard to name yourself cad, Damien. A true cad wouldn't, you know. You ought to be whispering loving sentiments and stealing kisses about now. I'm certain I'm as susceptible to both as any other maiden."

He laughed. He couldn't help himself. He wanted to hug and kiss her and tell her he never was such a fool as to try to get past her. But he was, and he would, and she just made it that much more challenging with remarks like that.

"I shall do just that, if you wish, my lady. I aim to please. Shall we visit the bootmakers first or just repair to the park where I shall start on those kisses?"

"The bootmakers," she announced firmly. "I wish to be quite splendid before you're seen about with me."

By the time they returned to the house late that afternoon, Melanie felt quite drained. She refused to acknowledge her exhaustion to Damien who had become more pensive as the day wore on. She knew she had spent an enormous amount in just a few short hours, but she thought it vindicated a lifetime of saving. He really shouldn't worry. She had more than enough for herself and whatever debts he'd run up. She supposed they should have gone to the bankers first, but the temptation of new clothes had diverted all good intentions. Besides, she kept waiting for her father to appear, roaring over his discovery of their lack of marriage lines. Or for Jane to come back and fall at their feet to plead her love and apologies. She just really couldn't believe all this was happening and wanted to grasp every opportunity as it was offered.

A groan from Damien made her look up from her ruminations to discover where his thoughts had strayed. When she saw he'd covered his eyes with his hand, she glanced out the window.

Strangers sat on her doorstep. Not elegant strangers, although she couldn't imagine even Damien's rakish friends stooping to sitting on a doorstep. These men wore round hats and garish waistcoats and smug grins as the carriage approached. They very much seemed to be waiting for them. Melanie sent Damien a questioning look.

"The cent percenters," he groaned. "They've come to collect already. Someone at the papers must have tipped them off. I'm sorry, Melanie. I'd meant to fob them off a while longer so you wouldn't need to see them."

"Oh, you mean loan sharks!" She looked out the window with curiosity at the smug, smiling faces grinning up at them. One man had a nose that looked as if someone must have battered it extensively. Another had a decidedly ugly red scar down the side of his face. Despite their smiling exteriors, she feared these were very rough men, indeed. "Well, I suppose it's too late to visit the bankers. You will have to tell them to send their bills 'round to my solicitor in the morning."

Damien gave her a look of amazement. "You don't even know the extent of my debt. Why should you pay what you do not owe for someone who isn't really your husband?"

"Do you gamble?" she asked with upraised brows.

"With what?" he asked dryly. "With my life, with my good name, with my family's reputation? Yes, I do that. But with money? I haven't any."

"Then once these debts are paid, we'll have only our living expenses, won't we? It seems fair trade to me. Your time must be worth a great deal, and I mean to claim a good lot of it while I can."

"You make me feel lower than a snake's belly," he growled, flinging open the door. "Stay inside while I clear this lot away."

With a few curt words he had them scattering. Damien had a very forceful way about him when called upon, Melanie noted with almost as much satisfaction as trepidation. She had always thought of him as something of an elegant rattle, but he'd changed these last years. She'd encountered him once or twice in the village when he visited his family, but she'd not really noticed the changes until now. When he returned to lift her from the carriage, her heart did a strange little flip-flop inside her chest.

"I'm sorry to have embarrassed you like that, Melanie. I meant for your first day in London to be special."

He didn't murmur the words softly and sweetly in her ear but announced them coldly, as if by keeping his distance he could pretend they came from someone else. She thought he meant them. He just didn't want to admit it to himself. She didn't know what to make of that, so she ignored it all.

"I can't remember ever having more fun," she said sincerely as they entered the house. "I feel like a fairy princess with a dashing prince for escort."

He gave her a flicker of a smile as he helped her with her pelisse. "Perhaps you ought to just keep me about for a storybook time and pretend I'm not here otherwise. We might rub along quite well that way."

She frowned slightly as she tried to determine the meaning behind that. She knew her own parents went their own ways most of the time. The only time she ever saw them in the same room together was when they entertained, or at dinner occasionally. They each had their own friends and pastimes. She had neither. Perhaps that's what he was telling her: he had friends and interests that he would pursue when she didn't want him around. She supposed she couldn't expect him to always be at her beck and call.

She didn't have time to dwell on this discovery. Mr. Watson, the caretaker, had hurried up to take their walking sticks and Melanie's pelisse. "The others are awaiting your convenience, my lord, my lady. Where do you wish to see them?"

Melanie blinked, unable to comprehend this request, but Damien seemed to have no problem. He gave her a concerned look and asked, "Do you wish me to do the hiring? You look as if you need a rest. Just tell me how many you want and I'll do what I can, but you'll have to choose your own personal maid."

The servants. Of course. Mr. Watson had called in staff. She really didn't wish to have to make these decisions now, but she couldn't make Damien do it all. Besides, she needed to learn the duties of a wife. Running a household was one of them.

She nodded reluctantly. "Just give me time to freshen myself, and I will join you."

Mrs. Watson had stripped off the covers in the salon. Melanie found Damien there a little while later. Mrs. Watson had brought in tea and sandwiches to refresh them, and Damien now sipped at a cup while perusing a list of staff the caretaker had provided. He looked up at her entrance and smiled, but she saw a lingering look of concern behind his eyes. She wondered if her appearance made her look haggard, or if something else bothered him.

"Is it an enormous undertaking?" she asked lightly, taking a chair beside the tea table and serving herself.

"An expensive one. I should not think we'd need half these people." He handed her the list.

We. He'd said "we," as if he truly thought of them as a couple. Melanie danced a quiet little jig in her head while pretending to gaze thoughtfully at the list. It seemed quite reasonable to her. She handed it back to him. "I cannot say I have a good grasp of my worth, my lord, nor do I have a sound understanding of my future income. I just know that my trust allots me more than I have ever been able to spend, and the cost of these few people will not change that to any degree. I should think it our duty to employ the less fortunate and keep them off the streets."

Grimly, he rang for Watson. "I think we had best visit your bankers as soon as possible. You cannot go along in complete ignorance forever."

She wanted to ask him what he knew of investments and such, but Watson showed in the first maid, and they had no time for further privacy. The only thing she accomplished in the next few hours was to make certain her own personal maid was young and cheerful and nothing like the elderly termagant she'd left behind who reported everything to her parents. Since Damien assured her he had managed to keep his own valet over all these years, she relaxed and watched him question the rest of the staff. She really would have been lost without him, she decided, as he turned away a handsome young footman who gazed on her with too much interest. She would have hired the fellow for his jolly smile.

Before the next person could enter, she whispered across the tea table to him, "Why did you turn him away? He seemed quite a nice young man."

"Because he worked for Lady Douton last," Damien answered enigmatically, ticking off one more position on his list.

"That is a fault? I should think that meant he had experience."

Damien looked up with a sigh of exasperation. "Melanie, I'm not about to explain the deviations of an evil-minded woman to an innocent such as yourself. Just leave it understood that the man had ambitions above and beyond his duties as footman."

She didn't understand, and she didn't like being treated like a simpleton, but she realized he protected her because she was a maiden and not a wife. Wives apparently had a great deal of understanding of the world simply due to whatever the marriage act entailed. Melanie had only vaguely wondered about that in the past because she had long since given up any dreams of becoming a wife. Now entire new horizons opened before her. Damien said he would have her as a wife. She still didn't quite believe him, but the possibility existed for the first time in her life. She might actually learn the secrets of the marriage bed. The thought so amazed her that she scarcely noticed who Damien hired after that.

When the room finally cleared of the last potential servant, Damien turned and gave her another of his concerned looks. "I've exhausted you, haven't I? I should have sent you to your room to rest."

Finally waking from her trance, Melanie shook her head vehemently. "No, not at all. I am just learning that freedom involves a great deal of responsibility. I had never thought about it clearly."

He gave her an approving smile. "Some people never learn that, I fear. They live for the moment and ignore the results of their actions."

She thought he might be speaking of Jane, but she didn't want to hear a word against her sister. She knew Jane had always been the tiniest bit selfish, but their parents had made her so, doting on her as they had. But Jane had never hurt anyone that way. She just knew how to enjoy herself more than Melanie did. She couldn't find a flaw in that.

Damien stood and helped her from the chair. She found herself standing much too close to him, but he didn't back away as was proper. He continued holding her hand and looking down at her with an expression she couldn't quite read.

"If the modiste delivered that gown as promised, would you care to go to the theater with me this evening? I'll send one of our newly hired footmen to a friend of mine for his box seats, if you'd like."

Any thoughts of exhaustion vanished. With a cry of delight, Melanie hugged his neck. As she limped hurriedly from the room to check on the gown, Damien watched her leave, a look of sadness haunting the shadows of his eyes.

"I have never seen anything so absolutely marvelous in all my life," Melanie said with satisfaction as she sat back upon the carriage squabs the next day.

Damien gave her an indulgent look as he took the seat across from her. "You have never been to the theater in your entire life," he reminded her. "You are scarcely a fair judge."

She pouted playfully. "Then you shall have to take me every night to a different production so I might become one. Shall we go to the Drury tonight?"

Damien shook his head. "After the announcements appear in the paper today, you will find your drawing room deluged with callers and invitations. We will be the current gossip sensation of society. I think an evening of rest is called for while we choose our next battlefield carefully."

Melanie's eyes widened. "Invitations? I don't know anyone yet. I haven't been presented. I haven't had a come out. Why would anyone send invitations?"

Damien just continued to shake his head at this ingenuousness. "You really do have crackers for wits, don't you? Perhaps I ought to find a place in the country and abscond with you there. Perhaps if I keep you to myself for a while, you'll see what an eminently wonderful husband I will be."

"You are already an eminently wonderful husband, albeit a borrowed one. Jane is the one with crackers for wits. Surely once she sees the announcements she'll return and all will be right again. I just hope it takes a few days for the papers to reach her. I really am enjoying this much too much." She gave him a look of inquiry. "However do you mean to explain to the world that actually Jane is your countess and not me? Perhaps we ought to stay out of society until it is all straightened out. You could say the papers made a misprint."

"If I were not content to have you as my countess, I would not have put the announcements in the paper, Melanie," he informed her firmly. "You may deny it as much as you wish, but in the eyes of the world, you're mine. You need only say the word and we'll make it so in the eyes of God, also."

"Faradiddle," she said tartly as the carriage drew to a halt in a narrow city street. "You cannot take a cripple as wife. I cannot dance or ride or do any of those things your countess ought to do. I'm just being shamelessly selfish while I have the opportunity. I'm perfectly aware you'll return to Jane the moment she snaps her fingers. I'll quietly disappear from the picture when that time comes."

Exasperated, Damien didn't open the carriage door but glared at her. "If you have so little confidence in me, what are we doing at your solicitor's? You will have a hard time explaining that to him when Jane returns and you turn me over to her."

She scowled at him. "You're not a pet dog. You said you would help me learn about my investments. He's much more likely to answer questions from you than from me. We'll just brush it off as a jest by bored nobility later. Who is he to argue? He works for me."

He didn't try to explain that she played right into his hands every time she introduced him to another person as her husband. He ought to feel more remorse at trapping her so callously, but as he sat before her solicitor's desk a while later, he decided his trusting wife actually needed someone like him to look after her.

With incredulity, Damien flung the list of investments back on the desk and slammed his palm against them. "She is not making enough interest on these to stay ahead of rising costs! At this rate, you'll have her living off assets in a year or two. Devil take it, man! You've got her invested like an old lady of ninety-three."

The bespectacled man behind the desk squirmed slightly, cast a glance to Melanie who merely watched the scene with interest, then returned his attention to the Earl of Reister. "Of course, we always understood . . ." He squirmed some more, then looked again at a radiantly healthy Lady Reister. "Her father always made it plain . . . Well, we thought the lady an invalid, my lord. And since she never spent what she earned, it seemed unnecessarily risky to invest in anything but certain income."

They'd thought her at death's door. Grimly accepting that explanation, Damien stood and pulled Melanie up with him. "I'll expect you and your banker in my office by tomorrow with a better plan of action than this. I have a few suggestions of my own I will make at that time. The lady will need to live off her income in the future, so keep that in mind."

The solicitor coughed into his hand as they prepared to depart. Damien turned and raised a questioning eyebrow.

"Ahem. There is the matter of the marriage lines, my lord. We will need them for confirmation that the lady's fortune is now in your hands. There are transfers to be made, you understand."

Damien gave a curt nod, placed a hand at Melanie's waist, and steered her out. He'd known the subject would arise. He had just hoped it could be postponed for a while. The awful danger of this whole scheme tumbling down on his head still loomed in the murky future. Melanie might not realize it, but this whole charade rested on a house of cards that could blow away with any gust of wind. He wondered how he would persuade the archbishop to change the name on the special license he still carried in his pocket.

Melanie glanced up at him uncertainly as they entered the carriage. "Does that mean we can't change the investments until we have the marriage lines drawn?"

"You would do better to look at it another way, gosling. Once I persuade you to the altar, everything you own becomes mine. Are you ready to run back to your papa yet?"

She stared at his blank expression with concern. "This gets very complicated, does it not? I'm of age. If we tell him we left our marriage papers with my father, will he let me sign the transfers until he receives them?"

"Not if you insist on saying you're married. I'll just go over with him the changes I want made, and you can make them if you decide to heave me out. I think I can earn my keep in the meantime just by increasing your return on investments. I wouldn't have thought your father would have been so bumble-headed."

Melanie shrugged. "The fortune came mostly through my mother's family, and he paid it little mind. He gave Jane a generous dowry when she married in addition to her own fortune." She gave him a wry smile. "Marriage papers or not, I don't think he'll do the same for us. It's not as if we asked his permission or anything."

"I'm sorry, Melanie. Your generous act of saving me from myself will cost you more than you can understand. I wish I knew how to make myself a better man for your sake."

She gave him an apprising look. "I wonder how I should go about improving you? You are already dangerously good-looking. Any more so, and I would have to fear fighting off all the ladies in London for you." She ignored the way his eyebrows rose in surprise. "You take no exception to my lameness. I have yet to find a man capable of that particular piece of goodness. You are not a gambler or wastrel that I can discern. You are intelligent and not a coward. You have dealt very well with my domestic and financial problems. In what way could I improve you, sir?"

He was grinning now, laughing at her, she supposed, but she could not slight on honesty. Other than the fact that he wanted her beautiful sister, she could not think of a better man for husband.

"All right. You have me convinced. If you will not have me, I shall go into the marriage mart believing I am superior to all others. I will not need Jane. I shall no doubt find wealthy women aplenty ready to throw their fortunes at my feet."

"Don't be facetious," she returned, disgruntled. "I am only saying we are in this equally. Neither of us is perfect."

Since she had absolutely no idea how imperfect he was, Damien kept silent. When they returned to the house, he helped her inside, then departed to go about some long-neglected business. Knowing he had no right to the money in his pocket, he still went off with a lighter heart than before.

Melanie welcomed the opportunity for a few hours of her own. Accustomed to loneliness, she didn't know how to act with so many people about and so many things to do. As she took off her hat, a maid rushed in to ask if she wished all the covers in the house lifted, or if she wished some of the rooms closed off for now. Declaring boldly that she would have all the covers lifted, she limped up the stairs to her own chambers. She would like to see some of the ancient fabrics changed in there, but she hesitated about redecorating those rooms first. If she truly entertained the fantasy of marrying Damien, they would share the master chambers at the other end of the hall. Now that she'd directed those rooms uncovered, it would look odd if she didn't see to them first. The servants would expect them to have adjoining rooms.

That thought made her exceedingly nervous. With the intention of overcoming her foolish fears, Melanie made her way down the hall to the dark back chambers where maids were already dusting and polishing and sweeping. Someone had decorated the master's room in heavy browns and golds that faded with too much light. For that reason, apparently, they'd kept the draperies drawn. She ordered the draperies pulled back and the windows opened to air out this room while she inspected it.

If they were truly married, she'd ask Damien how he would like the room furnished. They could go out to the warehouses together. But if he had no intention of staying, it would be foolish to waste money on changing anything. She would never use this room on her own. The huge bed on the raised dais alone intimidated her. Or perhaps the thought of what must happen on that bed to make a marriage scared her.

She had no illusions about her lameness. Damien had her fitted for a boot that would keep her from limping quite so much. She appreciated the gesture, but it did not undo the fact that the leg in question was twisted and ugly. Men didn't like taking ugly women to bed. She supposed Damien might do it for the necessary heir if they married, but then he would find someone whole and perfect with whom to spend his time. She didn't think she could bear that.

No, better that she find Jane and bring the two estranged lovers together. She just hoped Jane would be forgiving when she discovered what Melanie had done.

She informed Mr. Watson that she would not be at home to visitors today. She had no desire to meet perfect strangers without Damien at her side. She didn't know if she ought to meet them until the matter of Jane got straightened out. She had only envisioned the freedom of seeing London. She had never dreamed of entering society as a countess. Her one act of rebellion had landed her into hot water deeper than she had ever dreamed.

But she wasn't yet ready to give it up. She hadn't seen all of London yet. She hadn't gone driving in the park. She wanted to see the opera and the circus. Perhaps Damien would take her to Hatchard's when he returned. If she only had a few days to enjoy this freedom, she would squeeze in everything she could.

She didn't even bother to go down and inspect the cards that had arrived while she hid on the upper floors. They were Damien's friends. He could decide what to do with them. She happily made lists of changes she wished to make in her new home.

When Watson actually came upstairs to knock on her sitting-room door, Melanie glanced up from her desk with surprise. "What is it, Watson?" She'd already approved the cook's menu, directed Mrs. Watson to the rooms she wished cleaned first, and given orders for the dinner hour. What else could they possibly need of her?

"There is a personage at the door, my lady," Watson intoned formally. "She insists that she must see you."

Melanie's hand instantly went to her hair. "Jane? Has Jane come?" She wished more of her new gowns had arrived. She wanted Jane to see her as a sensible adult, not the child she remembered.

"I don't believe so, my lady. She says her name is Pamela, and the hackney driver is awaiting payment."

Pamela! Pamela was just a baby. This couldn't be. Surely Pamela was with Jane. Or her nanny. Or someone besides a hackney driver! Thoroughly bemused, Melanie started to leap from her chair, and caught herself on the desk when her weak leg wouldn't allow such a hasty movement. Cursing softly, she emptied some coins from the desk drawer where she had placed them this morning, and dumped them in Watson's hand. "Pay the driver, Watson, I'll be there directly." She let him take the stairs at a faster pace than she could manage.

When she finally arrived in the foyer, a child of immense girth wearing a straw hat with ribbons streaming down her back watched her from small eyes lost in a pudgy face. Melanie could only stare. Surely this . . . exceptionally large child could not be Jane's precious little baby.

"You must be my Aunt Melanie," the child stated with satisfaction. "I have come to live with you."

Melanie thought she might sink to the chair beside the hall table to catch her breath at this declaration, but she thought better of it. The child didn't look scared, but surely adults shouldn't show weakness at moments like this. Taking a deep breath, she asked carefully, "Where is your nanny, Pamela?"

"Oh, I got rid of her a long time ago," she said with that same satisfaction. "And I told the maid that I received a letter from you asking me to come. Mama read me your letters. You do want me to come, don't you?"

Oh, my. Oh, dear. Melanie looked helplessly to Watson, who remained as stoic as ever, seemingly not heeding this conversation at all. She glanced back at the child who didn't look at all like the lovely Jane of her memory except for the long blond curls. Despite the child's much too adult complacence, she sensed a certain wariness behind those small eyes now. Without another thought, Melanie offered her hand.

"Why, of course. I have wanted to meet you for ever so

long now, just as I've said in my letters. Let us go up and find you a room, and then we shall have a nice coze over tea, shall we?"

She could practically see the miniature giant fight back an expression of relief as she nodded haughtily and took her offered hand. When Melanie used her cane to help her up the stairs, the child looked at her with interest. "Mama said you was a cripple, but you have a stick to help you walk. Does it have a sword in it like Lord Aberdeen's?"

Leave it to a child to consider a handicap as something excitingly innovative. Melanie bit back a smile and answered seriously, "No. One needs two good feet to fence with a sword. How did you know to come here?"

"I heard the maids whispering that Lord Reister had married Mama's sister. When he came to call, I went down and took his card. He'd scribbled this address on the back. I showed it to the driver, and he took me right here," she answered proudly.

Alarmed at the precociousness of a child who could only be . . . Melanie tried to count back. Nine? Surely not already. Jane always spoke of her as an infant. But she'd been married ten years ago . . . Shaking her head, she returned her thoughts to the child now obediently following her down the corridor. "That was a very dangerous thing to do," she warned in her sternest voice. "Ladies never go out by themselves. Hackney drivers might sell them to the gypsies if they catch them alone. Don't ever, ever do that again. Do you understand me?"

She could see obstinacy welling up in Pamela's face, but Melanie refused to back down. She didn't know who had responsibility for raising this entirely too precocious child, but someone had to put a firm foot down before she found herself in more trouble than she could handle. "I want your promise, Pamela. If you're to stay with me until your mama returns, you have to listen to what I say. Even grown-up ladies daren't go out in the city by themselves. We could have lost you. Do you know how unhappy that would have made me? I've wanted to meet you ever so long, but what if the gypsies had stolen you before I ever met you?"

"You could have come to meet me sooner," she answered defiantly, her bottom lip stuck out. "Nobody comes to visit me."

Melanie handed the child into a chair in her sitting room, then rang for a maid. "One is supposed to wait until invited before visiting. Your mama knew I couldn't come, so she didn't invite me. Would you like some tea?"

The child's face brightened immediately. "Oh, yes, please. Will we have little cakes? I love the ones with thick frosting Cook makes."

Cakes with heavy frosting were definitely not what this child needed. How could Jane let her eat so inappropriately? Or had Jane even noticed what her child ate if she was not there to supervise the meals?

Not wanting to think a thought that sounded too much like something Damien might say, Melanie ordered the maid who appeared to bring up some lemonade and watercress sandwiches.

Pamela's expression immediately grew mutinous. "I wanted cakes. I don't like nasty old watercress. And I like tea with lots of sugar. And cream. Nanny says cream is good for the complexion."

"Sugar is bad for the complexion. It makes it all spotty. And my cook doesn't know how to make cakes because I can't eat them. We shall have strawberries for dessert if you eat your sandwich all up."

Torn between the desire to have her way and curiosity at the lady who couldn't eat cakes, Pamela wiggled restlessly in her chair. "Why can't you eat cakes?" she asked sullenly.

Good question. Lying to a child wasn't as easy as she thought. Frantically, Melanie tried to come up with a reasonable answer that wouldn't pull her deeper into a web of deceit.

"Because if she gets too fat, she won't be able to climb the stairs," a voice from the door responded. "Hello, Pamela, what brings you here?"

The child in the chair brightened perceptibly, turning to peer around the chair's wing to investigate the newcomer. "Damien!" she cried happily, leaping from her perch and rushing to meet him.

With ease, he caught all six stone flung at him, whirling the little girl up in his arms before depositing her back in the chair where she belonged. Amazed at the lordly gentleman so apparently at ease with the difficult child, Melanie merely sat back and watched as Damien placed both hands on the chair wings and trapped Pamela between them.

"Now tell me what you are doing here. Did your mama bring you?"

Pamela immediately became belligerent, crossing her arms over her chest and glaring back. "No, and the gypsies didn't sell me either. I'm gong to stay with Aunt Melanie. She told me I could." She didn't even look at Melanie for confirmation.

Neither did Damien. He merely stared disapprovingly at the child. "That is very good of your Aunt Melanie, but she doesn't know what a spoiled little brat you are. If you're going to stay here, you're going to behave yourself. You'll do exactly what your Aunt Melanie tells you, or I'll personally paddle your little bottom."

"You would not dare!" she shouted back. "My mama said she would shoot your brains out if you take one hand to me, Damien!"

Shocked, Melanie could only stare. Damien had no right to punish the child, although admittedly, the child needed firm guidance of some sort. But Damien's behavior was no less shocking than Pamela's. She'd never heard a child talk to an adult so. And how could she possibly have heard Jane say such a horrible thing?

"Then if you want your mama's protection, you can go right back to her," Damien informed her resolutely. "I will not have any spoiled brats in my house."

Deciding this was the point where she ought to interfere, Melanie interrupted smoothly, "I'm certain Pamela isn't a brat, Damien. She just misses her mama. Now have a seat, do. We're just about to take tea."

Damien straightened and gave her a glare. "You have no idea . . ."

"I'm certain I will soon enough," she interrupted before he could continue. "Pamela's nanny has apparently left her with a maid, so she is more than welcome to stay with us until her mama comes home. You can show Lord Reister how well you behave, can't you?" She asked this last of the child who clearly absorbed every word said.

"If you feed me cakes," she declared promptly.

"Strawberries," Melanie reminded her firmly. "And perhaps Lord Reister will take us to Astley's. I have always wanted to see a circus."

Distracted by this happy thought, Pamela bounced in her seat and sounded almost like an excited child as she bombarded them with questions while eating the dreaded watercress sandwiches. Damien raised a puckish eyebrow but genially complied with the undertaking, although he consumed almost everything on the tea tray in the process. Watercress and strawberries did not appease a hungry man.

Once they finished tea, Melanie sent her niece off to a hastily prepared room, sent a footman to inform Jane's servants where the child could be found and to fetch some clothing, and rose from her seat to follow Pamela to see that she got settled. Damien stood in front of her, blocking her path. She looked up at him with surprise.

"I can't think of another woman in the world who could

manage that obnoxious child so well, or who would even take the time to bother," he said softly, with almost an air of puzzlement. "Do you have any idea at all what you have let yourself in for?"

Melanie bit her bottom lip and looked skeptical. "I'm afraid a great deal more than I am able to handle." She turned a defiant look to him. "But I could scarcely do less, could I? She's just a *child*, Damien. A shamefully neglected one, I fear to say, I don't understand Jane at all."

"No, someone as good as you wouldn't," he murmured.

Then before she had any notion what he was about, Damien pulled her into his arms and kissed her.

Too utterly surprised to protest at first, Melanie quickly found herself caught by the myriad pleasures of Damien's embrace. She leaned against his strength, absorbed the masculine scents of tobacco and shaving soap, and fell headlong in love with the sensation of his lips pressing along hers. Before she knew what she was doing, she circled his neck with her arms. He rewarded her with a low groan as he lifted her closer against him, and his tongue lapped gently along the seam of her lips. Before she could part them in an exclamation of excitement, he stiffened and set her carefully back to the floor.

"I apologize, Melanie. I should not have done that. As much as I wish to convince you to marry me, I don't want you to feel as if you must."

Dazed, she gazed into the stark lines of his face, searching for answers that neither of them possessed. "If marriage means more kisses like that, I think you've convinced me," she answered somewhat breathlessly. "I had no idea, Damien . . ."

Lifting one eyebrow, he grinned a trifle rakishly. "That good, am I? Behave yourself, and I'll give you another for dessert."

Laughing shakily at his ability to take such a soul-racking moment and reduce it to a jest more easily dealt with, Melanie stepped away from his dangerous proximity and picked up her walking stick. "Then we shall have to have dinner half a dozen times a day," she replied, striving for the same light tone. She didn't think she was very successful.

Damien stood straight and tall as he watched her stride bravely away, her weak foot dragging only slightly. Only when she was completely out of sight did his shoulders sag, and he crumpled helplessly into the nearest chair.

She had taken in Jane's obnoxious child without a qualm. Drawing a shaky breath, Damien wished for a cigar and a glass of port right now. He needed to do something to calm this wildly escalating wave of hope. Of course she would take in Jane's child. Jane was family. She would feel obligated to help family, no matter how much she despised the burden. He'd rather thought of his "wife" as a helpless child herself, but she wasn't. Lord, after that kiss, he couldn't convince himself she was a child anymore. She was more woman than Jane would ever be. More woman than he deserved.

He closed his eyes and tried to concentrate on his plans to seduce her and sweep her into marriage, but he couldn't get any farther than the feel of her slender waist in his arms, the warm, eager pressure of her lips on his. The realization that she knew no other man but him in that way made his lungs constrict with the burden of responsibility laid on him. She would be completely, wholly his. He'd never possessed anything untarnished and complete before. He'd scarcely known his drunken father. His mother's memory faded into the distant past. He'd had to put his home out to let when his father died because he couldn't afford the upkeep. He'd lived off that small income and his wits ever since. He had nothing. Melanie could give him everything.

If she never learned of his reprehensible past.

That didn't seem very likely. He could try to keep the

truth from her until the vows were said, but then he fully meant to present her with the facts in all their dismal glory. That was one of the main reasons for his decision finally to sell his title in marriage. He didn't need just the money. He needed to establish a real home, a place to live, with a woman to run it properly. He would be the first to admit that Jane made a mighty poor bargain in that department, but he didn't have a great deal to trade beyond his title. The possibility of obtaining someone like Melanie nearly took his breath away.

She still thought of herself as inferior to Jane. He would have to show her otherwise, then perhaps he could convince her that he really, truly wanted her for his wife. He felt as if he grabbed for the stars, but a man couldn't be blamed for trying when they seemed so close at hand. She thought her lame leg put her beyond the pale, but he didn't see her lameness at all. With specially constructed shoes, she could even learn to dance if she wished. He didn't ask for perfection in bed either. He needed forgiveness and understanding and a great number of other things, but he didn't need perfect physical beauty. He, above all others, knew the uselessness of beauty.

He didn't know if he was adequate to the task. He'd spent the better portion of his life idling it away in pursuit of pleasure like the rest of society. He couldn't do that any longer. He had responsibilities he meant to uphold. If it meant waiting on Melanie hand and foot, he would do it. The odd part was, she really didn't know how much she could demand of him right now. She had some strange idea that they were equals. Sooner or later, events would dissuade her of that notion.

"I heard you got shackled, Reister, but did you have to grovel for a cripple with a kid? Even the fair Jane would be better than that."

Melanie gave the man credit for not intentionally saying

the words loud enough for her to hear. They just unfortunately fell into a lull in the crowd noise and some trick of their surroundings sent them wafting her way. She couldn't imagine why a fop like that stood outside with the noisy throng entering Astley's, but she didn't pretend to understand the whims of society. She just muffled a gasp when Damien caught the man by his starched cravat, hauled him to his toes, and nearly throttled him.

Staring avidly at the food vendors noisily selling their wares to the crowd, Pamela noticed none of this. Hastily, to divert her own attention as well as the child's, Melanie signaled for an orange vendor. Surely an orange couldn't hurt anything but the front of her niece's dress.

When Damien finally caught up with them as they pushed into the amphitheater, Melanie pretended she hadn't noticed anything, but he caught her elbow in a tight grip and whispered in her ear, "I apologize for the scene. I keep meaning to curb my temper, but there are times . . ."

"You needn't explain to me, Damien," she answered without inflection. "I realize I have asked a great deal of you. I do not wish to be a burden to your conscience as well. Do not change yourself for my sake."

She had to find some way to distance herself from him. He had wreaked chaos with that kiss, but it had been a thing of the moment, some spontaneous action that he couldn't control, like his temper, no doubt. She wouldn't allow herself glorious dreams of love and happy-ever-after. Damien would do as he pleased, and so would she.

Beside her, Damien fell silent. As he helped them into their seats, Melanie felt as if her words hadn't met with his approval. She had tried to release him from any obligation he may have felt to defend her, but he didn't seem particularly pleased about it. She didn't like being at odds with Damien. With curiosity, she watched his stony expression as he took his seat next to her.

"I heard what the man said, Damien. I *am* a cripple. You

needn't take his head off for stating the facts. You are kind to pretend that I am the countess you deserve, but you needn't, you know. Anytime you wish to call off this charade, I will understand."

Damien exploded. She couldn't put it any other way. He slammed his hands down on the seat in front of them, clenched his fingers into his fists, and bit back a reply with such difficulty that his jaw muscles strained from the effort. He finally leaped to his feet, and still clenching his hands in fists, stared coldly into the crowd rather than at her.

"I will fetch some lemonades and be back directly."

Melanie gaped at this display, but she said not a word as he strode off into the crowd. She would never understand the male mind, she decided as the first horses rode into the arena and she turned her attention to the performance.

Damien sat on the other side of Pamela when he returned, pointing out the clowns dancing in the wings, explaining how the riders did their tricks, agreeing that she needed a pony of her own if she wished to learn to ride properly. He would really make a wonderful father, Melanie thought sadly. And for just a moment, she felt a bitterness that Jane had all the luck.

But she let the excitement of the performance and Pamela's enchantment sweep away the bad thoughts. How could she feel bitter when she was having the most exciting time of her life? She would have these memories to cherish forever. She could even allow herself a little hope. Perhaps now that she had reached London, her father wouldn't have the power to drag her back home, even when it became obvious that Damien belonged to Jane and not to her. She thought Damien might help her stay.

He remained silent on their return journey when Pamela fell asleep in his arms. In sleep she did not seem so much a giant as a lonely little girl, and Melanie pushed the blond curls back from her childish brow with affection.

"You would be a better mother for her than Jane," Damien said coldly from his corner of the carriage.

Startled, she glanced in his direction, but the carriage lantern only sent his face into shadow. "Jane needs to remarry and settle down. A child needs two parents."

"I agree a child needs two parents. Jane isn't even one. I'd thought she might change, but I made a very large mistake. I think Jane realized that before I did."

Puzzled, Melanie tried to find the meaning behind his words, but it was late, and she was tired. She shook her head. "I don't understand you at all, you know."

He sent her an enigmatic look over the head of the sleeping child. "Don't call yourself a cripple anymore, Melanie. You are far less crippled than most. Your flaw is just more obvious than others."

"Is that what is bothering you?" she asked with relief. She smiled a little. "You can't catch me by my cravat and shake me when I call myself names. It must be very frustrating."

He raised his expressive eyebrows. "I'll find other ways of stopping that sharp little tongue, my lady. Beware."

The thought of just how he might do that sent a pleasurable shiver down Melanie's spine. She met his gaze boldly, and felt the stir of something sensual below her middle when Damien's gaze drifted to watch her mouth. He was trying to seduce her, just as he'd said!

She really thought she would like to be seduced. When would she ever have another opportunity? So with more courage than sense, she smiled back, and let her own gaze drop to his mouth.

He didn't touch her. He couldn't, not with his hands full of Pamela. But by the time the carriage stopped, Melanie felt warm all over just from the things his gaze spoke. When a footman rushed to take Pamela, and Damien lifted Melanie from the carriage and carried her to the house, she felt more than warm all over. She felt she might turn into steam.

He returned her to her feet at the top of the stairs so she might see Pamela settled into her room for the night, but Melanie found Damien waiting for her in the sitting room when she returned. He had a bottle of wine and two glasses in his hands.

"Will you share a drink with me before we retire?" he asked politely, but she didn't think there was anything polite about the look he gave her. He made her feel as if she wore a daring evening gown, or nothing at all.

"If I do, what do you mean to do with me?" she asked without shyness. Damien had never said anything to discourage her from speaking as she thought.

He filled the glasses and handed one to her. "Kiss you, probably," he replied in the same tone as she used. "I fully intend to employ what is usually the woman's ploy to trap a man. I'll flirt and tease and drive you to want more, but I'll refuse until you agree to marry me."

Melanie's eyes widened as she sipped the wine and absorbed his message. He wouldn't seduce her completely. She could encourage his kisses and still remain a maiden. She found the thought somehow stimulating. She had no understanding of the marriage bed, so she feared it. But she understood kissing.

A few minutes later, with Damien's wine-flavored breath mixing with her own, Melanie decided she didn't know anything about kissing either, but she was more than willing to learn. She stood on tiptoe and wrapped her arms around him and let him play with her tongue again. Desire shot swiftly and surely through her veins, and she nearly lost her balance. Only Damien's strong arms kept her from falling.

He trailed his kisses from her mouth to her ear to give her a chance to recover. "There's more I can teach you, sugar plum, but I think I'll make you wait for another night.

I want you eager and anticipating each step of the way," he murmured against her ear.

"You plan on telling me in advance how you mean to seduce me into marriage?" she asked with a slight laugh, not moving away from his hold. Her breasts felt oddly full yet somehow deprived as they rubbed against him.

"I don't want to be a complete scoundrel." Damien raised his hand to release some of the pins holding her hair, capturing a tendril between his fingers. "I may be a gazetted fortune hunter, but I'll be an honest one."

"It's not honest if you truly want Jane and I'm just a substitute," she pointed out implacably. "I think we'd best send Jane an urgent message to return home."

"Do that," he answered, visibly annoyed as he stepped away from her. "If calling Jane home is what it takes to convince you that I am not a complete imbecile, then do so. I've made my choice. It is up to you to make yours."

He left the room quietly, taking the bottle of wine with him.

Utterly amazed, afraid to believe a word he said, Melanie stared at the closed door until her knees folded and she had to sit down.

Damien Langland, Earl of Reister, declared he wanted *her* for wife and not the glorious Jane. Something did not ring at all true here, she just couldn't figure out what it was. She would have to wait for Jane.

In the meantime, he left her longing for something she didn't understand except to know that she couldn't have it.

"'Tis a pity a man of such noble countenance and title must be reduced to marrying an unfortunate cripple for money. I suppose she can claim no family, either?" the voice behind Melanie asked haughtily.

"Her father is a country baronet, but exceeding wealthy. Lady Morgan is her sister. Reister will survive," the second voice replied dryly. "They all do somehow."

The women moved on, leaving Melanie sitting on the park bench staring at the overhanging leaves of a maple in front of her. She supposed the women hadn't seen her there. She doubted they would recognize her if they did. They just gossiped as all society must gossip. They meant nothing by it.

They just left a hollow yearning behind. Melanie knew she was no match for an Earl of Reister. She had never held any such illusions. Damien deserved a beautiful woman like Jane on his arm. Pamela needed a father like Damien. Had she truly ruined his chances at having the countess he deserved?

She watched as Pamela ran and chased a hoop with some other children by the river. Melanie had brought one of the younger maids along so she might keep up with the child better than she could. With a little exercise and a proper diet, Pamela would be lovelier than Jane one of these days. Why had Jane neglected her only child so that she thought of food as her only companion?

It didn't make good sense. Since she had allowed her dreams to drive her to the altar with Damien, very little made any sense at all. She had made a childish decision and found herself burdened with adult responsibilities for the first time in her life. She had thought to help Damien out of an awkward situation and help herself in the process. Instead, she had unwittingly trapped him as well as herself. But he appeared not to mind while she spun dizzily, not knowing what she dared to ask.

She carried the pain of the women's scorn with her as they left the park to return to the house. Damien wished to introduce her at a grand social occasion, but Melanie couldn't do it. She would wait for Jane. She wanted Damien and Jane to be happy. She didn't want to feel responsible for destroying their lives. She wasn't at all certain anymore that could be arranged, but she'd have to try.

She found her men of business just coming out of the study when she returned to the house. They took off their hats and bowed to her as if she truly were a countess, and Melanie had to smile at her own playacting.

"You are very fortunate to find a man of intelligence like the earl, my lady," the banker declared boldly. "He will double your fortune within the year, mark my words."

She didn't know what to do with the wealth she already had, but she supposed Damien knew how to spend it. She had never thought paying his debts a bad bargain, but he seemed determined to square them somehow. She smiled pleasantly in agreement, not knowing how else to respond. She watched as Watson let them out, then turned to find Damien in the doorway, studying her.

"I have more business to attend to this afternoon," he said quietly, politely, as if they hadn't exchanged passionate kisses the night before. "Will you ride with me in the park this afternoon when I return?"

She didn't want the whole world to despise him for his unfortunate "marriage," but she hated to refuse him anything. Carefully, she asked, "Isn't a traveling coach a little unfashionable for the park?"

"I need to return that one to its rightful owner sometime. I thought you might enjoy a landaulet. I know of one for sale and thought you might like to try it out."

Melanie's spirits rose at the thought of owning her very own carriage. She stared at him anxiously, not certain how to take his toneless suggestion. "Do you think you could teach me to drive?"

This time, a smile lightened his demeanor. "Not a landaulet. You will need a driver for that. But once you've decided how you mean to go on, we might find something a little smaller for you." He frowned as she bounced with delight. "You will still have to take a tiger with you. You cannot go about alone."

"I will! I will, I promise. But if I could just learn quickly—"

He caught her hands and stilled her bouncing. "You cannot learn quickly enough to avoid your father should you choose to denounce me. There are still some things you have to face."

That still didn't bring her down completely. She envisioned many happy days before her father learned anything. And now that she was happily ensconced in her own home, perhaps he could do nothing at all but rant and rave. Even Jane might teach her to drive.

"Denounce you! As if I would ever do such a thing. Where do you come up with these words?" she asked mockingly, standing on her toes to kiss his cheek. "I shall love you dearly for the rest of my life."

The Earl of Reister held a hand to his cheek long after his innocent "bride" swept happily to her room.

The ride in the park had been a glorious success, Melanie thought contentedly as she sipped her morning tea and perused the stack of invitations that had assembled on the hall table these last few days. She knew she didn't have herself to thank so much as the modish carriage gown of luscious peach with the flattering neckline that made Damien look at her as if she truly were a peach ripe for eating. And of course, sitting in that lovely landaulet with all the plush velvet seats, no one could see her hobble, so perhaps she almost did look good enough to be Damien's countess. He'd showed her off proudly to everyone they met, and his friends seemed to greet her graciously. Perhaps she wouldn't be so very bad for him, after all.

Of course, that was last night talking. Melanie sat back dreamily and remembered how he'd held her as they sat on the love seat. He'd talked of the future of steam engines, if she remembered correctly, not precisely a romantic topic of conversation, but one she'd found as intriguing as he did.

He'd told her how he'd like to invest in a company that had produced a particularly workable engine suitable for moving wagons of coal, but by that time, she'd been listening more to the sound of his voice than the actual words. Damien's hands had taken to straying, and the occasional kiss to the nape of her neck or the lobe of her ear had her tingling in more places than she'd thought possible. He hadn't undressed her, but she'd wanted him to before the evening ended.

She blushed at the indelicate dreams that had flourished in her sleep after that. Damien had a way of making her feel as if she were the only woman in the world for him. She knew she wanted to believe that so strongly that she could easily fool herself into accepting him. She wanted to accept him. She wanted to ask him to take her back to the church and the vicar and repeat the vows in truth. But she wasn't a foolish child anymore. She knew Damien hid things from her. She knew Damien wanted her for her money. She wasn't quite certain that Damien still loved Jane, but she found it hard to believe that she would make an adequate substitute. She needed to know the truth, and she thought Jane would have it.

So while Damien went out on his mysterious errands of business and Pamela slept happily in her bed upstairs, Melanie perused stacks of mail addressed to the earl and countess and indulged in daydreams.

The clock had only struck the noon hour and Pamela had just come down dressed for another romp in the park when Watson came to Melanie to announce callers. She had left standing orders that they were not to be at home to callers, so she understood that these were not the usual type who left their cards and passed on to the next house on their list. She lifted an inquiring brow as she'd seen Damien do.

"Lady Morgan and Sir Francis Berkeley to see you, my lady. I put them in the yellow drawing room."

Jane and her father, together! Oh, my. That didn't bode

well at all. Jane and their father did not get along at all. The fact that they came together raised clarion calls of alarm. Nervously, Melanie glanced down at her new morning gown, removed a scone crumb, adjusted a ribbon, and pushed herself carefully to her feet. She hadn't quite learned to adjust to the higher heel of the new boot Damien had the cobbler make for her, so she held her walking stick as usual. She gave Pamela's worried look a smile, as if Jane's appearance here was perfectly natural.

"Shall you come down and make your curtsy before your grandfather, my dear? Or would you rather wait in the library and read a good book until your mother calls for you?"

The worried look didn't go away. Pamela glanced nervously at the door as if ready to bolt, but she bit her bottom lip and said politely, "I shall wait in the library, if you do not mind, Aunt Melanie." She sent Melanie another anxious glance. "You will not send me away, will you? I will behave, I promise. I shall not even chase away a governess if you wish to find one."

Melanie found that an extremely odd sentiment, but too worried about her own problems, she didn't pursue it. She merely pressed a kiss to her niece's hair and sent her off in the company of the young maid. She would prefer to have the explosion over with before she brought the child into her grandfather's company.

She almost had the rhythm necessary for keeping her new shoe in line by the time she reached the yellow salon. Clutching the walking stick but not relying on it, Melanie allowed Watson to open the door for her, and she did her best to glide in without a hitch to her step. The two people waiting for her didn't even seem to notice.

"Melanie! My baby sister! I'm so dreadfully sorry I have got you mixed up in all this!"

The woman rushing toward her in no way resembled the young girl who had so eagerly departed the country for the city sights ten years ago. Jane's lithe young figure, creamy complexion, and bounteous curls had somehow matured to a caricature of that long-ago image. Powder and a hint of what appeared to be rouge created the complexion. The curls had an oddly brassy shine which did not precisely duplicate the health and vigor of youth. But it was the figure that held Melanie speechless. Jane's once perfect hourglass figure now more carefully resembled their father's stout barrel shape. Melanie blinked and allowed herself to be wrapped in the suffocating envelope of French violet perfume and Jane's arms.

"You poor baby! We'll get you right out of here. I cannot believe that man! Of all the cruel, callous, despicable—" The tirade threatened to continue, but Melanie politely pulled herself away, casting a glance to her father.

"Hello, Papa. What brings you here?" She had the frightening notion that she knew, but she refused to admit anything. He had only to ask the vicar, and the vicar would have to tell him. She dreaded the disappointment she expected to see in her father's eyes, but she was prepared to stand up to him. She would tell him that she and Damien planned to marry as soon as they had the license. Unless Jane protested he belonged to her. That thought made her tremble.

"I've come to take you home, child. I'll not allow any daughter of mine to be slandered by the likes of that young cur. If he were worth anything, I'd have the law on him now. As it is, I'll just make it so hot for him here that he will have to flee to the Continent for the rest of his born days."

She didn't like the sounds of that at all. Nervously, Melanie bit her bottom lip much as Pamela had done earlier. Her father's side-whiskers quivered as he spoke, not a good sign at all. Reminding herself that this was her home, she took a seat in the yellow damask chair nearest her. She would hold out much better if she didn't fear her legs would crumble under her.

"If you speak of Damien, he is my husband, Papa. If you drive him to the Continent, you drive me with him." She thought she said that very well. The fury rising to her father's eyes did not confirm her opinion.

"He is not your damned husband! Do not give me that faradiddle, girl! He is a fake, a scoundrel, a fortune hunter who has ruined your good name and made us laughing stocks in front of all society. Were I not too old, I'd call him out and have done with him entirely. Now call your maid to pack and we'll be gone from here."

Knowing better than to argue with her father in one of his tirades, Melanie turned her attention to the sister she hadn't seen in ten years. "Do you wish me to call for Pamela? I'm certain you must have worried about her, but I didn't know if my message had reached you."

Jane gave an impatient huff and threw herself into the nearest seat. "The child is a trial. I think she'll be better off in the country with you. You can take her with you when you go. I don't know why it didn't occur to me before. Ring for some refreshments when you ring for your maid, will you? I declare, I'm quite exhausted by my exertions. I cannot believe you have done such a thing as to run off with Damien. Papa's quite right. He's a thorough scoundrel. When I read the announcement in the papers . . ." She rolled her eyes and shook her head as if the effort to continue was too much for her.

"You left him standing at the altar," Melanie reminded her, making no effort to summon anyone. "That was very badly done of you. If you did not want him, you should have told him so to his face." She found herself growing angry in Damien's defense. How could they call him names like that when he was the only man she'd ever met who had treated her as if she were a real person and not a broken doll to be kept in a corner? If anyone were to blame for her current situation, it was herself.

Outrage identical to their father's rose in Jane's eyes. "Do you know why he wanted to marry me? Do you?"

Melanie shrugged. The reason seemed quite obvious to her now. She didn't think it included beauty or love. "For the money?" she suggested.

"For the money, yes!" Jane screamed. "So I could raise his bastard child because he didn't have the money to support her. Your charming earl already has the woman he wants. She just doesn't have the money he needs."

Melanie thought the blow of those words must have pounded her into the seat. After that, nothing else seemed to quite register. She didn't remember calling a maid. She didn't remember ordering her bags packed. These things just miraculously happened around her until she found herself bundled into her father's traveling coach with Pamela, rumbling down the road out of London.

She thought she'd left a lot of things undone, but she couldn't quite recall them now. She was still trying to come to terms with the notion of Damien having a child and a woman he couldn't marry because he couldn't support them. The pieces fit awkwardly. She'd known he had secrets. She'd known he needed money. He'd made no pretense of that. He had made small objection to taking in Pamela when she supposed another man would have raised an uproar. That made a little more sense now if he expected her to raise another woman's child of his own. She just couldn't believe Damien would do that to her without telling her.

And she couldn't believe Damien had made such sweet love to her while keeping another woman behind her back.

It did not seem quite credible somehow, but then, it hadn't seemed quite credible that the Earl of Reister would take a plain spinster with a crippled leg as his bride either.

Melanie felt sick as the carriage churned on down the road to the house she'd lived in all her life, the prison she had so briefly escaped. She had known her freedom would be brief, but she had expected to turn Damien safely over to Jane. She hadn't expected this. She hadn't expected this at all, and she didn't know how to handle it.

Across from her, Pamela still looked worried as she watched the passing scenery, but the child remained blessedly silent. The notion that she would have Jane's child to raise helped relieve some of her anguish. She wouldn't be entirely alone again. She would have someone who needed her.

She supposed she'd had a narrow escape, that Jane had saved her from a dreadful mistake. She just wished she could make her heart accept that as her brain must. She had played the part of foolish, idle dreamer, allowing Damien to seduce her as he'd said he would. She just couldn't believe his kisses could lie so well.

Damien held the precious bundle in his arms, watching a milky breath breathe in and out of tiny bow lips, occasionally caressing a tiny silken curl. He'd given his heart at first sight of her, opened himself up to the onslaught of emotions he'd denied the better part of his life. Because of this tiny bundle, he'd learned to love. It made him feel awkward and vulnerable at times, particularly now that he'd been stricken twice by this malady, but it made him strong in ways he'd never been strong before. He didn't know how to deal with the emotion very well. No one had ever showed him how to express it. But he knew the iron courage it gave him when it came time to protect the women he loved. He needed it now, as he prepared to open his heart and let it bleed before the one woman he wanted more than any other.

He closed his eyes and gave a silent prayer as the hackney pulled up in front of Melanie's town house, the town house he prayed she would share with him and this inno-

cent bundle he held in his arms. He had thought to wait
until he had her bound safely to him before giving her this
evidence of his perfidy, but he found he couldn't do it. He
loved Melanie too much to treat her that way. He loved his
daughter equally. The battle to protect her first had been a
strong one, but he didn't think he could live with himself if
he sacrificed one love for the other.

The way Melanie had taken in Pamela had given him
hope. Surely she couldn't reject this innocent child, despite
the ignominy of her origins. He knew Melanie too well to
believe that. The woman who couldn't leave him standing
at the altar or starving in the streets, the woman who would
take in an obnoxious child she didn't even know, that
woman couldn't deny a babe in arms. He counted on that as
much as he counted on his own ability to make Melanie the
happiest woman alive once she accepted him with all his
faults and flaws.

Nervously, he carried the infant into a strangely silent
house. The child's wet nurse straggled shyly along behind
him, staring up at the grandeur of her new surroundings.
With a strangely pattering pulse, Damien took the steps two
at a time. Watson appeared in the lower hall before he
reached the top.

"Lady Reister has gone, my lord," he intoned cautiously
from below, eyeing the young nursemaid askance.

Damien's heart sank instantly. He recognized that tone
of voice as well as he recognized the man's disapproval.
Whatever Watson had learned this morning, the sight of the
child and nursemaid had confirmed it. Slowly, he turned
around and walked back down the stairs.

"Where did she go, Watson?"

"With Sir Francis and Lady Morgan, my lord. They left
orders for the house to be closed up and the servants turned
out. I believe Sir Francis mentioned selling."

Ah. He had something the old fraud wanted after all.
Watson wouldn't want to leave his comfortable position.

He'd no doubt padded the payroll with half his relatives. He might disapprove, but the servant would do whatever necessary to keep this house open. Damien smiled cynically.

"Thank you, Watson. In my wife's behalf, I countermand those orders. You will keep the place open and staffed. I greatly fear my wife has been abducted by well-intentioned fools. She will have need of you when we return. Send for her maid. I want her to travel with Miss Snipes here. I'll send around for the coach directly. Send one of the footmen for my horse."

Damien snapped out the orders curtly, quickly, as he made a mental list of all he would need to do. He'd had the world in his hands just hours ago. He wouldn't let it escape again without a fight. He didn't know what Jane had said to Melanie to make her flee like this, but he could very well imagine. She wasn't going to get away with it.

He hated to drag a child and a nursemaid across country roads in pursuit of a dream, but he couldn't leave them behind. Melanie had to see the truth with her own eyes, not wait until he carried her off and brought her back here. He wanted her to come willingly, with eyes wide open. He patted the pocket with the newly acquired special license in it. He wanted her full agreement this time.

He rode ahead of the carriage, leaving its lumbering gait well behind as he raced his horse past fields and meadows on the course toward home. Home. The house he'd inhabited as a child had never been a home. He'd vowed never to raise a child of his as he had been raised, but that had been when he'd never had any intention of having children. Now that he had one, the vow became even more important. A child needed two parents, Melanie had said. He could amend that somewhat. Children needed parents who loved them, who gave them the attention they needed. He didn't want to fail at that, but he might. Melanie wouldn't. And Melanie could keep him from failing too.

Damien didn't even have to repeat that refrain as the miles rolled beneath him. Melanie filled him. She had seeped into his soul and stayed there. He could feel her in every fiber of his being. He didn't know how it had come to pass, and he wouldn't question it. Melanie could save him. He had to save Melanie first.

That's how Damien looked at it as he rode up to the front door of the country manor he'd known since childhood. He'd used to ride up here to court Jane in his heedless youth. He thanked God he'd failed at that as he'd failed at so many other things over the years. He refused to believe he could fail at his current mission. He couldn't let all that life and loveliness that was his Melanie languish behind those cold doors and dark draperies.

He pounded the knocker and pushed past the butler when he asked for his card.

"Where's Melanie?" he demanded. "Where is my wife?"

The butler stared at him blankly. "The family is not at home to callers, my lord."

So the blamed man recognized him, Damien thought coldly. Good. Let him see the Earl of Reister breathing fire and fury. "I'm not a caller, man, I'm family. If you do not tell me where my wife is, I shall tear the place down until I find her."

The butler stepped back passively. "I'm sure I cannot say, sir."

"Fine then. Stay out of my way." Roaring with rage, Damien stormed down the hall, flinging open doors right and left. The library, she had said. She spent her time in the library, staring over the lawns. The library must be in the back of the house or she would be out here now. Melanie wouldn't ignore him. "Melanie!" he screamed at the top of his lungs. She would hear him. She would come running. It would just take her a little time.

He found a second passage leading to the rear of the house. He ought to remember where the blamed library was, but Jane hadn't spent much time there. Neither had he, for all that mattered. Where did one hide the blamed library?

He was aware of heads peering around doors and peeking down stairs at him as he rampaged through the silent halls. He didn't care. He needed Melanie. He needed to explain. He needed to make things right with her. Even if she didn't want him, he had to explain. He wouldn't have her thinking badly of him, or of herself. He knew that was what it was all about. Jane had said something to make Melanie doubt herself.

That thought filled his head as a familiar figure suddenly darted from the shadows at the rear of the hall. Too round and too large for flitting, the child merely pointed at a closed door and sat heavily on an antique boot bench by the side door. Damien blew Pamela a kiss and threw open the door indicated.

With draperies drawn, the room held only dusky shadows at first. Gradually he made out the floor-to-ceiling shelves, most of them half empty. Sir Francis didn't spend much time reading, nor had his limited selection of ancestors, Damien suspected. No one used this room, he knew instantly from the uncluttered library tables to the unburned wicks in the lamps—no one but a lonely woman who escaped into her own fantasies amid its dreariness.

He stalked to the drapery-covered windows. He didn't yell anymore. He would never yell at Melanie. Or maybe he would, occasionally. She had a stubborn will that needed opposition once in a while. But he could think of much better ways of opposing that will than by yelling.

Gently, he drew back the drapery hiding the window seat. She slept curled against the window frame. Tears sprang, unwelcome, to Damien's eyes. He wanted to pick her up and carry her out to the carriage that would arrive shortly, take her away from here, and never come back. But she wasn't a child like the one he'd held in his arms a few hours ago. She was a woman grown. She was entitled to make her own decisions.

"Melanie?" he spoke quietly, not wanting to startle her.

Her lids flickered, and her glance first went to the window. Perhaps he should have climbed in the window after her, Damien thought with amusement. That's what a gallant knight would do. He wasn't any gallant knight.

Then she woke more fully and turned to look up at him as if she'd expected him there all the time. "Damien," she said flatly.

"Not Sir Lancelot, I'm afraid," he apologized, jerking back the drapery so the sun flooded the dismal room. "But I've come for you anyway. You should have waited. I didn't want you to have to face your family alone."

"They're my family. I have nothing to fear from them." She watched him with curiosity now. She sniffed delicately as he sat beside her. "You smell of . . ." She tried to put a name to the odor she no doubt would have difficulty associating with him.

"Babies," he supplied the word for her. "My daughter spit up on me on the way to the house. I didn't exactly have time to change when I found you gone."

He loved the way those lovely violet eyes widened with surprise. In some ways, she was still a child. He thought that might be a good thing when it came to raising children. One needed to think like a child sometimes.

"Your daughter?" she asked questioningly, not coldly, not with condemnation, just asking explanation.

Damien took her hand and traced the delicate lines of her palm. "I thought I made it clear that I'm a cad without scruples. I'm sure Jane confirmed it for you. I had every intention of doing the same thing to you that I did to her. I was afraid if you found out before we were wed, that you would turn your back on me. I couldn't afford that. I was willing to do anything for my child. Her name's Arianna, by the way. She's three months old today."

"Arianna." She stared at him blankly. Damien knew he was doing this badly, but he didn't know any other way. He didn't want Sir Francis running in here shouting before he'd had time to explain. He had to speak hurriedly.

"I was bringing her to you when you disappeared. I couldn't lie to you, Melanie. I didn't want our married life to start out on a lie. I gambled my daughter's future for yours. But I lost before I had either. I'm not only a scoundrel, I'm a failure at everything that meant anything to me. I can see why you would turn your back on me. But don't turn your back on yourself, Melanie. Give yourself a chance. Go back to London. Call yourself countess. I won't contradict you. I can find a small place in the country for Arianna and myself. I've seen enough of London to last me a lifetime, but you deserve more than burying yourself here and wasting away. Find someone you can love. You deserve that. You deserve far more than I can offer you."

Tears streamed down her cheeks and Damien had the ridiculous impulse to kiss them away. He held himself back, though. He had to. If he ever had her in his arms again, he would never let her go. Love might have given him courage and strength, but he was only human. He wanted her too much to let her go. Right now, she wasn't his, so he could find the strength to hold himself back somehow. He'd forget all reasoning once he held her.

"You're doing it again, aren't you?" she asked, spoiling the coolness of her tone with a small hiccup at the end. "You're calling yourself names. Shall I grab you by the cravat and shake you?"

He managed a smile at the thought. "I could think of much more pleasant things to do if you'd like to grab my cravat, but if shaking me makes you happy, please do. I deserve far worse than that."

"Oh, stop it," she said crossly, starting to swing her legs down from her perch only to discover he blocked her way.

"You can't seduce me anymore, Damien Langland. Babies don't come into this world by magic. Where is Arianna's mother? If you truly want to take care of your daughter, you will marry her mother. The three of you can live just as easily as two in some cottage in the country. Perhaps you could take a position as someone's bailiff. Or I could give you some kind of commission for taking care of my investments. There are any number of alternatives besides shackling yourself to a wife you don't want. You ought to be quite glad Jane left you at the altar. She's become a terrible harridan since I saw her last."

"She was always a terrible harridan," he answered mildly. "I just had the strange notion that money would make life easier. I know better now. And if you won't have me, I'll accept your offer to make a commission on your investments. I'll gladly swallow my pride for Arianna's sake. But I want you. Perhaps I didn't make that clear enough. I don't want any other woman but you. Arianna needs a mother, but I need a wife more. I suppose, if you are happier looking for someone more honorable, I could learn to live with that. I might even find some comfortable farm woman to teach Arianna all those things about love that you already know. But it won't be quite the same as having two parents who love each other. Would you care to live in a cottage with us? I really don't need the town house or the carriages or such. I just need a wife, a lovely wife, a loving wife who understands I'm not perfect but loves me anyway. Do you think you could ever love me?"

She clenched her hands in the muslin of her skirt and looked out the window again. "Arianna's mother? Why can she not give you these things?"

"I'm not doing this very well, am I?" he sighed. "Arianna's mother is a"—he sought for a polite term—"a soiled dove. She took off shortly after Arianna's birth. She knew I couldn't keep her the way she wished to be kept, and she'd found an old man who would. Of course, he wouldn't keep the child. I've spent everything I had finding a wet nurse and providing them with a place to stay. It's extremely expensive living in London. I had no notion how much it took to raise a child. I had to borrow from the cent-percenters when Arianna ran a fever and I had to hire a doctor and buy medicines. I'll find some way to pay you back over time. Now that I have those debts off my back, I'm certain I can find a place for us where my income can support us. For that alone, I owe you. I will gladly do anything to see that you have the life you want, Melanie. Just tell me what you want."

She jerked her leg away from where his hand so casually rested upon it. "You can't make me whole again, Damien. You can't make me the kind of countess you deserve. You'll need an heir someday, and as much as you may protest now, I'm certain I'm not the woman you would choose to provide one. I mixed you up in my foolish dreams and made a hash of everything. I'm sorry I've caused you such confusion, but I won't go back to London and pretend to be your countess any longer. You need one in truth. Tell them I died, if you wish. Tell them the truth, if you prefer. And find a lovely mother for Arianna, one who will love you for who you are and not for your blasted title. You have a lot to offer, Damien. Don't sell yourself cheaply."

Damien suffered a brief flare of anger, and he clutched his fingers into his fists. He controlled it, however, when he saw the streaks of her tears. Catching her chin with his hand, he made her face him. "I don't want to sell myself cheaply. I want to sell myself to you. I'm the one who's making a hash of it. I love you, Melanie. That's what I've been trying to tell you. I couldn't lie to you because I love you too much. You have no idea how easily I could get an heir on you, if you wish to be crude about it. If it makes you happy to hide your leg, then hide it for your own sake, but not for mine." Boldly, he jerked up her skirt to expose two stockinged limbs sprawled across the pillows of the window seat. He ran his hand up the withered one, contrasting the brownness of his skin to the whiteness of her stocking. "You have nothing to hide from me." He kept his hand on her leg but met her eyes firmly. "I want you as my countess in all sense of the word. I want you in my bed, Melanie. I want you to bear my children. I need you to save me from everlasting damnation. Marry me, Melanie."

The library door slammed open, revealing a furious Sir Francis wielding an ancient battle-ax and a bevy of stalwart footmen carrying cudgels and muskets. The baronet's roar of rage filled the room as he discovered the Earl of Reister with his hand up his daughter's dress.

"You bastard! You son of a fiend! You bloody damned—"

Melanie brushed her skirt back down and leaned over to wrap her arms around Damien's neck. "I think I've borrowed Damien long enough, Papa. I want him for my own now. Do you think we might ask the vicar to do it proper this time? I want flowers and my family there. And Pamela can be my flower girl." She turned a loving look to Damien, who sat still and watched the armed footmen warily. "Will you need time to ask your friends?"

As he saw the way his little devil had brought her father and his army to a standing halt, Damien relaxed and wrapped his arm tightly around her waist. "What if we just ask your father to stand up for me this time? If the vicar isn't busy, we can have the business done by evening. I'll pick the flowers personally."

A maid ran frantically down the hall crying, "There's a carriage coming, sir. There's a carriage and a baby!"

Damien sought her eyes questioningly, and Melanie smiled back. "Let us go meet your daughter, my lord. Perhaps Pamela would hold her while we take our vows."

Sir Francis and his army of footmen stood back, gaping,

as Damien helped her to her feet and the couple glided without a hitch through their ranks, looking for all the world like expectant parents as the sound of a crying baby wailed through the previously silent corridors.

As they reached the astonished baronet, the Earl of Reister placed his arm around Melanie's shoulders and held his hand out to her father. "I want to thank you for raising such a beautiful daughter. I hope I can do half so well as you have."

Melanie pinched him for this conceit, and he laughed. He was a scoundrel, no doubt, but there was no reason he couldn't be a charming one.

As if she read his mind, she whispered heatedly, "One more whopper like that, Damien Langland, and I'll make you change your daughter's nappies."

"May I still have kisses for dessert?" he whispered back.

The look she gave him in return made him thankful he had a license in his pocket. He didn't think this groom could wait much longer for his wedding night.

SOMETHING BLUE

~

Edith Layton

It wasn't as if she was eavesdropping. It was her wedding they were talking about, after all.

If it was someone else's wedding it would be eavesdropping, June told herself. And it wasn't as if she was *lurking*, or anything like that. Her hand was on the door when she heard her name and she paused, that was all. She'd just stepped out to visit the Necessary and was returning to rejoin the company. And it was her home—her aunt's house, to be exact, and they were her guests—her aunt's guests, really—since she herself didn't know that many people in London yet. But Aunt had said she should consider it her home, and they had all *said* they were her friends . . .

But no matter how she convinced herself she was right— the old saying was even more so. She heard ill of herself. Worse, she heard ill of him. And that made her ill.

" 'Something old'?" one female voice said merrily. "Why, our June's already got that—her name, of course. Her family's been around since the Conqueror."

"As has his," another put in, with a hint of jealousy in her voice.

" 'Something new' is easy enough too, they've ordered up enough wedding clothes to see her through a decade—

and doubtless, he'll buy her anything she likes for that new home of theirs . . ."

There was a silence as the girls in the drawing room contemplated that. Few brides of their station actually got to move into new homes. They did move into ancestral piles and often shared the family mansion with their husband's parents or his other siblings. But the gentleman in question was a younger son with no entailed properties who had enough money to buy a new estate for his bride. And he'd gone and done it. A huge place, it was said, with many acres.

"As for 'borrowed,' I suppose there's no problem there, anyone will lend a bride anything," another voice finally said peevishly.

"Nor does she have to worry about anything 'blue,' " some one of them snapped spitefully, "for there's her bridegroom, isn't there?"

June's hand flew to her stomach as though she'd been punched and she froze on the other side of the half-opened door.

"Yes! He has had the blue megrims lately, hasn't he? Did you see his face last night at the theater?" another voice said gleefully. "Everyone was talking about it. Nothing could make him smile. Not even the pantomime!"

"*Certainly* not the thought of his coming marriage," one of them added with immense satisfaction.

"He is blue-deviled these days, isn't he? In spite of the fact she's got many a sixpence in her shoe," another girl said with a laugh.

"And there's our rhyme complete: an old name, new clothes, a borrowed trinket, a blue groom, and all the sixpence she needs! She's got it all, what a *lucky* bride," one of the girls said, giggling.

"It might be just the opposite of what you're thinking"— a soft voice chided them—"because she didn't look very merry either. Maybe they'd had a spat, and he was worried she'd change her mind."

Gales of laughter greeted that.

"About marrying *him?*" one of them shrieked. "You said, 'change her mind,' didn't you? Not *'lose'* her mind?"

They dissolved into merriment again.

"Ah, I see your guests are enjoying themselves," Aunt Maida said approvingly as she came down the long hall to the drawing room and heard the chorus of girlish laughter. "Go on, child, join them."

June's white face flushed. The footman she now saw standing near the door could have told her aunt the truth, she realized. But he simply stood, his face immobile, as silent and cold as her own heart felt now. But he knew. They all knew. Except for Aunt, and she wouldn't understand. But then, June didn't either.

Still, she was a Heywood, she told herself, and the Heywoods had faced Romans and Vikings, Normans and Roundheads. A roomful of stylish young women from London would be nothing to them. But none of her ancestors ever had to paste on a false smile and go into a room to sip tea and take little cakes with any invading hordes. June would have been happier with a horse and a lance. She'd definitely rather be holding a pistol now than a fan. The absurd thought helped her. Laughter always did, even if she had no one to share it with . . . and now not even him, it seemed, not anymore. That thought almost routed her.

But she put up her chin, tried to imagine what those cats would look like if she was armed to her teeth, as she wished she was—and entered the room again, smiling through the invisible saber she held in those clenched white teeth.

"My goodness," one of the girls said quickly, seeing her, "what an amusing story, Alice. Now then, June, dear, what were you saying about that delightful place you'll be moving to? Only sixty miles from London? Lucky girl."

"It isn't completed yet," June said, as she took a seat.

"How long will it take?"

"I—I don't know. They're working round the clock, Lawrence says."

"Then wherever shall you live? For the wedding's only two weeks off—Ah . . . I mean 'away,' " the girl named Alice asked with a show of eager interest.

"I don't know," June admitted.

"Ah," Alice said, as the girls all exchanged significant glances.

"But if worse comes to worst, he says we'll just extend our wedding trip—and then if we must, stay in an inn in the village until the house is done," June said quickly.

"But you don't know," Alice persisted.

"No," June said, "I don't." She hated how forlorn she sounded even more than the way the other girls were eyeing each other. She raised her head and looked all the sharp and blunt instruments she wished she had in her possession at them. "But faith!" she said lightly, with a brittle laugh she forced up from somewhere near her toes, "I do know I'll be married in two weeks' time, and to Lawrence at that, and that is enough for me!"

The other girls' secret sparkling looks faded. They fell silent. For indeed, she was going to marry Lawrence, Lord Morrow, and that would be enough for any of them too. They would have him if he was blue—or green or any other color in the rainbow, and she knew it too. It was only that now she didn't know if *she* would.

He didn't look any happier that night—at least not to June's anxious eyes. But it didn't make any difference, she thought. He still caught the eye of every woman at the dinner table. Unhappiness became him, as did every other emotion. Because he was an uncommonly handsome man. No, she thought, he was not. He was simply magnificent.

Dark gold hair. Dark golden eyes that were long and

dark lashed and turned down slightly at the corners. Slight sun wrinkles there when he smiled—which he was not doing now—because that clear skin was lightly tanned from all the riding he did. A strong face with hard high cheekbones and a jutting nose. But that nose was perfectly sculpted, as was his tender mouth. There was softness where a woman wanted to see it: in his lips and eyes. Hardness where a woman wished it to be, in his strong chin and determined gaze.

Add the fact that the noble head was well-matched by the graceful, slender wide-shouldered body, and it was easy to understand why June had doubted she'd be able to so much as speak with him when she'd first seen him. And why she now feared he regretted his mad, rash rush to marriage with her. He looked preoccupied, grim around the mouth, and there was no laughter in his eyes. That wasn't how he'd looked when they'd first met.

It had been at an Assembly. June's first in London.

Meeting an Adonis was the last thing she had expected. It wasn't even a particularly exclusive affair. Aunt Maida might come from good family, but her last daughter had been married off years before and she didn't know anyone in the marriage mart now any more than her rustic niece did. Still, she'd wangled an invitation to the Swanson's assembly—they were always having some kind of "do," she'd told June—with seven daughters on their hands, they had no choice, poor things.

Nor did her aunt know how to launch anyone into Society anymore, June realized. All she'd done was to get her niece dressed to the nines in a fashionable new French gown, have her own maid give a finishing touch to her hair, and hire a carriage to carry them to the affair. And then she'd settled back with a contented sigh to watch things happen.

"There's no need to exert ourselves, for you're pretty as a picture, June, my dear," she had said happily, "just like your mama. They'll come swarming around you, you'll see."

But June knew too well she was nothing like her mama. And even if she were, there had to be more to it than that. Why, even at home someone would take a newcomer around and introduce her to everyone. Not that it mattered, she told herself. She hadn't come to London to snare a husband. She'd been *sent* to London for that purpose, which was a whole other kettle of fish, and not very fresh ones at that.

It was true she came from a small village in a remote district. But there were young men waiting at home if she wanted to get married. They'd been asking since she'd turned eighteen, two years before. But she didn't love any of them any more than she did the idea of marriage.

Her own parents hadn't liked marriage much, they'd parted company soon after she'd been born. Mother blamed her loss of beauty on it. Father only looked uncomfortable when he came to visit, as if even being reminded he was married was painful for him. Because he didn't stop by often, and never stayed long when he did, June never got around to asking his precise opinion of marriage. And she couldn't visit him, after all, not when he was living in sin with his *other* family.

It was true Grandfather never stopped talking about Grandmother and the joys of their union. But Grandfather had been dead since June had been a toddler. And as June's mother often said—rather enviously—it was probably wonderfully easy to love a dead spouse.

So, June had decided long ago, there were definitely worse things than being single—like standing alone and friendless, looking at a parcel of strangers, wondering what on earth to say to whoever these people were that were goggling back at her, for example.

It was a fine high-ceilinged London town house, or at least the parts of it that could be seen in the press of people looked fine. Those parts were primarily the ceilings, because the house was crammed to the doors with well-dressed ladies and gentlemen. An orchestra was playing from somewhere in the next room, which might have been a ballroom. And since some people were moving their mouths without any sounds coming out, June assumed there was food somewhere in the vicinity too.

She decided to find a chair. Aunt Maida hadn't let her sit down next to her, had only shooed her off to join the company. So June turned and searched the crowd, looking for a vacant corner.

And saw him, instead.

In all those people, with all that to-do, still he stood out like a beacon to her, as though there was a light shining on him. In a way, there was. The light from the hundred candles on the chandelier above him bounced off his clean dark-gold hair. He was a jot taller than most of the other men, and his sudden smile was white and bright. That wasn't all. He drew the eye and generated his own glow. He was dressed like any of them, in a tightly fitted fashionable black jacket over snowy linen, but he shone out above them all.

When he happened to glance in her direction, he saw her looking back at him. She could hardly believe her good fortune, even days after, when she hugged her happy thoughts to herself in the night. Because he had promptly smiled. At her. *At her!*

And then, if that weren't astonishing enough, he started to walk toward her, still smiling. She knew it was true because she looked behind herself and didn't see anyone else smiling at him. Just a few gentlemen grinning at her. And why not? How foolish she must look spinning around and staring like that. But when she turned around again, he was even closer, and closing fast.

Well, what could she say to such a man, if she found the courage to speak at all? She wouldn't flee, because she was

a Heywood and Heywoods were better than that. They
could face up to anything, even a dream come true. She
wouldn't coo, or giggle or simper either. She refused to
make a fool of herself. Nor would she flirt. The man was
likely immune to the best flirts by now. Besides, she didn't
know how, and she'd probably start laughing at herself if
she suddenly tried.

But laughter wasn't such a bad idea. She could joke to let
him know she wasn't taking his attention seriously. She
could let him know she knew how ridiculous it was to think
he'd even be interested in her. *Her*—Little Miss June Heywood, a poor echo of the greatest beauty who had ever
graced London town—and who always let her daughter
know it.

June braced herself, because he came right up to her and
looked down at her with a quizzical smile.

"Ah, you waited. Good. This *is* my dance?" he asked.

Which was perfectly absurd and wonderful, and she felt
no awkwardness as she threw her head back and laughed,
full out. His eyes kindled.

"Of course," she answered. "Why look, I haven't moved.
I wouldn't budge a step without you."

Now it was his turn to laugh. No one in that press could
move. They were all crowding in around June and the
golden gentleman, and they all seemed to be listening to
them too.

"I'm Morrow," he said, "but it would be wonderful if you
would call me 'Lawrence'—or something even sweeter."

"Why, what could be sweeter than 'Lawrence'?" she
asked with an excellent mockery of flirtation.

He grinned. "And you, my dear Incognito?"

"Oh, I'm Unknown, but you may call me 'Miss Heywood'—or something louder—it's so noisy in here," she
said and grinned right back at him.

He angled closer, smiling so warmly her pulses leaped
even higher. "You are 'Miss—chief' unless I miss my

guess," he murmured. "Mischief, you are delightful. And very lovely. I couldn't help staring, forgive me. But you shine here, even in this sparkling company. And not only your beautiful eyes. May I have the next dance?"

His offer staggered her, but the compliments gave her balance. Why did men always think compliments were necessary? She was not her mother, after all. She didn't believe the flattery any more than she liked it, but it was the only thing about him that she didn't like. That was good. It gave her a tiny bit of disapproval to weigh against the absolute stark terror of being so impressed by him. It gave her the courage to not take him seriously, and to continue being flippant.

"My dear Morrow," June said without her voice shaking, which pleased her very much, "of course, you may dance with me. That is, if my aunt, Mrs. Captree—the lady in violet who is watching us over there—approves. And by the way, you are very lovely yourself, sir. I admired your neckcloth from halfway across the room. And your jacket is perfection. Not to mention your hair."

His smile widened. "Ah. I see. You won't let me flatter you?"

She smiled just as widely. "You may, of course, if you like. It's delightful. I just thought you might like to hear what it sounds like too. Why should it always be the ladies who hear such enchanting things?"

"That does it," he said, offering her his arm, "I won't say another word. It's time for action. I will win over the lady in violet, and take you in to dance, Mischief . . . 'Mischief Heywood?'—unusual name," he mused as he led her back to her aunt.

But the feel of his hard arm under her hand robbed her of speech, and she heard him laugh as her aunt exclaimed, "Oh, no, my lord, her name is 'June.' "

"June?" he said, light dancing in his golden eyes. "Oh. I see." Then: "May we dance, June?"

She found it impossible to look away, impossible to keep looking into his warm and tender eyes. But she knew what to say, had said it before.

"Certainly, if they play a March."

He roared with laughter. "Not fair," he protested, still laughing, "you've had a lifetime to practice that one. Come, give me a chance, will you?"

She would give him anything he liked, any girl would, and she suspected he knew it. So she had to make sure he didn't think she took him that seriously. "Gladly, but I'm not sure we get more than one lifetime, sir."

"One would be more than a man could ask—with you, I think," he said seriously, gazing down at her as intensely as she was staring up at him. Then he seemed to remember himself. He smiled. "Early days for such talk with the girl of the month, I agree. You're absolutely right to glower at me. Come, they've struck up a waltz."

She took his arm, and he led her into the dance, and didn't let her out of his sight for the rest of the evening. Oh, he had to let her go, to other partners, eventually. She was swamped with them, because he had made her popular, she thought smugly. But every time she danced by him, she saw him looking back at her. And everytime she danced past her, she saw him watching her. He took her in to dinner and they talked a lot of nonsense. She didn't remember much except that she tried to make him laugh and did, and he made her laugh back at him.

And she thought of him so much when she got home that it was like he was still with her.

It was only when she was undressing for bed, as the sun was struggling up over the rooftops of town, that she came back down to earth again. She caught sight of herself in the mirror in the dawn's rising light. She saw a slight girl with shadowy hair, for her hair didn't take on life until light really touched it, being merely brown and needing the sun to show up glints of red. The face in the looking glass was in shadows too—which was for the best, she thought. She sighed. She was not her mama, the famous beauty.

No, because the daughter had a heart-shaped face, not a perfect oval. Her eyes were the exact color of the mists of dawn, or dusk: gray as a pair of field mice, not Mama's famous blue orbs that all London's gallants had written such bad verse about. She had a small nose, not Mama's noble one. Nor did she have Mama's famous deep bosom and swanlike neck. She took inventory of her own slender body and noted glumly: breasts—two, and in the right places, at least. A waist, a definite waist—there was that. A small rear, a flat tum, and legs: two, and in the right places too. Adequate. But not much there to entice such a fellow as Lawrence, Lord Morrow.

But the laughter! June thought as she sat in bed. Now that was something. She could always make people laugh. First Mama—because Mama was so often sad and self-involved that it was the only way to distract her. And then, everyone else she knew as well. Because as a shadow of her mama, she had learned to watch and listen, and doing so, had found life absurd.

But it seemed he did too. Was it because he so often received the same transparent flattery that Mama did? And for as little reason? Mama doted on it, it was the absence of it that made her blue. But a sensible man might find it ridiculous to be praised for something as fleeting as beauty, June thought. No matter. She'd bet no one else made him laugh like she had tonight. He'd even said so. He might have even meant it.

She had used her sense of humor to prevent herself from gaping like an idiot and stammering like a fool in his presence. She had used it to give herself courage, as she always did. But if it drew him further into her orbit, if he sought her out again at parties . . . she would treasure every minute of it. And if she brought nothing back from the great city but the remembrance of his laughter, it would be enough.

Thinking that, she cuddled down into her covers and slept at last, with the sun—warm as his bright smile—shining directly on her own smiling face.

He called on her the very next day. And the one after that, and that. Before she knew it, he was part of her every day as well as her dreams each night. Because even with all her sense of the absurd and in spite of all the laughter—or perhaps because he shared it—she couldn't help tumbling deeply and irrevocably into love with him.

How could she prevent it? He was as clever as he was handsome. He smelled of sandalwood and clean linen. He was six years older then herself, a younger son from a good family in the West country. He was educated and well traveled, having been at University and on the grand tour. He'd been in the army with Wellington and served with distinction, but sold out when the war was over. He traveled with the Corinthian set when he was in London because he loved to ride and spar and drive his carriages. He liked to read and sing, and loved the theater. He liked London, but longed for the countryside. He was a sportsman and a scholar and a brave man too.

There was nothing he was not, to her. Except honest, perhaps—a little, she thought. Because he often flattered her. She said he must not. He asked how he could help it when she was so lovely? And nothing she could say convinced him she was not.

"My mama was the beauty," she insisted.

"You have no eyes," he said.

"I most certainly do," she joked, "it's just hard to notice them. They're gray as squirrels, not the 'limpid pools of azure' my mama has."

"Ugh," he said, "bad poetry and a terrible image too. Who needs all that running blue? Your eyes are opals, pearls in a mist."

"Rodent gray," she said with a straight face, and suddenly grew serious. "Why do you feel you must offer me false coin?"

"Yes, coins—good image, that. Silvery Spanish coins, that's very apt. That too. They're gray as smoke, silver as the dawn."

"Oh, Lawrence," she said, half-laughing, half-appalled at such nonsense.

"And a man can see your soul come and go in them," he said.

She'd stopped laughing then, unable to look away from the sincerity in his own intent eyes.

"And they are set in a face like a flower," he whispered, tracing the outline of her face with his fingertips, lightly, with wonder. "Infinitely charming, always changing, lit with laughter and sometimes, too often, inexplicably, so sad—like now."

"I wish you would not," she said. "I really don't like compliments."

"They're not false," he said, frowning.

"Maybe not—but I don't trust them," she said miserably, hanging her head.

"Do you trust this then?" he whispered, tilting her chin up with one hand. He cupped her face in both of his hands and brought his lips down gently, lightly to hers. And then much less gently, but no less carefully. Then, far longer, less carefully, and more breathtakingly.

That was the night he'd asked for her hand in marriage.

She'd been too dazed to scoff, too moved to protect herself with laughter, too overwhelmed to speak at all. His lips were persuasive even without words, and with the solid warmth of him in her arms she could only breathe in the scent of him and sigh, "Yes." Though she wanted to add, ". . . yes, of course, oh, *please*."

If it was true that he could see her soul in her eyes, he must have seen all the other things she wanted to say midst the delight and wonder, fear and confusion he could read there. Because he didn't speak at once. He only nodded.

After a moment he said, "Yes. We must marry, and soon. Because I've never met a girl like you before and know there's no other one for me."

They set the day, and waited for the date. Three months had passed since that night.

And now their wait was almost over. He should have been joyous as she was. But tonight, watching him as he sat tight-lipped and silent beside her, June saw for once cruel gossip had been kinder than truth. Because he wasn't merely blue, as they'd said. He seemed under a black cloud of sorrow. With their wedding day less than two weeks away, she looked at him and saw nothing but misery in his face.

Well, she wouldn't have it. Even if it meant she wouldn't have him. She'd never really believed she could, anyhow. Not really, not in her heart of hearts. He'd always been too good to be true.

She waited until the evening was over, when they were left to their five minutes alone together—the privilege of an engaged couple. They usually stretched those five minutes to twenty—twenty increasingly exciting, frustrating, and memorable moments. As soon as they were alone he usually stretched out his arms and she came tumbling into them, and they kissed and touched and held each other until they drove each other to the brink of distraction. Then he'd remember their time was up. And each night, she regretted it more.

But lately he'd seemed distracted, even in her arms. And tonight he sat beside her but apart from her, lost in his thoughts.

"What is it?" she asked softly. "And don't say 'nothing,' and don't be polite or even kind," she added when he looked up. She went on quickly, while she still had courage: "Something is eating away at your heart and I must know what it is. Don't worry about my feelings, for it will be far, far worse for me if you don't tell me now."

He frowned. "What are you talking about?"

"Something's worrying you, I think I know what it is. You mustn't worry about how I'll take it. I'll understand," she said, sitting up very straight, keeping her voice even. But she couldn't help the fact that all the color left her face, for her blood seemed to have turned to frost.

"Understand what?" he asked in fascination.

"That you"—she swallowed and then blurted, looking everywhere but at him—"have had second thoughts about our wedding. Which I understand I assure you, there's no reason anyone should be trapped for life with someone just because of one moment of madness and—"

But she couldn't say more because he reached out and pulled her into his arms.

"One moment of madness? Are *you* mad?" he asked in amazement. "Why, love, we haven't had our moments of madness yet."

Before she could answer, he kissed her, very thoroughly. His mouth was warm and ardent. The touch of his tongue and the caress of searching hands was as reassuring as it was thrilling. She shivered with desire and forgot all her fears in the tumult of her emotions—for the moment.

Because when he drew back he didn't settle her even deeper in his arms and deepen their embrace the way he usually did. Instead, he drew a shaky breath, released her, and sat back. "Now, then," he said, with an edge to his voice, "what was that all about? Bride nerves? Or have you changed your mind?"

The absurdity of what he said helped her shake off the fuzzy, restless feeling his kisses left her with.

"What?" she said. "Me? Of course not! But you look so sad lately, everyone's noticed. More miserable every day in fact. As every day draws us nearer to being married, I thought—"

"I am an idiot!" he muttered. "No, no—it's not you, how could it be? It's just—well, the truth is that I've got word there's a problem in my family, an illness. It's nothing dire, but it might upset some travel plans. I get daily bulletins from home, but we live so far from London they're a day late. The thing is there may be a problem with them all being able to come to the wedding. Don't bother yourself about it, I'll know more tomorrow."

He rose and paced a few steps. When he swung back to her he was frowning again.

"But—are *you* having second thoughts?" he asked. "Because truthfully, I've seen you looking merrier than you've been lately."

"It's only that I've been worried about you!"

"Don't be," he said abruptly.

"Oh. Certainly. I'm supposed to watch you fret yourself to pieces and make jests then? Would you like that?" she cried, stung at the unfairness of his request.

He stared at her furious face. "Blast," he murmured, "are we fighting? And if we are, then over what: which of us is the more worried about the other's happiness? What nonsense! Come over here, little fussbudget, and let's see if we can remedy things," he commanded, holding out his arms to her.

She did, and they stood there together, holding each other tightly, not saying anything. But not kissing either, she thought later as she walked him to the door and said good night.

He must have thought about that too, because after he'd shrugged into his greatcoat, he waited until the footman shrank back into the shadows and then turned suddenly and gazed at June. Without a word, he pulled her into his arms and kissed her almost desperately, his mouth opened hard against hers, his tongue questing, as though he was looking for a way to enter her soul. She responded with shock and then equal urgency, opening her lips to him as though she wished she could drink him in and keep him there.

Then he'd looked at her for a long moment, and left.

She went to bed, and lay there with her eyes open for a very long time. His kiss still burned on her lips, and troubled her heart. Because he hadn't looked much happier when he'd left than when he'd arrived. And that wasn't very happy at all.

Lawrence walked home. It was a long way, and very late, but he didn't notice the time or the place. He didn't worry about footpads, he worried about a slip of a girl, because he didn't have an idea as to what to do about her now.

He had bachelor quarters, a whole three floors of them in his rented house, and it seemed to him that the halls echoed in their emptiness when his footman closed the door after letting him in. He was wrong—as he was with everything these days, he thought wearily.

"Someone to see you, sir," his butler said. "I took the liberty of allowing him to wait in the salon."

But he smiled as he said it, so Lawrence knew he hadn't taken any liberties—his guest had taken them all. He hurried to meet him.

"Brother!" he called as he threw open the door to the salon before he even got a good look at his guest, because the odds were in his favor. He had four excellent chances of being right.

"Laurie!" his brother Heath said laughing, rising from his chair and enveloping him in a bearlike clasp. Then the brothers stepped back, clapped each other on the shoulders, and grinned at each other. They stood boot toe to toe; they were almost the same height and their white-toothed smiles were replicas of each other. Yet although they were similar, they didn't look alike. Heath was the older by five years, the heavier by several pounds, his closely cropped curly hair was the color of bright sunlight, and his eyes brilliantly blue.

"You're here!" Lawrence said with pleasure, but then his smile slipped. He paled. "Nothing's gone wrong, has it?" he asked.

"No—no, nothing's changed at all," his brother assured him. "Except I'm here—and at the height of sowing season at that. I shudder to think what a botch they'll make on the south acreage—but bother the crops. What the devil do you mean by all those messages, lad? They drew straws and so you drew me in answer to your demand for someone from the family. I'm not complaining, mind. I want to know what's going on with you, for my ownself."

"Sit down—a cordial: brandy, whiskey?" Lawrence asked, waving his brother to a chair. He turned and saw crystal decanters set up on a nearby tabletop. "Oh—I see you've already answered that for yourself. I'll join you."

He poured himself a healthy jot of amber spirits, noting his brother's eyes measuring the amount in the glass, and then sprawled down in a chair opposite him. "To us, to health, and confusion to our enemies," Lawrence said raising his glass, "and don't look at me like that, my problem's not drink."

"Never was," his brother agreed, "so—what is?"

Lawrence drank, wincing at the burning taste. He leaned forward, cradled the snifter between his spread knees, and hung his head over it. "I've fought in a war, I've been in society, I've found my way around ballrooms *and* battlefields in my past—"

"Not to mention bedrooms," his brother muttered into his own glass as he took a swallow of his drink.

"Yes—that too—but what am I supposed to do now? It's a damnable situation. I feel stupid as a day-old chick in this, Heath. I keep messengers wearing out horses between here and home. There—you heard it? I live here in London—but that's still home to me."

"Always shall be," his brother said, "wherever you end up. That's how it is. Salmon swim back to where they were spawned, a man knows his home ground too."

"I'd better be able to learn more than a fish can," Lawrence said ruefully. "My new house is being built, even as we speak. And I've promised to make it my new home—and home to my children."

"Ah!" his brother said, his light brows going up. "Well, I am surprised! You seemed so happy. So were we, although we never met the girl, of course, but we heard nothing bad about her. More than we could say about the father, of course. But it's a good family, even though the old man played fast and loose with the name, not to mention the female he got his hands on. He has her and a parcel of bastards tucked away up north, they say. At least he's discreet about it. His lady wife was a great beauty in her day too. No accounting for some men's tastes. But if you've changed your mind, there's a problem."

"No," Lawrence said, "I haven't changed my mind. I could't."

"Ah—so that's how it is—trapped are you? Sprained her ankle, did she? Well, fatherhood's not bad."

Lawrence's expression grew cold, his fists clenched as he half rose from his chair. Seeing his brother's look of alarm, he sat back. He gave a bitter laugh. "Fatherhood's not bad, but death is—I'd kill any other man for saying that, and not only because it's not true. But how could you know? You've never met her, or you'd never even think such a thing. Lucky thing for me that you never did meet her, at that—you'd steal her from me."

Heath shook his curly head. "No, I wouldn't have a chance with her after she saw you. Aside from the looks—you're the one with the wits. But you'll never believe it so I'll save my breath to cool my porridge. Well. So then, if there's no problem, what's the problem?"

"The wedding's only days away," Lawrence said quickly. "How can I leave her now?"

"Then don't."

Lawrence raised his head. His handsome face was set in lines of grim despair. "You know the situation. Tell me, do you think it will change for the better in the next week?"

His brother shifted in his chair. Then he spoke, but his voice was sorrowful. "Wish I could say so, but I can't."

"Then," Lawrence said sadly. "I must go, and now."

"She said you wasn't to do it," Heath said quickly.

"What did you expect her to say? No, I must. But what can I tell June? I don't know when I can return."

"Take her along then, lad."

"Yes, that would be wonderful for her reputation, wouldn't it? No, I have to leave her here—but I worry that if I'm gone too long I'll lose her."

Heath chuckled. "Not likely, lad. But then, why not marry her double-quick and take her with you?"

"What?" his brother said in amazement. "Did you ride here so fast you left your head behind? Even if I could marry her before I left—what about that little matter of the wedding guests, the chapel, and all the festivities they've planned? But that's all nothing to what would await me at home. Think about it: *She* knows all the plans too, doesn't she? What do you think *she* would say if I suddenly waltzed home with June and said 'behold, this is my bride'?"

There was a long silence as his brother gazed into his glass as though he were looking for an answer there. When he raised his eyes, he raised his shoulders in a shrug.

"She'd die, lad," he finally said in a deep voice. "I really think she would. She'd give it up if she thought you'd given up on her."

"Yes," Lawrence said softly, "that's what I think too. There you are. Oh, God, brother, what am I going to do? I'm trapped between two women, and God help me but I love them both. And yet whatever I do, one of them is bound to be hurt by me. And whichever way I turn, it makes no difference—I think I'm bound to lose one of them."

"Nonsense, lad, she adores you! Always has, we weren't supposed to know, but we all did. As to losing her—well, that's not in your hands, lad, nor in hers, anymore. But as for the other? Are you the one who's run mad? You—losing any female's interest if you didn't want to? I was jesting before, thought you'd got that bug out of your head long since."

Heath began to laugh heartily, but seeing his brother's expression, his own face fell into a frown. "So then," he said heavily, "what will you do, lad?"

"Do? Nothing immediately. Nothing yet. Nothing until I have to. I'm going to wait a day—I have that long, at least—I think?" He looked questioningly at his brother.

"Yes, certainly," Heath said, "at the least. But not much more—I can't even stay to see your London lady. I must go soon as the light returns. I'll send word, if not return myself. But you have another day—*that*—I think I can promise you."

"Then I'll wait. I'm going to wait on it as long as I can. And hope the fates settle it for me by then."

"Aye, there's a good plan," his brother said eagerly.

"No. It's not a plan—it's a prayer," Lawrence said.

All his brother could do was nod, and sigh his agreement.

"It's a *monstrous* fine affair," the red-headed girl remarked to her friend as the two stood fanning themselves at the sidelines of the ball, "such food! M'father says the wine is excellent too. And the musicians! One can actually dance to them; as for the dancing—for once the ballroom floor is big enough to move upon. Such a clever idea to hire a public hall for a ball. I mean, a home is charming, but this place is grand!"

"Trust the Merrymans to do it right. Everyone is having a grand time!" her friend said enthusiastically.

"Except for the Duke of Austell, of course," the redhead commented. "Do you see his face? Because that Turner woman is here too, eyeing him."

"Remembering him, more like," her friend said slyly.

"Yes," the redhead answered gaily, "and so her husband knows! That's probably why he's looking at him with murder in his eyes!"

"Yes." Her friend giggled. "He's staring at almost every other gentleman here too—and for the same good reasons."

"And look—there's poor little Kitty Kenyon—no partner for the last three dances, she doesn't look too merry, either."

"Well, of course not. With her lack of fortune *and* inches—she'll be lucky to get a footman to ask her to dance."

The girls tittered, but June frowned. There was such a crowd and this was such an enormous place that when she'd left the Ladies' Necessary she had to walk around the fringes of the throng looking for a way back to Lawrence. He was somewhere in the middle of it, waiting for her. She paused, trying to figure out the best way to get to him, and heard the two girls. They were close by, but behind a huge marble urn filled with flowers. She hesitated, wanting to avoid them; she thought they were cattish and trivial, and they'd gossiped about her before. But until she found a way to move on without them seeing her, she was forced to listen to their inane chatter once more.

She wasn't eavesdropping this time, she was only trying to find a way away from them, But she heard ill of herself again anyway.

"Speaking of people who are *suffering*," the redhead

purred, "have you seen Morrow tonight? Blue as can be, poor fellow—as usual for him these days."

"Not as blue as *she* is though! She looks like she lost her best friend—or maybe she's worried about losing her groom? What I wouldn't give to know what was eating at them!" the other girl said greedily. "Due to be wed in a few weeks' time—but some lovebirds they are! Blue as a pair of crabs, the two of them."

June shivered with rage. Her face grew hot, her hands grew cold. Well, she thought fiercely, she'd step out of the shadows right now! She'd confront them—and say:

"I heard that! It's much better to seem *blue—than to be redder than a baboon's bottom—like your faces now!"*

No, she thought furiously, no—better to say:

"Blue is *he? Well, it's better than being green with jealousy, like some people here, methinks!"* —and then snap her fingers right in their astonished faces.

No, that was lowering herself to their level. Maybe she should saunter out, wearing a half smile as though it was all *so* amusing, and say:

"Blue? Heavens! Maybe you need spectacles, my dears, because no one is blue—except you . . ."

. . . Except they were right, she thought miserably.

So she slipped back the way she came, and circled halfway around the room before she looked for Lawrence again. By then she was on the other side of the room from the gossiping girls and had her shame and indignation under control. But not her wild sorrow. And not her temper.

"I must speak with you," she told him as soon as they stepped into the waltz together.

Lawrence tilted his head to the side. "Yes? So—please do," he said, smiling.

"Not here," she hissed through clenched teeth.

He usually enjoyed dancing with her, and had looked forward to it tonight. There were precious few times when he could actually hold her in his arms. At night, when all

the household left them together, of course. But those
nights were becoming less of a pleasure; they were almost
physically painful lately because of the frustration he felt
on leaving her. Here, he could hold her warm supple body
in his arms in front of all the world, and move with her in a
poor simulation of how he most wished to move with her.
There was frustration too, but it was bittersweet, because
here at least, he knew his limits.

But suddenly it was no joy to dance with her. Tonight,
her body was rigid, she moved woodenly and gripped his
hand hard as she spoke. He felt like he was dancing with a
powder keg.

"Then later, I promise you," he said, gazing down into
her eyes—which blazed with rage, he thought uneasily.

Afterward neither of them knew how they managed to
get through the long night. A successful party ended near
dawn. And this was a very successful party.

He wanted to take her home and find out what was troubling her immediately. But he knew if they left early it
would cause talk. Amused talk. He knew men, and knew
that even gentlemen would jest about how the engaged couple couldn't wait to be alone together, and amuse themselves by speculating about it. In the ordinary way of
things, it would be nothing. But given his fears, and the
way things were going, he wouldn't do anything to jeopar-
dize her reputation further. Instead he suffered her long,
angry silences and spent most of the night restraining himself from either kissing or shaking her out of them.

She wanted to leave early, but every time she glanced at
her aunt she saw what a good time that lady was having.
And they couldn't leave without her. Of course, Aunt
Maida would go, if her niece insisted—but June didn't
know how to explain why she wanted to leave. So she
danced and ate and drank, without really knowing what she
was doing, all the while rehearsing what she was going to
say when she could say something personal to him.

When she could, it was like steam escaping from a boiling pot.

She wheeled around and spat it at him the second they were finally alone together, in her aunt's salon.

"Everyone! Everyone sees how unhappy you are," she cried. "That's all they're talking about. There's no hiding it anymore. So don't tell me it's nothing and it will pass—or anything like that. What is it? Why are you so blue? And don't tell me this time that . . . that: 'It's nothing dire' and that it won't upset our wedding plans. Because I won't believe you!"

His face was drawn, his eyes filled with sorrow.

"I won't," he said softly, "because it isn't."

She stopped and held her breath, and tried not to cry. Suddenly she didn't want him to say another word. It was bad enough suspecting something awful. She didn't want to hear it. She choked back a sob and waved her hands distractedly, as though that could stop what he was going to say.

He didn't see it. "I have to leave London," he said, looking down at his boot tops, slapping his gloves against the blameless edge of a table in his frustration. "I'll know better tomorrow, but it looks like I must go, after all. And probably immediately, at that. I can't say when I'll be back. I wish I could, but I can't."

He heard her gasp and glanced up, and saw her stagger. Her face was chalky white and her eyes glittered with tears. He strode to her and caught her up and held her close, although she tried to push him away.

"No, no," he said appalled at her wild misery, "what is this? Shout at me for upsetting your plans, be angry—but this? Don't cry, June, please."

"Why?" she asked, tears falling from her stormy gray eyes.

He had sisters; even when he'd been little and they'd teased him and richly deserved punishment for it, he couldn't tell on them because he hated to see a female weep. This was worse. This was June crying.

"Hush," he said, holding her close, feeling her body trembling, hardly knowing what he was saying, "don't cry. There's nothing tears can do but make it worse and Lord knows it's bad enough as it is. I must go, and there's an end to it."

She dragged in a harsh breath, and held it hard, so she could speak. "What did I do?" she finally asked in a ragged whisper. "Just tell me, I must know."

"You?" he asked in astonishment, his head going back as though she'd slapped him. He stared at her. *"You?* Good God! You've done nothing. It's my grandmother. She's sick, and failing. I have to go home and see her, I've put it off and I don't think I can anymore. It breaks my heart. I didn't say anything before because I think I thought if I didn't, it wouldn't be as true. But I can't deny it anymore. And it's not good news, in any way. Home is two days' hard ride from here. With the best of luck, that's cutting it close: two days there—two back—and the time spent at her bedside in between. I may not be able to make the wedding on time."

He shook his head, his eyes distant and filled with sorrow. "And if she—if things don't work out, I'll have to stay to see it all through. We're a close-knit family, they wouldn't leave then either. So the wedding would be ruined in any event, should worse come to . . . But even if she rallies I might have to miss the wedding, given the time it takes to get there and back—given that I might have to wait it out . . ."

June grew very still. She stared up at him, memorizing his handsome face; even in his arms, she felt the distance between them lengthening. She'd never really believed he would be hers. Whatever had caused him to offer for her— he'd obviously realized his mistake. She'd been expecting this for a very long while.

Hadn't Mama been reluctant to take her to London in the first place for fear of tarnishing her great reputation as a beauty by presenting such a little dab of a daughter? She'd put off bringing her daughter to London until she was almost on the shelf and everyone said there was no choice in the matter anymore. Hadn't she been ecstatic when her sister offered to do the job? And hadn't Mama's reply to the announcement of her daughter's engagement been shocked surprise that she'd landed such a fellow?" *Little June,"* she'd written, *"and the catch of the Season?"*

So it was over. So, it probably had never really been at all.

But some tiny voice in June clamored to be heard. Some pride, some speck of self-esteem she'd hoarded up that her mama had never found and crushed, was there for her now. She dashed away her tears, stepped out of the comfort of Lawrence's arms, and confronted him. He *had* asked for her hand—if only because of a whim, or the way she'd looked in a certain play of light, perhaps—but he had, after all.

He was probably trying to spare her feelings. Her inclination was to hear him out, and then run away and hide and cry all her fears into her pillow. It was what she did whenever her mama rejected her, and what she did each time her father left her home. But that would leave her empty, and worse, unaware. She deserved a real answer from him.

"But I remember," she said carefully, "you told me your grandmother was strong as an oak: she gardens and rides every day, you said, didn't you?"

"So she does—did," he said, "but she caught a fever, anyone can. It's turned to a pneumonia, or so they fear. If so, then the next seven days will tell the tale. That's what my brother said yesterday. That means six days—as of today—five as of tomorrow—you see I can't put it off any longer."

"Your brother was here?" she gasped. "Why didn't you bring him to meet me?"

"He'd have liked that, but he came at night—had only just time to sleep and then left at dawn to get back home again. I wanted to go with him, but decided to wait until tomorrow to hear what happens next. But if things don't change for the better, I won't be able to wait any longer."

Her eyes grew wild. She threw her pride out the window. Because if she was going to weep about losing him, weeping over lost pride wouldn't make it much worse.

"I'll go with you," she blurted.

"Love," he said tenderly, "it won't do. What about your reputation? You can't just run away with me. What will your aunt say? Your family? All the invited guests? You see?"

"But if your grandmother is so ill—we can marry there!" she said in a burst of invention.

He hesitated, and then said heavily, "I've thought of it. Don't think I haven't. But you don't know her. If I appear with you in tow, she'll know how sick she is. She'll think the game is up with her. What would you think if you were old and had an invitation to your grandson's wedding and you fell sick. And then he suddenly turned up with his bride at your bedside, with a minister hovering in the background? You'd wonder which service he was really there to read, wedding or funeral, wouldn't you? No, I've seen it happen on the battlefield: if a fellow thinks he has no chance—he has none. How can I do that to her?"

He paced a turn around the room as she watched in dumb misery. "June," he finally said, "the question is: should we cancel the wedding date outright, or hold off and wait on events? I mean, it will be hard rescheduling the ceremony . . . and Lord! Your aunt's anteroom is already filling up with gifts." He ran a hand through his hair, disarranging the dark gold mass of it.

"Gifts can always be returned," June said absently.

She hardly heard him. His grandmother ill? Unto death? She had only his say-so for that. She hadn't even seen his brother—or any of his family—there'd always been something to prevent it, now she thought of it. He loved them, he said, and so would she, but he never gave her a chance to see if she would. His family was so numerous there was no room for newlyweds to live comfortably at his family home, he said. He'd bought a new house because he'd wanted her to himself, to build a new life for them together. Or so he'd said. She'd been flattered, but now she wondered why he'd felt he had to live apart from them, even then.

Clearly, she couldn't rely on what he said anymore. She had to go by what she knew. His attentions had flattered her, his kisses had muddled her, his face still bemused her. But she had to deal with the facts now, and the fact was that he didn't want to marry her now.

Not in the West country, or in London.

That was all she knew for certain, and she had to deal with that. That—and what she knew of herself. She was not an heiress or a beauty. But she had good sense and courage, no one could take that from her. Not even him. Everyone was talking about how unhappy he was. There would be no more grist for the gossip mill, she decided, straightening her shoulders.

She wouldn't make a fool of herself, it was bad enough that it looked as though he would.

"No," she said, "I think we should just call it off. Now."

"Reschedule then?" he asked, absently.

"Call off," she said.

"Postpone?" he said, thinking about that word and not liking the sound of it either. "No, we're in for a penny, in for a pound. Let it stay. If it comes to that—if we have to reschedule I'll give you a day's notice so no one will show up at the church expecting a wedding. At least, that. But give me time."

Give him time to get far away so that when the ax fell, his neck would be nowhere near it—is what June heard. But what could she say? One more word and she'd bawl like a baby.

"Maybe time will be on our side," he mused.

She could only swallow and nod. And offer her cheek instead of her lips when she showed him to the door. But he was too preoccupied to notice. She closed the door behind him, but was too distraught to hold back the tears until she got to her room. Which gave the servants something to talk about as they tidied up the house that morning. And gave her aunt something to think about when her maid came in with her chocolate, and the news, when she awoke.

The gown was heavy silk, as white and smooth to the touch as the thick pearly nacre that clung to the inside of an oyster shell. But it was soft and lustrous and made to grace a young girl's slender form. Two breathless maids carefully lowered the long gown over June's head, and it flowed down over her lithe body, caressing every one of her elegant curves. She turned this way and that to catch sight of herself in a long looking glass.

The rich creamy silk of her gown whispered as she moved, murmuring like the sighs in a contented lover's throat. It was altogether a sumptuous gown; it glowed like a pearl, except where old lace the color of a dove's breast graced its sleeves and flowed from the train of it. And so it was odd that the young woman wearing it also wore the expression of someone in funeral black.

"Gardenias, I think," Aunt Maida said decisively as she considered her niece, "nothing less to honor that gown."

"Fine," June said, and dashed away a tear.

"We shall talk, I think," her aunt said. She cast a significant look at the maids, and said, "Girls? If you please."

They scurried from the room, leaving June alone with her aunt.

Aunt Maida gazed at her niece reflectively for a moment before she spoke. She was June's mother's older sister, and as unlike her as two sisters could be. June's mama was tall and elegant and though she now had lines in her face and her hair had turned white, she still had a trim figure and moved with languorous catlike grace. Aunt Maida was small and round and looked very like a plump brindle tabby cat, and moved about as seldom as a drowsy old tabby would, at that.

June's mama was neither a widow nor a single woman, and had little use for men, except for their compliments. Aunt Maida was a widow and numbered many elderly gentlemen among her friends. June had always liked her aunt; she was as comfortable to speak with as she was to look at. But she'd seldom seen her while she was growing up. London was a long way from home, and Aunt Maida said she never liked to travel far from her doorstep. June had hoped to get to know her better in London, but they hadn't had much time together. June's social life had occupied her at first, and Lawrence had taken up her every moment since then.

"You wept this morning, you weep now. Come, my dear," Aunt Maida finally said in her calm, soothing voice, "if you've changed your mind about the match, tell me now. I thought he was an excellent catch but you may know something about him I don't. So if you want to cry off, there'll be a breath of scandal, to be sure, but it will be forgotten by next season. In fact, I'm not sure it mightn't make you all the more desirable then—not that you couldn't attach any young man you wanted this year, of course."

June gaped at her.

"Don't look so astonished. Young Audley wanted you, as did old Hightower—as if I'd let that old rogue within a yard of you—and Lord Putnam was enamored of you, as were Brightcastle and Wallace and—"

"Are you mad?" June asked, and then clapped a hand over her mouth and stared at her aunt wide-eyed. Because the words had just slipped out and she didn't want to hurt her aunt. Especially if she *had* run mad—as she strongly suspected.

"No, of course not. I have eyes, don't I?" Aunt Maida said, smiling slightly, for nothing ever seemed to upset her very much. "And ears," she added, "and all those gentlemen requested an audience with your papa, you know. But he's so far from town it was next to impossible to get word to him—not that it was necessary. In town a week—and you met Morrow. Three weeks after, you were promised to him. Most irregular, but so romantic, but as I—"

"They did?" June squeaked, interrupting her. "Brightcastle *and* Putnam? But—but why? Has father dowered me *that* well?"

Her aunt gave a warm chuckle. "You're no heiress, my dear, if that's what you're thinking. But then, none of those gentlemen, except Hightower, of course, are in need of one. Thank goodness for that. For though your papa is well off, there *is* the fact that he has that other family to feed."

June's cheeks grew rosy. No one ever mentioned her father's other family so casually to her, not even her mother. But everyone talked about them, of course.

"Then why in the world do you think I had so many suitors?" June wondered.

"Well, aside from your charm and ready wit, just look into that mirror and answer yourself, my dear." Aunt Maida chuckled.

June frowned at her image. The gown fit her just right, giving her a charming figure. There was that. She looked very well in it, she decided, but then who wouldn't in such a gown? She shook her head.

"I wish you would tell me straight out, Aunt," June said, "because if you're trying to tell me it's my looks, I thank you, but it can't be. Mama was the beauty, not me."

"Indeed?" her aunt said. "Your parents' match was the most talked about, that's true. Your father was the most handsome gentleman of the Season, just as your mama was its acclaimed beauty. You have the best of both of them. For you've your father's eyes—so speaking, my dear! As well as many of his features; indeed, you're the most lovely creature. I was so pleased to see how you'd turned out, for it meant less work for me. All I had to do was bring you to your first assembly. As I suspected, I didn't even have to take you round to introduce you. They all flocked to you, you see.

"But best of all, apart from that, you've more than your father's beautiful eyes. You've got his tender heart. Which is very good. For your mama, of course, has none."

June spun around and stared at her aunt.

"I knew your father well, my dear," Aunt Maida said carefully, "and though I know he has behaved very badly—it cannot be easy for his children, or for his . . . ah . . . companion—in many ways I do believe he is more sinned against than sinning. Because I know your mama quite well too. How could I not? She is my sister. And so I know that when they met, she was already very much in love, and there was no room in her heart for anyone else."

"Oh," June breathed, "poor Mama, I never knew!"

"Of course you did, my dear. For it was her own image in the mirror that she doted on—and still does," Aunt Maida said calmly. "And so it must still be. Why else would such an exquisite creature as yourself refuse to believe in her own beauty? At first, I thought it merely modest and charming in you. Now I see it's ignorance, and like all ignorance, crippling to you. Beauty is not everything, indeed, just look at the story of your mama's life to see that for yourself. Indeed, I think *not* believing in your own beauty may have made you as clever and interesting as you are. But the fact remains: you are far more than you think you are, my dear.

"Now then, that said—I repeat: if you don't want Lawrence, say so now. I'll help you through the awkwardness of it, and get you right back into Society."

"Oh! But I do want him!" June cried, forgetting the shocking things her aunt had said. "It's that—oh, Aunt, I think he doesn't want me!"

"Now I think it's you who has run mad," Aunt Maida said in astonishment. "Why in the world would you say such a thing? Have you never looked in his eyes? My dear, he scorches everything in his path when he gazes at you. Lord North complained that he got his collar singed the other day simply by happening to walk between the two of you at the Merryman's ball."

"Oh, Aunt," June wailed, sinking to her knees in front of her aunt, "you don't know the half of it!"

"Then I think you'd better tell me the whole of it," her aunt said gently.

Crouched there at her aunt's feet, June told her all: about the gossip, the awful jokes about her "blue" bridegroom, Lawrence's story about his grandmother, and finally—his fear that they'd have to postpone the wedding. She also told her how she knew he really wanted to cancel the wedding altogether. When she was done, she rocked back on her heels, wiped her eyes with the heel of her hand, and waited for her aunt to speak.

"My dear niece," Aunt Maida said after a moment, touching the side of June's cheek, "there's nothing you can do about japes from the envious. I advise you to discount gossip—it is seldom correct, and always cruel. But as for Lawrence . . . He says his grandmother is sick. He says he can't marry you at his home because he doesn't want to frighten her by doing so when she is ill. He says he can't ask you to go with him otherwise. Nor can he swear to get back on time. But you don't believe him. You believe gossip instead."

The older woman heaved a sigh. "Tell me, you did offer to break off with him?"

June nodded.

"And he refused?"

June nodded again.

"Ah. And do you *truly* love him?"

June gazed at her aunt, her wide eyes filled with suffering.

"Ah, yes," her aunt said sadly, "I see that's so. Well, then, I myself, would believe him. But then, I believe in myself. I think, my dear, that you can't ever believe him until you do believe in yourself. For if you've no faith in yourself, you can't have faith in any other person, can you?"

June cocked her head to one side. She thought for a long moment. Then she gave a sniff, and rose to her feet. "I don't want to presume on him," she said slowly. "I don't want to look like a fool . . ."

"How odd," her aunt said with a little smile, "most people do, of course."

"But I don't want to just sit and wait for him either. That will be as embarrassing as canceling the wedding altogether. I don't see why I can't go with him!" June said in sorrow, but with a hint of growing anger. "I mean to say: if he wishes, I could marry him at his home without his grandmother knowing, or not marry him at all until we return to London. It doesn't matter to me. I just want to be with him. But he says he can't ask me to go with him."

"Quite so," her aunt agreed. "Of course, he can't. But that doesn't mean you can't. Or does it?"

June stopped, and thought. And then she smiled so radiantly her aunt wished that she could truly see herself in that moment.

"I see," June said. "You're right. Then you would understand? I mean—if I were to pack and go—this very night? Because he said he was waiting for a message, and that after it came he might have to leave at once. I know it's not what's done, but I think it's what I have to do—don't you?"

She waited, expectantly. She knew what she yearned to do, and it was a mad thing. But she needed only a word from her aunt to back her up in this moment of rash bravery.

Her aunt hesitated. "I believe you must be a lady, true. But there are times when a lady should act as a woman," she finally said, "just ask your father, if you doubt me."

But she said the last to thin air, because her niece suddenly had her ears covered over with yards of whispering silk. She had pulled her beautiful wedding gown up over her head and was wriggling out of it.

"I hope I'm in time," June wailed when she emerged, before she ran to her wardrobe to root out her traveling bag.

And I pray I am right, her aunt thought as she watched her.

Lawrence paced his drawing room as he waited. His carriage was waiting, his traveling bags were packed, everything was ready for his journey. He only wished his mind was as neatly arranged and prepared to go. When he heard voices in his hallway he stopped pacing and strode out into the hall. He expected to see any one of his brothers, or a servant from his parents' house. But he was stopped dead in his tracks by what he actually saw.

"There he is!" one of the men shouted joyously.

"Ho, Laurie, my lad, we've come to save you!" another chimed in.

"It's not every day one of our friends decides to tie the knot," one of the less drunken gentlemen who were crowding into the hall said when he saw Lawrence's astonishment.

"We're here to regale you, maybe change your mind," another chorused, as he tried to fumble off his greatcoat and hand it to an astounded footman.

"And if not that—why then, to have ourselves a time with you and your other . . . guests, before you swear off such times! And we even brought 'em with us, to save you the trouble of inviting 'em!" another cried, and they all laughed.

"Cor'! Is 'e the one? Then this won't be work at all!" a pretty young creature with far too much face paint cooed as she slipped off her cape to reveal far too few clothes.

"Too true," a dark-haired young woman said, stepping out from the knot of gentlemen and boldly assessing Lawrence where he stood arrested, staring back at her. She slipped off her cape and proudly threw back her shoulders to show him how nicely her high breasts just barely held up the thin excuse for a gown that she wore.

"Maybe," she said, never taking her eyes from Lawrence, "we should pay the nice gentlemen for bringing us here, instead of the other way around."

A chorus of giggles greeted that as other women showed themselves, standing on tiptoe to see their host, peeping out from under the encompassing arms of several of the gentlemen.

The scent in the crowded hall was of perfumes and liquors, both of which Lawrence usually liked. But both were secondhand and stale and hung too heavy in the air. Lawrence shook his head to clear it, and eyed the group before him. He recognized several of his old schoolmates and a few fellows from his club. Some of the celebrants were men he'd never seen before. He didn't want to see any of them tonight. They were mostly drunk, and all excited. He nodded to his alarmed butler and his footman. He would handle this himself. He only wanted them to leave in orderly fashion—and fast.

"Gentlemen, *ladies*," Lawrence said with a forced smile. "I thank you kindly, but I haven't the time or inclination for such sport tonight. I must ask you to leave, please."

"What?" a chubby fellow gasped. "But, Laurie, old boy—itch—itsch—'tis Tradition, man!"

"Too right!" another said with the awful dignity of the seriously drunk. "For the bloke who is about to lose his freedom—a last sweet taste—of life's finest—liquors—and lips!" he said in inspiration, before he leaned down, grabbed the young woman at his side, and gave her a long open-mouthed kiss.

The other gentlemen cheered.

"Now then, my lord bridegroom," the dark-haired woman said as she sauntered up to him, "let me give you a taste of what you'll be missing once you're married too— or maybe not, since arrangements can always be made," she whispered before she shrugged her precariously balanced gown off her shoulders entirely, reached up, and dragged his head down to her own opened lips.

It was only an instant before he freed himself. Only a heartbeat, really. But in the way of such things, that was the instant in which June saw him, as she walked in through his opened front door, wondering at the crowd of people who were there.

June had flown out of the hackney cab and raced up the front steps to see if Lawrence was still at home. When she saw the crowd in his hallway through the opened door, she hesitated, her heart sinking. At first, she thought they'd heard his grandmother had died and were there to give consolation. She wondered how they knew about it, and why they'd flock to his house to commiserate with him even if they did. It might be a death in the family, but still—a grandmother, and one who lived half a kingdom away, at that?

She feared some other harm had come to him and heart in her throat, pushed through the crowd—and frowned. The gentlemen gave way easily because they were in high spirits—hooting and laughing. Very high spirits, she realized, because they had drunk so much of them. Most of them were bosky. If their actions didn't tell her that, her nose did. And then her eyes showed her worse. She saw the women who were there.

She seldom saw such women from up close. Sometimes she spied them from her carriage at night, near the theaters, or loitering under London's new gaslights. But they were here tonight—in Lawrence's house. And they were laughing like jaybirds. Except for those who were otherwise engaged with some of the gentlemen. June whipped her appalled gaze away from one of those outrageous couples.

Something was terribly wrong. Her heart picked up its beat as she looked around for Lawrence. She found him. That was when her heart almost stopped beating.

Or so it felt, because she couldn't breathe when she saw Lawrence locked in an embrace with a strange, half-dressed woman.

June gasped. He couldn't have heard it. Still, when he lifted his head, he looked straight at her.

It was an extraordinary moment. Even the most drunken of the revelers seemed to sense it, and fell silent.

"June!" Lawrence said in dismay. He unwound the woman's arms from around his neck the way he would discard an old cravat, without even looking at her. Then he sucked in a long, sustaining breath.

"Gentlemen," he said with deadly calm, addressing the crowd but never taking his eyes from June's agonized ones, "I appreciate your efforts, but not the result of them. Leave, please. *Now*. This sport is not my way, nor my wish. I don't enjoy such games, I don't like this kind of surprise. I accept that the thought was well intentioned. But it was ill-conceived. Let's have an end to it. Thank you, and good night."

His words sobered most of the gentlemen. The look on his face discouraged most of the women. The dark-haired girl who had kissed him shrugged, backed away, and picked up her cloak again. The others began putting on their capes and coats as well. A few of both sexes, however, grumbled and shifted their feet, but made no move to leave his house.

"I might add," Lawrence said in a harsh voice, "that if you leave now, I will consider it a jest gone wrong. If you remain, I fear I must take it as an insult."

That cleared the hall. The last hesitant gentleman herded out the last complaining woman. Their reluctant host was known to be a crack shot and a prime swordsman. The would-be revelers swept past June, hardly noticing her in their hurry to be gone. Soon she stood alone in the doorway, still staring at Lawrence.

He grimaced. "June," he said wearily, "I'm not the best of all men, and never claimed I was. But just think about it. Whatever else I am, am I the kind to have orgies in my hallway? I mean to say, if I had such plans, give me credit at least for knowing enough to go up to my bedchamber, at least. At least, that!"

The fact that he seemed angry rather than apologetic made June start to breathe again. He must have seen the tension disappear from her stiff shoulders, because he signaled for the butler and footman to leave, and stepped closer to her.

"Seriously, my love, I wouldn't play you false," he said softly, "not even in the guise of a jolly 'bachelor farewell.' Infidelity is infidelity, in jest or not, and I'm not that sort of man. I hope you realize that." He put his hands on her shoulders and looked straight down into her worried eyes. "It was as much of a surprise to me as it was to you. A badly conceived notion carried out by some merry fellows. The sort of thing that gets cooked up late at night between one bottle and another, and the girls were obviously hired on for such sport—but wait! It *is* late! What are you doing here?" he asked in alarm. "I was so confused by those idiots, I didn't think. Is anything the matter?"

"I came to go with you," she blurted.

"What?"

"I can't sit and wait and worry," she said all in a rush, her gray eyes wide and bright as they searched his. "I must go with you."

His expression changed; she saw warmth and light reappear in his eyes. He touched her hair. "You are a wonder," he breathed, "not a word of censure, not a complaint, though you walk into a scene that would have other women screeching like banshees. No, none of that. But only a word to tell me that you're going to fling your cap over the windmill for me. I can't let you though."

"Can't?" she asked. "Or won't?"

"I won't let you run off with me and shock the stockings off Society," he said. "Is that so wrong of me?"

"But the wedding . . ." she said, her courage evaporating.

"May be delayed," he said, "better than you being disgraced. Now, I'll see you home before anyone hears of you being here. My brother's due soon, I'll leave word for him to wait for me. Don't worry about those drunken louts— even if they remember they saw you when they wake tomorrow morning, they're too worried about my anger to dare let me hear they've been gossiping."

"I see," she said thoughtfully. "Is *that* it?" she asked, standing firm and looking straight into his eyes, "Are you ashamed of having me meet your family?"

"Ashamed?" he asked in shock.

"I never have met any of them, you know," she said wistfully. "First, you said they lived too far for easy travel so they never came to London. But your brother did come here and still, I never met him. Now you're leaving and you say I can't travel so far with you."

She tilted her head to the side, considering. "But how will you keep me from them if you really intend to marry me?"

"Of course I intend to marry you," he said in confusion. "All I want to do is to keep you from the gossip mill. How can you say such things? How can you even think them?"

"Easily!" she snapped, the injustice of it melting away fears of being brazen. "I'm supposed to be marrying you within days, how could my leaving with you now, or even marrying you before the wedding, cause gossip? Pray be honest with me! There's no earthly reason why I can't go with you.

"If you're afraid your grandmother seeing me will hasten her death," she went on courageously, "then don't let her see me! I'll wait in the inn, or hide in the gardens—or something," she said a little wildly, not seeing his lips quirk at the picture her words painted for him.

"But I want to go with you, and why shouldn't I?" she insisted. "You have our wedding papers all ready. But you don't want to marry me there? Fine. Even if we don't marry at your home, at least I'll be with you. We'll marry soon enough later—or so you claim . . . No, Lawrence, what you say makes no sense at all. I think you want to be rid of me. I think you must be ashamed of me, that must be it!"

"Hasty weddings cause gossip," he argued, his humor vanishing. "And I just want to . . . I just want to . . . No—you never have met any of my family, have you?" he asked suddenly as a strange expression crossed over his face. "It was always one thing or another, wasn't it?

"Think of that!" he murmured to himself, a faraway look in his eyes. He laughed. "Love, you've surprised me into surprising myself. Do you know, when I think . . .

"June," he said decisively, coming back to the present, smiling down at her. "I never did let them meet you, did I? And do you know why? How could you? I think I only know why now, myself.

"Come, sit here, next to me," he said, leading her to the salon, and a settee. "Well then, how to say it?" he murmured when they sat. He took her hands in his.

She watched him anxiously, very aware she was alone in the night in his house with him, as no respectable girl, engaged or not, should be. But his mind was clearly not on lovemaking. That worried her even more.

"You see," he finally said, "as you know, I'm the youngest of five sons. And, June—I'm the runt of the litter. There's no other way to put it."

Her head cocked to the side as she stared at him, obviously uncomprehending. He grinned, but ruefully.

"You should see my brothers!" he went on. "Or—I suppose I wish you would not! They're famous in our home county. One is more handsome than the other. Blond as Vikings, blue-eyed and tall, all of them. The jest in our family always was that we could run windmills on the strength of the local lass's sighs when they walked into a room. And three of them are as yet unwed! I'm the only dark-haired one—"

"Your hair is gold!" she cried, interrupting him.

"Their is flax," he said, "and I'm the only brown-eyed one—"

"Gold too," she said heatedly, "they're light brown gold."

"Brown: the color of earth—exactly," he said, "theirs— the color of a summer sky. But even worse for a growing lad—I'm the smaller by three inches from the rest of them."

"They must be giants," she muttered, "that is *not* attractive."

He grinned. "They are not, and they're very attractive. Or so I always thought, along with the rest of our immediate world. All my life I've measured myself against them in more ways than looks. It wasn't a bad thing, actually. It made me push myself farther, made me do things I might not have, trying to be their equal. Yet, in the case of looks, at least, I always knew I never could be. Chalk can't be cheese.

"So I tried to outdo them in everything else. It's why I fenced and raced carriages, and became expert with pistols too. I did a dozen other foolish things to prove I was as good or better than them. Some not so foolish things too. It's why I struck out on my own. That's why I went into the army; why I went into business ventures and speculated with my funds—I've made quite a bit of money on my own, by the way. I haven't done badly for myself with my futile competition. Still, I thought I'd got over it long since.

"I must not have. I don't think I was aware of it," he said pensively, "but I think I never arranged a meeting between you and any of them because somewhere in the back of my mind, I must have been worrying about what you'd think about me when you met them. I look very no-account next to them, you see, my love. And you—why you could have any man in the kingdom."

"Oh, my," she said, her hand going to her heart. "Lawrence, you are the best-looking man I ever met in my entire life. Truly, that is so! It is I who am nothing. That's why I was glad instead of being hurt when Mama decided not to bother coming to London until our wedding day. She's so lovely—I'm nothing compared to her. Everyone says so. I've passed my life in her shadow, and I didn't want to see you comparing us in your eyes."

"You are beyond compare," he said simply.

"No, it's you who are," she vowed. "Why, I'm plain, compared to her."

Whatever he was about to say next went unsaid. Because he muttered gruffly, pulled her close, and kissed her hard. It was a long while before he spoke again, and then, all he could manage was a word.

"Plain!" he breathed in wonder against her smooth white neck, when he finally stopped for breath.

"Runt!" she whispered in astonishment against his hard jaw.

"Idiot," he murmured lovingly, into her hair.

"Fool," she sighed against his chest.

And then they laughed. And then they kissed again. And again.

The bed was half in shadow, because the heavy drapes were drawn against the evening light. The first thing Lawrence saw as he came to the door of the bedchamber were the dim shapes of all his brothers and sisters grouped around the high bed. He held his breath. Then he glanced back before he squared his own shoulders and walked into the room.

But the first thing he heard was the voice of his grandmother, strong and annoyed, coming from within the bed.

"Is that my Laurie? So 'tis! Open the curtains, so I can have a look at him! Laurie, love," she crooned as he came close and took her hand, his eyes serious, searching her face, "did these fools convince you to come posthaste? But I am better. Tcha! Don't look like that! I've lost a little flesh, but I feel like a spring lamb. Even the wretched doctor agrees, I'll do. The fever broke, and I will live to make him regret all those foul potions he poured down my throat.

"Now give us a kiss, and then turn yourself round and get yourself back to London town, and your bride. Running off and leaving her like that! What must she think of you?"

"Why don't you ask her?" he said proudly, motioning for June to step out of the shadows and enter the room.

The first wedding of Lord Morrow and his lady was held in a bedchamber, as they always ever afterward were fond of telling their children. This was because it was important for the bridegroom's grandmama to see the ceremony. Recovered though she certainly was, she wasn't strong enough yet to make the journey back to London with them for their formal wedding.

What they didn't tell their children was how quickly they repaired to their own bedchamber after the ceremony.

"The advantage of a ceremony at home," the groom told his bride rather breathlessly, as he helped her remove her shift, "is that there isn't much of a walk to the honeymoon. Lord! Look at you!"

Then he didn't say very much at all for a long while, except for murmurs of "lovely," "beautiful," and "beyond beautiful," which were balm to his bride's blushing ears. But when he became too overcome with pleasure to speak a word, she was even happier. Although the feelings his hands and lips and body brought to her were so much more than "happiness" that she thought she'd have to think up a new vocabulary to describe them.

Then, after, lying dazed and delighted by his side in their borrowed wedding bed, she was able to tell him how very beautiful she thought he was.

"Runt, my foot!" she muttered indignantly, as she studied the whole magnificent naked form of her new husband.

And then she giggled as he stirred around in bed and captured one of her little feet, lifted it, and planted a kiss on it, murmuring, "Ah—a place I forgot, thank you for reminding me."

"No, I meant it," she said, stretching out beside him with a happy sigh. "Not that your brothers aren't handsome, for I suppose they are. But they are pale copies of you, my dear. What are blue eyes to gold? Or that whitish flyaway stuff they all have compared to such glowing golden hair as you have?" she said with a dismissive wave of her hand. "And," she said dreamily, stroking his hard muscled chest, "there's not a one of them so strong as you!"

"Blind," he said in a loving whisper as he sat up and then bent over her again, "how lucky I was to find a blind girl to marry."

"The only thing I regret," she mused, long after, as she trailed a finger through the dark gold fuzz on his chest again, "is that I didn't pack my wedding gown. Oh, Laurie, it's so beautiful. Wait until you see it! It really makes me look worthy of you."

"Shall I have to spend my life undoing what your mama has done?" he wondered, capturing her hand and bringing it to his lips. "I tell you: you are lovely. I tell you I adore you, and would, whatever you might look like. Because your mind is as beautiful as your body. I'm just lucky you are so very lovable in all ways. Do you still doubt me?"

"No more," she said gladly, "and even *they* shall see it now!"

"*They?*" he asked idly, as his hands roved her slender form.

"Oh—the girls I met in London," she said, shivering deliciously at his touch. "They were the ones who first made me feel badly about us, you know."

"Did they?" he asked with some more interest.

"Yes, they kept talking about how blue you looked, and saying how you must be regretting your offer."

"Now that, I didn't know," he said, frowning. "I was worried about my grandmother, that was all."

"Now I know that—but then? Then," June said sadly, pleasurable sensations fading as she remembered the great pain of it, "I did not. It was worse after I overheard them talking about us. And they kept doing it. I tried to discount it, but it was hurtful to think about. And worse to overhear. Once . . ." she said hesitantly, for even though she now knew it wasn't true, it was still distressing to talk about.

"Once I overheard them jesting about the old wedding rhyme," she continued softly. "You know the one—about something old, something new—for brides? They said I had the old name, the money for sixpence for my shoes, as well as enough to buy new things. And that anyone would lend me something for the 'borrowed.' But they also said I didn't need anything blue—because I had you. They laughed so hard I thought they'd hurt themselves after they said that. They never stopped jesting about my 'blue' bridegroom."

"Did they not?" he asked with great interest. But since he was dragging her down to his kiss again, she knew where that interest would lead them—and went willingly with him.

Lord and Lady Morrow never had to tell their children about their second wedding, because it became famous in its own time, and would be remembered for many generations after.

The church, one of London's most prestigious, was filled to overflowing. Everyone there knew the bride had run off with the groom the week before, though none dared say it aloud. She and the groom had not been seen in London since. The groom's expertise with pistol and sword was a mighty deterrent to that sort of gossip. But to no other kind. Because all the assembled guests wondered if the pair would make it back to London in time for their scheduled wedding. Or if they even planned to anymore, now that the bride had run away from London with her lover, without benefit of clergy. Especially considering how blue the fellow had been before she'd thrown her cap—and her reputation—over the windmill. There wasn't a scandalmonger in the *ton* who wanted to miss out on the drama.

It was said that the couple had already married at the groom's grandmother's bedside.

But no true gossip believed that; it was just too convenient an excuse in case the pair didn't appear on the day planned for their formal wedding. And so the guests came to the church early, and sat craning their necks and whispering, waiting eagerly to see if the bride would show up, much less the groom. It was the social event of the Season because it had everything in it gossips most adore: personages of high birth who might do something of low repute, plus tension, suspense, and the possibility of someone else's misfortune and heartbreak.

There was a stir when the bride arrived. And not only because of the gossip about her. But because she was luminously lovely.

It wasn't just her gown, which was a masterpiece. It was the glow about the girl: a radiance, an aura of such beauty and—satisfaction—that the guests had to catch their breaths in envy or delight. Her soft brown hair was all twined around with gardenias, baby's breath, and seed pearls. Her charming figure was swathed in yards of lustrous pearly silk, her fine wide gray eyes were filled with joy, and misty with remembrance of some glorious scene of love. She glowed like the pearls at her slender neck did.

The assembled company was so rapt in looking at her that no one noticed the famous beauty who was her mama, much to that lady's chagrin. Because no beauty could compare to this bride this day. Truly no one had ever seen such a lovely bride—nor such a *fulfilled*-looking one, either.

And so, no one saw the groom secretly and stealthily position himself at the altar. No one saw him at all. At least not until the bride herself did.

She stopped in the aisle and laughed aloud when she spied him standing there waiting for her. It was such a joyous sound that it made even the solemn minister's lips quirk.

But all the guests could do was stare. They actually turned their heads away from the most beautiful bride of the Season in order to goggle at her bridegroom.

Then some of them looked shamed. Some others finally laughed. All quickly understood. They'd all heard the gossip, of course; some had seen the caricatures on sale in the bookstalls. And so, it seemed, had the bridegroom.

Because he was the bluest groom anyone had ever seen. Literally. He wasn't dressed in the usual dove grays or pastel colors that were proper hues for a groom to wear at a morning wedding. Instead, he was blue. Extremely blue. Incredibly blue. Gloriously blue. He could not have been more blue, one wag commented, if he had dipped himself in woad, as his ancestors might have done.

He wore a blue superfine jacket fitted tight across his wide shoulders. Blue unmentionables clung to his muscular legs. His elaborate waistcoat was a symphony in shades of blue: embroidered blue hummingbirds dipped their blue beaks into blue flowers all over it. Somewhere, he'd gotten himself a blue neckcloth too. He wore blue flowers in his lapel. But his grin was wide and brilliantly white, and filled with unholy delight when he saw his bride's expression.

Which became dazed, and delighted, and filled with sensual wonder as she gazed up into the face of her groom when she met him at the altar.

And that was why, down through the generations, the Morrow bridegrooms were always blue. And why their brides always wore the same expressions of dazed delight. Which, given the nature of the sons who issued from that happy couple—with their fascinating gray eyes, their dark blond hair, and their ready smiles—was perfectly understandable.

Or so everyone ever after always said—and happily, whenever they remembered the groom who gave his bride something truly blue for luck on her wedding day. And all the sunny years thereafter.

. . . AND A SIXPENCE FOR
HER SHOE

by Anne Barbour

It was a glorious day in Hampshire. The June sun spilled its warmth on parkland and fields, bees buzzed contentedly among the blossoms, birds filled the air with song glorious enough for a cathedral, and a soft, scented breeze stirred glossy green leaves in the trees that sheltered a certain country residence.

The watcher in an upstairs window, however, remained oblivious to the beauty that lay before her. She stood, tall and slender, the polished coils of her auburn hair reflecting shafts of sunlight. She stared intently at the carriage that approached the house down a long, graveled drive, and instinctively, her hand went to a small pendant tucked, as always, beneath her gown of jonquil muslin.

"Drew." Catherine Edgebrooke breathed the name. In just a few moments, he would enter her home for the first time in three years. Would he greet her courteously, taking her hand in his and brushing her fingertips with his lips? Or would he merely murmur a careless, "Good morning," as he handed his hat and gloves to the butler. Lord, what if he would not speak to her at all? It would hardly be wondered at, she thought with an uncomfortable squirm.

Sighing, Catherine turned away from the window, glancing at her image in the mirror. She had taken a great deal of care in preparing for this visit. Perhaps it had been foolish to array herself in her most becoming gown, for it certainly would not matter to Drew. She moved to the other side of the room and reached for the handle to the door of her bedchamber, only to be brought up short as a vigorous knock sounded. It was followed almost immediately by the entrance of a tall, lithe gentleman whose red hair seemed to blaze ahead of him into the room.

"Cathy! He's here. Are you ready?" The young man grasped her arm and turned her about for his inspection. "Well, you're looking quite toothsome, indeed. If Drew doesn't respond to that very fetching gown, we'll know you're in trouble."

"Oh, for Heaven's sake, John." Catherine wrenched herself from her brother's grip. "You know perfectly well he hasn't come to see me at all. And what we are to tell him when he finds out that Helen—"

"Never mind that," said John peremptorily. "The thing you must keep in mind is what you'll say to Drew when you see him. He is changed, you know. War does that to a man, even without the—the disfigurement he suffered. You'd hardly recognize him. His face—Well, the scar is not as bad as he described to me. Even his arm—there is some mobility there, even though his left hand is almost totally useless—and the rest—Lord, I don't know. He's changed—inside, and outside. He seems totally ruined. As for Helen"—he added after a moment—"Drew will have to be told the truth almost immediately."

"Dear God," whispered Catherine. "How am I—"

But they had reached the head of the main staircase that led to the entrance hall below. John patted her arm. "I'd better go hunt down Mama and Papa. They will want to be on hand to greet Drew." He turned away.

"No!" Catherine clutched at him, panic-stricken. "Don't leave me."

"Nonsense," replied John reassuringly. "I'll be back momentarily."

The next moment he was gone, leaving Catherine to stare after him in agonized indecision.

The sound of voices in the hall below caused her to whirl in that direction. Seldon, the butler, had just opened the door to admit a man who limped noticeably as he entered.

Andrew Carter, the second son of the Earl of Barnstaple, replied gravely to the butler's murmured words.

"Yes, thank you, Seldon. It's good to be home."

It was not, of course, thought Drew, but one glance at the servant's horrified demeanor led to this hurried assurance. Damn, it was still hard to get used to the effect his face had on people, or to the sick sensation their response created within him. Handing his hat and gloves to the man, he proceeded into the hall and then toward the morning room that he knew lay to his right. He halted suddenly at the sight of the slender figure moving toward him down the great front stairway.

His throat constricted despite himself as he watched Catherine's approach. God, she was more beautiful than ever. He had expected that her willful selfishness would have displayed itself by now in a sharpening of her features or a hardening of her expression, but no, her eyes were still glowing pools of silver and her face—with its straight nose and wide, generous mouth—was that of an engaging gamin. She was all the vital warmth of the summer day, wrapped in a gown the color of sunshine.

Almost defensively, Drew's thoughts flew to Helen. His gaze swung about the hall. Somehow, he had expected that she would be the first person to greet him at Greengroves.

"Drew."

He started at the sound of his name. Her voice, too, was unchanged, still retaining that unique blend of melody and a certain seductive smokiness. He turned back to her and lifted his face. Silently, he absorbed the expression of shock in her eyes and the revulsion that surely lay beneath it.

"Catherine," he said, as she floated toward him down the stairs.

Catherine felt her insides clench. She couldn't do this. She simply could not do it. She could not bear to utter vapid nothings as though Drew were a stranger come to call. Though, he was, of course. A stranger. Dear God, if she had met him on the street she would not have known him. John was right. The laughing young man she had known since she was a child had been transformed into a gaunt, stony figure who fairly radiated pain and weariness. He seemed larger than when she had last seen him. Certainly, his shoulders had broadened during his absence, she mused almost abstractedly. His hair, dark as midnight was longer than he had used to wear it, and slightly shaggy. His eyes were as expressionless and black as coal chips. And then there was the scar. It ran, harsh and jagged from high up on his left temple to a point just under his jawline. Her gaze dropped, only to encounter the sight of his left arm, hanging uselessly at his side. She almost put out a hand to him, before withdrawing it quickly. What he must have suffered!

"It's good to see you, Drew." She almost cried aloud at the inanity of her words. What must he think of her? Once again, she noted his searching glance about the hall. Of course. He was not thinking of her at all. She took a deep breath. "Please, let us go into the morning room and I'll ring for tea."

Without waiting for a response, she swept past him, and, wordlessly, he followed. In the morning room, Catherine gestured Drew to a comfortable settee and took a chair near him.

"John will be here presently," she said. "He has gone to

fetch Mama and Papa." She hesitated. "I am so sorry about—what happened to you, and—" she lifted her hand, only to be met with a furious scowl.

"It is not necessary," he growled, "to mouth meaningless platitudes, Catherine. I know precisely how grieved you must have been at hearing of my, ah, contretemps."

"Oh, Drew! No! I would not—"

"Never mind," he continued impatiently as she lifted a hand in protest. "I remember, even if you do not, your singular benediction when I left, after, of course, your vows of vengeance." Catherine flinched, and he took a deep breath. "In any event, I am here this morning to—"

"My dear boy, you are here at last!"

The voice issued from a plump, middle-aged woman who bustled into the room. Behind her hurried a gray-haired gentleman, and, bringing up the rear, was John.

The woman fairly flung herself into Drew's arms, but a moment later, when she tilted her head to look up at him, she gasped. "Drew! Oh, heavens, what have they done to you? My dear boy, does it hurt terribly?"

As though embarrassed by his wife's gaucherie, the gentleman surged forward.

"Rose! That will do."

Gently thrusting the woman aside, he grasped Drew's good hand and shook it awkwardly. "Never mind, my boy, she means well. And we *are* glad to see you, of course."

Drew bowed courteously. "As I am to see you, Sir Martin—and Lady Edgebrooke." He widened his greeting to include the plump little woman, now twittering in agitation.

"Yes—yes, but do let us sit down," she said breathlessly, fairly hurtling into the settee next to Catherine.

"Please do not distress yourself, my lady," continued Drew. "I appreciate your concern. No, the pain is minimal now, except for an occasional twinge." He bent a reassuring smile on Lady Edgebrooke, who returned it with unspoken gratitude.

"Still," she continued, patting his knee, "it must have been perfectly wretched for you."

"Yes, Mama," interposed John, "and I'm sure Drew would rather not discuss it just at the moment. I say," he continued hastily, turning to his friend, "now that you're here, perhaps we can steal away for a little fishing. We have plenty of time before luncheon."

"Oh, for heaven's sake, John," said Lady Edgebrooke in some displeasure, "Drew will wish to talk with Catherine. They have much to discuss."

Sir Martin nodded in agreement, and everyone glanced expectantly at Drew, except for Catherine, who flushed and cast her gaze to her fingers, twisting in her lap.

Drew said nothing, however, and an awkward silence fell. When Seldon arrived with refreshments, he was greeted with an almost audible sigh of relief. Over the cups, however, the silence seemed to grow louder, and when Drew spoke at last, Catherine jumped.

"I do not see Miss Carstairs," he said, an odd note in his voice.

Catherine's breath caught and a chill flooded through her.

Sir Martin and his wife stared blankly at Drew. "Why," said Lady Edgebrooke, "Helen is no longer in my employ. She left us not two weeks ago to be married."

"Married!" Drew almost gasped the word. "Helen Carstairs is—? But she never—I don't understand."

Oh, God, thought Catherine, he looked as though someone had just struck him a terminal blow. Oh, God, oh, God. What had she done? She turned her attention to her mother, who had continued in the bright tone of one trying to control a conversation that is slowly unraveling.

"Oh, yes, Mister Dench fell head over tail in love with Helen the first day they met. That was"—she swung toward her husband—"oh, almost a year ago, wasn't it, Martin? Of course, he was so shy—Why, if it hadn't been for Catherine, I don't think he ever would have brought himself to the sticking point, and poor Helen would have spent the rest of her life as a lady's companion."

Drew's blank gaze shifted to Catherine. "Indeed?" He spoke the word through clenched teeth.

Catherine tried out a light laugh that was not wholly successful. "Really, Mama, all I did was make opportunities for them to be alone once in a while."

"And to make sure that dear Mister Dench sat next to Helen at the harvest festival last fall, and the choir recital, and last Christmas you did all but push them under the mistletoe together. And do you remember Valentine's Day? Why, you—"

An almost inaudible sound made Catherine turn toward Drew. He was glaring at her with a malevolence that shocked her. His voice when he spoke, however, was cool and sardonic.

"You seem to have devoted considerable energy, my dear, toward bringing the two together. Now, I wonder why."

This time Catherine eschewed the light laugh, making do with a bland smile. "They were so obviously in love, of course. It would have been a shame to keep them apart." Drew's eyes darkened and Catherine gave a small gasp at her maladroitness.

"Ah, yes, you always were an advocate of true love, weren't you?"

Catherine clenched her cup in whitened fingers and murmured incoherently. Drew rose, and it seemed to Catherine that hurt and disappointment, blended with his rage at her, fairly radiated from him like tremors from a simmering volcano. He bowed to Sir Martin and his lady.

"I really must not stay. I only stopped in to pay my respects, for I have—business in the village."

Lady Edgebrooke's face puckered in dismay. "But, you just arrived, and I know that you and Catherine . . . That is—"

"It's all right, Mama," interposed Catherine hastily. "Drew must have a great deal to see to. We will speak later."

Drew turned to leave and John followed, as though to escort him to his carriage. He was forestalled, however, by a sharp nip from his mother. She nudged Catherine before saying pointedly, "Dearest, after you have seen Drew out, do come to my rooms. I wish your opinion on that new scarf I purchased to go with my puce muslin."

So saying, she grasped both her son and her husband by an elbow and hustled them from the room via another exit.

Drew had not halted during this exchange, and, after a moment of indecision, Catherine followed him outside. When he prepared to enter his carriage without so much as looking at her, she laid a tentative hand on his sleeve.

"Drew—I am so sorry. I—"

Drew swung about, and for the barest instant, Catherine thought he might strike her.

"Sorry for what?" he snarled. "Sorry for removing the only bright spot in my life? Tell me, Catherine, how did you know? Did Helen confide in you that we were corresponding? Perhaps she even showed you some of my letters. Knowing me so well, you must have divined instantly that I was growing attached to her. That knowledge must have been most gratifying, for it suited your plans so well. Was it you who encouraged her not to tell me of her growing devotion to this—Dench, is it?—so you could watch me disintegrate in front of you when I found out?"

"Drew! It wasn't like that. Truly, I—"

Drew shook her hand from his arm. "Well, you've had your revenge. And now, let me conclude the real purpose of my visit. I realize I am a few years late with this, but I have come to grant your dearest wish. You may, with my blessing, at last declare our betrothal at an end."

Catherine almost gasped with the pain his statement caused her. She knew now that this was going to be more difficult than she had dreamed. What in the world was she to say to him?

Her gaze dropped for a moment before she lifted her eyes to his.

"Drew, I know I have given you cause to—to be angry with me, but, believe me, I have no wish to dissolve what our families have put in place."

Drew stiffened. "What? You cannot be serious! 'Cause to be angry' with you? Why, how could I be angry with one who informed me she'd like to see me dead rather than marry me, whose most devout wish was that I never return from the Continent?"

Catherine placed her hand on his sleeve. "Drew, you must know I did not mean any of the dreadful things I said. My temper—"

"Ah, yes, the famous Catherine Edgebrooke temper. You always blamed it for getting you into trouble as though it were some sort of foreign entity over which you had no control."

"Yes, I did," replied Catherine quietly. "But I do so no longer. Since that miserable episode, I have strived, with reasonable success, to master my temper. I tried to apologize to you, Drew, but you never even read my letters—at least, that's what you told John."

Drew smiled tightly. "Quite true. I felt I had enough chaos in my life without adding your particular brand of venom to it." He paused before continuing. "Apologized did you? Well, I am sorry I missed that. Your efforts at wriggling out of the consequences of one of your tirades would have been entertaining, if nothing else. At least, they always were."

Catherine sighed. "I know you do not wish to hear this right now, but we are betrothed, and, as you said so many times to me, that is a fact. If you cannot bring yourself to actually marry me, I shall certainly not force the issue, but, I remind you of our families' feelings in the matter."

Drew smiled sourly. "Oh, yes, I had it dinned into my head since I was in leading strings that it was the fondest wish of dear Papa and Sir Martin that our families someday be joined. We're fairly trapped, aren't we? You in your family's desires, and me in Ceddie's sensibilities. He is bound and determined, you must know, that the wedding will march forward as scheduled. Now, of course, it's all in honor of dear Papa's memory. Or perhaps"—for a moment his sardonic grin gleamed whitely against the scar—"perhaps, you have formed a tendre for me. Am I not, after all, the answer to a maiden's prayer?" He turned away from her with a grimace and swung into the carriage, slamming the door behind him. As the vehicle prepared to rattle off down the driveway, he thrust his head through the window. "It's too bad *you* couldn't have married Ceddie."

Catherine shrank within herself. He was, she knew, referring to his older brother, Cedric, the present earl. The elder Barnstaples had decided that Ceddie, of course, as the heir, could not be wasted on the modestly endowed daughter of a baronet, and he instead offered for the hand of the Duke of Brentmore's daughter. No, it was Drew who must marry Catherine. Not that Drew had objected. He was by no means smitten with her, but as much as said that if he must marry someone, he wouldn't mind being leg shackled to his childhood friend. No, it was she who had taken exception. She might have been just as amenable as Drew if she had not already fallen madly and wildly in love with Randolph.

She smiled ruefully. She had not thought of Randolph Sills in months, which was perhaps not altogether surprising since her infatuation with him was as brief as it was intense. Not a month after Drew's departure, she had discovered that what everyone said about Randolph Sills was true. He was a gazetted fortune hunter who had worn out his welcome among the wealthy families of the *ton* and had turned to the modestly endowed baronet's daughter in his desperate need for funds.

No one could convince her of this, however, while the flame of passion burned bright in her. She was appalled when she discovered her parents' plans for her and Drew. She had flailed out in all directions, sparing no one her outrage and her temper. Drew had remained remarkably equable throughout, although in the end, she had alienated him to the point where, if he were not bound by his sense of duty, she was sure he would have acquiesced in her desire to be free of him.

Her hand went once again to the pendant she wore concealed beneath her gown. It was a gesture that had become increasingly frequent in the last few months, as though even a brief contact with her talisman could make her troubles disappear. Her eyes filled, and, shaking her head at her own foolishness, she turned and entered the house.

In his carriage, Drew stared unseeing at the fields passing before his view. He had noted Catherine's stricken expression at his words, and a pang of regret shot through him at the realization of the pain he had caused her. He shook himself. What nonsense! After the anguish she had caused him, he should feel nary a twinge that he had discomfited Catherine Edgebrooke.

For, indeed, it was not just the thought of her machinations in his relationship with Helen Carstairs that caused a slow burn of anger and heartache to rise within him. He had truly loved Catherine—or, at least he thought he had. Not, perhaps, when the idea of his betrothal to her had been presented to him. He'd been only three and twenty at the time, poised on the threshold of an army career and all the other challenges and rewards of adult life. The idea of his marrying anyone, let alone the chit he'd known since she wore her unruly hair in plaits, seemed ludicrous. When the plan was put to him, however, with the proviso that the betrothal would not interfere with his joining the army, he began to think it a very good thing. The fact that little Cathy Edge-brooke of the knobby knees and toothy smile, the barely tolerated little sister of his best friend, had blossomed into an attractive, vibrant young woman, about whom the other sprigs in the neighborhood buzzed like so many bees, was of some influence in his decision, it was to be admitted. A fellow had to marry someone, after all, and both sets of parents agreed that the actual marriage should be held when his service in the Peninsula was concluded and, hopefully, he would be safely embarked on a career in diplomacy. The notion of carrying against his heart the miniature of a pretty girl as he rode off to war, of receiving tender billets-doux from same, and knowing there was someone back home besides his mama and papa worrying about his well-being appealed to the admittedly overdeveloped romantic side of his nature. Thus, he agreed, with the utmost goodwill, to his parents' plans.

He was completely astonished at Catherine's response to the arrangement. When he had arrived at Greengroves, shoes polished and cravat starched to within an inch of his life, she met him at the door. Her gray eyes, red and swollen with angry tears, flashed at him like warning beacons, and he had no sooner begun his carefully prepared proposal than she began railing at him like a Billingsgate, using language he didn't even think she knew. She loved another, she said. She was not about to be forced into a marriage, the idea of which revolted her very soul, she said. She said a great deal more, all of it apparently dredged from particularly awful Gothic novels and all of it at the top of her lungs.

Despite his best efforts, Catherine's heels had remained firmly dug in against the prospect of becoming affianced to him, and over time, her insults and her diatribes began to wither the seeds of his newly burgeoning passion. As the date of his departure grew near, he had become heartily sick of her, and, if it were not for his obligation to his family, would have called the whole thing off with a great deal of relief.

His thoughts drifted to that last afternoon with her. Chivvied by his mother, he had come to Greengroves, the Edgebrooke's estate, for a duty call, and Lady Edgebrooke had lost no time in bustling the beleaguered couple into the garden. Catherine had been stiff and uncommunicative, remarking only that if he had the slightest trace of backbone, he would inform Lord Barnstaple that the betrothal was a colossal mistake.

He had turned to grasp her arm, and giving it an impatient shake, he growled, "For God's sake, Cathy, can't you get it through that stubborn head of yours that you are going to marry me? Our betrothal is a fact, and you can't escape it—not unless you want to break the hearts of two sets of parents."

"Oh, what fustian, Drew! They care nothing about my heart—why should I care about theirs? I just wish you'd stop pretending that all this is agreeable to you. I know you don't care tuppence for me—"

"If that's true," interrupted Drew rudely, "it's because you've effectively destroyed any scrap of affection I might have felt for you. I hope that by the time I return from the Peninsula, you will have grown up a little. I must say I do not look forward to being married to a spoiled brat."

At this, Catherine had fairly exploded. She would have struck him if he had not grasped her other hand, thus effectively spiking her guns. He released her after a moment, and she remained glaring at him. He smiled grimly. Even at such a moment, he had observed with a quickening of his pulse the rise and fall of her softly curved bosom, her flashing eyes, and the glints that shimmered in her polished mahogany hair.

He walked away, and after a moment she followed him, still muttering mutinously. As he strolled along the path, his eye was caught by something small and glittering that lay in the blossoms bordering the graveled area. Stooping, he picked up a sixpence, shiny and new, and he turned to hand it to his betrothed.

"Here you are, Cath," he said mockingly. "A sixpence for your shoe. No bride should be without one."

To his appalled astonishment, her cheeks reddened even more furiously and, raising her clenched fist, she hurled the coin at him. It struck his cheek, and rattled faintly as it fell into the small stones at their feet.

"Damn you, Drew Carter!" she had shrieked. "I *will* get out of this betrothal, and I'll make you sorry you ever agreed to enter it. I—I hope you never come back from Spain!"

Breathless, she had picked up her skirts and run back into the house, leaving him staring after her. He did not see her again before he embarked for the Peninsula.

It was with some degree of satisfaction that he had burned unopened the few letters she had sent. He corresponded with John regularly, and when he told his friend that he had no wish to hear from Catherine, the letters had ceased. It was not long afterward that the first missive from Helen had arrived. He had been slightly acquainted with her since the time she had arrived to serve as Lady Edgebrooke's companion. She was in her early twenties, small and quiet and attractive, with short, dark hair that curled becomingly about her pale cheeks. That first letter had been almost apologetic in tone. She knew, she said, that she was committing a solecism in writing to a gentleman, but because of his association with dear John, she quite thought of him as one of her family. She feared he might be lonely in such an alien environment and wondered if he might like to hear news of the neighborhood, items that perhaps young John would not think to include.

Drew had, indeed, found himself unexpectedly overwhelmed by the strangeness of his new life. His fellow officers were all the best of fellows, but he was used to

companions he had known all his life. Later, as the horrors
of war invaded his life, her letters had become a lifeline.
Then came the incident that changed his life forever. During the battle of Toulouse, he was caught in a hail of gun-
fire and fell beneath the wheels of a battle wagon, loaded
with rifles and ammunition. He had been left crushed and
broken, and awoke to find himself a monstrous caricature
of the man he had been.

Of all the expressions of sympathy he had received from
friends and family, it was only Helen's understanding and
friendly good sense that he could bear. Her gravely comforting words strengthened him and saw him through the
darkest of the hours following his desperate struggle for life
and the ineffectual efforts of the surgeons to make him
whole again. He had grown to depend on the arrival of her
letters as a starving Israelite must have awaited his daily ra-
tion of manna in the desert.

He was not sure when he had begun to love Helen. While
he was technically betrothed to Catherine, he certainly
could not speak to Helen of his growing need for her or of
the feelings that were swelling within him like a spring
bud. He had been so laughably sure that she felt the same
way, and when at last they came face to face, she would see
beyond the obscenity of his face and form to the man beneath. How could she have gone off to marry this Arthur
Dench, when she had never so much as mentioned the fellow to him?

And now Catherine insisted she wished to marry him.
Lord, when he was whole and reasonably personable, she
would have nothing to do with him, but now that he was
deformed and hideous, she declared her steadfast intention
to be his bride. Why, for God's sake?

John had written him that her infatuation with Randolph
Sills had, not unexpectedly, faded in the light of reality, but
surely that could not account for her about-face.

The carriage had by now arrived at Graymore Abbey, the

seat of his brother, the Earl of Barnstaple, and Drew descended wearily. Ceddie had come out to meet him, rubbing his hands briskly at Drew's approach.

"Did you find the Edgebrooke's well?" he asked anxiously. "Sir Martin appeared to be coming down with a putrid sore throat last week, and I was concerned that he would not be in health for the house party."

"The house—? Oh, good God, Ceddie. Are you still planning to go through with that nonsense?"

Cedric, Lord Barnstaple was a tall, jovial man. He had acceded to the title a scant year ago on the death of his father, and all his neighbors and tenants agreed that in that time he had taken up the reins of his authority with industry and dedication. He was not blessed with an abundance of intelligence, but his nature was sunny and he was a genuinely good person. Also, he had the gift of choosing his staff well, a trait that served him in good stead as master of Graymore Abbey, one of the premier estates of the country. Added to that was the fact that his wife was as sharp as she could hold together, and ran her household with the efficiency of a sergeant at arms.

He gazed now in consternation at his brother. "Nonsense?" he gasped. "Drew, invitations have gone out to half the county, not to mention the people from London. They'll be arriving, some of them, this afternoon. The wedding is less than three weeks away, after all, and it's high time for the celebrations to begin."

"Ceddie, I told you when I arrived, I do not wish to marry Catherine—and that's putting it mildly. I'd sooner ally myself with a ring-tailed catamount. And, don't you remember? She has no real wish to marry me."

Ceddie's forehead creased in a troubled frown. "That was before you went away. After she discovered what a bastard Sills really was, she mellowed considerably. And, even before that—well, she told me she was truly sorry for what she said to you on that last day. You know," added the earl thoughtfully, "I don't think she's lost her temper—at least, not really—since."

"Ump," replied Drew skeptically. "I don't care if she's turned into a plaster saint, I don't want to marry her. Why can't I get anyone to listen to me? You tell me it's all for the best—John merely pats me on the head and tells me not to be surly—Sir Martin and Lady Edgebrooke burble all over me, and even Catherine—"

"But, it is for the best, my dear boy. Every man needs a helpmate, after all. I mean where would I be without Miranda?"

Drew smiled despite himself. Where indeed? It was generally assumed that Ceddie did not so much as choose a cravat without the advice of his perspicacious wife.

"Miranda is a pearl beyond price, brother. Catherine is Spanish coin." He grunted. "Are the Edgebrookes arriving tomorrow, as well?"

"Of course. The celebration would be pretty hollow without the presence of the bride-to-be. Now, Drew, I want you on your best behavior. Give Catherine a chance. And yourself, for that matter."

Drew stiffened. "Meaning?"

Ceddie shifted uncomfortably. "Nothing, only that you seem to consider yourself as—completely worthless now—and you're not, Drew." His brown eyes were almost pleading as he faced his brother.

Drew knew an urge to lift his face to the sky and howl. He turned on Ceddie and snarled, "My God, I am possessed of a face that scares little children. I cannot tie my own cravat—can't so much as cut my own meat. Only the fact that I am an aristocrat with an inherited substance is saving me from starving in a gutter, for my hopeful career as a diplomat will never come to pass, and I am fit for nothing else. So, tell me, Ceddie—what precisely is your definition of the word 'worthless'? And do I not fill it beautifully?"

He turned on his heel and walked into the house.

*   *   *

Lord Barnstaple had been correct in his estimate. The first guests arrived not an hour before dinner that night, and by the next day, the abbey began to fill with friends and relatives. The process of greeting those he had not seen since his departure from home three years ago was not quite the ordeal that Drew had dreaded. Evidently, Cedric and John had told everyone what to expect. Reaction to his appearance was apparent, but no one actually flinched upon greeting him. To his sour amusement, one or two of the younger, sillier ladies apparently considered him rather a romantic figure.

Thus, it was with a reasonable degree of equanimity that he greeted Sir Martin and Lady Edgebrooke and their offspring on their arrival the following day. Catherine, he noted unwillingly, looked like a gift from the heart of the forest in a simple gown of pomona green sarcenet embroidered with leaves of a darker green. She smiled at him when she stepped from the carriage, but he merely offered a brief hello before turning to John. Pulling his friend aside, he whispered, "You wanted to go fishing—well, now's the time. If I don't escape from this parcel of determined well-wishers I may well go screaming mad before your very eyes."

Catherine, who had moved toward him, halted abruptly, and Drew could have sworn the pain in her eyes was genuine. Swallowing, he turned his back to draw John off toward the house. He was forestalled by the approach of a young man, tall and personable, with fair, modishly curled hair and bright, blue eyes. He was dressed in an ensemble that might have been considered by some a little excessive for the country. He strode past John and Drew.

"Catherine!" he cried delightedly, pressing a fervent kiss on her hand. "I have been waiting for you to arrive. You are looking radiant today as usual."

The gentleman turned, then, and addressed Drew.

"Hallo, coz, good to see you again." He stretched out a hand with apparent cordiality and Drew accepted it with a shade less heartiness. Why the hell had Ceddie invited Theo Venable to the festivities? He was family, of course, although the relationship was fairly distant. Drew had never liked him above half, considering him spoiled and too knowing for his own good, but he had always maintained a cool courtesy toward him. It appeared the young man and Catherine had become friends, he mused irritably.

"It's good to see you, too, Theo, but if you will excuse me, John and I are off for a spot of fishing." Once again, he pulled John in the direction of the house, and less than an hour later they stood together on the banks of a small stream that flowed nearby. For some moments they did not speak, and all that could be heard was the rippling of the brook, the singing of their lines as they cast, and the faint plop of lures landing on water. At last John spoke.

"Being a little hard on Catherine, ain't you?"

Drew did not reply for a moment, concentrating his attention on the placement of his lure. Fishing was just one more activity that was proving almost impossibly more difficult without the full use of his left arm. "Are you going to lecture me, old friend?" he drawled at last. "I've had enough of that from Ceddie since I came home."

John laughed easily. "I'm the last man in the world to be giving lectures to anyone on anything, as well you know. All I'm saying, is it ain't like you to give hurt where it ain't deserved."

Once more, Drew was silent for a few moments before he turned to face his friend. "I think we have a difference of opinion here on what's deserved. But, I apologize. I don't wish to speak ill of a man's sister. The fact remains, however, that I remember her as a termagant of the first water." He sighed heavily. "I know it would create a terrific row if I were the one to cry off, but I'm hoping I can persuade Catherine to do so."

"But she doesn't want—"

"I know. She doesn't want to hurt our families. Well, I don't either, but I'm not willing to sacrifice my well-being for the sake of this charming but totally unrealistic fantasy they've created. Nor do I think Catherine should be expected to do so, either. Good God, John, I'd think you'd be rooting on the sidelines for this betrothal to die a natural death. Surely you want more for your sister than a lifetime shackled to half a man."

"I want only for her to be happy," replied John slowly. "And from what I can gather, marrying you is what she wants to do."

Drew snorted. "Fustian!" He gathered up his tackle. "I think we shall have no luck this afternoon. Shall we go back to the house?" Without waiting for an answer, he turned and strode away from the river. After a moment, John sighed and followed him.

Conversation was desultory among the two men as they walked. Drew felt a moment of regret for his outburst. It was natural that John should take Catherine's part, but Drew was not the acquiescent boy who had marched off to war with a head full of brass bands and flying banners. He was older now, by several centuries, it seemed, and he was not, by God, going to be pushed into an arranged marriage with a woman who had sent him off with the strident hope that he not return.

His lips curved into a bitter smile. Not that it hadn't been a near thing. He did not blame Catherine for the disaster that had befallen him. That would be superstitious nonsense, but—

His unpleasant reverie was interrupted by the sound of high, excited voices. Looking toward the sound, he found that he and John had emerged from the woods surrounding the house and had entered a small terraced area. A few hundred yards away a group of children played, and in their center was Catherine and another young woman.

They were playing ball, and Catherine was laughing with
joyous abandon. Her hair had escaped the confines of the
pins and ribbons of her coiffure and it hung down her
back in a heavy molten fall. The lithe splendor of her
form was outlined clearly as she strained upward to catch
the ball.

Once again, Drew experienced a treacherous tightening
of his throat. As he watched, his cousin Theo ambled onto
the scene and moved close to Catherine. She seemed to
welcome the young man's approach and soon his laughter
blended with hers. Turning away from the sight, Drew
strode toward the house.

Watching his progress surreptitiously, Catherine's heart
sank. How could she reach Drew if he would not so much
as speak to her? Unable to maintain her pretense of frivolity, she withdrew from the ball game, ignoring Theo's
protestations, and made her way into the house. Restless,
she entered the library, and for some minutes simply stared
blindly at the volumes displayed for her perusal in this elegantly paneled chamber, furnished with comfortable chairs
and footstools.

Reaching for a volume entitled *Martyrs and Their
Deaths,* a tome she felt precisely reflected her mood, she
was stayed by the sound of the door opening behind her.

"Ah, there you are, Catherine. I wondered where you had
got to."

Miranda, the Countess of Barnstaple, entered the room,
her step purposeful, as always. She was a small woman, but
moved with such authority that one had no difficulty in en-
visioning a legion of distinguished forebears arrayed at her
back. Drawing Catherine to a satin striped settee, she settled herself beside the young woman with a brisk crackle of
skirts.

"Now, tell me," she continued, "about your meeting with
Drew yesterday."

Catherine smiled tightly. "It did not go well, to put it mildly."

In a very few words, she related her conversation with her betrothed. Miranda shook her head.

"I suspected it would be so. I would not have believed a man could change so drastically—and I do not refer to his physical impairments."

"I am sure it is not to be wondered at," replied Catherine slowly. "Aside from the horrors that have been inflicted on him, he has watched his comrades fall and die in unimaginable agony. I do not believe that those of us who have not experienced it can even remotely comprehend the effect of such carnage on the human spirit."

"I'm sure that is true, but Drew is home now, among his family, and"—Miranda bent a significant glance on Catherine—"and those who love him. Yet, he remains as bitter and defensive as though he were still facing the enemy. I don't think I have seen him smile since his arrival, and he meets every pleasantry with a caustic reply."

"At least he will speak to you." Catherine swallowed the lump that rose in her throat. "He has made it more than plain that he would rather not so much as remain in the same room with me."

"Oh, my dear." Miranda placed her hand on Catherine's. "This must be terribly difficult for you." She lifted her eyes to gaze directly into Catherine's. "I do not wish to pry, of course, but we have, I hope, become friends as well as neighbors, and it seems to me that after Drew left—and after Mr. Sills—that is, once you—Well," she finished hastily, "it appeared that your feelings for Drew have grown—" She stopped short and lifted her hand in an impatient gesture. "Pah! How I hate roundaboutation. Catherine, it is my belief you have come to love Drew."

Catherine felt herself go first very cold, then exceedingly warm. She had never discussed her feelings for Drew with anyone, not even John. An automatic denial sprang to her lips, but in the face of Miranda's obviously sincere concern, she replied hesitantly, "I—I am not indifferent to him."

Miranda smiled. "An understatement, I believe, but I am glad to hear you say it. I must, however, confess to some puzzlement. You and I were not acquainted at the time of your, er, infatuation with Mr. Sills, but by all accounts you expressed your displeasure with Drew at some length. I am wondering how you underwent such a profound change of heart after Drew left."

Catherine's heart thudded uncomfortably and her mouth went dry. "Oh. Yes. Well, I have known Drew since we were both in leading strings, and I always liked him." She laughed awkwardly. "At least, when he was not pulling my hair or perpetrating some ghastly joke on me. He was a very good sort of boy," she concluded lamely. She twisted her hands in her lap under Miranda's waiting silence and forced herself to continue. "As we grew older—well, if the truth were known, I phased into a period of violent infatuation for him. He could not see me for dust, of course, but I wove all sorts of fantasies about him when I was in my early teens. I had outgrown such feelings by the time I was sixteen or so, but we remained friends. In fact, if it were not for my ridiculous—and very temporary—infatuation with Randolph Sills, I should probably have agreed willingly to a betrothal with him, even though at the time my agreement would have been based solely on the fact that one must marry, after all, and I held Drew in great affection."

She drew a deep breath. "After Drew left, and I saw Mr. Sills in his true colors, I was terribly sorry for the way I had treated Drew. I thought about him a great deal—the, um, admirability of his character—and all that—and I realized that he is all that a woman could ask for in a husband."

Catherine's gaze remained locked on her fingers, still

clenched in her lap, but she was aware of Miranda's silent skepticism.

"Of course," replied the countess smoothly. "Purity of character and high moral purpose are just the qualities that would entice a maid to fall head over heels for a man."

Sudden tears flooded Catherine's eyes. She was a private person and had never allowed herself a true confidant. Even John, who was aware of the details of her perfidy, was not privy to her feelings about Drew. But Miranda had become a good friend in the two years since she had come to Graymore Abbey as Ceddie's wife, and Catherine knew a sudden, overpowering urge to open her heart to this kind, no-nonsense little woman.

She sat very still for a long moment before she spoke again.

"Tell me, Miranda, do you remember Helen Carstairs?"

"Of course. She visited here often with your mother. A nice young woman, if rather quiet. Wait," Miranda said, arrested. "Drew mentioned her just recently. In fact, he spoke her name almost as soon as he got in the house. Ceddie told me later he had been writing to her." Her brow creased slightly. "I gather the correspondence became somewhat warm. He seemed quite devastated at the news of her marriage. I must say, I was rather surprised. Miss Carstairs seemed so very proper—not at all the sort that would embark on a clandestine correspondence between a betrothed gentleman and an unmarried lady."

"She didn't."

"But—"

"It was I who wrote to Drew—using Helen's name."

The countess fairly gaped. "You! You carried on a correspondence with your own fiancé—under a pseudonym?"

Catherine shrank into the settee. "Yes—I did. Oh, Miranda," she cried, "I know how it sounds. I don't know how I could have launched on such an outrageous charade. Not that I regret any of it, of course. I could have bitten my wretched tongue off at the roots right after I hurled that vicious tirade at Drew. When John had told me of his refusal to so much as open my letters, I knew I deserved nothing better, yet I longed to make amends. It was John who had made the suggestion—only as an irony—that I might try writing Drew under another name.

"I responded with suitable mockery at the time, but later the idea slowly took possession of me. John brought up the notion again, with the additional hint that a letter from, say, Helen Carstairs, our mother's prosaic companion, would no doubt be received with platonic gratitude by a lonely soldier."

"And you did not think of what would happen later—when Drew came home?"

Catherine flushed. "No. I plunged into my pretense, with no thought as to its ultimate consequences. I suppose you cannot understand, but I was so delighted by Drew's willing reception of and response to 'Helen's' chatty missives. He told me that my insights and warmth came as a delightful surprise—and it was not long before he began to share his innermost thoughts with me—with Helen, that is."

Catherine's expression became dreamy and she gazed unseeing at the landscaped lawn beyond the library window. "I found I had more in common with my brother's friend than I had ever dreamed and—and I was touched as I had never been before. I filled pages with my own response, and when Drew received his grievous wounds I cried with him and did my best to provide balm for his ravaged spirit."

She straightened and turned to look directly at Miranda. "The day came at last when I realized I had committed the supreme idiocy of falling in love with a man whose regard I had effectively destroyed. And now"—her eyes filled with tears once more and her voice sank to a whisper—"and now, I don't know what to do."

"Oh, my dear." Once more, Miranda reached to touch Catherine's hand. "How awful for you."

They sat thus for a few moments, then Miranda straightened and continued in her customary brisk tone. "Well, there's no use crying over spilt milk. What's done is done, and we must consider how to bring the matter to a happy conclusion."

Catherine stared at her in surprise. "Happy conclusion? How can you say so? There can be no such outcome for me."

"Nonsense. Drew is in love with the woman who wrote those letters, is he not?"

"Well—I don't know. He never breathed a word of his feelings in his letters, though I sensed that he . . . But, what does that matter? If he has given his heart away, he believes it is to another woman."

"You are not listening," responded Miranda patiently. "He loves the woman who wrote the letters, and that woman is you."

"But—"

"All you have to do is apprise him of that fact. It may take him a few days to accustom himself to the idea that the woman he loves is actually the woman he is to marry in three weeks' time, but I'm sure he will understand your reasons for deceiving him so delightfully."

"Delightfully? I am not at all sure Drew will see my little masquerade in that light. Really, Miranda, you have no concept of the depth of his loathing for me right now."

She rose and paced the carpet for several moments. "But you are right," she continued at last. "I must tell him what I have done. I can continue my lie no longer."

She bent a tremulous smile on the countess, who also stood, just as a gong sounded in the distance. "It is time to dress for dinner," she said. "Let us hope that by the end of the evening, you and Drew will have resolved your difficulties and we shall all be looking forward to a happy wedding day."

Catherine's smile faded. She was not nearly so sanguine as Miranda on Drew's response to a confession of her perfidy. In any event, she could not possibly tell him the truth so soon. She would see what transpired over dinner, and then perhaps tomorrow . . .

Leaving Miranda in the corridor outside the library, she made her way wearily to her room.

Drew's heart sank as he entered the dining room along with the other family and friends trooping in for the evening meal. It must have been Ceddie who ordered that he be placed next to Catherine.

He had successfully avoided her in the preprandial gathering in the blue salon. Not that she was easy to ignore. Tonight, she wore a deceptively simple gown of blue silk that clung to her lithe curves in a sweep that began just under her breasts and fell to the tips of her matching kid slippers.

God, she would be a witness to his inept struggle to feed himself. She would watch as he had to summon a footman to cut his food, and she would see his pathetic efforts to butter his roll. He almost turned and fled the room, but, taking a deep breath, he took his place at the table. He must not give in to his stupid panic. This is how he was now, and he must face down his humiliation. His lips curled in a bitter smile. Perhaps his crude performance as a dinner partner would be enough to disabuse Catherine of her avowed wish to marry him. Turning to Catherine, who was now seated beside him, he raised his wineglass to her.

"You are in looks tonight," he said shortly.

Did he imagine the flash of pleasure that shone in her eyes for a moment?

"Thank you," she said simply, then after a moment,

added, "did you enjoy your fishing expedition with John this afternoon?"

He grimaced. "We came home empty-handed, I'm afraid, although I enjoyed getting out to the brook."

The conversation languished until Drew, in a spurt of desperation said, "The abbey is looking prosperous. I was struck by how green everything is—especially compared with Spain."

"Oh, yes," breathed Catherine. "I remember—" She stopped, appalled. She had almost said she remembered his descriptions of the heat and dust of the endless Spanish plains. "That is, I have heard that the climate in Spain is very nearly insupportable."

He uttered a sharp bark of laughter. "That is hardly the word. The grit blew into one's very skin, as did the suffocating heat. Sometimes our column seemed like a serpent, writhing along the plain, caked with dust and withering with thirst."

He paused abruptly, surprised that he had unburdened himself to such an extent. He had not spoken so before except to Helen. He became aware of a footman at his shoulder, proffering a platter of roast beef. To his surprise, the man deftly scooped a portion of meat onto his plate, already cut into bite-sized portions. The vegetables that followed were green beans and sliced parsnips, both easily managed with one hand, and another servant provided him with rolls, already cut and spread with butter.

He supposed he had Ceddie to thank for this, he thought. Or—no, it must have been his sister-in-law, he surmised as he intercepted an understanding smile and a slow wink from the countess. His returning smile was rigid. He should be grateful for these little attentions, but they only served to remind him, in mortifying detail, of his present situation.

When he looked again at Catherine, she had turned away to converse with the partner on her other side. Drew bent over his plate, devoting himself to his dinner.

Catherine gave scant attention to Squire Bentwaters. All her senses seemed riveted to the conversation taking place on her right. Drew was speaking to Mrs. Portlarington, a middle-aged matron who had known him all his life. To Catherine's surprise, he appeared to be responding courteously to the lady's pleasantries. She grimaced inwardly. Perhaps it was only with her that Drew elected to vent his spleen.

After giving a proper amount of time to Mrs. Portlarington, Drew turned back to Catherine. His conversation was bland and unexceptionable. At the end of the meal, when the ladies withdrew to leave the gentlemen to their port, she breathed a small sigh of relief. Perhaps Drew was getting over his antipathy toward her. Perhaps there was a chance she might reach him after all.

This pleasant delusion continued until the gentlemen joined the ladies again in the gold salon. Drew had just entered the room, his eyes going directly to Catherine, but upon sighting her, he had moved in another direction. Lady Barnstaple reached out a hand to intercept him.

"Lovely evening," she said in a minatory tone.

"Yes, it is," replied Drew warily.

"The moon is full and the stars are out. You will wish to enjoy a stroll on the terrace with Catherine," continued Miranda, her tone brooking no dispute. She beckoned to Catherine, who was standing in conversation with her mother. Lady Edgebrooke, her gaze meeting that of the countess, gave her daughter a slight push and, blushing, Catherine moved forward.

Theo Venable also moved forward, as though he would intercept Catherine, but a threatening glance from Miranda halted him in his tracks.

Thus, a few moments later, Drew found himself strolling on the terrace beside his betrothed, her hand tucked in his arm. He noted with some surprise that he felt comfortable with Catherine at his side, though her closeness brought a most unwelcome response. He guided her to a stone bench.

"It is time we talked," he said after a moment's hesitation.

Catherine drew a long breath. "I suppose it is." She placed her hand on his and Drew fancied he could feel its warmth spread over his body. "I know you have cause to dislike me, Drew," she continued. "My behavior before you left was inexcusable. I can only offer in my defense that I was young—and spoiled—and fancied myself desperately in love with someone else. I have been granted my every wish since I was a child, and I simply could not conceive that my parents actually intended to make me do something I did not want to do."

Lord, he wished she weren't so beautiful, thought Drew. The moon, as advertised, beamed brilliantly, drawing glints of deep fire from her hair. Her eyes were starshine on velvet and it seemed to him that they were filled with the ineffable sweetness he remembered from the days when he had fancied himself falling in love with her.

He pulled away slightly, so that her fingertips fell from his sleeve.

"And Helen?" he asked tightly.

Catherine made no attempt to reestablish the brief contact, but she leaned toward him. Drew immediately became aware of the familiar scent of her, a combination of flowers and, he thought, a hint of lemon.

"Please believe me," she replied, "I did not encourage Helen in her romance with Mr. Dench in order to spite you, nor did I keep her from telling you of her marriage plans."

Again, Drew pulled back.

"That's as it may be, but you see"—he struggled to maintain control of his voice—"I rather lost my heart to her."

He rose abruptly and stood before her.

"I'm sure you will understand." He could not keep a hint

of sarcasm from his tone. "I do not wish to contemplate marriage to one woman while I—while I have these feelings for another."

Catherine did not seem as cast down by his words as he might have expected. She stood, and her smile enveloped him.

"I do understand, Drew. Is it possible you might have mistaken your feelings—as I did mine?"

"No." He said the word uncompromisingly, and Catherine sighed.

"This is most unfortunate, my dear." She paused for a moment as though uncertain how to continue. "The wedding—"

"Good God," Drew cried. "Can you not get this one fact through your head? There will be no wedding!"

Catherine flinched as though he had struck her, and he continued in a quieter vein.

"Surely you do not wish to marry one whose affections are placed elsewhere. You, of all people should understand my sentiments."

When she remained silent, he went on awkwardly. "You have been the belle of the neighborhood since you were sixteen. In the time we have been separated, has no one touched your heart?"

"No," she lied, her throat tight with unshed tears. *Only you!* she longed to cry out. *Only a man I have come to know as prideful and passionate—a man of wit and vulnerability and a great capacity for love.*

Unthinking, Drew lifted his good hand to grasp her shoulder. She looked up at him, and her brimming eyes glittered in the moonlight. Once more, her scent filled him, and when she lifted a slender hand to touch his cheek, something seemed to explode within him.

"What the devil do you want from me?" he growled. He pulled her toward him and for a long, suspended moment, she stared up at him before he bent to cover her mouth in a savage kiss. Almost immediately his mouth softened, and the kiss became one of seeking urgency.

She stiffened, and for an instant, she struggled before melting against him. The feel of her softness pressed against him created a frenzy of desire within him and he wrapped his arms about her more tightly. Suddenly, he became aware of the constraint caused by his withered limb and he pulled away from her abruptly.

"You see?" His voice was a bitter rasp. "I cannot even hold a woman properly. Is this the sort of creature you want for a husband?"

He stared at her for a moment, his eyes hard, the scar on his cheek very white against his skin, before whirling away from her. Catherine watched as he strode into the house. She pressed trembling fingers against lips that felt swollen and bruised. It was the first kiss she had received from him—she had not allowed so much as a buss on her cheek in their former relationship, and as a first kiss, it left a great deal to be desired. It had been violent, and insensitive and vengeful, yet it had shaken her to the center of her soul. What would it be like, she wondered as she listened in the silence of the night to her pounding heart, to be kissed by him in earnest? A kiss of tenderness and passion—and of love.

Slowly, she followed Drew into the house. When she entered the gold salon, she discovered that Drew had retired for the night. Miranda eyed her sharply, but said nothing, and after a few moments, Catherine said her own good nights and made her way to her bedchamber.

The next morning, she rose unrefreshed, determined to seek Drew out once again. Surely, there must be something she could say that would convince him that he was still a man, despite his impairments. Having accomplished that, of course, she must confess her deception to him. Despite Miranda's bracing words, she knew Drew would be furious. Just how furious, she could not know, but it was not a discovery to which she looked forward with any degree of anticipation.

Her quarry, however, proved to be singularly elusive, and it was soon borne on her that Drew was taking great pains to avoid her. They did not meet again until just before luncheon, which was to be a picnic, held in the south meadow. Unfortunately, Sir Martin had fallen victim to a return of the sore throat that had plagued him earlier in the week, and he and Catherine's mother had departed for Greengroves that morning with instructions that Catherine was not to worry, and that she was to enjoy her reunion with her betrothed. Catherine knew her father's illness was not serious, but she missed their support, tenuous though it was, under the circumstances. She affixed a smile to her lips as she joined the others for the picnic.

The guests were transported in laughing groups in open gigs, and both Ceddie and Miranda made it their business to see that Catherine and Drew rode together.

It was not difficult to sense Drew's continued withdrawal, for his conversation both with her and the other occupants of the vehicle was minimal. Catherine made uncomplicated chatter with Lord and Lady Whitestone and their two children and smiled and laughed until she thought her face would crack. In the south meadow, tables had been set up beneath a stand of oaks, and cold chicken and salad were being dispensed by liveried servants. Cutlery clinked delicately against fine china and, despite Drew's best efforts, he was ushered to a seat next to Catherine. For a moment it looked as though he would bolt, but his training as a proper English gentleman held fast and he flung himself grudgingly into his seat. After a moment, as though the social setting recalled to him his responsibilities as a son of the house, he began to speak courteously to those placed near them, all except, of course, Catherine. She noticed that his mannered smile never reached his eyes.

When the meal was concluded, Catherine rose quickly, and, unable to maintain her composure in the face of Drew's continued rebuffs, prepared to flee from the group still chattering beneath the trees.

She was intercepted, however, by Theo Venable, who grasped her elbow. For once, he was not smiling.

"Catherine, what is it? My dear girl, why are you so troubled? Or, perhaps I can guess the reason." He drew her arm through his and pressed it close to his side. Catherine instinctively jerked away from him.

"Theo, I thank you for your concern, but I really wish to be alone right now."

"And I wish to be alone as well—with you."

Catherine glanced around, somewhat dismayed to note that the other picnickers had drifted away, leaving the two alone in the shadow of a great oak.

"Catherine," continued Theo, "you know how I feel about you. I would not speak, except that I have seen you and Drew together. You cannot tell me yours is a match made in heaven."

"Perhaps not, Theo, but it is the match I am entered into and I intend to honor it."

Theo grimaced petulantly. "I cannot believe you mean that. Very well," he sighed, as Catherine opened her mouth to remonstrate. "I shall say no more now, but I shall not give up, my dear. There are three weeks before your so-called wedding, and I shall spend every second of them trying to make you see reason."

The smile had reappeared, and with a graceful bow, he turned away from her. Catherine gasped in indignation, almost giving in to the urge to hurl an imprecation after him, but instead she whirled about and, picking up her skits, ran as though pursued by demons. In a few moments, she had reached the edge of the meadow, and she plunged headlong into the forest. She did not stop until she had reached the banks of a sparkling little brook that wound through the woods. Dropping beside a tree, she breathed deeply as though she might absorb some of the peace of her surroundings.

In the meadow, Drew had watched her abrupt departure, and after a moment, he drew a deep breath and proceeded after her. In his distraction, he bumped into someone headed in the same direction.

"I beg your—" he began. "Oh, it's you," he concluded as he recognized his cousin. He continued walking.

"In the flesh," responded Theo, moving with him. "You seem to be in a brown study, coz."

"I was thinking of something."

"Of your coming nuptials, perhaps?"

Drew stiffened. "I hardly think that is any of your concern."

"Now, that is not very friendly, coz," responded Theo softly, "and you see, I have made it very much my concern."

Drew halted. "Yes, I have noted your attentions to my fiancée. I would very much appreciate it if they would cease."

"I think that is for Catherine to decide." His tone was gentle, almost meditative, but it seemed to Drew that a certain smugness lay beneath it.

"Are you saying that Catherine welcomes your smarmy compliments, coz?"

Theo smiled. "Let us just say that she seems to enjoy my company, as I do hers."

Drew was hardly aware that his fingers had clenched into fists. "By God, Theo, you will leave Catherine alone, or I'll—"

Theo laughed. "Or you'll what? You will forgive me, Carter, if I do not perceive you as much of a threat."

By now, Drew was ready to do murder, and he stepped forward, hands clenched. He overbalanced on his bad leg and staggered. At the same moment, he became aware that he was poised to strike with a fist that was shriveled and useless. He halted, humiliation and rage boiling within him in a maelstrom of futility.

"Very wise of you, Drew." Theo's mocking laughter washed over him like acid. "Never attempt what you cannot complete." His gaze drifted to where Catherine had disappeared into the forest. He made a swift gesture of farewell, and strolled off to join a group of young men playing darts nearby.

Drew was trembling so that he could hardly stand. A year ago he could have pounded the likes of Theo Venable into a satisfying smear on the ground. God, how he hated what he had become!

Crouched beneath her tree, Catherine failed to find the peace she sought. How stupid she'd been to think that she could win Drew back to her. He had made it plain, in every way that he could—including that brutal kiss of the night before—that his only feelings for her were of contempt, and that he had no intention of going through with their marriage. When she told him of her duplicity regarding the letters, his dislike would turn to hate, if it had not already done so.

The sound of footsteps interrupted her unpleasant ruminations, and she knew without turning to whom that limping stride belonged.

"Catherine," said Drew. "Catherine," he repeated as he threw himself down beside her. "Are you all right?"

She made an effort to smile coolly at him. "Not precisely, but I was hoping that a few moments of solitude would bring me to rights."

"Meaning that you wish I would go away, I suppose. I shall do so momentarily, but not before I have apologized to you." He shifted uncomfortably. "My behavior last night was inexcusable."

Catherine essayed a light laugh. "Surely it is permissible for a man to kiss his betrothed."

Drew frowned. "Possibly. But, as I believe I have mentioned once or twice, I do not consider us betrothed. Besides, that wasn't a kiss, it was an unforgivable display of ill temper and—and retaliation."

"For what? I have already told you I did not urge Helen into marriage simply to cause you pain. Or did you wish revenge for my own display of infantile temper—which occurred three years ago and for which I have already apologized profusely? And which, I might add, you must have known I did not mean."

Drew's lips curved in an acid smile. "Did you not? But your wish almost came true, didn't it? In fact, you should be pleased, for death would have been preferable to the fate that befell me."

Catherine gasped. "Drew! What a dreadful thing to say!"

"Yes, I suppose it is—but you must know I do not mean it," he replied, mimicking her tone. His face grew serious. "Because, of course, I realize the petty curses of such a budding virago would be insufficient to cause the calamity that befell me."

Catherine twisted to face him directly. "For God's sake, Drew. When are you going to stop feeling sorry for yourself?"

Drew whitened. "What" he growled.

"You came home maimed and scarred. But you did come home—which many did not. And many who did return are a great deal worse off than you." Catherine's voice began to tremble in its intensity. "You behave as though life is over for you now—that you might just as well curl up and die. Have you really looked at yourself? The scar is bad, but it has not turned you into a monster. So far I have not seen little children run screaming from you. In case you had not noticed, your little cousins and the children of your guests behold you no differently than the other rather boring adults in residence. In addition, according to John, it is not nearly so inflamed as it was. In a year or two, people who know you will have forgotten it's there, and strangers will find it hardly remarkable. As for your arm, again according to John, the doctors told you that you will regain more mobility with exercise. Certainly enough to accomplish most routine tasks. So, as far as I can see, the only limit to your future activities, besides your own self-destructive state of mind, is that you probably will never be able to dance very well again.

"Drew," she continued, almost breathless, "a terrible thing has befallen you, but everything that makes you what you are is still whole. You can think, and you can appreciate fine wine or a good book—or good conversation. You still possess the intelligence and the skill that your superiors recognized as the makings of a fine diplomat."

She paused, her breath coming in great, painful gulps. Drew continued to stare at her, speechless, his eyes glittering darkly against the pallor of his skin. When he made no response, she sagged suddenly, a wave of exhaustion sweeping over her. "And another thing," she said dully. "Your apology, such as it was, is accepted. Furthermore, I have been brought to the realization that there is nothing so tedious and humiliating as trying to persuade a reluctant male into marriage. Therefore, as a reward for your noble deed, I shall release you from your obligation to marry me." Catherine listened to herself disbelievingly. Good God, she had not at all meant to say such a thing. She knew, however, that every word she spoke came from the heart. At any rate, she seemed incapable of stopping herself. She rose and glared down at him. "You may consider yourself a free man, Andrew Carter. Free to wrap yourself in your little cocoon of self-absorption and free to give up on life. I shall miss you, for I had grown rather fond of the Andrew Carter I used to know, but then, I have at last come to learn that in this world we cannot have everything we want."

Unable to say more because of the tears that gathered in her throat to choke her, she whirled and ran, fleeing the furious, stricken expression in Drew's eyes. She halted when she came to the meadow's edge, then moved ahead more slowly. By the time she rejoined the picknickers, she had regained a modicum of composure, and seated herself in a spot somewhat removed from the main group. Distractedly, she watched a desultory game of ball taking place some distance away.

"Are you all right, Catherine?"

She started, to observe Miranda approaching the table. Good Lord, her demeanor must indeed be lugubrious to cause everyone such concern this afternoon.

"Yes," she replied shortly. "Behold me unbetrothed, Miranda." At the countess's expression of dismay, tears rose once again, and her smile was brittle as she described the scene that had just transpired.

"Oh, my," was Miranda's only response.

"Indeed," said Catherine. "I do not know how soon you will wish to make a formal announcement, but surely everyone will have to be told that the wedding they have come to celebrate is no longer on the schedule." She rose. "If you will excuse me, Miranda, I think my supply of social chatter has dwindled to nonexistence."

She turned away, but was stayed by Miranda's hand on her arm.

"Do not give up, Catherine. I believe Drew's feelings for you are stronger than you realize."

Catherine laughed shortly. "Oh, no, I am well aware of precisely how strong his feelings are, for he has told me repeatedly since his return."

With a dispirited wave of her hand, she set off for the house.

Some distance away, Drew emerged from the forest, feeling rather like a hibernating bear just emerging from its den. For Catherine's monologue had had a profound effect on him. His first reaction had been one of white-hot anger.

How *dare* this pampered daughter of privilege lecture him on a subject on which she had not the smallest understanding? But he had listened, paralyzed by the sting of her words—and a vague familiarity in them. When she concluded her monologue by breaking off their betrothal, he felt no sense of victory or relief, merely an overwhelming sadness over a relationship that had gone terribly wrong.

She was talking with Miranda. He made a move to go to her, but something stayed him. His pride, perhaps. He had just made one apology to her for his behavior; he was damned if he'd make another in the space of half an hour. She had told him that her temper tantrums were a thing of the past. He laughed shortly. She had flared up at him like an incendiary rocket, all because he had told her a few home truths. Seeing Catherine walk away from Miranda toward the house, he moved slowly forward only to be brought up short as an idea struck him.

She had been angry, yes, but she had not really lost her temper, had she? She'd been giving him a few home truths of her own, if he were to be completely honest with himself. It was not, after all, as though he had not heard those sentiments before. He continued walking. It was Helen, he realized suddenly, who had also told him he was in danger of falling into a morass of self-pity. Lord, was he so transparent that any perceptive woman could read him like a novel?

How could Catherine have fathomed his trouble so deeply, when heretofore it was only Helen who had understood his agonies of soul? She had understood and cautioned him not to let his tragedy overwhelm him.

That is precisely what he had done, and Catherine recognized his bitter ravings for what they were—the imprecations of a hurt child.

He should be pleased, he supposed. He had accomplished his purpose. He was free of his betrothal to Catherine Edgebrooke, a consummation he had devoutly wished for three years. Yet now that his purpose was accomplished, he felt nothing beyond a forlorn emptiness.

He cast his thoughts to Helen, and found, to his surprise, that he had difficulty in recalling her face. This was not surprising, he supposed, for he had been only slightly acquainted with her before their correspondence. Now, when he tried to bring up her image, Catherine's face was superimposed.

Catherine.

She truly did seem to have changed, he admitted grudgingly. He thought of her laughing gaiety with the children the day before. She had been tactful at dinner, managing not to say all the wrong things as he ate. She was courteous and heedful of the wishes of the other guests, even going out of her way, he remembered with a smile, to play whist with old Lady Bensham, a tartar of the first rank.

Had she changed, he wondered, or was this her true character, with the chaff of her spoiled youth winnowed away?

He shook himself angrily. Why did he continue to dwell on Catherine and her attributes when he should be thinking of Helen? She was no longer available, but surely he should be pining for her—should he not? Still, there was no denying he had come to enjoy Catherine's company, and there could be no harm in being friends with her—could there?

His thoughts flashed back to last night's kiss. There had been nothing of friendship in the bruising punishment he had inflicted on her. Yet, the instant his mouth had touched hers, he had been almost overcome by a wave of longing tinged with tenderness. Despite Catherine's initial resistance to his embrace, there could be no mistaking the response that shuddered through her. Did she truly feel something for him? The thought was, of course, unwelcome, but he felt a stirring in the pit of his stomach at the idea.

He moved forward, at last, crossing the meadow toward the picnickers, only to be intercepted by a militant Miranda.

"How *could* you?" were her first words to him, uttered in a tone of deep indignation. When he made no response beyond a blank stare, she continued brusquely. "Is it true? Catherine says she has ended your betrothal."

Drew still said nothing, but nodded briefly. He made as though to push past her, but she restrained him with her hand.

"You must talk to her, Drew. The wedding must go forward. Oh, dear," she sighed, "Ceddie will be devastated."

Drew stiffened. "I do, of course, regret discommoding Ceddie, but I trust you will forgive me if I tell you that my brother's sensibilities are not my primary concern at the moment."

"Of course not," replied Miranda quickly. "The ones to whom this marriage are most important are you and Catherine."

Declining to dispute this ludicrous statement, Drew contented himself with a cold stare.

"If you will excuse me," he said icily, "I must apprise my brother of Catherine's decision."

Ceddie reacted to the news as Drew had expected.

"My God!" He paled. "I don't believe this. She simply set you adrift? I don't understand." His pale gaze shot toward Drew. "This is absolutely unacceptable, you know. You and Catherine must marry. It was the dearest wish—"

"Yes, I know," snapped Drew impatiently. He grasped his brother's arm and led him to the closest chair. "You just do not understand. Catherine doesn't give a good, healthy damn about the dearest wishes of our parents. She never has, and now I see why. They claimed to have our interests at heart, but it was only theirs that concerned them."

Ceddie's spaniel eyes filled with concern.

"You're wrong, Drew. Father wished for a union of the

families, as does Sir Martin, but they would never have gone ahead with the betrothal if it were not the best thing for you two, as well. As for Catherine, Lord, she used to worship you."

He grinned as Drew stared blankly at him. "Don't you remember? She followed you about like a Tantony pig. The highest delight of her life is when you allowed her to carry your game bag."

Drew flushed. "Perhaps. But that was a long time ago—when she was a child. Believe me, any worship she might have felt for the friend of her older brother dissipated shortly after she went into long skirts."

"I'm not so sure. She awaited your return with the greatest anticipation, you know."

Despite himself, Drew felt a stirring of interest. "Did she?"

"And have you not noticed how she looks at you? No, I suppose not, for her glances are always surreptitious, when she thinks you will not notice. Just as yours are toward her."

Drew opened his mouth to protest, but closed it immediately with a sheepish grin. He realized, almost with a shiver of discovery, that when he and Catherine were in the same room, he could not keep his gaze from her. Why was that? he wondered in some irritation. He had no real interest in the pestilent female beyond a desire to get her out of his life. Yet, his thoughts, his senses centered on her in a manner he would not have thought possible when he returned home.

It was not merely her beauty that drew him, although her storm-colored eyes and piquant features were enough to rivet the attention of any man. Nor was it her charm of manner, although when she put herself out to be agreeable, she could entice bees from the hive. It was all, as he knew to his cost, false as paste jewelry. She wielded her assets to her own advantage.

Was that it? he wondered, suddenly arrested. Had Catherine possessed an ulterior motive in her desire to marry him? Had she abandoned some cherished plan when she released him? If so, what could it be? She had lost Randolph Sills—or at least, she had realized that the hedgebird was only after her substance, and she was forced to let him go. Was she now desperate for a replacement?

Surely not. She had the pick of every eligible male in the neighborhood. Look at Theo Venable. He was sniffing after her like a randy weasel. Good God, had she formed a tendre for him? He was only slightly more eligible than Sills, for God's sake.

A marked feeling of distaste swept over him at the idea of Catherine succumbing to Venable's oily flattery. On the other hand, perhaps she did not see the encroaching mushroom as husband material. Perhaps she envisioned a future with him as her secret lover. He certainly might be available for dalliance were she married to a complaisant husband. And who more complaisant than a man she had married for convenience, only to please her family? A man who openly disliked her?

That scenario certainly made sense, although it did not jibe with what he knew of Catherine's character. Subterfuge had always been foreign to her nature. It would have been just like her to announce to her supposedly uncaring fianceé her intention to carry on a liaison after her marriage.

He shifted uncomfortably. Somehow, this did not seem like Catherine, either.

He came to with a start, aware that Ceddie was still staring at him in a troubled fashion.

"I see no reason," said his brother, "to inform the rest of the guests of Catherine's little, er, flutter of apprehension. She will no doubt have changed her mind again by this afternoon."

Drew laughed shortly. "You have an infinite capacity for

self-delusion, Ceddie. Now that Catherine has given me my congé, I consider myself a free man, and, even in the unlikely event of yet another reversal of feeling on her part, I have no intention of allowing myself to be re-lashed to the altar of familial duty."

Ceddie's lips curled faintly. "Methinks you protest too much, brother. Tell me, truly, would marriage to Catherine be such an intolerable fate?"

For a moment, Drew experienced the astonishing sensation that his universe had suddenly skewed sideways. Inexplicably, it was as though he had never considered this concept before in his life. A lifetime with Catherine! His disillusionment with her had been complete, and the resulting emotional vacuum had been filled almost immediately with his growing attachment for the empathetic Helen. Now, Helen was gone, and he was almost appalled to discover that he was no longer devastated at this turn of events. Was he a callow youth, then, fickle in his affections as summer sunshine playing with rain clouds? A lifetime with Catherine. The words hummed through his mind again, with an increasing lilt, and an image rose before his eyes of the laughing girl he had beheld yesterday, playing ball with the children. In the few nonconfrontational conversations he had held with her, he had found himself enjoying her company, despite himself, and somehow it was beginning to seem less and less difficult to picture her at his side in the years to come. She had apparently managed to overcome her revulsion to his appearance. She would have him believe he should consider it a minor inconvenience!

He turned to Ceddie.

"Very well. I shall say nothing to the other guests, and in the meantime, I shall make an effort to reconcile with Catherine—at least to the point where we might be friends."

Ceddie blew out his cheeks happily.

"Good lad!" he cried. "I must tell Miranda. She will want to discuss this with Catherine. I mean, we do not want your betrothed to be spreading the precipitate news that the engagement is off."

He laughed heartily and stumped off to where Miranda stood in conversation with several of the guests. Drew watched his departure, a small crease forming between his eyes. Good God, what had he just done? Catherine had just granted him the consummation of his most devout wish. He should be shouting it from the treetops.

He took a deep breath. No, he had promised Ceddie he would try to reestablish a friendship with Catherine—if not a betrothal. He would pursue that goal in good faith. It would not be difficult, after all. He thought of Catherine as he had last seen her in the forest glade. Soft tendrils of hair had escaped their sculpted coils to catch fire in the early afternoon sun and her gray eyes had glittered with unshed tears. Distress had radiated from her with every appearance of sincerity and, despite his own fury, he had known an almost mindless urge to draw her close to him, to press his lips against her fragrant hair, and to brush away those incipient tears with comforting fingers.

Sighing, he limped toward the house in search of his elusive destiny.

"But, Miranda, they must be told!" Catherine blurted out the words with ill-concealed exasperation. She sat with the countess in a small salon just off the manor's long gallery. Dinner would be announced soon, and Catherine had fully expected Miranda to come to her with the news that Ceddie would announce the dissolution of the betrothal at that time. Instead, Miranda had pulled her aside to inform her that Ceddie had, "persuaded dear Drew to withhold any action on your ill-advised offer to release him."

Catherine had almost gasped in astonishment. "But Drew could not have said anything of the sort! He—that is, I left him before he had a chance to respond to my severing of the betrothal, but there is no doubt in my mind that I have granted his dearest wish."

Miranda smiled patiently. "Of course it is not his wish, my dear, and he knows it—at least underneath."

"But—but this is abominable," sputtered Catherine. "Does Drew believe he is doing me a favor by keeping quiet about the breakup of our engagement? How very condescending of him, to be sure!"

She was so angry she could hardly speak. What sort of game was he playing? First, he raged to the heavens that he wished to be free of her, then, when she acceded, he blushed coyly and said, "Well, perhaps not."

"Where is he?" she asked in an unpleasant tone.

"Why, I believe he and the other gentlemen went out for some shooting, but they should be back momentarily."

"Out shooting? Our future hangs by a thread, and he goes out shooting?"

"Now, Catherine . . ." But Lady Barnstaple spoke to the empty air, for Catherine had turned on her heel and stalked from the room.

It was perhaps just as well, thought Catherine an hour or so later as she descended to the blue salon to join the other guests for dinner, that she had been unable to find Drew. She had been ready to disembowel him, but in the hour or so since she had left Miranda, her seething sensibilities had subsided somewhat. She knew that when she encountered Drew in the company of the others, she would be cool and controlled.

Approaching the blue salon, she tensed as Drew moved down the corridor toward her from another direction.

His mouth curved in the smile that always caused a melting sensation in her interior. "Ah," he said, "just the person I wanted to see."

Catherine returned his smile warily. "You'll forgive me," she replied tightly, "if I beg leave to doubt that."

He did not reply for a moment, but gazed at her assessingly for a moment. "Do I sense a faint hint of censure in your tone? Perfectly understandable, I'm sure. However, now that I have found you—"

Catherine knew a resurgence of the anger that had simmered within her all afternoon. "Found me? But I have been right here. Did you expect to find me lurking among the shooting party?"

"Shooting party?"

"Yes, Miranda told me where you spent the afternoon," replied Catherine with some asperity.

Drew laughed, a little shamefacedly. "Oh, that. Well, I started out with John and Ceddie and the rest, but my mind was elsewhere, and when we passed—" He halted suddenly. "In fact—" He moved to her suddenly and caught her hand in his. Sparks of something disturbing danced in his dark eyes. "Catherine, come with me—right now. Please."

"But—but . . ." She sputtered. "The dinner hour is on us. People will be coming down any minute."

"Yes." He pulled her along the corridor, bending on her a smile that was both mischievous and tender. "That's why we must make our exodus quickly."

Catherine said no more, but allowed him to draw her into the library and through the double doors that stood at one end of the room. Once outside, he hurried across the lawn until he came to a stand of oaks that stood between the parkland of the manor and the open field that marked the boundary of the home farm.

"Drew, where on earth are we going?" expostulated Catherine. "I am not dressed for a country excursion. And we will miss dinner! Whatever will everyone—"

She fell silent suddenly, for Drew had pulled her beneath one of the oaks, and in a moment had made his way to the far side of the trees, where the branches bent low over a spreading hedge of hawthorne and brambles. A sort of cave was formed there, in which were set three crumbled stone benches and a rotting wooden table. Catherine gasped.

"Why, it's—"

Drew turned to her and pushed her gently onto one of the benches.

"Do you remember this? Our secret place. Yours and John's and mine." He sank down on another bench. In the cramped confines of the little enclosure, he was very close.

Catherine was forced to laugh. "Well, it was really yours and John's—and whatever select friends you chose to let join you here. I was the interloper. I remember the day I discovered your secret club meeting here. I crept up with all the stealth of a red Indian—or so I fancied—and when I sprang upon you crouched over your latest treasure—a dead badger, if I recall correctly, I thought my short life had reached its end."

"Well, of course we were somewhat disconcerted to find that a female—a grubby six-year-old at that—had penetrated the fastness of our lair."

"Disconcerted! You threatened me with horrors too awful to speak aloud—although, I think you did mention decapitation."

"Nonsense. We let you stay, did we not?"

"Only because I threatened to tell Nurse where you could be found all those times she called for you in vain."

"Nevertheless, you eventually became a full-fledged member of the group. We had some marvelous times in here, didn't we?"

Catherine smiled. "Yes, it was a splendid place for hiding away from the adult world. Goodness, we planned explorations through the jungle and over polar caps—and planned battle strategies, and—"

"And the horrible revenges we would wreak on certain footmen and grooms and gamekeepers and tutors and anyone else who persisted in keeping us buckled under the intolerable rules and regulations of childhood."

Catherine laughed and then fell silent. "We did have good times together—you and John and I—didn't we?"

"Yes." Drew took her hand in his. "I was thinking about that when I was here earlier today. Where did it all go, I wondered—the friendship, the camaraderie? What happened?"

"We grew up, I suppose," replied Catherine, her eyes suddenly moist. "Only, some of us did not grow up quite enough."

"I think you're right. We both thought we were fully mature and capable of directing our own destinies in the weeks before I left for the Peninsula, and we both acted like children."

A vision rose suddenly in Catherine's mind of the little sixpence, flashing through the air just before it struck Drew's cheek. She nodded, without speaking.

"And I'm afraid I haven't been behaving much better now," Drew continued, and Catherine glanced at him, startled.

"You're right, you know. I have allowed myself to sink into a morass of self-pity ever since my, er, unfortunate incident at Toulouse. It seemed as though everything in my life had gone wrong—the woman I planned to marry had rejected me, and then when I thought I had found love again, that turned out to be a fool's dream, as well. I lashed out at everyone around me, particularly you, whom I had by now come to think of as my evil genius."

He drew a long breath.

"I guess I am trying to apologize—again, and I'm wondering if we could not make a new start in our lives. You have granted me my freedom, and I appreciate that. Ceddie convinced me to keep the pretense of our betrothal alive, and I'm not so sure that was a good idea, but I did agree. What do you think, Catherine?" He was very close to her, and she was aware of the familiar smell of him permeating her senses. "Can we at least be friends again?"

"I—" began Catherine, then fell into a helpless silence.

"Perhaps friendship will lead to something more—for there is still the betrothal to consider—and perhaps not. Our families still wish us to marry, and there is the succession to consider, for so far, Ceddie and Miranda have produced no children. I must marry someone—and—Oh, God—" He rose abruptly. "I'm making the most wretched mull of this." He sank down onto the bench again. "What I'm trying to say, is that neither of us appear to have a great love waiting in the wings, and that being the case—perhaps we should each consider marrying a friend."

"Yes," whispered Catherine, her throat suddenly dry, "we could consider that, I suppose."

"I propose we simply let ourselves drift in this situation for a week or two. Then, if either of us feels that we cannot go through with the marriage, we will call it off. It will raise a tremendous rumpus, of course, but we shall just have to stand together."

There were a hundred objections Catherine knew she should make. She should say something about loveless marriages, at the very least. But it would not be a loveless marriage, would it? At least, not on her part. A voice rose in the back of her mind, clear and unpleasant.

And what about your Great Lie? He believes himself to be in love with another woman. What would he think if he knew the truth? Would your famous friendship stand up under the revelation of your perfidy?

As though in counterpoint, another voice made itself heard almost at once, whispering slyly.

But does he need to know at all? We have progressed from outright loathing to an admission of friendship in just two days. He fell in love with the woman who wrote those letters. Do you not think you could make him fall in love with her again?

No, of course not. Such a course of action would be contemptible. She would have to tell him—but not now. Not now, when their new relationship was still in the bud, fragile and shiny. She would wait for a more appropriate moment—a few days from now, perhaps. She lifted her gaze to his.

"I have never ceased being your friend, Drew, even in my worst moments." Her heart beat so loud in her ears, she thought he must hear it. "I will certainly agree to your proposal of—continued amity." For, he had not really proposed marriage, had he?

He said nothing, but in the depths of his coal-chip eyes, a disturbing light shone. He bent to kiss her cheek. Just a butterfly kiss, really, and she expected that he would draw back immediately. But, he did not. His lips trailed, still with that feather-soft touch until he reached hers. Slowly and deliberately, his mouth moved on hers—almost teasing, and from somewhere deep within her, Catherine experienced a shudder of response. As the kiss deepened, his right hand caressed her back, moving upward to cup her head so that the pressure of his lips fairly burned its way into hers. Catherine felt as though she were drinking in Drew's very essence, and that she was imparting hers to him. At last, he drew back and simply gazed at her for some moments.

"Well," he said quietly, his tone bemused, almost startled.

"Yes," she replied, willing her heart to stop its absurd leaping in her breast.

Drew said no more, but rose, and taking her hand once more, led her back toward the house.

The days that followed were the first truly happy ones Catherine could remember since Drew's departure for Spain. Although there was no repetition of the scene in the tree cave, she and Drew spent endless, idyllic hours with each other. Nothing more was said between them of marriage, but when other guests teased them with the usual jokes directed at betrothed couples, there was no thought of denial. They merely laughed and, when the jibes grew ribald, Catherine blushed adorably.

Theo made two or three attempts to insert himself into their intimacy, but even he seemed to sense that his efforts were futile.

This blissful state of affairs lasted for almost a week.

Catherine had no portent of disaster the morning she awoke to find the skies leaden and opened her bedchamber window to discover a sharp, disagreeable wind blustering about the casement. She merely smiled, recalling the archery tournament that was to be held today. Perhaps, she thought dreamily, the gentlemen would decide on a shooting party instead, and the ladies would shop in the village, leaving Drew and her to dream by a cozy fire in the library.

Similar thoughts occupied Drew's mind as he stood at his own window, clad in shirt and breeches. Too bad about the tournament, he thought. He'd rather been looking forward to giving assistance to his betrothed, his arms about her shoulders, his body pressed against her softly curving back. However, there was much to be said for tea by the fire, or perhaps a brisk walk to the cottage ornée situated in a spinney not far from the main house. All sorts of magical things might happen in a snug cottage, for two people taking haven there against the elements.

Was he wrong to have let things progress as they had? he wondered. He was teetering on the brink of parson's mousetrap. Should he not be more concerned? Somehow, the rage he had built up at Catherine had dissipated like ghosts in the first shaft of morning sun—and after only a few days in her company. She had always held this power over him, even as a very young girl. How many times had he been furious with her over some trick she had played, or her latest display of temper, only to be won over moments later by her laughter and her teasing?

He was beginning to fall in love with her—again, he realized with a start, and it appeared she once more found the idea of marriage to him appealing. Why? he asked himself once more. Why would a lovely, vibrant woman, who could have her pick of any man in the country, want to shackle herself to a ruin of a man? His breath caught as he recalled the kiss of a few days ago. She had seemingly opened herself to him—given of herself as a woman would to the man she loves. A flame of hope shot through him, only to be squelched with a cold burst of realism. What a daft idea. She had certainly never said in word or gesture that she loved him. And yet, her passion had seemed genuine. God knew his had certainly been. It had taken everything in him to draw back from the sweetness of her mouth—from the pliant warmth of her body. She had made no move to prolong the moment. And yet . . .

It was in a thoroughly confused state of mind that he resumed dressing and left the room a few minutes later, whistling thoughtfully.

As it turned out, there was to be no intimate chat before a cozy fire that day. True, the others in the house party drifted away to find their own cold-weather amusements, but when Catherine and Drew headed toward the library, they were corralled by Miranda into a game of charades with several of the children in the house party.

It was with some irritation that Drew scribbled words and phrases for the youngsters to act out, but as he watched Catherine laughing with the little ones on her team, he experienced a peculiar stirring within him.

My God, he realized, with a heartstopping thud of finality, he wanted to spend the rest of his life with this woman, to make babies with her, and to squabble and laugh together as they had for the past few days. In short, he concluded with a startling lightening of his being, he wanted very badly to marry Catherine Edgebrooke. Was she still willing to have him—for whatever reason?

He bent a tender glance on her. She was whispering instructions to a dark-haired moppet, and she turned her head to laugh into his eyes. She caught her breath at his expression and for an endless moment, they simply gazed at each other.

Her hair, burnished in the light of the candles that had been lit against the dismal morning, had escaped from the confines of her coiffure. Oblivious to the chatter about them, he moved to her and reached to brush a stray tendril that curled along her cheek, and his fingers stayed to play with the curl, following the curve of her jaw and brushing her lips. She gasped a little, but did not pull away. Her eyes grew large and luminous until it was as though the candlelight had pooled in them, turning them to molten silver.

"Are we going to play?" piped up an exasperated little voice as a small boy tugged at Catherine's sleeve, "Or are you and Drew going to stand there looking silly at each other?"

Hastily, Drew withdrew his hand and the game continued without further incident until the gong summoned them to luncheon.

The meal was a convivial affair, family and guests behaving rather like survivors of a great storm as they regaled the company with tales of how they had passed the chill morning indoors.

Catherine admitted to herself that she could have been served boiled shoelaces by the staff and she would not have noticed as she consumed her meal in a blur of dazed happiness.

The glow in Drew's eyes this morning had been unmistakable. She had set him free of his vow, but the realization fairly sang in her blood that it would take only a word from her to reinstate the betrothal.

After luncheon, Drew approached her and, grasping her

hand, began to steer her purposefully from the room, only to be waylaid by Squire Melford and his lady who claimed them for a game of whist. While he hesitated, Catherine accepted with good grace, knowing that to refuse would be an act of rudeness on their part. Shooting her an exasperated glance, Drew bowed with good grace, and followed her and the Melfords into the green salon, where tables, cards, and counters had been set up for the guests' pleasure.

An hour or so later, as their pile of counters grew steadily, he turned to compliment his partner.

"You have brought me luck, my dear." He caressed Catherine with his gaze. "I am usually a disaster at the gaming tables."

Blushing like a schoolgirl, Catherine giggled. "But do you not remember?" she queried, almost giddily. "You told me of winning almost a hundred pounds in that little village—I forget the name—from—who was it—a Captain Butler, I believe. Why, I—" She clapped her hand over her mouth and stared, frozen, at Drew. He returned her gaze with one of blank puzzlement.

Oh, God—oh, God, what had she done? She felt sick, suddenly, and as she watched a dawning comprehension fill Drew's eyes, she leaped to her feet.

"Good gracious!" exclaimed Mrs. Melford. "What is it, Miss Edgebrooke? You're white as a sheet. Are you—" She moved as though to come to Catherine's assistance.

"No!" Catherine choked. "Please—I'm sorry—I—" She whirled then, and fled from the chamber. Behind her, she could hear Drew's footfalls in pursuit.

He caught up with her in the crimson salon, the first room she came to in her flight. She sank into a chair and flung her hands up before her in a protective gesture. "Please—" she said again, but Drew grasped her wrist and pulled her to her feet.

"Perhaps you would care to explain." His eyes were flint striking on granite.

"Ex—explain?" She was shaking so badly she could hardly form the word.

"Yes, how you happened to be aware of my good fortune with the pasteboards. I certainly do not remember telling you of the incident."

"No," Catherine replied numbly. She felt as though time had slowed to a crawl and that she stood on a precipice, beginning an interminable plunge into a black abyss.

"On the other hand, I do recall regaling Helen with the tale in one of my letters to her. Tell me, Catherine," he continued conversationally, "was Helen in the habit of sharing our correspondence? Or perhaps you read my letters to her without her knowledge."

"No," Catherine said again through dry lips.

"You surprise me, my dear." Drew still spoke in that chill, almost abstracted tone, yet Catherine could almost feel the tension that stretched between them. "You never used to number lying among your character flaws."

Catherine opened her mouth, but she could not utter a sound. How incredibly stupid she had been—and wicked as well—to embark on her charade with no thought of the moment of reckoning that would come. Now, that moment was here, bringing the end of all her foolish hopes. She drew a deep breath, schooling herself to face the inevitable.

"Drew." She spoke in an incomprehensible croak, and tried again. "Drew, you never received any letters from Helen." She lifted a hand to still the astonished protest in his eyes. "They were all from me."

She bowed her head, and listened to Drew's quick, startled breath.

"But, that's impossible!" The words seemed to explode from within him.

"It's true," replied Catherine, lifting her eyes to the storm that rose in his. "Oh, Drew—I never meant to deceive you—that is, well, of course, I did, but I meant no harm."

She cursed the inanity of what she had said, but plowed ahead determinedly.

"I was so desperately sorry for the awful things I said to you just before you left—but you would not read my letters—so I thought—that is—"

"Are you telling me you wished to salve your conscience?" asked Drew, his tone hard and distant.

"Well, yes," admitted Catherine. "And—and I did not wish to lose you as—as a friend. You must know how I have always felt about you!"

Drew snorted. "From all accounts you looked on me as some sort of hero—a notion which you outgrew long ago, as you made very plain. By God, Catherine, I cannot believe you would serve me such a trick."

He stepped away from her, his gaze hot and anguished. In the next instant, however, the cold, bitter smile that she had hoped never to see again, curved his lips.

"But, I should not be surprised, should I, pet? For after all, you did vow revenge. You had already driven me away with your vicious tongue, so the only avenue of retaliation was to try to make me form a relationship with another woman—a relationship that you could destroy at a time of your choosing. How very clever of you."

"No!" cried Catherine. "No, it was not like that at all. Yes, I may have begun the correspondence to make amends, but your letters grew to mean a great deal to me. No, more than that. Drew, I came to lo—"

"For God's sake!" His eyes blazed once more, and Catherine fell back before a rage that she thought might consume her. "If you dare to say the word 'love,' I think I may vomit, for on your lips it is an obscenity. You do not have the slightest inkling of the concept."

"No," she said pleadingly. "I tell you it was not like that."

"Catherine"—he continued as though she had not spoken—"do you have any idea what you have done? Or do you merely amuse yourself by creating havoc in the lives of others? Those letters—those letters were my lifeline. I *believed*, Catherine. I believed in the goodness and the warmth and wit I perceived there. Good God, I actually—" He stopped abruptly and drew a long breath. "Were you ever going to tell me, if you had not tripped yourself up? But, of course you were, or what would be the point? Timing, as you are so acutely aware, is everything, so you were no doubt going to wait until the night before we were to be married to spring the fruit of your jest on me."

"Oh, dear Lord, Drew. Is there not anything I can say to convince you that I was not playing some ghastly joke? Do you really think me capable of such monstrous behavior?"

"But you see, my dear, I do not know you at all. Every time I think I have come to understand you, you reveal yet another surprising facet of your character. Although"—he grimaced and continued in a harsh growl—"I should have known. These past few days have been—extraordinary, and I had come to believe, despite that nagging inner voice that warned me of what you are, that you were actually—that you could—oh, God!" he snarled. "Despite the premature revelation of your little prank, you may consider it a complete success, Catherine. Congratulate yourself on my complete humiliation."

He turned on his heel and the next moment, he was gone, leaving Catherine to gaze after him in consternation.

Dear God, it was worse even than she had thought it would be. She would never make him understand. He would never believe her. She had lost him.

She sank into a nearby chair. How could what had seemed like such a good idea have gone so wrong? And how was she to get through the rest of her life? A life that now stretched ahead of her, empty and gray. At long last, she rose slowly and made her way to her bedchamber.

Here, she sat before an unlit hearth as the hours passed with no lightening of her thoughts or her heart.

In his own chambers, Drew stood before a window, staring out into the rain that beat steadily against trees and parkland. He searched within himself for the fury that should be rising in him like a tide, but his whole being seemed filled with a chill despair, leaving no room for anger. He should be filled with a desire to punish Catherine, but he felt only a desolate sadness that she was gone from his life—permanently this time. He just wished that he didn't want so badly to believe her.

He thought about the letters she had written to him. He had fallen in love with the writer of those letters—with her warmth, her empathy, her intelligence, and her sense of fun. Could it all have been false? He had been so sure that she had found much to love in him, as well. The idea, however, that beautiful, vibrant Catherine Edgebrooke could actually want to marry him was ludicrous. Good God, he could not even button his own shirt, and he was unable to so much as mill down a man milliner like Theo Venable. In short, despite her salutary little speech on the day of the picnic, he was of no use at all. No, Catherine's desire for retaliation was the only explanation for her actions that made sense. After all, she had spurned him once before—though, granted, her rejection of him had lacked the subtlety of the method she had chosen to rid herself of him this time. Lord, he wondered dully, what could there have been in his simple acquiescence those three years ago to his family's wishes that he marry her to spark such a virulent thirst for revenge?

Not that any of it made any difference. She had betrayed him, and the pain of that realization was so great that he knew an urge to cry out his anguish in great, gulping sobs. He stiffened. No, at least he was still man enough to keep his emotions in check.

He stood staring out the window for some time, until the

dinner gong sounded faintly through the door to his chambers. He knew he would not be going down to dine with the others, but, he must put an end to this business once and for all. He turned stiffly, as though he had just risen from a long confinement in a sickbed, and rang for his valet.

When the muted tones of the dinner gong reached Catherine in her bedchamber, her first impulse was to simply ignore it. She had never felt less like eating, and she could not possibly face Miranda and Ceddie, let alone the assembled guests. By the time her maid had arrived to dress her, however, it had been borne upon her that she could not hide here forever. She must face Drew again, and, perhaps, she might have the opportunity afterward to plead her case with him again.

It was with a mixture of hope and dread that she awaited his arrival in the blue salon. She waited in vain. Drew did not make an appearance among the company until the meal was over, the covers had been removed, and the ladies were about to rise to depart for the music room.

He entered the chamber slowly, his limp more pronounced than ever.

"Drew!" said Ceddie. "Where have you—"

But Drew merely lifted his hand.

"I do apologize for my intrusion, brother, for I realize that I am late beyond pardoning, however, I have an announcement to make."

He surveyed the guests, his gaze passing over Catherine as though she were not there.

"I feel it is necessary to inform all of you that the betrothal between Miss Edgebrooke and myself has been—withdrawn." He spoke the words as though he were announcing the cancellation of a race meeting.

"Drew!" gasped Ceddie once again, echoed in anguished accents by his wife. "You can't mean—Surely this is neither the time nor the—"

"I am sorry for any inconvenience"—Drew continued as

though he had not spoken—"but I could not let this charade go on any longer."

He bowed, then, and turned, and left the room.

Catherine, oblivious to the startled murmurings about her, ran after him. She spied him at the end of the corridor, but when she called his name, he neither slowed nor hastened his step. He might not have heard her at all.

Running to catch up, she placed herself in front of him.

"I really have nothing to say to you, Catherine," he said in a tone of great calm, belied by the desolation in his eyes. "There is no need to demean yourself by chasing after me like—"

"Like a hero-worshipping child? It is hard to break old habits, I fear." She tried out a smile that went painfully awry. "Drew, let me say this one thing to you, and then I shall trouble you no longer. It is something I have not said—and perhaps should have. I love you. I have loved you, first as a child—even, I think, through my brief lunacy with Randolph Sills. I began writing the letters because it was the only way I knew to reach you. During the course of our correspondence, I began to love you as a woman loves a man. I wanted to tell you what I had done, but I feared your anger—rightly, as it turned out.

"I believe that you came to feel something for me, as well—or at least for the writer of the letters. Since you have been home, the feeling between us has grown—you cannot deny it. Oh, Drew, please do not turn your back on love! We will both regret it for the rest of our lives if you do."

She halted, breathless in her intensity, but drew from him no response other than yet another slow, acid smile.

"How very affecting, my dear. I might almost be tempted to believe you had I not chanced to look in the mirror before I came downstairs. I cannot conceive why you are turning yourself inside out to apologize—and to continue your laughable protestations of love. Is it that you wish to gain the sympathy of Miranda and Ceddie and all the others thronged to the old homestead for the festivities? Am I to be cast as the villain of the piece? Mmm, yes, I suppose that would complete your plans to a nicety, would it not? If that is the case, I am sorry to disappoint you, but I fear I have contributed quite enough to your little plots and schemes. Now, if you will excuse me . . ."

He bowed and, turning, walked swiftly away from her.

"Oh, my dear, I am so sorry about all of this." Miranda spoke mournfully to Catherine in the abbey's airy breakfast room the morning after Drew's dramatic announcement. "What a perfectly dreadful thing for him to have done."

"But perfectly understandable, you will agree." Catherine pushed her portion of eggs and York ham about her plate in endless circles. She looked about the room, empty except for the countess and herself. "I suppose everyone is upstairs packing."

"Yes. There has been a steady procession of footmen back and forth between various bedchambers and the emerald salon, where all the wedding gifts had been placed on their arrival. Oh, dear," she uttered a small, hiccuping sob. "I just cannot bear it."

Catherine rubbed her eyes wearily. She had spent a sleepless night pondering on what she might have done to avert the calamity that had befallen her. Her thoughts had circled in an endless, futile maelstrom, and she had cried endless, painful tears. When the first traces of morning had begun to show against her windowpanes, she had risen, exhausted and miserable.

"I suppose I had better do the same," she said to Miranda. "Pack, that is."

"Please do not be in a hurry to leave, dearest. Unless—of course, if you feel uncomfortable staying in the same house with Drew, I understand perfectly."

"Well, yes, I do rather. And I should imagine Drew feels the same." Odd, she thought distractedly. Even saying his name caused a wave of hurt to sweep over her. She rose and moved toward the door, halting as she heard Miranda speaking to one of the hovering footmen.

"Yes, James. Please send someone to the summerhouse. I must have left my spectacles there yesterday—or no, it must be the day before, and I shall need them this morning for my embroidery."

Catherine turned. "I shall be happy to do that for you, Miranda. I would welcome a turn out in the fresh air."

"Oh, but—Very well, my dear. That is kind of you."

Wrapping the shawl she had brought into the room with her against the early morning chill, Catherine hurried from the house via the double doors that gave out onto the north lawn.

Miranda, too, rose from her chair and stood at the door for some moments watching Catherine. A slight frown gathered between her brows as she noted a slender figure glide from another exit and follow Catherine as she rounded the corner of the house.

She turned at the sound of footfalls behind her, and broke out into a broad smile.

"Why, good morning, Drew. I was just hoping a stalwart male would come to my rescue. I hope you will not mind postponing your breakfast for a few moments, for I have a small favor to ask you."

The clouds of yesterday lingered like unpleasant memories, but the day was warmer. Catherine inhaled the fragrance of summer blossoms and freshly-mown grass. She was pleased that she had taken on this small task for Miranda. Perhaps a walk surrounded by nature's beauties would provide balm for her wounded spirits.

Nature, however, had failed in this purpose by the time she reached the summerhouse, and she opened the door with a sigh—only to be brought up short by the sound of someone approaching behind her.

"Why, good morning, Theo," she said in some surprise.

In a black humor, Drew trudged across the grass toward the summerhouse. Blast Miranda, anyway. Why did she need her damned spectacles right this minute, for God's sake? There were squads of servants milling about the place, but his sister-in-law had claimed they were all busy at appointed tasks and could not be spared.

He had not come to the breakfast room to eat. He had merely stopped to collect a cup of coffee on his way to the stables. After pounding his pillow all night long in a futile courting of sleep, he had risen with the dawn, determined to ease his troubles with a bruising gallop over the downs. He would ordinarily not have minded a detour to please Miranda, but this morning he was in no mood to do anyone a favor.

As he topped a small hill that overlooked the summerhouse, he was surprised to observe that someone was there before him. Who could be out and about at this early hour?

With an uncomfortable churning in his stomach, he recognized Catherine. And she was with a man! Good God, was he witnessing an assignation between his ex-betrothed and the man she truly loved? He expelled a sudden gust of breath, as though he had been kicked.

Oh, my God, the man was Theo Venable. He was shaken with fury, followed by a surge of helpless misery as Theo's arms came up to gather Catherine into an embrace. Unable to watch, he swung about to return to the house. But . . . no . . . wait! She was resisting—pushing against Theo, but the smarmy little worm was paying no attention to her protests. He had her clutched in a damned death grip and was fairly raining kisses on her hair, her cheeks, her mouth, and anywhere else he could manage to plant them. Catherine struggled in his grasp to no avail.

Blindly, Drew hurtled down the hill. His mouth opened

in a mindless, atavistic howl as he approached and, startled, Theo released Catherine.

"Drew!" Catherine gasped, as she attempted to repair the damage done by Venable's onslaught. By God, he had torn her dress!

Drew advanced with both fists raised, but Theo seemed unperturbed.

"Morning, coz," he drawled. "What brings you out at this unseasonable hour? Must say your appearance is extremely inapropos. The lady and I wish to be alone."

Still in an unthinking fog of pure rage, Drew did not answer—did not so much as hesitate in his course toward Theo. He pulled back his good fist and let fly with a single blow, one in which he packed all the frustration, humiliation, and anger of the past several months.

Theo crumpled like an empty sack of meal, and Catherine stood motionless with shock as Drew stood over him menacingly. It was several seconds before Theo stirred, and when he did it was to scuttle on elbows and posterior as far away from Drew as he could manage in such a position.

"If you ever," growled Drew, "molest Miss Edgebrooke again, I shall repeat the lesson—times ten. Do you understand, you unconscionable snake?"

Theo had by now managed to struggle to his feet. He had fished a handkerchief from his pocket to press to his streaming nose, and he nodded.

"At least," he said, somewhat unintelligibly, "admit that if you had not taken me by surprise, you would have not managed such a hit."

"Possibly not," admitted Drew, with a mirthless grin, "but I'll certainly be willing to try."

Behind the kerchief, Theo attempted a small smile. "I believe you would. And it is equally apparent that I have made a gross error. My apologies—to both of you."

He turned and walked away, with a rather unsteady gait.

Drew turned to Catherine, who gazed at him wide-eyed.

"Drew, that was—that was magnificent."

He gazed down at his hand in some wonderment. "It was, rather, wasn't it? I did not know I could do that."

"Well, I did. And I am so glad you appeared. The wretched toad simply refused to believe I was not delighted by his attentions. If you had not come, I don't know . . ." She forced a laugh. "It appears you are still my hero, after all."

Drew's returning smile was rigid. "Doing it rather too brown, my dear. Still"—he continued, still in a tone of bemusement—"I fancy perhaps I am not quite useless, after all."

"No," she breathed, placing her fingertips on his arm. He stepped back abruptly, and she caught her breath. In the turmoil of the moment, she had almost forgotten that he would no longer welcome her touch. She dropped her hand and began to turn away. "Oh, dear," she said suddenly, noticing for the first time that her bosom was barely covered by her torn gown. Drew removed his jacket in some haste.

"Allow me," he said, draping it around her shoulders. The next moment, he found his arms were around her shoulders as well, and despite his best efforts, he could not seem to remove them.

With a groan that seemed to come from the center of his being, he caught her in a rough embrace and pressed his mouth on hers. He ground her lips beneath his until she thought he must be drawing blood, but she did not pull away from him. Instead, she pressed her body into his, exulting in his strength and the scent of him that seemed to fill her senses.

He thrust her away from him abruptly and stood staring at her for a moment. His breath came in gasps, and when he spoke, his voice was ragged.

"I—I did not mean to do that."

"No?" she said, her own voice breathless. "You seemed quite purposeful."

"Nothing has changed between us, Catherine."

"You are right, Drew. Nothing has changed to alter the feelings we have for each other. For, as much as you may try to deny it, you love me. And I love you."

He groaned again, and spun away from her. In a moment, however, he turned to face her again. "If only I could believe that."

She stared at him mutely. This was how it was going to end, then. Despite everything she had said—despite whatever he might feel for her, he could not believe her. It was over, she thought dully, aware of the pain that waited to descend as soon as she fully assimilated those impossible words.

She became aware in a remote corner of her mind that the sun had come out. How odd, that the sun could still shine on a world that would never contain happiness for her. She turned to walk back to the house, but was stayed by Drew's hand on her arm.

"What is that?" he asked, reaching for the chain she wore about her neck.

"What?" she asked blankly.

"This little circlet. The sun caught it just now. It—it looks like—"

Her fingers curled protectively about her talisman. "It's nothing. Just a silly trinket I have kept by me. Please excuse me now, Drew, I must leave." She must get away before the tears banked behind her eyes began to spill over. He must not see her cry.

But he had clasped her arm with one hand, while with the withered fingers of his other, he scooped up the little pendant.

"Why, it is!" He lifted his gaze to hers. "It's a—"

"It's a sixpence," Catherine's voice broke on a sob she could no longer contain. "It—it's the one I threw at you."

"You kept it all this time?" Drew's voice was tight with an emotion she could not name.

"Yes."

"But—why?"

"Why do you think, you idiot?" Tears streamed down her cheek now, like rain sliding down the fronds of a garden flower. "To remind me of what an awful thing I had done—to help me remember never to do it again—and—and later to remind me of what I had tried to throw away—and, later still," she whispered brokenly, "as a remembrance of the man I had come to love."

Drew stared at the coin. His fingers were very warm against her breast.

"My God, Catherine," he breathed at last. "Ever since I left? You wore it all this time?"

Something stirred within her at the expression in his eyes—something very like hope. She scarcely dared breathe as he gathered her in his arms once again. She lifted her face for his kiss and this time it was gentle and infinitely tender—at least at first. His mouth moved on hers with increasing urgency until, after several moments he drew back to gaze at her, and now the expression in his eyes was unmistakable.

"Oh, my God, Catherine," he whispered exultantly, "I do love you so very much. And you do love me. You really love me."

The tears still fell from Catherine's eyes, but the smile that shone through them was blinding.

"What have I been telling you all this time? Do you not listen? Of course, I love you. I always have and I always will."

He enfolded her in his arms once more and it was many more minutes before he lifted his head from hers again.

"I expect we had better get back to the house or we will have no guests left to attend our wedding. They're all getting ready to leave." He brushed a tendril of hair away from her cheek, and the smile he bent on her was open and so full of love that Catherine thought she might very well explode with joy.

She said only, "Yes, indeed. Oh, Drew—do you know— if you had not happened along just then to save me from a fate worse than death, I would have been packed myself and gone within an hour or so."

Drew chuckled. "I did not just happen along. My busy sister-in-law sent me out here to retrieve her spectacles."

Catherine shot him a puzzled glance. "Oh, but—" She laughed. "Never mind."

She would thank Miranda later.

Having found the spectacles on a little table in the summerhouse, they began to make their way back to the house. As they walked, Catherine removed the sixpence from around her neck. Drew glanced at her in surprise.

"What are you doing?" he asked in surprise. "You are not going to throw it at me again, are you?" He cringed in mock dismay.

"Oh, no, my love, but the clasp seems to be loose, and I don't want to lose it." Her eyes twinkled mischievously. "I shall need it for my shoe, after all."

"Of course you will," he said promptly. "No bride should be without one," he added solemnly. "Now come here and let me kiss you again."

She did and he did, and the little sixpence, dangling from her fingers, tumbled and glittered in the morning sun.

BREATHTAKING ROMANCES YOU WON'T WANT TO MISS